LAU
HANEY

Author of *Flesh of the God*

A PATH OF
SHADOWS

AVON

U.S.$6.99
CAN.$9.99

RETURN TO AN ANCIENT TIME OF GODS, MYSTERY, AND MURDER WITH

LAUREN HANEY's

LIEUTENANT BAK

Also:

ISBN 0-06-052190-2

9 780060 521905

50699>

EAN

Praise for the Lieutenant Bak mysteries by LAUREN HANEY

"Haney's Egyptian police lieutenant is appealing, sympathetic, and totally convincing in a setting drawn with expert skill."
Dr. Barbara Mertz

"Remarkable . . . full of intrigue, confusion, plots, and missteps. [Her] characters are well drawn, and the details convincing."
Contra Costa Times

"What might seem an alien culture is drawn in human terms, and Haney limns her characters in loving detail as she weaves an intriguing tale of murder and human frailty."
Publishers Weekly

"An engaging hero in an exotic locale."
Ventura County Star

"In a sea of romanticized visions of Egypt's ancient past, Haney's work stands out among them all with a gritty realism that rings true to life . . . The heat, dust, and sweat of Hatshepsut's Egypt rolls off each page in a sensory barrage which is pure delight."
Dr. W. Raymond Johnson, Field Director, Epigraphic Survey, Chicago House, Luxor

"Elizabeth Peters and Lynda S. Robinson will need to 'move over' to make room for Lauren Haney."
KMT: A Modern Journal of Ancient Egypt

LAUREN HANEY

A PATH OF SHADOWS

A MYSTERY OF ANCIENT EGYPT

AVON BOOKS

An Imprint of HarperCollins*Publishers*

This is a work of fiction. Names, characters, places, and incidents are products of the author's imagination or are used fictitiously and are not to be construed as real. Any resemblance to actual events, locales, organizations, or persons, living or dead, is entirely coincidental.

AVON BOOKS
An Imprint of HarperCollins*Publishers*
10 East 53rd Street
New York, New York 10022-5299

First Avon Books paperback printing: October 2003

Avon Trademark Reg. U.S. Pat. Off. and in Other Countries, Marca Registrada, Hecho en U.S.A.
HarperCollins® is a registered trademark of HarperCollins Publishers Inc.

Printed in the U.S.A.

10 9 8 7 6 5 4 3 2 1

Acknowledgments

As always, I wish to thank Dennis Forbes, Editorial Director of *KMT: A Modern Journal of Ancient Egypt,* for his generous support and for giving so freely of his time and knowledge. I also wish to thank Tavo Serina for reading the first draft of this novel and making his usual astute comments.

Thanks are also due to Dr. W. Raymond Johnson, Field Director, Epigraphic Survey (Chicago House in Luxor, Egypt), Oriental Institute, University of Chicago, for generously allowing me access to the library at Chicago House when last I visited Egypt, and to librarian/Egyptologist Steven Shubert for searching out the appropriate books and for researching a few questions at a late date.

Finally, I wish to thank those few men who have explored the land through which Lieutenant Bak travels in this novel and have published accounts of their journeys. I've seen many of the places Bak visits, but not all. Without their books, this one would not have been possible.

Any errors are mine.

Cast of Characters

From the Fortress of Buhen

Lieutenant Bak	Egyptian officer in charge of a company of Medjay police
Sergeant Imsiba	Bak's second-in-command, a Medjay
Sergeant Psuro	Medjay sergeant lower in status than Imsiba
Commandant Thuty	Officer formerly in charge of the garrison of Buhen
Troop Captain Nebwa	Second-in-command to Thuty
Nebre and Rona	Medjay policemen who serve as scouts and trackers
Kaha	Medjay policeman who serves as scout, tracker, and inexpert translator
Minmose	Medjay policeman responsible for the donkeys and the camp

Kaine and the Eastern Desert

Commander Inebny	A ranking officer posted to the garrison at Waset, a longtime friend of Commandant Thuty
Minnakht	The son of Inebny, an explorer of the Eastern Desert
Senna	Minnakht's nomad guide
User	A longtime explorer of the Eastern Desert who is leading a party of inexperienced men
Amonmose	A merchant who has a fishing enterprise on the Eastern Sea
Nebenkemet	A carpenter planning to build a fishing boat and huts for Amonmose's fishermen
Ani	A jeweler from the royal house in search of beautiful and precious stones
Wensu	A young man seeking adventure, fame, and fortune
Dedu	User's nomad guide
Unknown Man	The first to die, a stranger to all
Ahmose	A long-missing explorer, Minnakht's friend
Nefertem	A nomad chieftain
Imset	A child of the desert
Hor	Nefertem's brother
Captain Kheruef	Commander of a cargo ship plying the waters of the Eastern Sea

Nufer   Master of one of Amon-mose's fishing boats

At the port and mines beyond the Eastern Sea

Lieutenant Puemre   In charge of the port that serves the turquoise and copper mines

Lieutenant Nebamon   Leads supply caravans to the mountain of turquoise

Sergeant Suemnut   Nebamon's sergeant

Lieutenant Huy   In charge of the camp at the base of the mountain of turquoise

Teti   Overseer of the turquoise mines

Nenwaf   Overseer of the copper mines and smelters

Those who walk the corridors of power at Kemet

Maatkare Hatshepsut   Sovereign of the land of Kemet

Menkheperre Thutmose   The queen's nephew and stepson; ostensibly shares the throne with his aunt

The Gods and Goddesses

Amon   The primary god during much of ancient Egyptian history, especially during the 18th Dynasty, the time of this story; takes the form of a human being, with the ram as his symbol

Maat   Goddess of truth and order; represented by a feather

Hathor	A goddess with many attributes, but in this case the Lady of Turquoise; shown as a woman with cow's ears
Sopdu	Patron god of the eastern frontier
Set	An ambivalent god generally representing violence, chaos, and the desert; usually shown with the body of a man and a doglike head
Inheret	God associated with war and hunting, represented by a man carrying weapons of the hunt

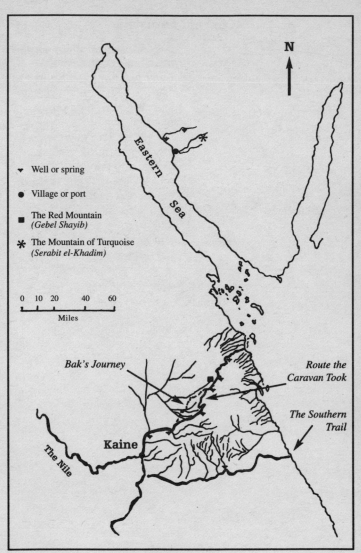

- ▾ Well or spring
- ● Village or port
- ■ The Red Mountain
  (Gebel Shayib)
- ✳ The Mountain of Turquoise
  (Serabit el-Khadim)

0 10 20   40   60
|—|—|———|———|
Miles

Eastern Sea

N

Bak's Journey

Route the Caravan Took

The Southern Trail

The Nile

Kaine

KEMET

A PATH OF SHADOWS

SHADOWS

A MYSTERY OF ANCIENT EGYPT

Chapter One

"Get him! Now!"

The words rang through the air, carrying an edge of cruelty.

"We'll teach him a lesson," another voice, equally vicious, snarled. "Show him a thing or two."

Lieutenant Bak, officer in charge of a unit of Medjay police until recently posted on the southern frontier, was instantly struck by the meanness he heard. His head snapped around and he looked along the waterfront. His Medjay sergeant Imsiba and Lieutenant Karoya, head of the harbor patrol, followed his glance. They saw three men in the distance, standing at the mouth of what they knew was a dead-end lane. The object of their hatred had to be trapped inside.

A third voice shouted, "Cast him back into the desert he came from."

"Not enough!" the first man snapped. "We must send a message to others like him. They've no right to defile the streets our sovereign treads."

Exchanging a quick glance of mutual agreement, Bak, Imsiba, and Karoya raced up the broad, open street, lined on their right by ships moored along the riverbank and on their left by several blocks of interconnected buildings.

"Let's geld him," the second man yelled.

"Yes!"

The three ruffians, so intent on their victim they failed to notice the approaching men, slipped into the lane.

Bak slowed as he neared the opening and raised a finger to his lips, urging silence. Followed closely by his companions, he crept to the corner and peered down the narrow passage that, hugged between two rows of adjoining buildings, lay in deep shadow. Though the three scoundrels blocked the way, he could see at the far end a man clad in a brownish kilt, with a wrap of a darker color around his shoulders. He held a long shepherd's staff horizontal to the ground as if to bar their way. Behind him, a woman stood half-hidden by a laden donkey, clinging to its rope lead.

"Look what he's brought with him!" one of the ruffians chortled. "As dirty as the desert she came from, but a choice bit nonetheless."

"Get him out of the way," the most dominant of the three said, brandishing a short whip that ended in several thongs knotted at the ends to hurt more. "Then we'll take her."

"You'll take no one!" Bak, his tone as hard as granite, stepped into the broad shaft of sunlight that reached into the mouth of the passage. He was a man of medium height with short-cropped dark hair and broad, muscular shoulders. Senior to his two companions, he carried only his baton of office. A symbol of power that, when used with purpose, could be a deadly weapon.

The men swung around, startled. Their leader, the quickest to recover, sneered, "Who are you to tell us what to do?"

"Drop your weapons!" Karoya moved up beside Bak, brandishing his spear and holding before him, so none could mistake his authority, the black-and-white cowhide shield of the harbor patrol. The young Medjay officer was tall and slim, with a tribal tattoo on his left upper arm.

Imsiba took his place beside them. The Medjay sergeant, the tallest of the three, was as lithe and graceful as a leopard. He carried a long spear and the black shield the men of Bak's company had chosen as their own while posted at the frontier fortress of Buhen.

"Are we supposed to be afraid of three men?" the leader of the ruffians scoffed. "Bah! The odds are in our favor."

Bak had to smile at how highly the man overrated himself and his friends.

One of the men said, "Kames, maybe we'd better . . ."

Kames laughed harshly. "Don't worry, my timid friend. We'll give them something they'll not soon forget." He swaggered toward the policemen, raising the whip and slapping the hard-packed earth on which he walked.

"One's a harbor patrolman, Kames."

"So?"

Bak shifted his grip on his baton and eyed the trio, the leader approaching with malicious purpose, his friends drawn along behind, one willing if not eager to participate, the other dragging his feet. He cocked his head as if measuring the men he faced. "How long will it take the three of us to teach them to respect their fellows? A count of ten? Fifteen?"

"Ten or less, I'd say." Karoya grinned at Imsiba. "Will you offer up your weapon, or shall I?"

"He knows you're official and most likely thinks I'm not. If he believes he's disarmed the better-trained man, he'll become overconfident."

"I'll provide the distraction," Bak said. With so many donkey caravans crossing the southern frontier, he and his men had often used the technique of which they spoke to disarm drovers who applied their whips too freely to man and beast.

Suddenly he stubbed his toe. Karoya caught his arm, saving him from falling and giving Imsiba time to slip a couple of paces ahead.

Kames, imagining a weakness where none existed, ran forward. Mouth clamped tight with purpose, eyes glittering, he drew the whip back, shoved aside the point of Imsiba's spear, and struck out at the sergeant with all his might. Imsiba ducked sideways and, at the same time, Karoya leaped forward and thrust his spear diagonally between assailant and intended victim. The lashes wrapped themselves around the point and shaft. Kames tried to jerk the whip free. Karoya twisted his spear, winding the lashes tighter. Bak moved in and slammed his baton down on the man's head. The scoundrel tumbled in a heap, senseless.

Bak leaped past his fallen opponent and ran with Imsiba toward the two remaining men. The sergeant whacked the nearest on the side of his head with the flat face of his spear point, felling him. Bak lunged forward to disable the third man, who had turned away in a futile attempt to escape. The man with the shepherd's staff bounded toward him, holding the simple tool as if it were a club. The ruffian could not have missed the fury on his face. Panicking, he swung around again and raced toward Bak, who rammed his baton hard in the pit of his stomach. With a whoosh of escaping air, the man dropped to his knees and bent double, moaning.

Karoya walked to the mouth of the lane and gave a loud, piercing whistle, summoning the men who reported to him. The sound of pounding feet heralded their approach and within a short time, they hauled away the three scoundrels.

As quiet descended on the lane, the man they had aided bowed his head in a show of gratitude. He was tall and thin, emaciated almost, and darker than Imsiba. His kilt was made of leather and the rough shift covering his shoulders was worn and ragged. His hands were callused by hard labor, his bare feet toughened by a lifetime of walking on sand and rocks. He looked to be about thirty years of age, but was doubtless younger. Bak recognized him as a nomad from the Eastern Desert.

"We owe you our lives." The man spoke slowly as if the tongue of Kemet was unfamiliar to him—as it undoubtedly was. Nomads sometimes grazed their animals along the fringes of the valley, but rarely came into the city.

"You owe us nothing," Bak said. "We're policemen. It's our duty to serve the lady Maat, to see justice done." Maat was the goddess of right and order.

"They would have slain me. As for my wife . . ." The nomad nudged the donkey, urging it against the wall so he could place a protective arm around the young woman. She stood, her head bowed, her hand resting on her swollen stomach and the unborn child within. "She would have suffered a different kind of death."

She must have understood a few words, for she glanced up to receive his brief, reassuring smile. Her hair and shoulders were covered by a length of red fabric, framing a remarkably pretty face. Her eyes fluttered toward the men who had come to their rescue, then she turned her head away, whether out of modesty or embarrassment Bak did not know.

Nomad women customarily remained with their flocks, while their men presented themselves to the world when necessary. Bak wondered what had prompted this man to bring his wife with him. The question sat on the tip of his tongue, but he could not decently pry. "When will you return to the desert?"

"We were getting ready to leave when they came."

"I'm Lieutenant Bak, a police officer passing through Waset. I stand at the head of a company of Medjays who at present have nothing to do. If you'll permit me, I'll send for a few of them. They can ease your path through this city."

The man stood proud and unyielding. "I thank you but no. We've been here four days and this is the first . . ." The woman laid a trembling hand on his arm and gave him a pleading look. "We'll accept your kind offer," he said.

"I'm grateful for your help," Karoya said. "If I'd had to summon my men, those vile rogues would either have heard my whistle and gotten away or, in their eagerness to hurt a man they considered of no account, would've . . ." He shrugged. "The lord Amon alone knows how far they'd have gone."

"You couldn't have faced them alone," Imsiba said in a grim voice.

"Thanks to the gods, we came upon them when we did." Bak veered around a scattering of reddish pottery shards lying in a puddle of oil spilled by one of the many merchants who had come to Waset for the recent celebration of the Beautiful Feast of Opet. During the festivities, a greatly expanded market had lined the waterfront. Now back to normal, a dozen or so stalls served the needs of the nearby dwellings and the sailors passing through. "That kind of senseless hatred can drive a man into an uncontrollable and vicious frenzy, almost impossible to rein in."

The three friends walked on in companionable silence. Thoughts of what could have happened were driven away by the pleasure they took in each other's company and the sporadic breeze that almost made bearable the stifling midday heat. The ships moored along the waterfront rocked gently on swells so shallow they barely rippled the river's surface. Their hulls creaked, a loose corner of sail flapped against a yard. Ducks, their heads hidden under their wings, rested in the shade cast by the vessels, while a lone egret walked from rock to rock along the water's edge, searching for insects. Sailors assigned to guard duty sat with drooping eyes or lay snoring in any bit of shade they could find.

"When do you sail north to Mennufer?" Karoya asked.

"The day after tomorrow, I suspect." Bak looked upstream toward the large cargo ship Imsiba's wife had recently purchased, the vessel that would carry them to their new post and a life far different from that on the southern frontier. Two smaller ships moored nearby would accompany them, carrying men and supplies too numerous for the one vessel. "Commandant Thuty must first appear before our sovereign, Maatkare Hatshepsut herself, to offer obeisance as the new commandant of the garrison there. The vizier suggested he report tomorrow morning to the royal house."

"I can't tell you how much I'll miss you."

"I, too, will feel a loss." Bak, who disliked saying goodbye, made his voice light, teasing. "We'll surely meet another time. Perhaps you'll someday be posted in Mennufer."

Karoya chose to ignore the jest. "I'd counted on going hunting with you in the desert. If I ask Commandant Thuty to come along, do you think he'd delay your departure?"

"Best we leave right away," Imsiba said, only half joking, "before Amonked finds another excuse to keep Bak in Waset."

Amonked was cousin to Maatkare Hatshepsut. He had grown fond of Bak, and had also come to depend upon him to solve any serious crime occurring in the southern capital. Thuty, who was determined that Bak and his Medjays would serve with him in Mennufer, would not rest easy until he was well on his way to his new post, with officer and men by his side.

"Amonked bade goodbye to all of us last night," Bak said. "You were there; you heard him."

"Nonetheless . . ."

Bak had to laugh. What could possibly happen at this late date to prevent his accompanying his Medjays and his commandant to Mennufer?

"I'm amazed at how many possessions you men have collected since arriving in Waset. You've been here a month, no longer." Scowling, Bak looked around the courtyard of the building where they had been quartered since coming from Buhen. Much of the area was stacked high with baskets and chests and bundles. "I've always believed women to be more easily lured by wares than are men. I see I err."

The entire company of Medjays stood among their belongings, looking everywhere but at him, unable to meet his eyes.

"I know you were on the frontier for a long time, far from a market displaying the innumerable desirable objects found in Waset, but you'll find as many if not more available in Mennufer. I suggest you get rid of . . ."

Moans, groans, and yelps of dismay cut him short. Sergeants Psuro and Pashenuro exchanged a glance, each silently urging the other to speak up for the men. Bak wondered how many of the bundles belonged to them.

Pashenuro, a short, stout man, second among the Medjays to Imsiba, cleared his throat. "Sir, you gave the men garrison tokens to use as they wished during the Beautiful Feast of Opet. It's to their credit that they chose to buy objects they especially like or can use in the future rather than waste them on beer or women."

"We thought it best to use the tokens here, sir, close to the garrison that issued them." Psuro, thick of body with a face scarred by some childhood disease, looked as if even he was not convinced by that feeble argument.

Bak smothered a smile. "Commandant Thuty and his wife will not be pleased to find no space left on deck for their household goods."

"They're already on board," Imsiba said, striding through the portal from the lane, "as are my own household items. I fear all heavy objects you men have acquired must be stowed in the holds of the smaller ships, the rest wherever we can make room."

The chubby police scribe Hori, followed by the large, floppy-eared white dog the youth had rescued as a puppy, hurried through the entry. "You're all packed? Good. We're ready to load your belongings, everything but your sleeping pallets and cooking bowls. Keep them here with you; you'll need them tonight."

Bak stood aside to watch his men gather up and carry off the weapons in the police arsenal and their personal belongings. His own clothing and weapons had been loaded earlier, along with Hori's possessions and the few police records they had brought from Buhen. He planned to cross the river at dusk to spend the night and bid goodbye to his father and the two fine chariot horses he had kept as his own when he had been exiled to Buhen. He had thought to take them with him to Mennufer, but had decided to wait to see what the future held. A future of promise, he was sure. He felt sad about parting from his father, but looked forward to the journey north and a new life in the northern capital.

As he watched the men and listened to their chatter, so comfortable in his presence they had no need to guard their tongues, his heart swelled with an affection he knew they shared. Thanks to the generosity of Commandant Thuty, they had all been given the opportunity to remain together and serve in Mennufer as a single unit.

A tall, tough-looking Medjay policeman strode toward the exit. He carried a thick bundle of spears on his shoulder and held a wooden cage containing two doves, which he treasured above all things. At the sound of footsteps in the lane outside, he backed away from the portal.

Thuty walked into the courtyard, let his eyes slide over the Medjay, who was too burdened to salute, and stopped in front of Bak. "Here you are, Lieutenant. We've been looking for you." He was a short, broad man with well-defined muscles that rippled beneath his oiled skin. His mouth, normally hard-set, was more unyielding than usual.

Troop Captain Nebwa, second-in-command to the commandant, crossed the threshold behind his superior officer, clapped the Medjay on his free shoulder, and nodded at Bak. With the way ahead clear, the policeman carried spears and birds out into the lane.

Nebwa was a coarse-featured man who had no patience for the small things in life. As a result, his appearance suffered. His broad-beaded collar hung askew and a strap on his sandal was pulling loose from the sole. His failure to smile was as telling as Thuty's dour expression.

Bak studied the pair, puzzled. "I thought you'd be at the garrison, sir, bidding goodbye to the men you know." And introducing Nebwa to men in Waset who could aid his future progress in the army. The troop captain had grown to manhood on the southern frontier and had been posted there throughout his military life. He was a child where the politics of advancement were concerned, and Thuty had been giving him an intensive course not merely on surviving but on thriving in a difficult environment.

Thuty glanced around the rapidly emptying courtyard at men who, in his lofty presence, had lost the power of speech. His eyes settled on the hearth and the pot nestled among glowing coals. A strong smell of lamb and onions wafted from the container. "Is that stew, Lieutenant?"

"Yes, sir. Would you like some?"

"Haven't tasted a good Medjay stew since we left Buhen."

While the commandant and Nebwa seated themselves on the ground and dipped chunks of bread into the thick meaty concoction, Bak broke the dried mud plugs from three jars of beer and sat down with them. Thuty was clearly troubled and Nebwa none too happy. What could be bothering them? Thuty had been looking forward to his exalted new position, and Nebwa, who had been promised a promotion, would certainly share in Thuty's added importance and influence.

"We've spent the past hour with Commander Inebny at the garrison," Thuty said, fishing around in the stew as if seeking one particular scrap of meat. He trapped a piece of lamb against the side of the pot and lifted it out on a piece of bread. "He's a long-time friend. A man sorely in need of help. His son Minnakht has vanished." Taking a bite, he looked at Nebwa, whose clear disapproval offered no help at all. He chewed longer than necessary, but finally swallowed and said, "You're aware, Lieutenant, of how much I've counted on you sailing north to Mennufer with me. But of all the men I know, you'd have the best chance of finding him."

Bak noticed the commandant's reluctance to state his appeal in a plain and straightforward manner. No wonder. He was probably embarrassed. He had been adamant that Bak would not remain behind to satisfy Amonked's wishes, now here he was, asking him to delay his departure.

"Exactly where did he vanish, sir? What were the circumstances?" Bak asked the questions reluctantly. If he failed to sail north with his Medjays, would he ever be able to rejoin them in Mennufer?

"Minnakht is an explorer." Thuty washed away any embarrassment he might have felt with a long drink of beer. "He vanished somewhere between Kaine and the turquoise mines across the Eastern Sea." Kaine was a village located on the bend of the river downstream from Waset. It was situated at the near end of a lesser-used trail that crossed the Eastern Desert to the sea.

Bak stared, appalled. "I know nothing of the desert east of here, sir. How can I hope to find a man who may've become lost in that wild and barren land?"

"Inebny is expecting you within the hour." Thuty dunked his bread into the stew, the matter settled as far as he was concerned. "He'll tell you all you must know."

"My son is a fine man. I'm proud of him, and with good reason." Commander Inebny rose from his campstool to pace the length of the tent, not a great distance, but far enough to show his agitation.

"How long has he been missing?" Bak asked, trying not to reveal how unwilling he was to go out in search of Minnakht. The mission needed a man with far more experience than he in the ways of the Eastern Desert.

"I last saw him four months ago." Inebny dropped heavily onto the stool. He was a large man, tall and broad, and the lightly made seat creaked from the strain. "The day he left Waset to sail north to Kaine. He was checking the supplies and equipment he meant to take into the desert, making sure he hadn't forgotten anything." He smiled at the memory. "That was like him: checking and double checking. He left nothing to chance."

Bak exchanged a silent thought with Nebwa, who stood beside him facing the commander: Minnakht had left something to chance or he would have returned to Kemet.

"Who reported him missing?" he asked.

"His nomad guide, Senna by name."

"Minnakht has vast experience in the Eastern Desert, so Commandant Thuty told us," Bak said, thinking to draw out further information.

Inebny raised his head, listening to the blare of a trumpet signaling an order to the troops perfecting an exercise on the sandy plain on which the tent had been raised. Rather than listen to his friend's tale a second time, Commandant Thuty had gone out to observe the soldiers' performance. Inebny had watched his friend leave with a touch of resentment, and had been either too annoyed or too self-absorbed to offer seats and refreshment to Bak and Nebwa. A breeze ruffled the fabric roof and walls, but with the doorway covered by a length of linen, not a breath of air could get inside. The tent was stifling.

Evidently satisfied the exercise was proceeding as it should, Inebny said, "He's journeyed into the desert two or three times a year since his first expedition eight years ago." His breast swelled with pride. "When he made that initial journey, he was seventeen years of age. A young man of uncommon courage, with a remarkable quest for knowledge."

"Has he always used the same guide?" Nebwa asked.

A slight frown creased Inebny's brow. "Until a year ago, he used an older man, one he felt as close to as an uncle. That man died, of what ailment I've no idea. Senna has accompanied him since."

"Did Minnakht remain in Kaine for long?" In spite of grave doubts, or maybe because of them, Bak found himself caught up in the puzzle.

Inebny rose again to pace. "He stayed for two days. Long enough to purchase donkeys and a few items he preferred to get from the nomads who go there to trade." The commander lifted the fabric covering the entryway and peered outside, where barked instructions and the sound of marching men could be heard. "The guide joined him there and accompanied him across the desert to the Eastern Sea."

Bak scowled. "Commandant Thuty said Minnakht vanished somewhere between Kaine and the turquoise mines on the far side of the sea. Did Senna not travel with him all the way?"

"He crossed the sea with him, yes, but he had no need to go beyond the port." Inebny dropped once more onto his stool. The creaking sound was louder, alarming almost. "My son joined a military caravan delivering supplies from the port to the mines, and he returned with a caravan bringing turquoise and copper back to the coast. I've talked with the officer in charge of the port, Lieutenant Puemre."

"Exactly who was the last man to see Minnakht?" Nebwa asked, unable to conceal his impatience with the slow progress of the questioning.

"Senna—so he says."

Bak looked thoughtfully at the officer. "You doubt the guide's honesty?"

Inebny shrugged. "How far can you trust these nomads?"

"I suspect they're like the rest of us," Nebwa said, not bothering to hide his irritation. "Some are honest and reliable, others are not."

Bak leaped in with a question before the commander

could register Nebwa's near insolence. "Where exactly did Senna last see Minnakht?"

"At the port a day or so after my son returned from the mines. He . . ."

"Sir!" A young officer swept aside the hanging over the doorway. He saw Nebwa, took note of his rank, muttered an apology, and retreated.

Patently annoyed by the interruption, Inebny said, "The guide claims to have watched my son sail away with the intent of crossing the sea to the Eastern Desert. He meant to retrace their footsteps, returning to Kemet by the same path."

"Would striking off alone like that have been safe?" Nebwa asked.

"He's explored that stretch of desert many times and wouldn't have been a stranger to the route." Inebny's eyes followed an ant making its solitary way across the floormat, but Bak doubted he saw the insect. "He probably thought he could travel faster by himself." He paused, nodded. "Yes, I'll wager he thought another man and several donkeys would slow him down."

"Why would he have been in such a rush?" Bak asked. "He'd already been gone for many weeks. What difference would a few more days make?"

A sharp exchange between two men outside the tent momentarily drew Inebny's attention. "I suspect he grew impatient with the slow pace of the donkeys. Or he might've wished for some reason to dispense with Senna's services."

Bak thought he heard Commandant Thuty approaching. Nebwa must have thought so, too, for his gaze shifted from Inebny to the entryway. "How long ago did he leave that port?"

"Two months, Senna told me, a fact verified by Lieutenant Puemre."

"Two months to cross the Eastern Desert?" Bak asked, raising a skeptical eyebrow. "It's my understanding that one or two men not overly burdened with supplies and donkeys can cross in a week by the southern route the caravans travel from Waset."

Inebny permitted himself a meager smile. "My son preferred a longer, more challenging path, one untrodden by other men of Kemet."

Bak heard a soft snort from Nebwa. He could understand his friend's irritation. That the commander was proud of his son, one could understand, but such extreme pride was aggravating. It made one wonder how much Inebny's tale was colored by his feelings. "Exactly which way did they go?"

"They followed a series of wadis that took them in a northeasterly direction around the southern flank of one of the highest peaks in the desert range and thence to the sea. Their path ran at a diagonal to the trails our caravans customarily use. Their journey, according to the guide, would've taken no more than two weeks if they hadn't continually gone off to investigate interesting landforms along the way."

Nebwa spoke up, voicing Bak's thought. "You told Commandant Thuty that you've known of Minnakht's disappearance for five days, yet your son left the port across the Eastern Sea two months ago. Why did Senna take so long to tell you?"

Inebny stood up, strode to the doorway, and lifted the fabric. The back of his kilt, Bak noticed, was stained by sweat, and one of the stool's legs was bisected by a long, irregular crack.

"He claims to have spent weeks questioning wandering nomads and searching the land for signs of my son." The commander draped the fabric over a pole supporting the roof. The breeze immediately found its way inside, bringing slightly cooler air with it. "He said Minnakht would often see a wadi or a ridge or some other landform he believed promising and would, without thought to man or beast, spend many days looking for signs of precious minerals or stones. That

I've no doubt. I know how obsessed my son could be when something attracted his interest."

"What exactly was he looking for?" Bak asked. "Gold?"

"He always sought gold, of course, but other valuable minerals and stones as well." Inebny turned his back to the outside, but remained in the doorway. "He hoped one day to present to our sovereign a map showing the whereabouts of a mine or quarry worthy of her divine father, the lord Amon himself."

Always the skeptic, Nebwa asked, "Has he ever found anything of value?"

"Not in sufficient quantities—unfortunately—to make mining on a large scale worthwhile." An unexpected smile brightened Inebny's face. "This time, however, he was very optimistic. He said nothing about what he had found, but I caught him many times with a secret, rather smug smile on his face. The same smile he wore as a child when he'd learned a secret he could barely contain within his heart."

"Did he ever before seem so confident?" Bak asked.

Inebny's smile grew rueful. "Often.

"I'm the wrong man for the task, sir," Bak insisted. "Commander Inebny should seek someone who knows the Eastern Desert, an explorer like his son."

Thuty stopped in the intersection where he, Nebwa, and Bak would part company. "If you can't find Minnakht, Lieutenant, no one can."

"Bak's right, sir," Nebwa said. "He'd be entering the desert blinded by ignorance."

"You'll sail north with the rest of us in two days' time." Thuty's tone was strong and decisive, a man making an official pronouncement. "We'll go as far as Kaine, and there we'll speak with Senna. Minnakht disappeared without paying him his due, and Inebny vowed to return with the livestock and supplies he's asked for. He'll be there waiting, I feel sure. Once you hear him out, you can decide for yourself if you wish to go. I'll not press you further."

Bak muttered a curse beneath his breath. Sooner or later, Thuty always had his way. An empty feeling in the pit of his stomach told him that the same would hold true on this occasion.

Chapter 2

"I fail to understand why you let my son sail alone." Commander Inebny's voice was harsh, angry.

Senna bowed his head, not quite concealing the flash of resentment in his eyes. "He insisted, sir. Would you have had me force my wishes upon him?"

"Don't be impertinent!"

"Sir!" Bak could not blame the nomad for taking offense at the commander's attitude. "That you're frustrated and angry at the uncertainty surrounding Minnakht's fate, I can understand, but to berate a man who's trying to help can serve no purpose."

"Frustrated, yes. Angry, no." Inebny, his complexion as flushed as a radish, glared at the guide. "As for trying to help . . ." His loud, cynical laugh was echoed by the bray of a donkey, further enflaming him.

Commandant Thuty flung a quick look at Bak, an apology of sorts for his friend's behavior, then placed an arm around the commander's shoulders. "Come, Inebny. We've asked Bak to speak with Senna. Let him do so." Allowing for no refusal, he firmly ushered Inebny away along the high wall that enclosed Kaine.

The cargo ships carrying the commandant and the men and women traveling with him had sailed north from Waset early the previous day. They had made good time and, shortly before midday, the crews had moored the vessels alongside the mudbank at Kaine, a small unimposing village of single-story mudbrick houses baking beneath the unforgiving sun. Inebny's sleek traveling ship, which had followed them downriver, had moored at the stern of the largest cargo vessel. At least thirty children had gathered along the shore to gawk at so rare a visitation.

Thuty and Inebny had immediately set out to locate Senna, with Bak, Imsiba, and Psuro trudging after them. They had found the nomad outside the village wall, where the weekly market was coming to a close. All that remained were a few farmers packing up produce wilting in the heat, unsold livestock—a cow and calf, a couple of donkeys, and a few sheep and goats—and scattered groups of men and women chatting with friends they might not see for a week or a year. Small children ran laughing and shouting among bundles and baskets, broken and crushed fruits and vegetables, animal waste. Four boys played leapfrog beside mounds of reeds, palm trunks, and sun-dried mudbricks lying beside the knee-high walls of a building under construction.

Bak shifted position, placing the sun at his back, and beckoned Imsiba and Psuro, who had preferred to stand aside while the two senior officers were there. "I'll not apologize for Commander Inebny's behavior, Senna. Only he can do that. All I can say is that I do believe you're trying to help."

The nomad managed the briefest of nods, a signal of understanding rather than trust. "Minnakht's decision to leave as he did was his alone, sir. You must believe me." Senna, a few years older than Bak's twenty-five, was a man of medium height with stringy muscles on a thin body. A puckered whitish scar ran down his right shoulder, beginning at the top and ending beneath his arm, as if someone had tried to cut off the limb.

"He surely had a reason for not taking you with him."

Senna dropped his gaze to his hands, folded together at his waist. "He failed to say."

Bak felt certain the guide was evading the truth, and he could see that Imsiba and Psuro felt the same. "You'd traveled with him before, I understand. Two men alone night and day, walking across the barren desert with nothing better to do than get to know one another. Even if he didn't give a reason, you must've known in your heart why he left you."

"He gave no hint, I tell you."

"Still . . ." Bak let the question hang between them, a heavy veil of silence that no one but Senna could lift.

The nomad was slow to answer. Finally, staring at the earth beneath his feet, he spoke with visible reluctance. "He left me behind for a reason, yes, one I'm not proud of."

"Tell me."

Senna raised his eyes to Bak's. "While he was away at the turquoise mines, I grew ill. Something I ate, I suspect. I was pale and weak when he returned, not fully recovered. He wanted to leave right away, but thought me too sick to accompany him. He said we'd meet later, and so I believed we would."

A pack of dogs came racing along the wall, barking at a small yellow cur Bak assumed was an outsider invading the territory of the village mutts.

"Why do you feel shame?" Imsiba asked. "Any man can become ill."

"I'd agreed to accompany him throughout his travels. To break such a vow is not a thing I do without regret."

Psuro crossed his arms and leaned a shoulder against the wall. "It was he who broke the vow, not you."

"You agreed to meet at a specific place?" Bak asked.

"At a spring below the red mountain, which we bypassed on our eastbound trek. A place where the people of many tribes water their flocks." Senna licked the sweat from his upper lip. "I waited there for over a week, and I talked with all who brought their animals. No one had seen him."

"Seems simple enough to me," Psuro said, wrinkling his nose at a sour smell carried on the light breeze. "Whatever happened to him took place somewhere between the port where you last saw him and the area grazed by the eastern-most tribe whose members you spoke with."

"Between the mountains and the Eastern Sea?" The guide shook his head. "Someone should've seen him. No one did."

Bak knew how barren the desert was around Buhen and assumed the Eastern Desert was equally empty of life. He also knew how far and wide nomads ranged and how they gossiped. In spite of the desolation, Minnakht could not have traveled far without someone seeing him. Unless he chose not to be seen. "Did he set off in the boat by himself?"

The nomad shifted his feet, uncomfortable with the question. "He left with two fishermen, men I didn't know."

"Do you think he knew them, perhaps from the past?"

"He didn't say. He merely assured me they were honest men."

"My son has not journeyed to the netherworld." Inebny stood close in front of Bak, fists planted on his hips. "I know he's alive and well. I'd have felt his passing."

"Senna is certainly worried, sir."

The commander's laugh was brusque, cynical. "I'd be worried, too, if I'd allowed the man I was hired to care for to vanish in the wilderness."

Bak could not avoid Inebny's belligerence, but he could elude his physical proximity. He stepped a couple of paces back along the narrow path between the cargo and the ship's railing and sat on a large woven-reed chest marked with a dried mud tag identifying the contents as linens belonging to Commandant Thuty's household.

Except for aisles left for the crew, the bow was piled high with similar chests, baskets, bundles, and bags. The sailors and the other passengers sat in the stern, waiting to journey onward, among cargo as densely packed as that stowed forward. The ship's master paced the rear deck, impatient to be on his way.

"He feels responsible, of that I've no doubt, but I don't believe he's to blame for whatever has happened to your son." Bak shifted his rear so he could push a sliver down in among the woven reeds beneath him. "If he were, why would he not vanish as Minnakht has?"

Thuty, seated on the steps leading up to the forecastle, scowled. "Bak's right, Inebny. If Senna injured your son in any way, he'd not be here now. The Eastern Desert is vast, a place he knows well. He could hide there for years, until he died of old age and infirmity."

"He's a nomad," Inebny snarled. "Those people know nothing of our lady Maat, of law and order and common decency." He sucked in a breath, snorted. "My son trusted them as he would his own family, but I warned him. More than once. Do I believe this one abandoned him at a time of need? Indeed I do."

Bak knew that nothing would change the commander's attitude, nor would anything change his own certainty that Senna feared something. Or someone. Inebny, probably. "What do you think, Imsiba? Psuro?"

The big Medjay sergeant chose his words with care. "I've nothing of substance to base the feeling on, my friend, but I lean toward his being sincere."

"He has every reason to be worried." Psuro, standing at the railing beside Imsiba, glanced toward Senna, seated cross-legged on the scruffy grass of the riverbank, waiting to collect the goats and supplies Inebny had promised, all being held on the afterdeck of the traveling ship. "He's not been paid for the time he spent with Minnakht, and the way Commander Inebny's acting, he can't be sure he will be."

"You think him innocent?" Bak asked.

"He may be, but if I were to travel with him in the desert, I'd sleep with one eye open."

"I know Inebny can be difficult, Lieutenant." Thuty spoke in a low murmur so the commander, standing at the top of the gangplank, talking with the master of his traveling ship, would not hear. "I've often suspected that his son's wander-lust has more to do with the urge to be free of his parent than with curiosity about the world beyond the horizon. Nonetheless, he's a friend. A good friend. And you're the sole individual I know who has a chance of finding the missing man."

"Sir . . ."

Thuty raised a hand, staving off objections. "You've no wife or family to care for, no responsibilities other than to me. You won't be leaving any task undone and, upon your return from the Eastern Desert, your new task will be awaiting you in Mennufer."

"How many times must I remind you, sir? I don't know the Eastern Desert."

"A problem easily solved, Lieutenant."

Bak could have continued his plea, but the futility of argu-ing—and, though he hated to admit it, an urge to know the truth—silenced him. Against all reason, in spite of the excite-ment of a new task at a large and important garrison, in spite of the difficulties of seeking a man in an unfamiliar and for-bidding landscape, he wanted to know what had happened to Minnakht—and to see the Eastern Desert and the turquoise mines. He noticed Imsiba watching him, saw the hint of a smile on the Medjay's face. His friend had read his thoughts.

Thuty strode to the gangplank to speak with Inebny. After a brief discussion, the commandant beckoned Bak and the sergeants, walked down the gangplank with his friend, and headed across the grass toward Senna. The trio looked at each other, not sure what to expect, and hurried after them.

As the five men descended upon the nomad, he scrambled to his feet and eyed them uncertainly.

"Lieutenant Bak has agreed to go into the desert to search for Minnakht," Thuty told Senna. "He'll take you as his guide."

"Sir?" Senna asked, startled.

Bak was equally surprised, but should not have been. The choice of guide must have been obvious to a man as open and straightforward as the commandant.

Thuty plowed ahead, allowing for no objection. "You'll follow the path you took on your eastbound journey to the turquoise mines, searching all the while for signs of the missing man."

The nomad shook his head vehemently. "Sir, I want nothing more than to take my due and go home. I'll not lead a man who has no knowledge of the desert to what might well be his death."

"You lost my son," Inebny snapped, "now you'll help Lieutenant Bak find him. I won't give you the goats and supplies I promised until after you return."

Senna's eyes darted toward Bak and flitted on toward the animals penned on the deck of the commander's vessel. "They're mine, sir. Minnakht promised and so did you."

"They're not yours—make no mistake about that—and they never will be if you don't guide the lieutenant through the desert."

Bak felt certain Thuty had suggested the ungodly bargain, but even he seemed shocked by his friend's malevolence.

"How will I know you'll give them to me when we return?" Senna asked. "Will you find another reason to keep them from me?"

"You've no choice but to trust me," Inebny snarled.

The guide's face closed down, shielding from those who watched the mistrust and helplessness he had to have felt. The impotence of a poor man facing a man of wealth and power.

Bak sympathized with the nomad, who had come to Kaine expecting payment for a task performed. Instead, he had to accept the promise of a man who had failed to live up to his word and also must repeat the task. "I'll see that you receive fair return, Senna."

"I'm grateful for the thought, sir, but how can you help me if something should happen and you perish in the desert?"

"I don't intend to perish." To Imsiba Bak said, "I wish to take along the four men in our company who best know the desert: Rona, Minmose, Kaha, and Nebre."

"If you must go, my friend, and I see that you must, you couldn't have chosen better men." Imsiba flashed a wry smile. "I'm bound to admit my knowledge of the desert is limited, but I've some talent in the use of weapons. I'd like to go with you. You might need a man with a spear more than one who can read footprints in the sand."

Bak clasped the sergeant's wrist. "I'd be more than pleased to have you, Imsiba, but someone must take charge of our men. They'll be entering a new garrison and taking on new tasks. They'll need a man they like and trust to stand at their head. I can think of no one who can fill my sandals better than you."

"Take me, sir." Psuro, who knew Bak almost as well as Imsiba did, flashed a smile. "I've a strong desire to see the Eastern Desert."

Bak, suspecting he would need someone to watch his back, accepted the offer. Other than Imsiba, he could think of no man more loyal and devoted than Psuro, no man more dependable.

Thuty stared at the nomad guide, his face grim. "A word of warning, Senna. If my men vanish as Minnakht did, you'd better vanish with them."

Bak and the five Medjays bade goodbye to their friends and stood at the water's edge, watching them sail away. Feeling rather like children cast aside by their parents, they turned their backs on the vessels they had thought would carry them to Mennufer and strode into Kaine. The garrison tokens Inebny had given Bak to purchase whatever they needed eased their path. In no time at all they had seven donkeys, one for each man, the minimum they would require for the trek across the desert. They bought food and supplies, the large jars in which they would carry the water they would need, and a few sheaves of hay for the animals.

Bak was standing at the village well, watching Senna and his Medjays fill the water jars and goatskin waterbags, when Psuro called from across the small sandswept square. "Lieutenant Bak! You must hear what this man has to say, sir."

Veering around a dirty white dog scratching its fleas, Bak hurried to the sergeant's side. Psuro stood before a grizzled old man sitting beneath a sycamore tree, weaving reeds with gnarled hands to form a sandal. A matching sandal lay beside his skinny thigh.

"This man's name is Huy," Psuro said. "He's told me of a rumor that may have something to do with Minnakht's disappearance."

Bak knelt before the three pairs of sandals lined up in front of their maker. "Tell me, old man, what have you heard?"

"A rumor, no more, but one that might cause a man more trouble than he bargained for." Huy gave Bak a sly smile, revealing stained teeth worn down almost to the gums.

Bak well understood the pause and the suggestive smile. "Your knife is old, I see, its blade pitted. You look in need of a new one. One with a fine bronze blade."

The old man nodded, pleased. "They say he found gold. Somewhere in the Eastern Desert."

"I'll need more. Details."

"That's just it, sir. Rumors abound. Tales that bode ill for the young explorer, none with any substance. Each is built upon the one before, created late in the evening in the house of pleasure by men besotted by beer and a longing for riches."

"To earn that knife I promised, you must tell me all you've heard, each and every rumor no matter how unlikely. I must judge for myself what's worthy of belief."

The sandal maker obliged, repeating one tale after another. Most hinted at the discovery of gold; none pointed the way to finding it. Bak would have taken none seriously—except for the danger they posed to Minnakht.

As soon as he had rewarded the old man, he hurried to the well. "Senna, have you heard the rumors that Minnakht found gold?"

"How could I not have heard? From the moment I set foot in Kaine, I was besieged by men demanding that I tell them what I knew. Nothing, I swore, yet they refused to believe me." The guide gave a derisive snort. "Rumors fly through this village as bubbles in the air, and have as much substance."

Late in the day, they walked away from Kaine. To their left, the river and its cultivated plain turned to the west and disappeared, hidden by high limestone escarpments. Ahead lay the first wadi in a series that Bak fervently hoped would lead them to Minnakht.

In less than an hour, they had left behind the rich black soil of the river valley, the fields blanketed with tender green shoots and dotted with birds, and had crossed the barren, lifeless sands of the low desert to enter the mouth of the wadi. One look at the vast dry watercourse rent asunder Bak's skepticism of ancient tales of pounding rainstorms tearing through the desert and of broad and deep rivers lined with plants and teeming with life. Over an hour's walk in width and fed, according to Senna, by a multitude of lesser wadis, it was the culmination of what had to be a vast drainage system. The thought of himself and his companions, mere men, walking through so immense a landscape filled him with awe.

Senna led them up the most recent channel to be cut through the wadi by water pouring downstream after thunderstorms and heavy rain in the mountains to the east. About forty paces wide and washed out to a depth of three or four paces below the wadi floor, its hard sand surface provided easy walking for men and donkeys. An irregular line of leafless, seemingly dead plants dotted the wadi floor, silla bushes that the smallest amount of water would bring to life.

Some distance to the east, they could see a large worn limestone mound, its profile softened by dust in the air. Farther north, a long ridge sloped steeply down into a gap between itself and the mound. The gap, Senna said, marked the location of the wadi up which they would travel during the next few days.

As dusk crept upon the land and the heat of the day waned, after the small caravan had settled into the rhythm of the journey, Bak fell in beside the nomad. Behind them, the donkeys walked in an irregular line led by Psuro, Rona, and Minmose. Kaha and Nebre, the most accomplished trackers in the party, had left the watercourse to range across the wadi floor, seeking knowledge of the landscape around them. The sounds of evening, a bird calling, a hoof striking a rock, a donkey blowing, the men behind talking together, were muted by the stillness of the vast expanse around them.

They spoke for a while of the trek ahead, a journey into an ever-more rugged landscape. With no lofty officers to question his every move, Senna was considerably more relaxed than he had been at Kaine and much less defensive when he spoke of the trip he had made with the young explorer who had vanished.

"I know nothing of Minnakht except what his father told me," Bak said. "He naturally spoke of the man he knew in the city, not of the explorer, and his eyes were most likely blinded by the love he feels for his son."

"Minnakht is a fine man, that I can tell you without reservation. A man of remarkable courage and determination."

"You sound like his father," Bak said in a wry voice.

Senna managed a sparse smile. "He's a good friend to the people who dwell in this part of the desert. They know him well, know how at home he feels with them and their land. They can't understand how he could vanish as he did."

Bak gave the nomad a sharp look. "You speak of the people here as if you're not one of them."

"I was born to a tribe that dwells many days' walk to the north. On this side of the Eastern Sea, but opposite the place where men of Kemet mine turquoise and copper." Senna must have sensed the query in Bak's thoughts, for he smiled, "You're wondering, and well you might: if I was born a stranger to the land through which we'll be traveling, how did I get to know it well enough to serve as a guide?"

"The thought struck me, yes."

"While a boy, I was servant to a man who wished above all things to find gold. Each cool season he explored the Eastern Desert, trekking farther to the south than the year before. His guide at the time, a man of infinite patience and wisdom, taught me all he knew."

"As an outsider . . ." Bak paused, not wanting to rub natron into what might well be an open sore.

"Do the nomads in this area blame me for Minnakht's disappearance?" Senna's smile was bitter. "Why do you think I spent so many days and weeks searching for him?"

A distant whistle sounded off to the left, drawing Bak's attention. Kaha or Nebre assuring him and their fellow Medjays that all was well with them. A second whistle followed, Psuro's response.

"You've no idea how much I regret the illness that prevented me returning with Minnakht," Senna said. "Worse yet, I argued with him about his decision to leave in such haste."

"He made the decision, not you."

"Still, I must live with what happened. If we should find him alive, I can make amends. If we find him dead or don't find him at all . . ." Senna shrugged. "How can I know how he felt about my absence? How can I myself know how I should feel?"

Unable to think of a suitable answer, Bak said instead, "What do you believe happened to him?"

"Someone must've made him their prisoner or, as reluctant as I am to think the worst, he may've been slain. Maybe by the fishermen he sailed away with or by bandits somewhere along the coast of the Eastern Sea."

Before leaving Waset, Bak had questioned a seasoned officer who had escorted prisoners and supplies through the Eastern Desert and across the sea to the turquoise and copper mines. He thought of all the man had told him: the long treks between watering places, the enormous and rugged wadis and mountains, the immense sea with its endless coastline and multitude of islands. How could he hope to find one small man in a land so vast?

Full darkness fell. The air grew cool and fresh. The stars sparkled with a crystalline brilliance and the moon, a pale half circle, lit the sand beneath their feet. A donkey shied and a deadly viper slithered away. Night birds called to one another, a fox barked.

Kaha and Nebre returned to the caravan as silent as the large sand-colored lizard Bak had seen during the day. If the donkeys had not turned their heads to look, he would not have noticed the two men sliding down the bank of the watercourse. Smiling, they loped across the sand to report.

Nebre, who was tall and slender, about forty years of age with woolly hair as white as his kilt, planted the point of his spear in the sand. "As far as we could tell, sir, we're the only men within shouting distance, but others have gone ahead of us. Earlier today, we believe."

Surprised, Bak looked up the line of donkeys toward their guide. "According to Senna, this path we're following is seldom used."

"Not long after we left you, we spotted the tracks of a caravan. Seven men—four barefoot, two wearing woven reed sandals, and one wearing leather sandals—walking with a dozen or so donkeys. They traveled a route parallel to this channel but closer to the eastern side of the wadi."

Bak frowned. "Reed sandals? They'll never last in this harsh landscape. Those two couldn't have been nomads."

"No, sir." Nebre glanced at Kaha, who voiced agreement, and went on with his tale. "Later, about two-thirds of the way between the mouth of the wadi and where we now stand, the tracks of two men wearing leather sandals and walking with four donkeys merged with the first set of tracks. Whether the later group caught up with the earlier or simply trod along the same path, we've no way of knowing."

"Were they also men of Kemet, I wonder?"

Nebre shrugged. "Nomads usually go barefoot, but a few have taken to wearing sandals. Leather sandals."

"Interesting," Bak said with a wry smile. "We thought to be walking alone into the wilderness and instead we find ourselves to be one segment of a procession."

"A procession with a spectator, sir," Kaha said, grinning. "Just before dark, high on the hillside to the east, I found a single footprint of another man, this one also wearing leather sandals." Smaller than Nebre and a few years younger, he was equally slender, with long arms and hands as delicate as those of a woman.

"By climbing so high, I'd hoped to see the men ahead. They were too far away, but I thought the print sufficient reward for such an effort. It was in a sheltered place overlooking this wadi. It hadn't been disturbed by a breeze or a passing animal and was very distinct. As its sheltered location might've preserved it, I'd make no bets as to how long ago it was made."

Minnakht? Bak wondered. No. If he were nearby and able, he would show himself. Who were the others? Men he surely would have heard of if he and his Medjays had taken the time to sit down and gossip with the men of Kaine. No matter. If they had stopped at the well ahead, he would learn soon enough who they were.

On this, the initial day of the trek when men and animals were fresh, they made good time, reaching their destination before midnight. Here, where a subsidiary watercourse opened into the main wadi, was the first of a string of wells that made travel possible along the route they meant to follow to the Eastern Sea.

A cluster of hobbled donkeys stood or lay near a stand of scrubby tamarisks that marked the location of the well. They saw no sign of a fire, so assumed the men traveling with the animals were asleep. Opting to remain apart, they made camp about fifty paces down the wadi beside a row of stunted trees that followed the watercourse for some distance downstream. Better to approach in the light of day when they would not be mistaken for bandits.

Rona, a hard-muscled young Medjay who had a slight limp, gathered broken twigs scattered around the trees. Minmose, shorter and broader, as cheerful as Rona was serious, whistled softly as he built a small fire on which to warm a slim but welcome meal of beans and onions, which they ate with dried fish.

While they enjoyed the food, a man emerged from the shadows by the well and walked toward them through the moonlight. "Good evening, sirs. My name is Amonmose.

This is my first night on the trail and I find I can't sleep. May I sit with you for a short while?"

Bak motioned him to join them. With luck and the favor of the lord Amon, this man might tell them of the men who had preceded them up the wadi. "Welcome to our humble . . ." He laughed. Home was not a proper word to describe their surroundings. He introduced himself and his men and offered to share the meal.

Eyeing their few donkeys and modest bundles of supplies, Amonmose shook his head. "You mustn't be too free with what you share. You're traveling too light for generosity."

Bak gave him a quick look. "You've previously crossed the Eastern Desert?"

"Several times, but always by way of the southern route traveled by our sovereign's caravans. I've never before traveled this far north."

Intrigued, Bak studied the visitor in the dim light of moon and stars. Amonmose looked more a man who enjoyed his comfort than one familiar with the desert wilderness. He was about forty years of age, of medium height and portly, with laugh lines at the corners of his eyes and mouth. In spite of his girth, he moved with a rare grace and seated himself on the sand with the ease of a child. Bak suspected the bulk was hard muscle rather than simple obesity.

"Soldiers, are you?" Amonmose asked.

"We've recently come from the southern frontier and are on our way to the mines beyond the Eastern Sea." Bak kept his answer simple, choosing not to discuss his mission, and flung a pointed look at Senna, making sure the nomad understood that he should not elaborate. He knew nothing of this man and the others camped near the well, but to find a half-dozen men following a route he had expected to be unused made him wary. "What brings you across this desert so often?"

"I've a fishing fleet that shelters in a bay on the near shore of the Eastern Sea. Six boats, but I hope over the next few years to increase the number." Pride filled Amonmose's voice to overflowing. "We've established a base camp some distance to the north, near a cluster of islands where the fishing is particularly good. The men live rough, in palm-frond shacks, but within a year or so, I'll see they have proper housing."

Psuro flung the bones of a dried fish onto the embers of the fire, making it crackle. "We've barely started on our journey and already I miss fresh food. I can well understand that a couple of fishermen, even in so unlikely a place, might find men who'll buy their catch. But six boats?"

Laughing, Amonmose swept several small pebbles from beneath his backside and settled himself more firmly on the sand. "We supply fresh fish to the port that serves the turquoise and copper mines, to ships that sail the Eastern Sea, and to nomads who come from inland. When the mines shut down during the hot season and fewer men are posted at the port, we dry a good portion of our catch and supply that to the caravans traveling back and forth between Kemet and the Eastern Sea."

"You've no end of business, I see." Bak sipped his beer, savoring the last jar he would see in a long time. Amonmose was so garrulous he doubted he needed prompting, but he asked anyway, "If you always travel the southern route, what're you doing here?"

"I met a young explorer a few months ago, Minnakht by name." If Amonmose noticed the sudden interest among the members of Bak's party, he gave no sign. "He swore he could show me a more direct and time-saving route between Kaine and my fishing camp. If he didn't exaggerate, I hope, several years in the future, to expand my fishing enterprise and transport dried fish to Kemet."

Delivering fish to Kemet and the great river that ran

through the heart of the land was very much like hauling rocks to a quarry, Bak thought.

"He said if I'd meet him in Kaine, he'd show me the way," Amonmose went on. "I arrived on schedule, purchased donkeys and supplies in the expectation of leaving right away—and heard he'd gone missing."

"When you found him gone, you came into the desert anyway?" Kaha asked. "You surely don't plan to travel this wasteland by yourself."

"A most foolhardy endeavor, sir," Nebre said, shaking his head.

"No, no." Amonmose waved away the very idea. "I've brought with me a man who'll build boats and huts at my fishing camp."

"A man unfamiliar with the desert." Nebre's voice was flat, disapproving.

"You misunderstand. I've traveled this land often enough to know that one should never make such a journey without a competent guide. That's why, when I learned that a man named User, a seasoned explorer, and several other men plan to follow a path similar to the one Minnakht described, I thought to seek them out. Their caravan had left Kaine in the early morning, I learned, so we hastened to catch up." A smile blossomed on his face. "And catch up we did."

"You know this man User?" Senna asked.

"Oh, no. But men I spoke with in Kaine said he knows the Eastern Desert as a man knows the curves of his wife's body. In addition, he's brought along a nomad guide, Dedu by name." Amonmose rose to his feet and brushed off the back of his kilt. "I'd best return to my sleeping pallet. We're to make an early start tomorrow."

Bak bade him goodbye and watched him walk away. He rather liked the man, but his tale of a fishing fleet so far from any town or city stretched the imagination.

Chapter 3

Bak awoke to the harsh braying of one of his donkeys. Two others answered from the direction of the well. The lord Re had not yet peered over the horizon, but pale yellow streaks rising above the ridge to the east heralded the god's ascension from the netherworld. Bak rose from his thin sleeping mat, yawned, and stretched. The night had been too short.

Awakened by the donkey as Bak had been, the Medjays scrambled to their feet. Following his example, they looked around at a world they had not been able to see clearly in the moonlight. The plateau that edged the wadi to the west looked taller than it had in the night, and closer. The row of tamarisks followed the modern watercourse around a gentle bend to the north. The secondary wadi up which they would travel—for no more than three days if the gods smiled upon them—led off to the east through the gap they had seen the previous evening between the ridge and the mound they had skirted for much of their journey from Kaine. An irregular row of scraggly trees meandered up that watercourse for a hundred or so paces

Senna, making no secret of his interest in the men camped near the well, watched them as they roused themselves from sleep and began to get ready for their day's trek. Bak, too, was curious. What had prompted so many men to journey along this particular trail, normally frequented by only a few nomads? Had they, too, heard rumors of gold? Had they been lured into this harsh and unforgiving land by the same tale of riches that he had heard in Kaine?

Minmose passed around a loaf of bread and the bowl containing the cold remains of their nighttime meal. The taste of onions seemed stronger in the light of day. As soon as they had eaten, Psuro and Kaha unhobbled the donkeys. Rona, Senna, and Nebre loaded water jars and goatskin waterbags onto the sturdy creatures, and the five men led their charges off toward the well. Minmose scoured the bowl with sand, rolled their sleeping mats, and gathered up their supplies for loading onto the animals. Content that all was well, Bak hastened along the row of tamarisks to speak with the men camped near the well. A pair of small black-and-white birds, wheatears, flitted from branch to branch, keeping pace with him.

"Lieutenant Bak." With a warm smile, Amonmose hastened to meet him and ushered him into the camp, where he presented him to a tall man about forty years of age. "User, this is the man I told you about, the officer who stands at the head of those Medjay soldiers."

He gestured toward Psuro and Kaha, drawing water from a well encircled by a waist-high stone wall built to prevent animals from fouling the precious liquid. Two donkeys were drinking from a rough-plastered stone trough, while a dozen or more waited nearby. The nomad tending them was carrying on a conversation of sorts with Kaha, who had some knowledge of several desert dialects, but was a master of none. Psuro lowered and withdrew the large red pot tied to the rope so quickly that the water had to be close to the surface. Kaha held each large jar until it was filled and plugged the top with mud that would dry quickly in the heat. Senna, Rona, and Nebre, while awaiting their turn at the trough, had led their animals upstream to nibble on some low green bushes Bak could not identify from so far away.

"This is User, Lieutenant," Amonmose went on, "the man who agreed to let my friend and me accompany his party across the desert."

Bak gave the explorer a genial smile. "Amonmose tells me you have considerable knowledge of the land between here and the Eastern Sea."

User greeted him with a nod. "I'm more familiar with the desert farther south, but I've done some exploring in this area."

His body was lean but muscular. His skin, weathered by sun and wind, was the color and texture of leather. He spoke in a voice so deep it sounded as if it had come from the depths of the netherworld.

Bak glanced around the camp, which looked to be in total disarray. Three nomads hustled about, packing up so they could load the donkeys. Two served as drovers, he assumed, and the third must be the guide. A large muscular man, obviously from the land of Kemet, was helping, while two other men of Kemet looked on. "You left Kaine early yesterday, I understand."

"At sunrise. We stopped here to rest through the heat of the day and thought to go on before sunset, but when Amonmose and his friend showed up, thinking to travel with us, I decided to remain overnight. They'd pushed their donkeys hard, and I thought it unwise to drive them farther without rest."

"If the truth be told," Amonmose laughed, "Nebenkemet and I were as tired as the animals. The delay was most welcome."

Bak noted User's fleeting grimace. The explorer had not been happy with the delay. He also recalled the wide-awake man who had come to their camp in the night, displaying no sign of fatigue. "From what our guide has told me, the next well is a long, hot march ahead of us."

"If he knows what he's doing, he'll take you up the wadi to

the east. There's no decent shade north of here." User queried Bak with a glance, as curious about the newcomers as they were about him, understandable in this cruel and desolate land.

"We plan to travel east, yes, and since you recommend the route, I assume you'll go that way, too?"

"Ah, here's my good friend Nebenkemet." Amonmose drew close the man who was helping the nomads break camp. He was a burly individual close to Bak in age. "He's the man I told you about last night, Lieutenant. He'll dwell for a year or so at my fishing camp, where he'll build at least one boat, hopefully more, and some huts."

Bak raised a hand in greeting. The man, whom he assumed to be a carpenter by trade, eyed him with the mistrust of many a poor man faced with authority. He wore a tunic so wrinkled it looked as if he had slept in it—as he undoubtedly had. His limbs were thick and muscular, and he looked as strong as an ox. His sandaled feet were heavily callused, his hands and lower arms scarred. He had lived rough in the not-too-distant past.

"Do you share Amonmose's enthusiasm for journeying through an unknown land?" Bak asked.

"Our trek has barely begun, sir." Nebenkemet's demeanor, like his voice, held neither humor nor warmth. "I've had no time to know."

"Nor have I," Bak admitted with a smile. "My men and I must learn to dwell in this land, so unlike any we've ever known."

Amonmose flung him a sharp look. "You were posted on the southern frontier. Is that not equally barren?"

"It is, yes, but unlike this Eastern Desert, the river that flows through the land of Kemet also gives life to Wawat. In many places, fertile plains hug the river, allowing for a considerable amount of farmland. The escarpments enclosing the floodplain can be high, and rocky mounds rise from the desert sands, but there are no mountains like those I've been told form the spine of this desert. I've heard of no great sheets of sand here or long, high dunes such as those found west of the river."

"You're well informed, Lieutenant," User said.

"Thanks to my nomad guide, Senna. During much of the trek from Kaine, we spoke of the land through which we'll pass."

"Senna?" User's head snapped around and he stared with narrowing eyes toward the guide. "He wouldn't be Minnakht's guide, would he?"

"User!" The voice was sharp, peremptory. "Shouldn't you be urging those wretched nomads to hurry?" A young man of about eighteen years, slapping his leg with a fly whisk, strode up to the explorer. He would have been handsome but for the scars on his face. Like Psuro, he had been marked by some childhood disease. He was one of the pair who had been watching the men toil, making no effort to help. "At this rate, we'll never set off up the trail."

Nebenkemet exchanged a quick glance with Amonmose, then slipped away to return to the drovers and the task he had left unfinished.

"This man you see before you is Wensu, Lieutenant. He wishes to become an explorer." User's face held no expression whatsoever and the words carried no hint of sarcasm, but Bak sensed animosity.

"A worthy goal." Bak formed another smile. "Not many men are eager to suffer the hardships of rough and solitary travel day after day."

"When I travel alone, I'll not suffer, that I vow." Wensu glanced at the explorer with poorly concealed contempt. "When I no longer need a man like User to show me the way, I'll take along enough men, animals, and supplies that I'll suffer no less comfort than my father does when he goes on a hunting excursion into the desert west of Waset."

User stared hard at the young man, then swung around and walked away. Wensu sputtered in impotent fury.

Acting as if he had noticed nothing amiss, Amonmose called out, "Ani!" He beckoned the short, rotund man watching the drovers break camp. "Come. You must meet the lieutenant I spoke with last night."

Ani, whose sole activity had been to hop from one spot to another, the better to peer at the men breaking camp, looked at Amonmose and at the nomads as if not sure where he was most needed. Flinging a last, reluctant look at the toiling men, he hastened to respond to the summons. User looked on from a few paces away, saying nothing, a faint but cynical smile on his lips.

While introductions were made, Bak studied the new arrival. He looked as soft as well-risen bread dough, and his pale skin was burned a bright red, betraying a man unaccustomed to the sun. Only his hands revealed a life of toil. They were callused and bore the pinkish scars of burning.

"Ani toils in a workshop in the royal house," Amonmose said with open admiration. "He makes jewelry for our sovereign and the men and women she holds close within her heart."

"I've a skill with precious metals and stones, yes, but I'm beginning to see how deficient I am in other skills." The craftsman threw a humble, almost apologetic smile at User. "After one day of walking beneath the cruel sun, after one night of sleeping on the ground and eating plain food cooked in a manner strange to me, I've come to realize how little I know of the hardships of life. I know nothing about the desert, about donkeys, about living beneath the sky. I'll do my best to learn, but I see many a trial ahead of me."

Why men such as Ani and Wensu, so obviously of the city, had chosen to travel so far from home, Bak could not imagine.

* * *

A sharp whistle drew Bak's attention to the well. The donkeys had drunk their fill and the nomad was leading his small herd toward User's camp. Amonmose, Nebenkemet, Wensu, and Ani hurried to meet him, thinking to oversee the loading of their belongings, Bak assumed. The signal had been Psuro's, summoning Senna, Rona, and Nebre. The trio hurried to the well to water the donkeys in Bak's small string of animals.

"Other than Senna, do any of your men speak the tongue of the nomads?" User asked.

"One man tells me he can get by."

"You're fortunate."

Bak did not like User's ominous tone. "Are you hinting that Senna may abandon us, as some say he did Minnakht?"

"I know the nomads in this area hold him to blame. They would, since he isn't one of them and Minnakht vanished while under his care. Do I personally think him guilty of wrongdoing? I've no idea." User watched one of the drovers lift several bundles one after another, testing their weight to be sure none was too heavy for a donkey. The man who had watered the animals began to load them. "All I'm saying is that not many nomads speak the tongue of Kemet. I've learned a few words over the years, but not enough. If anything were to happen to my guide and the drovers, I'd not lose my way. But should we need help, I doubt I could explain what we need."

Bak could see the weakness troubled him. "Which man is your guide?"

"The one wearing the faded red leather kilt. Dedu is his name."

Bak watched Dedu for a few moments. The guide, some years older than the drovers, toiled among them as an equal. He liked that. It signified a man secure within himself. Thus far, Senna had helped with the donkeys but had offered no assistance to Minmose. As if the many small household tasks were beneath him.

The sun rose fully above the ridge, sending long rays through the wispy branches of the tamarisks. A slight breeze blew the smoke from a makeshift hearth across the small encampment, carrying with it the odor of charred bread. A donkey brayed; its rear hooves shot through the air as it tried to shake off its load.

One of the nomad drovers separated a gray donkey from the rest and led it across the sand to a spot twenty or so paces away from the trees and slightly farther from the well and User's camp. He stopped near a clump of bushes, spoke a few words in his own tongue, a murmur from so far away, and repeated himself in a louder voice. Receiving no answer, he shouted to User, "He sleeps, sir."

"A man camped there through the night," User explained. "A stranger." Scowling, he strode across the sand. "You'd think by this time, we'd have awakened the dead."

Certain no man could have slept through a yell as loud as that of the drover, Bak hastened to catch up. Stopping with User beside the nomad, he stood at the edge of a small shallow cavity in the sand on the downwind side of the bushes. A man lay flat on his stomach within the hollow, his face turned away, arms and legs in a line with his body. A water jar, a goatskin waterbag, a couple of baskets in which to carry supplies, and a bow and quiver filled with arrows lay on the sand near him.

Too many flies were swarming around, Bak noticed, and the donkey was easing backward, pulling at the rope halter the drover held. He guessed the worst and muttered an oath, earning surprised glances from the two men beside him. "A stranger, you say?"

"He showed up at nightfall, watered his donkey and hobbled it with ours, and otherwise kept to himself." User snorted. "Amonmose came out here and tried to strike up a conversation. You'll have noticed how much he likes to prattle. Well, he got nothing in return but a few grunts."

The explorer was talking too much, a sure sign that he sensed something wrong.

Calling out to the man, User knelt beside him. He got no more of a response than the drover had. He clutched a shoulder, tried to shake him awake. Snapping out a sudden oath, he jerked his hand away and scrambled backwards. "He's cold!"

Bak knelt where User had been. He waved off the flies buzzing around, laid a hand on the dead man's shoulder, and felt the coolness of death. Giving himself no time for qualms, he eased backward and rolled the body onto its back. From the amount of stiffness, he guessed the man had been slain sometime early in the night, long before he and his Medjays had reached the well.

Clearly a man of Kemet, the dead man was about twenty-five years of age, of medium height and build. Other than his large dark eyes, fully open and turned Bak's way, his features were nondescript. His hair was dark and cut short. His deeply tanned body was well formed and his lower arms and wrists thick, like those of an archer. He wore a tunic, a knee-length kilt, and leather sandals. A thin gold chain encircled his neck and from it hung a golden amulet, the sign of life. The sheath tied to his belt was empty, the dagger missing.

"Is this Minnakht?" Bak asked.

"No." User cleared a roughness from his throat, repeated. "No. Minnakht is taller, not so plain, not so . . ." His voice tailed off and he shook his head. "No."

The flies began to settle around an encrusted wound below the dead man's breastbone. His life's blood had flowed onto the thin woven mat beneath him, leaving a large red-brown stain. The weapon—probably his own dagger—had been withdrawn and carried off. The sand around him had been thoroughly churned up, making it too soft to hold footprints.

Looking at the man's sandals, Bak wondered if he could be the one who had left the footprint Kaha had found on the hillside overlooking the wadi. "Did he plan to travel on with your caravan?"

"I told him he must. No man should go off by himself into this wilderness."

Bak glanced at the nomad drover, who was slowly backing away, as anxious to leave as the donkey was. "He came with a single animal?" he asked User.

"Like you and your men, he traveled light."

"Did any of the men with you know him?"

"They all greeted him as a stranger." User ran his hand back and forth over the sand, wiping away the feel of death, and stood up. "A nomad must've slain him. To rob him, I'd wager."

"You don't trust your guide? Your drovers?" Amazed, Bak also rose to his feet. How could any man travel in so risky a place with men on whom he felt he could not rely. The thought brought a cynical smile to his lips. He had allowed himself to be led into the desert by Senna, a man he was not sure he could trust.

"I've known Dedu for many years. He wouldn't slay any man, nor would the drovers he brought with him. They're his kin." User's smile was grim. "A nomad family camped several hundred paces up the secondary wadi. A couple of young girls brought their goats to the well shortly before dusk, and I glimpsed at least one woman up there."

"You noticed no men?"

"I didn't. That doesn't mean they had none with them."

"His name is nowhere to be found." Bak replaced the contents of the baskets, mostly foodstuffs, a few dried herbs that could be used for medicines, and a few personal items such as a razor and comb. The bare essentials needed for a journey.

"I suggest we bury him here and now." User swatted at a fly that had strayed from the body. "Many a man has vanished with his family none the wiser. An unfortunate occurrence, but what else can we do?"

"We're a few hours' walk from Kaine. I suggest you wrap him up as best you can and have one of your drovers take him back. Someone there may know who he is."

"Yes," User nodded. "Let someone else worry about him."

Bak eyed the men standing at the edge of the hollow. Ani and Wensu were staring at the body as if never before had they been so close to death. Ani looked appalled by what he saw; Wensu's face registered distaste. Amonmose appeared saddened by the death, yet curious. Nebenkemet looked on with the composure of a man inured to all life had to offer. Senna seemed mildly troubled, while Dedu and the drovers looked as if they wanted nothing more than to turn their backs and go on their way. Except for Psuro, who stood slightly apart from the other men, the Medjays had come and gone.

"Are you certain you never saw this man before yesterday?" Bak asked, not for the first time.

As a single unit, they chorused a denial.

"You surely don't believe one of us slew him," Ani said.

"Who are you to question us?" Wensu sneered. "You're a soldier, not a police officer."

Bak was not yet ready to divulge to these men that he and his Medjays were policemen.

"He never once revealed his name." Amonmose shook his head as if mystified that any man could die unknown. "Sitting around our fire last night, we talked about him, made guesses as to who he might be and what he was doing out here alone. That's one reason I came to him, tried to strike up a conversation. I felt sorry for him, thought he could use some companionship."

"I'd wager a donkey and foal that a nomad took his life," User said. "One of those people camped up the wadi could easily have slipped past us in the dark and crept upon him to rob him."

"Rob him of what?" Bak asked. "The golden amulet he still wears?"

"As none of us know what he brought with him," Ani said, "how can we know what might've been stolen?"

"If you're so determined to play policeman, Lieutenant, I suggest you question those nomads." Wensu slapped his leg with his fly whisk, a habit Bak was beginning to find exceedingly irritating. "If they didn't slay him, they'll certainly know who did. Another nomad who crept out of the desert in search of wealth."

A convenient theory, Bak thought. One highly questionable if this man's death was somehow tied to the disappearance of Minnakht. He had no reason to think it was, but experience had taught him not to trust coincidences. This death occurring here and now when a half-dozen other men had set out on the same trail Minnakht had taken looked suspiciously like a coincidence.

"The footprint I saw yesterday was not made by these sandals." Kaha, kneeling at the dead man's feet, ran his finger around the edge of a sole. "These are almost new and show no sign of wear. The print on the hillside was made by a sandal well worn, its sole beginning to curl to fit the foot of the man wearing it, and the outside edge had a slight cut near the small toe."

Bak studied the lifeless face, wondering exactly who this man was and why he had come into the desert alone. If he had not left the print, who had? Another man traveling alone? "You must go to User's camp, Kaha, and study the footprints left by the men who spent the night at this well."

Nodding his understanding, the Medjay rose to his feet.

"You wish to know if any of them made the print on the hillside, or if someone else was watching from afar."

"That, yes, and I also wish to learn if any nomad left the vicinity of the well to snoop around User's camp or the place where this man was slain."

"I doubt a nomad slew him, sir."

Inclined to agree, Bak looked thoughtfully at User's camp, which was in a state of disarray. About half the donkeys were loaded, while the rest awaited water jars and supplies with the enduring patience of most beasts of burden. The explorer was arguing with his nomad guide and the drovers. The other men were standing around in idle expectation that they would soon be on their way.

"We've come upon two groups of men recently merged to form a single unit," he said, "their intent to cross the desert on a route never before used by any man other than a few nomads and Minnakht. As if that doesn't tickle the imagination sufficiently, we also have two men who chose to travel alone through this wilderness, one who's disappeared and the other who's dead. That doesn't merely tickle, Kaha. It causes an itch that must be scratched."

Grinning, the Medjay walked off to do as he was bidden, passing along the way User, a drover, and a donkey. From the resentful expression on the nomad's face, Bak guessed he was the one selected to take the body back to Kaine. Beyond the trio, Dedu had begun to issue orders, setting his kinsmen to their tasks.

A distant movement drew Bak's glance up the secondary wadi. He spotted Nebre's tall, slim figure, returning from the nomad camp at a good fast pace. As soon as User and the nomad spread out a sheet in which to roll the body, he hurried eastward to meet the Medjay, preferring to speak with him alone than to air his suspicions to all the world.

*   *   *

"The nomads are gone, sir."

"So early in the day?"

Nebre wiped a thin film of sweat from his face. "Nothing remained but a few footprints and the marks of a crude shelter. The fire was cold. I'd guess they moved out long before dawn."

"They left in a hurry."

"So it would seem."

With Nebre beside him, Bak walked slowly toward the well, mulling over the news. Would the nomads have left in such haste if they had nothing to hide? "User said two young girls took their goats to the well. Other than their tracks, did you see any others along the way?"

"None."

"How many people were in the nomad camp?"

"It was a family group: one woman, the two girls who cared for the flock, a child learning to walk, and I found signs of a baby crawling on the ground."

"No sign of a man?"

"I found no footprints of a man, sir, neither a husband nor an intruder."

Bak smiled. Nebre had read his thoughts. The slain man could have forced himself on the woman and she in turn repaid him with death. "Unlikely slayers, that family, wouldn't you say?"

"The odds are much against their guilt, sir."

Bak looked down the wadi toward the well. He knew nothing of the men traveling with User's caravan. They all had pleaded innocence, but might not one among them be a murderer? "I've asked Kaha to study the footprints in User's camp to see if any match those he saw on the hillside yesterday and to search for signs of a nomad intruder. After he's finished, you and he together must make a wide circuit of the well and the campsites. I want to know if any outsiders have come near."

                    *   *   *

Bak parted from Nebre and hurried to the well, where
Senna and Rona were filling the goatskin waterbags. Upon
learning that they had almost finished the task, he went on to
the campsite where he and his men had spent the night. He
found Psuro and Minmose dividing the last of the supplies
among the donkeys. Assured that all was well with the packing, he told the sergeant of the tasks he had given to Nebre
and Kaha.

"What's the point of seeking tracks?" Psuro asked. "We
must travel on."

"Two thoughts have occurred to me. One is the possibility
that this death is in some way related to Minnakht's disappearance. The second is of more immediate concern. If a
slayer is lurking about who has no regard for right and order,
for the lady Maat, we'd best learn the truth and take precautions. Would you like to wake up some fine morning and find
one of us slain in our sleep?"

Psuro dropped a bag of dates into a basket and gave him a
long, speculative look. "You suspect one of the men traveling
with User?"

"I think it a possibility."

The sergeant knew Bak very well. "And you wish to snare
the slayer."

"Minnakht has been missing for two long months. What
are the odds that he still lives?"

"I'd not wager a grain of sand that we'll find anything
other than a shallow grave, and probably not even that."

"Now we've come upon a dead man. Do you not think we
should include his slayer in our quest?"

"Where do you go from here, Lieutenant?" Amonmose
hefted his goatskin waterbag, checking to be sure it was full.
He was not wearing his usual cheerful smile.

"We plan to travel northeast, following a series of wadis

through the desert mountains. I suspect our route is similar to yours."

Amonmose's face lit up. "If that's the case, why don't you come with us? The bigger the caravan, the safer we'll be."

Bak liked the suggestion. To travel with User's caravan would answer two of his needs. It would offer the safety of numbers and give him the chance to know better the men traveling with the explorer. "Do you fear an attack, Amonmose? Or are you afraid there'll be another slaying?"

"In all the years I've crossed this desert, I've never known the nomads to be dangerous. True, the tribes fight each other, but the people themselves are generous and kind, especially to a stranger. I've traveled farther to the south, to be sure, but I'm certain the nomads here are no different." Amonmose laid down the waterbag and picked up another. "Something's happened out here. I feel it in my bones." He managed a thin smile. "No, it's more than a feeling. In Kaine I learned that Minnakht has vanished. A seasoned explorer he was, one who took no unnecessary risks, a man reputedly beloved of the nomads. Now we find a stranger murdered in our midst. I don't like it, sir."

"Are you about ready?" User asked, approaching Ani. The jeweler stood a half-dozen paces away, holding his rolled sleeping mat as if not quite sure what to do with it.

"User, listen to this," Amonmose called out, overriding Ani's response. "Lieutenant Bak plans to travel a route much the same as ours. I've asked him to come with us."

Looking annoyed, User urged Ani to hurry and hastened to join Bak and Amonmose. "The smaller the caravan, Amonmose, the faster we'll travel and the easier it'll be to find forage for our donkeys. Did I not tell you that yesterday when you asked to accompany us?"

"You did, yes. But considering the circumstances, don't you think it to our advantage to join forces? Bak and his Medjays are well armed and trained to fight, while the rest of us are civilians. I can't speak for Ani or Wensu or for Nebenkemet but I, for one, have no aptitude in the use of weapons."

User planted his fists on his hips. "Considering what circumstances? The dead stranger? Bah! His death had nothing to do with us."

Amonmose's mouth tightened, betraying the determination that had led him to build a fishing fleet in an unlikely and formidable location. "Lest you've forgotten, User, no one has seen Minnakht for at least two months, which probably means he's dead and buried." User opened his mouth to rebut but the big man plowed on. "A merchant in Kaine told me another young explorer has also disappeared in this desert."

Another disappearance? Bak's interest sharpened.

"About ten months ago, that was," Amonmose went on. "He, too, must be dead, his body hidden where no one can find it. I'd not be surprised to learn that the first disappearance led to the second and the second to this stranger's murder. Do you want one of us to be the fourth victim?"

Bowled over by the torrent of words, User could think of no retort. He had to know that he had no control over Bak and his Medjays. He might not wish them to join his caravan, but if they chose to walk a few paces ahead or behind and to camp close by, he could do nothing but fume.

"Our donkeys won't be loaded for at least a half hour. You'll be ready to leave by then, Lieutenant?"

Bak stood with Senna and Psuro, watching the solitary donkey and drover plod south down the main wadi, taking the body of the unknown man to Kaine. It would be a long, hot trek for man and beast, but the rations token Bak had supplied, assuring a generous reward upon presentation to the nearest garrison quartermaster, should partly make up for so unpleasant a trek.

"Will we be joining User's caravan, sir?" Senna asked.

Offering a silent prayer that drover and donkey would have a safe journey, Bak turned to the guide. "What do you recommend, Senna?"

"We'd make better time without them. And . . ."

"And what?" Psuro asked impatiently.

Senna looked uncertainly at Bak. "Well, sir . . ." Again he hesitated, but a sharp look from the sergeant drove him on. "We'd have two guides and two masters, not a good idea at the best of times and especially not here in this harsh and desolate land."

"User and I would have to come to an understanding." Bak watched Psuro kick sand over the blackened remains of the fire, leaving no sign of their presence but the soft and uneven surface. "Tell me what you know of Dedu."

"I can't vouch for his honesty." Senna looked toward the well, where the guide in question was lifting a water jar onto a donkey. "He's from a tribe that ranges the land south of here and along the edge of the Eastern Sea. I've heard that in years past he served often as a guide, usually traveling with User but sometimes leading caravans across the southern route between Waset and the sea. He's since become a man of substance, with a family and flocks, and seldom strays away from his tribal territory."

If Dedu was capable enough to toil for the caravan masters entrusted to transport copper and turquoise, he could be depended upon to lead a small caravan through a less-traveled portion of the Eastern Desert.

"What do you know of User?" Bak asked.

"I've heard he's a hard man, one who doesn't hesitate to use the whip on men who fail to obey him. They say his honesty comes and goes, depending upon his needs. He doesn't trust most nomads, nor do they trust him."

Bak's donkeys were fully loaded and ready to travel when Nebre and Kaha returned to the camp. He told Senna, Minmose, and Rona to go on ahead with the animals, leading them up the secondary wadi. Whether or not they joined User's caravan, he wanted himself and his men at the head of the procession.

When they were well on their way, Bak asked the two Medjays, "What did you find?"

"I found no sign of the watching man in User's camp," Kaha said. "Not a man among them brought sandals that leave the print I found on the hillside. Nor did I find any recent sign of nomads other than at the well."

"What of your search farther afield?" Psuro asked.

"We circled far out around the well and the three camp-sites. You must've seen us from time to time." Nebre paused, awaiting Bak's nod. "We found no tracks of anyone entering or leaving the circle who didn't belong here."

Bak eyed the row of tamarisks that rounded the bend to the north. "Those trees are thin, but at night a man could've come from upstream unseen."

Kaha leaned his shield against his leg, freeing a hand so he could adjust the waistband of his kilt. "We took special care when looking for prints in that direction, sir. We found none."

"We came upon one other likely place," Nebre said. "A place where rocks have tumbled down and broken apart, forming coarse gravel on the bottom of a wash. A man could walk down the wash, leaving no trace of himself, but we found no sign of disturbance where the gravel tails off into the sand."

"In other words . . ." Bak looked from one man to the other, seeking their conclusion.

"We might've missed some sign, sir," Nebre said, "but if not, someone in User's party must have slain the stranger."

Crossing his arms in front of his breast, Bak stared up the wadi toward the well and the men and animals preparing to set out. He did not have to think for long. Two men had gone missing and another was dead. One coincidence had troubled him; two he found to be incredible. And here he stood, with an invitation—reluctant though it might be—to join the men most likely to have slain the unnamed man. How could he not accept?

"We'll travel with the other caravan. It's better to keep an eye on people you don't trust than to allow them to go their own way, giving them a chance to do further mischief."

Chapter 4

Bak stood off to the side of a rough track left on the wadi floor by what had to be hundreds of goats or sheep, mostly the former since they could survive the heat and harsh grazing easier than could the latter. He had tried to find signs of the nomad family after passing the place where they had been camped, but the sand had been so stirred up by the many sharp hooves that nothing remained but soft grainy undulations. The few clear tracks he found, those of animals that had wandered away from the path, could have been left in the early hours of the morning—or they could have been made a year or more ago. He suspected they and the mingled tracks on the path had been left by all who had come this way since the last water had flowed down from the mountains. Two years ago, so Senna said.

Nebre and Kaha had found footprints around dead bushes and a dying acacia where children had gathered wood, but they did not match those of the girls who had watered their goats at the well. He did not suspect their mother of slaying the dead man, but he had an idea that she or her children might know something of his death. Why else would they flee in the dead of night?

Resigned to the fact that they had evaded him, he sent Nebre and Kaha to scout out the surrounding landscape. He remained where he was, standing beneath the burning sun,

waiting for the caravan to catch up. As he raised his waterbag
to drink, sweat slid down his spine beneath his tunic, tickling
him. The day promised to be as hot as any he had ever en-
dured at Buhen.

Senna was the first man to draw near. He walked at the
head of the caravan, probing the sand with his long staff.
With luck, any lurking vipers would reveal themselves and
slither away. A half-dozen paces back, Rona and Minmose
led their string of seven donkeys.

"Are we making good time?" Bak asked the guide.

Senna ventured a wry smile. "User can make no complaint
that we're slowing his caravan."

"Excellent. We're not pushing too hard, are we?"

"Like you, sir, I wish to reach the Eastern Sea with every
man and animal safe and well."

Bak clapped the guide on the shoulder and walked back to
Minmose and Rona. After assuring himself that all was well
with them and the laden donkeys plodding along in their
wake, he let them walk on ahead. The outliers of the limestone mound to the south were closing in, narrowing the
view. He took a final look at the high escarpment that vanished in a bluish haze far to the southwest, following the
course of the river that gave life to the land of Kemet. He
bade a silent goodbye to the land he could no longer see,
tamped down a touch of homesickness, and turned his
thoughts to his quest for Minnakht.

About thirty paces behind the last animal, he fell in beside
User, walking with Dedu at the head of his string of donkeys.
The nomad murmured an excuse and slipped away.

"What are you doing out here, Lieutenant?" User asked.

"Crossing the Eastern Desert, as you are."

"Don't give me that!" the explorer scoffed. "You and your
men are like birds with broken wings, creatures out of your
element. You know nothing of this land except what you've

been told. Worse yet, you've placed yourselves in the hands of a man you don't know, one whose integrity may not be all it should be."

Bak resented being thought an innocent, but kept his tone level, untroubled. "You underestimate us, User. My men and I know exactly what we face. A cruel and waterless landscape, where the slightest accident can disable a man to a point where he can die. Where an unseen viper can leap out of the sand and doom a man to a most painful death. Where a much needed spring or well that men have depended on for years may turn up dry. Where . . ."

The explorer raised a hand to silence him. "I don't question your knowledge, Lieutenant. You look to be a man who absorbs information like a drunkard soaks up beer. What I question is your lack of experience and your judgment."

This time, Bak let his irritation show. "We've entered this desert, thinking to find Minnakht. And make no mistake: we will find him alive or dead."

An incredulous laugh burst from User's lips. "How were you drawn into that?"

"Commander Inebny, Minnakht's father, knows my commandant." Bak's eyes flashed anger. He could find no humor in the task. "I was sent out to find the missing man and here we are."

"You're obeying an order," User said, surprising him with a sympathetic look. "That accounts for your presence, but it doesn't explain your willingness to trust Senna."

"Let's just say that Minnakht's father left him with far less choice than my commandant left me." Bak eyed the explorer, measuring him. "What of you? What are you doing out here?"

Recognizing his own question thrown back at him, User smiled. "When Minnakht failed to return to Kaine, rumors began to fly, hinting that he'd found something of worth. Gold, they were saying, but they could've meant anything of value.

Silver, copper, some kind of beautiful and unusual stone." He shrugged. "Who knows? Anyway, I thought to take a look. To see if I could find what he'd found. If anything."

So User had also heard the rumor, Bak thought, and had believed it credible enough to follow Minnakht into the desert. Was the tale no more than hopeful thinking, as Senna had indicated, or had User's years of exploring the desert given him a greater insight? Could the young explorer have spotted something of value that he wished to keep secret? Could that be the reason he had left Senna behind? "You thought to ease your search by following in his tracks."

"All the world knows he's confined his interest to a slab of desert between the southern caravan route and the high mountains, between the wadi we traveled up yesterday and the Eastern Sea. This path we're taking runs diagonally between the southwestern limit of his range and the northeastern limit."

Bak could not fault User's logic. It followed his own. "Why bring along Wensu and Ani? They seem unlikely traveling companions to a man bent on searching for treasure."

"Treasure! I should be so fortunate." User laughed, at himself this time. "They'd both met Minnakht at one time or another—I don't know where or when. Nor do I know what promises he made, if any. All I know is that they assumed he'd take them on his next expedition. Then he turned up missing. They heard of me and asked to come along."

"I'm surprised you agreed."

User's expression clouded. "My wife is ailing, has been for a long time. Physicians are costly. They were both willing to pay a fair sum."

The man's pain was obvious and Bak preferred not to probe an open wound. "How well do you know Minnakht?"

"I've seldom crossed his path. Other than a knowledge of the Eastern Desert, we've had no reason to seek each other's company. He's younger than I am, the son of wealth. I grew to manhood in Gebtu, my father a drover. I first crossed this desert at the age of thirteen, leading a string of donkeys in a caravan transporting turquoise and copper along the southern trail. He came in search of adventure."

A sensitive subject, Bak could see. "He gets along well with the nomads, I've been told."

"They're as brothers to him and this desert is his home." User scowled, grudgingly admitted, "He grew to love it as I do, and since he's learned the tongue of the nomads, he knows its ways better. That's why his disappearance is so mystifying, why many blame Senna."

"His father said he's never found anything of value, but here you are, retracing his path on the strength of a rumor."

"Minnakht knows minerals and stones." User glanced across the sloping banks of the main flow of the wadi to scan the gray limestone ridges on either side. "He's wrong if he believes he'll find gold this far north. The only gold-bearing quartz I've come upon that wasn't long ago exhausted has been some distance to the south. But these desert mountains are full of other valuable minerals and stones. The trick is to find rock of sufficient quality in a quantity worth mining.

"For example . . ." He picked up several small black and gray chunks of rock and held them out so Bak could see. Their facets glittered in the bright sunlight. "These are granite washed down from the mountains of the central range. The stone's beautiful and of value to sculptors, but with so much fine granite available at Abu, where it need be dragged but a short distance for transport downriver, this is worth nothing."

"Where might Minnakht have vanished?"

User dropped the stones and brushed his hands together to wipe away the dust. "He could be anywhere. Look at the land around you. What you see is barren and rough, but blessed by the gods when compared to the land through which we'll pass in the next few days. The deeper one travels into this desert, the wilder and more forbidding the land becomes. I myself have journeyed into innumerable places where no man had ever trod before me."

Bak eyed the barren wadi up which they were trudging and the craggy stone ramparts fading into the haze ahead. How could he hope to find one man in so vast and rugged a land?

Bak stepped off to the side of the track to wait for Wensu to come even with him. The portion of the wadi they had traveled thus far was broad and straight, a long slope dropping down to the well where they had spent the night. As if solely to provide a background, the escarpment beyond the well, partially cloaked in a pinkish haze, rose as a series of high, steep steps in shades of gray from dark to light.

User had given him much to think about. If he was to be believed, he had not come into the desert in search of great wealth, yet he must have planned this journey as soon as he heard of Minnakht's disappearance and rumors of gold. Could anything less than riches have drawn him from a sick wife for whom he clearly cared? A passing donkey brayed, as if jeering at his puzzlement.

"Lieutenant Bak." Wensu raised a scornful eyebrow. "I thought you were firmly ensconced at the head of this caravan, free of the soft sand that marks this trail."

Bak fell in beside the young man, who walked alone in front of the drover leading User's string of donkeys and about twenty paces behind the explorer. Each time his right foot led the left, he tapped the leg with his fly whisk, betraying an impatience with the monotony. "Commander Inebny, Minnakht's father, requested that I search for his son. I need your help."

"Me? Help you?" Wensu asked, immediately on the defense. "I know nothing of his disappearance."

"How did you come to know him?" Bak pretended not to notice the adolescent break in the youth's voice. Was he younger than the eighteen years he had initially believed him to be?

"How can I be sure his father sent you?"

Bak made his laugh as cynical as he could. "Why else would I come into this godforsaken land?"

Wensu flushed. "You might've come for the gold Minnakht found."

This spoiled young man, it seemed, had also heard the rumors. "I'm here solely because Commander Inebny and my commandant have known each other for years and are as close as brothers. If not for that, I'd be taking a long, soothing swim in the river at this very moment." A movement caught Bak's eye far up the wadi, the golden-tan coat of a gazelle. The graceful creature bounded out of sight as fast as it had entered his line of vision. "Tell me, how did you come to know Minnakht?"

"I met him a few months ago. In a house of pleasure in Waset." As memory surfaced, Wensu's misgivings slipped away and a smile spread across his face. "He was surrounded by young women who were listening to his tales of the desert, accounts of the many wonderful and exciting adventures he's had. They sat as silent and still as stones, utterly enthralled." No less absorbed in his own tale, Wensu forgot the flywhisk he carried and waved off an insect with his free hand. "As was I."

Bak could picture the youth sitting in the shadows, awed by the more mature man, his way with words and women. Drawn in by tales of bold and stalwart behavior, of what he interpreted as being a romantic and heroic way of life. "Did you approach him then and there?"

"Oh, no! He went off with one of the women." Wensu flushed scarlet. "I waited outside in the lane, and when he appeared later that night, I spoke to him."

"And . . . ?"

Wensu flung a distracted look Bak's way. "I told him how much I admired him, of course. How much I'd like to become a man of the desert as he was. An explorer. He wrapped his arm around my shoulder and . . ." The young man looked away, bit his lip. "He told me I must wait. I must not simply gain in maturity, but I must come to hunger for the desert as a man hungers for a woman."

Bak pressed his tunic against his chest, blotting a rivulet of sweat trickling down his breastbone. "He made no promise to take you along on a future expedition?"

"Well, no, but he did imply . . ." The lie faltered. "No, he made no promise."

"Why, in the name of the lord Amon, did you travel to Kaine, thinking he'd take you with him?"

Wensu visibly wilted beneath Bak's incredulous gaze. "When I told my father I wanted to become an explorer, he laughed at me." The young man swallowed, his distress apparent. "He's a chief scribe, sir, a lofty and influential man who reports directly to the vizier. He wishes me to become a scribe as he is. He hopes some day that I'll become a man of note, attaining a rank equal to or higher than his." A bitter smile touched his lips. "He'd like to see me a vizier."

"You came anyway," Bak said, trying not to reveal the sympathy he felt. "You turned your back on your father's wishes. You ignored Minnakht's advice."

"I couldn't submit to a lifetime of boredom, Lieutenant!" The response, meant to be defiant, came close to being a wail.

Bak ignored the young man's anguish. "Wensu, you spoke earlier of the gold Minnakht found. Were you repeating something he told you or were you referring to a rumor you heard?"

"He told the women in the house of pleasure that he was looking for gold."

"He mentioned no specific discovery?"

"Oh, no. He merely said that was his goal. To find gold or some other precious mineral or stone." Wensu flashed a guileless smile. "When I arrived in Kaine and heard the rumor, I assumed he'd found it."

Wensu's dream was no different than that of many other young men. Bak doubted, however, that one as selfish and arrogant as he could ever learn to cope in an uninviting environment like the one User had described. In fact, he could not imagine the young man sneaking away unseen from User's campsite or creeping up to the stranger and taking his dagger without rousing him. He would have neither the patience nor the ability.

"Tomorrow, Wensu, you should turn around and return to Kemet. It's not too late. You can spend the night with us at the next well and go back in the morning. Within two days, you'll be sitting in a house of pleasure in Kaine." He did not wish to squash the young man's pride, but he felt sure User would agree to sending one of his drovers with him to make sure he arrived safe and well. If not, he would send a Medjay.

"No." A stubborn look descended upon Wensu's face. "If I can discover a new source of gold or some other valuable metal or stone, I'll attract the attention of our sovereign and my future will be assured. My father will have to accept me as I am, not as he wishes me to be."

When Bak walked back along User's string of donkeys, Ani was nowhere to be found. Looking worried, the nomad bringing up the rear pointed in the direction from which they had come. There Bak spotted the craftsman, lagging far behind the caravan.

Reassuring the drover with a nod, Bak left the softer sand trampled by the animals and, reaching firmer sand off to the side, hurried down the wadi. The caravan was slowly approaching the gap between the ridge to the north and the limestone mound that had lain off to their right since their trek began. The once broad, dry watercourse had begun to narrow, its walls to steepen.

Too intent to notice Bak's approach, Ani walked slowly along the base of the northern wall, studying limestone rocks and boulders that had broken away from the hillside or the harder stones that had washed down from the distant mountain range. He was carrying what looked like a white bag, bulging and heavy.

As Bak approached, the short, stout man picked up a small stone, examined it, and dropped it, scooped up another and studied it. A third stone brought a smile to his lips.

"What are you doing way back here?" The question was rhetorical; Bak could see what the jeweler was doing. "You shouldn't have allowed the caravan to get so far ahead. What if something happened to you?"

Ani looked up, startled. Recognizing Bak, he greeted him with a beaming smile. "Ah, Lieutenant. I thank the gods you've come. Look what I've found." He held out a pinkish stone for Bak to see.

"You mustn't walk so close to the wadi wall. A viper could be hiding among the rocks."

Paying no heed, Ani glanced around. His eyes came to rest on a flattish limestone boulder. Glistening white patches marked places where the weathered exterior had broken away when it had tumbled from above. He set what Bak had thought was a bag, actually a large, sweat-stained square of linen, on top of the boulder and spread the corners wide, revealing dozens of rocks, none larger than a duck's egg.

"If you have another square of linen . . . You do, don't you?" Allowing Bak no time to answer, Ani bubbled on, "You can carry these while I look for more."

Bak gave him a stern look. "You can't be serious."

Ani blinked, taken aback. "I came into the desert to seek

rare and beautiful stones for my workshop. Now you're trying to tell me I can't take them with me?" He stiffened his
spine, standing as tall as he could. "I can and I will."

"Who's going to carry them?"

"We've brought along plenty of donkeys."

"Those donkeys are carrying water and supplies, Ani."

The craftsman stood quite still, his face revealing one
emotion after another: realization, dismay, and a reluctant
acceptance. "Can I not collect a few?" he asked in a meek
voice.

Bak eyed the bits of rock displayed on the linen. Most
looked to his untrained eye like the granite User had showed
him. "Are any of these stones exceptional?"

"They're wonderful specimens, but . . ." Looking pained,
Ani shook his head. "Other than one or two, no."

"If you'll pick out those two, we can be on our way. We
must catch up with the caravan."

Faced with the inevitable, Ani wasted no time. With an expert eye, he searched through the rocks until he found three
he deemed worthy of saving. Openly saddened by the sacrifice, he pulled the square of linen from beneath the rest and
left them lying on the boulder. An offering to the lord Set,
god of chaos and the desert.

Bak strode up the wadi at a good fast pace, grateful that
Ani had accepted reality so quickly. The much shorter man
practically ran along beside him. They were a hundred or so
paces behind the donkeys when Bak noticed Ani's labored
breathing and how red his face had become. He stopped,
handed over his waterbag. "You should never stray far from
the caravan, but lest you forget and wander away, you must
always carry water with you."

Smiling sheepishly, the jeweler drank, allowed the water
to settle in his stomach, drank a second time. Bak reclaimed
the bag, pulled free the dusty square of linen tucked beneath

Ani's belt, dropped the rocks into the jeweler's hand, and trickled water on the fabric. "Wipe your face and neck."

With a grateful smile, Ani obeyed, smearing dirt across his cheek. "I wasn't thinking, Lieutenant. About the rocks, I mean. Minnakht assured me that there were many stones in the Eastern Desert that would enhance the jewelry I make. He said nothing about the practicalities of transporting them."

Bak took a drink of the tepid water. "When did you last speak with him?"

"I talked to him only the once. Eight months ago? Ten? I've no concept of time." Ani ran the damp cloth around the back of his neck. "He showed me a stone, an amazingly clear crystal. It came, he said, from this desert. It was lovely, perfection itself. He also showed me a chunk of turquoise a nomad had given him in trade. I told him I dreamed of traveling across the Eastern Sea to the mountain of turquoise, and he said that he, too, wished to see those mines."

"Did he offer to take you with him on one of his expeditions?"

"Not in so many words, but when I told him I dreamed of seeing the stones in their natural state, of picking and choosing myself rather than depending upon someone else's judgment as to which is the best and most beautiful, he said he thought we'd make a good team. Between his understanding of this desert and my knowledge of fine jewelry and stones, we'd surely find things overlooked by other men."

Noting that Ani's breathing had slowed and his color had almost returned to normal, Bak signaled that they move on. "Did he show you any stones other than the turquoise and the crystal?"

"Carnelian, jasper, milky quartz. Attractive pieces, but of less value."

"According to his father, he left Kemet to explore this

desert about nine months ago, returned in three months, and went off two months later never to return. Why didn't you travel with him on one of those journeys?"

"I was afraid." Ani gave Bak a sheepish look. "Yes, afraid. A thing I'm not proud of, but true." He looked down at himself. "Look at me. Do I have the appearance of a man accustomed to hardships? Do I have the demeanor of a brave and hardy soul?"

Bak grinned. He liked a man with no illusions about himself. "What finally brought you here?"

"Desire overcame fear."

After Wensu's blustering, Ani's modest admissions were refreshing. "You must've been disappointed when you heard that Minnakht never returned from his latest expedition."

"I can't tell you how disturbed I was." Ani looked up the wadi toward the caravan. "We can walk a bit faster if you like. I feel better now." As if he had not interrupted the thought, he went on, "I'd spent months convincing myself I could do this, and convincing my overseer that I should. What did I find when I reached Kaine? The man who'd urged me to come had vanished!"

"You must've heard the rumor that he'd found gold."

"I'm not a man who believes all I hear, Lieutenant, but when I heard that tale, my blood ran cold."

"You feared his life was at risk?"

"I toil in a workshop well-supplied with precious metals and stones. Even I am not immune to their value. I know from experience how quickly men's hearts can become inflamed by dreams of wealth."

Bak understood. True or not, the rumor had put Minnakht's life in jeopardy. "Did you and Wensu approach User together, or did you individually propose to travel with him?"

"We were in a house of pleasure, each of us alone, trying to decide what to do. We overheard a man speak of User, calling him witless for entering the desert after Minnakht had so recently failed to return. Foolhardy they called him, to travel alone with a single nomad to keep him company—as Minnakht had. Wensu asked where User could be found, and I inquired as to his appearance. We realized we were both after the same thing: a reliable man to take us into the desert."

Bak recalled Senna saying that User was not entirely to be trusted. "Did you inquire about his reputation?"

"Several men—merchants, drovers, men selling donkeys—vouched for his integrity and his knowledge of the desert." Ani looked at Bak, frowned. "Have you heard anything to his discredit, Lieutenant?"

Bak shook his head. He saw no reason to worry the jeweler. User might be the untrustworthy man Senna thought him. Or Senna might be as unreliable as User believed. Then again, both could be right—or wrong. As for Ani himself, he was a child in this harsh land, one whose every footstep would be torturous to him. Bak was willing to wager a jar of the finest northern wine that this man was as innocent in thought and deed as he appeared.

"I'll say to you what I said to Wensu. If you wish to abandon this adventure of yours and return to Kemet, it's not too late to do so. Kaine is two days' trek away. You can go on with us to the well, stay through the night, and turn back tomorrow."

"No, no, no." Ani's face held the same stubborn look Wensu's had. "I'm here, Lieutenant, and here I stay."

The caravan had come to a halt by the time Bak and Ani caught up. Leaving the craftsman with User's party, Bak hurried forward, seeking a reason. Not a speck of shade was to be seen anywhere. The heat of the sun, confined within the tall, steep hillsides, was merciless. This was not a place to rest.

He found, near the head of his string of donkeys, Minmose holding the halter of a stocky black animal while Rona probed a front hoof with a pair of bronze tweezers. Psuro looked on.

"She's gone lame, sir," the sergeant explained.

"Ah, here it is." Rona screwed up his mouth in concentration while he manipulated the tweezers. The donkey twitched, tried to pull away. The Medjay clamped the tweezers tight and pulled out a small stone. As he released the hoof, Minmose let go of the halter. The animal shook its head and blew, expressing its contempt for such treatment.

They'd no sooner started forward than Nebre and Kaha made their careful way down a steep cut in the rocky slope to the right and walked toward them. Perspiration poured from the men; their tunics were stained with sweat and dust. Each man carried on his shoulder a bow and quiver filled with arrows. Kaha carried a goatskin waterbag.

"You've been gone a long time," Bak said, greeting them with a smile.

"This land is endless." Nebre pulled bow and quiver from his shoulder and handed it to Minmose. "There's much to see. All different but alike."

"This is truly a barren land," Kaha said. "How the nomads find sustenance for themselves and their flocks, I'll never know."

"Did you see any sign of the people who were camped near the well last night?" Bak asked.

"No, sir." Nebre slipped his tunic over his head and shook the dust from it. "They've disappeared without a trace. I've a feeling they left the wadi long ago, probably not far from the well where we spent the night."

Sneezing, Kaha backed away from the cloud Nebre had created. "Twice we saw a man on a distant hillside. Like us, he carried a bow and quiver. He was watching this caravan."

"At first we thought him to be a nomad shepherd, moving his flocks and family through this area. Or a man hunting ibex or gazelle." Nebre slipped his arms through the sleeves of his tunic and pulled it down over his head. "The second time we saw him, we went to the place where last he'd been."

"We found the print of a sandal, sir," Kaha said. "It matched the one I saw on the hillside north of Kaine."

Chapter 5

The sun beat down with the ferocity of a wounded lion. Short gusts of wind failed to lift the coarse granules of sand on the wadi floor, but carried a fine dust unseen at close hand. The land around them shimmered in the heat, while the distant ridges faded into a dirty yellowish haze. Bak and the others drank frequently, consuming the tepid water from their waterbags, quenching a never-ending thirst. Sweat poured from their bodies, staining tunics and kilts.

The donkeys plodded forward, hooves now and again striking a stone, tails swishing away the flies. Bak walked for a while with Psuro, telling the sergeant what he had learned from the men with whom he had talked. He spoke softly, preferring that Senna not hear what he had to say.

"I'm certain Senna didn't slay the man at the well. We'd not yet arrived when he lost his life." Bak wiped the sweat from his face with the tail of his tunic. "But until we're certain we can trust him, I'd rather we keep our suspicions to ourselves."

"You've not told him we're policemen, I've noticed. Nor have you told anyone else."

"Initially, I didn't want him to know until he'd proven himself reliable. Now, with our circumstances altered and a dead man left behind, I'm convinced the decision was a wise one. Ofttimes people grow defensive with the police. They're more apt to speak openly to soldiers. We'll enlighten no one, at least for the present."

As the wadi walls grew higher where the ancient waterway had sliced a path through the hills, Bak walked back along the caravan. The donkeys looked half asleep, as if each followed the one in front by instinct rather than thought. From time to time one would shake its head to throw off a fly or pull back its lips for a soft whicker. He scratched each animal between the ears as he passed it by, grateful for the help it gave to man, the patience it exercised in the most trying of conditions.

Midway in User's widespread string of men and animals, he stopped to speak with Amonmose, who was trudging along beside a donkey laden with water jars. He carried a long staff as Senna did, and probed the sand in front of himself and his equine companion. Other than ruddy cheeks and a shift dripping with sweat, he seemed no more troubled by the heat than the other men, further convincing Bak that much of his weight was muscle rather than fat.

"You appear to be holding up well in this heat, Lieutenant," he said, as if reading Bak's thought and returning it.

"I must admit I prefer green fields and the northerly breezes along the river," Bak said with a smile.

Amonmose chuckled. "I've already begun to suspect I'll find the southern route to the Eastern Sea preferable to this path."

"According to Senna, we'll reach the next well by midday. After we leave it behind, we've two days ahead of us without water, then another well and two or three more dry days."

"User told us." Amonmose licked his lips, whether to moisten them or because he was concerned about the journey, Bak could not tell. "He also said the landscape will grow rougher each day."

"If your decision is nearly made, why not turn back? It's

not too late." Bak spoke with scant conviction; he doubted Amonmose would ever give up a task once begun. Certainly not this one. If Ani and Wensu, as green as they were, would not return to Kaine, neither would the more experienced man.

"Minnakht said this way was more direct, and he should know. I'll stay to the end."

"Our sovereign's caravans have traveled the southern route for many generations," Bak pointed out.

"So my wife reminded me." Amonmose spoke in a sour voice, as if his spouse had belabored the point.

If she had, Bak thought, nothing less than a catastrophe would make him retreat. "How long ago did you meet Minnakht?"

"I'm not sure exactly. Probably within a few days of the day he set off into the desert, never to return." Amonmose pulled a square of cloth from beneath his belt and patted the sweat from his face. "In Waset, it was, at a house of pleasure near the waterfront. My youngest son spends too much time there. Drinking, gambling, playing with the women. You know how a youth of fourteen years can be. Irresponsible. Totally absorbed with fun and games and relieving his sexual urges." A sudden smile spread across his face. "I find nothing wrong with women, mind you, but all things in moderation, I say."

Returning a quick smile, Bak asked, "Did you approach Minnakht or did he come to you?"

"I'd gone in search of the boy and found instead the explorer. I heard him talking to the women there. They were enthralled and, I must admit, so was I. He spoke with a knowledge of the desert that I could never hope to attain. I joined him, offered him a brew, and we talked. He'd heard of my fishing camp and said he'd thought a time or two of sailing up or down the coast on one of my boats, thinking to hasten his journey. Each time the desert beckoned and in the end he never took advantage of my men's generosity."

"Did he say anything about seeking gold?"

Amonmose laughed. "Isn't that every explorer's dream?"

Bak laughed with him. Other than an errand such as his own, what besides wealth or royal attention would entice a man into a land as grim and empty of life as this?

"He admitted he hoped to find gold or some precious stone," Amonmose said, "but he spoke more of the quest for adventure. And knowledge."

A vague movement caught Bak's eye, drawing his attention to a silla bush a dozen paces away. It looked dead, but small pale purple flowers studded its dry, naked branches. The sand was slightly disturbed under it, betraying the presence of a viper beneath the loose surface granules, waiting to ambush a passing rodent or bird. The serpent was far enough off the track to pose no threat to men or donkeys, so he let it be.

"Before your fishing enterprise, how did you support your family?" he asked.

"I was—and still am—a merchant. I began as a young man with the fish my father netted in the Great Green Sea. Fresh and dried, I traded them to nearby farmers. In exchange, I received the bounty of the land, fruits and vegetables, which I traded in turn to villagers for the products of craftsmen. Those I bartered at the estates of noblemen, getting in return goats, sheep, and cattle. And so it went. I ultimately traveled all through the land of Kemet, from the Great Green Sea to the land of Wawat. In the end, we grew quite prosperous."

"We?"

"My three brothers and I. Our families." With the tip of his staff, Amonmose turned over a flattish rock, revealing nothing beneath but sand. "My wife would have me stay at home now and play the country gentleman." A snort of derision burst from his lips. "What a life that would be! The nobility would look down upon me; the men who toil as I've done would think me acting above myself. No, thanks! Let her play the fine lady if she wishes, but that's not the life for me."

Bak liked Amonmose. He felt as the merchant did and could not imagine a life with no purpose. Could Amonmose slay a man? Most certainly. He had the determination and the strength to take a life should the need arise, and he was so light on his feet that he could probably slip unseen through a brigade of sleeping spearmen. Bak preferred not to think that he might have slain the man at the well.

Amonmose caught the bottom of his tunic, pulled it away from his sweaty belly, and flapped it up and down in a vain attempt to dry himself. "I hope you didn't mind my insistence that you join our caravan, Lieutenant."

"To travel together made sense."

"Thus I believed, especially with a slayer lurking somewhere close by."

Bak gave him an interested look. "You don't seem a man easily alarmed."

"Alarmed, no. Cautious, yes." Amonmose glanced up the line of donkeys toward User and smiled, obviously pleased that he had had his own way. "Why travel in two separate groups when we're all taking the same path? Not only are we safer, but we now have the benefit of your experience and the pleasure of your company."

"User believes we've no experience."

"He underestimates you. You and your men are soldiers, proficient fighting men. You may be unschooled in the ways of this particular desert, but you've a knowledge of the weaknesses of others that few men attain."

The words were spoken in so positive a manner they left no doubt of Amonmose's conviction—and more. "Exactly how far into Wawat did you travel?"

"The fortress of Kubban. No farther, and just the once. A man can grow wealthy in Wawat, but it takes time and patience. Time I preferred to spend in Kemet, trading with men I've known for years." All the good humor vanished from the merchant's face; his expression turned grave. "I heard at Kubban of a Lieutenant Bak posted at Buhen, standing at the head of a company of Medjay police. He was a man of honesty and decency, so they said, one highly respected by all who obeyed the lady Maat and greatly feared by those who didn't. One who never failed to snare the man he sought."

Bak muttered an oath. The gods were surely conspiring against him. What were the odds that he would encounter a man who knew him—not by sight but by reputation—in this sparsely inhabited wilderness? He smiled in spite of himself at the unlikely coincidence. "I've come into the Eastern Desert in search of Minnakht. I think it best we leave it at that."

"You can depend upon me to remain mute."

Bak nodded, accepting the pledge, praying the merchant would keep his word. "You mentioned yesterday that someone told you another young man had disappeared in this desert."

"So said a merchant in Kaine, yes."

"Did he offer any details?" With the point of his spear, Bak probed the sand around a bush near the path of the donkey.

"Like Minnakht, he was an explorer," Amonmose said. "I don't recall hearing his name, but the merchant had an idea that he knew the desert well."

"He didn't come out here alone, did he?"

"Evidently not. He told the merchant and other men in Kaine that he had a guide, a man he planned to meet at the edge of the desert. A nomad, they all assumed, but no one ever saw him. He set out by himself one morning, heading north. Who the guide was and whether or not they met remains a mystery to this day. A puzzle yet to be solved."

* * *

They reached the well soon after midday. There they stopped to rest in the narrow slice of shade cast by steep and high wadi walls. The well, a hundred or so paces away in the floor of the ancient watercourse, was surrounded by a dry-stone wall. How that wall would hold up to one of the rare flash floods, Bak had no idea.

While seeing to the setting up of his camp, he noticed Nebenkemet helping the drovers unload the donkeys of User's caravan farther down the wadi. The shade was too skimpy to share with the animals, so they stood in the sun, meekly allowing the men to relieve them of their burdens. Though the nomads spoke a different tongue, the burly carpenter seemed to communicate well enough with them, using hand signals and other gestures easy to understand. Did he choose their company because he felt uncomfortable with men of a more lofty status? Or did he simply prefer to keep busy, and to help with the loading and unloading was one of the few ways to do so?

After ensuring that his own animals were cared for, Bak walked down the wadi. As he approached Nebenkemet, the carpenter greeted him with a grunt and went on about his task. Struck dumb by the officer's presence, the drovers toiled on, watching with wary eyes.

"It's good of you to help with this task," Bak said.

Nebenkemet devoted his full attention to the water jar he lifted off the donkey. Holding it with ease, betraying the fact that it was empty, he set it beside the jar which had hung on the opposite side of the animal. "I've nothing better to do."

"Neither Ani nor Wensu is helping."

"Those two!" The carpenter laughed harshly. "Wensu wouldn't lift a hand to feed himself if he didn't have to, and Ani wouldn't know how."

"Have you noticed the scars on Ani's hands? He didn't get them by spending his days in idleness."

The carpenter lifted from the donkey's back the wooden frame from which the jars had been suspended and the soft pad beneath. "I've seen them."

Bak noted the edge of contempt in his voice. "You don't believe a man who creates beautiful jewelry can toil as hard and long as a carpenter?"

Nebenkemet did not deign to respond.

Watching him knead the donkey's shoulders where the pad had rested, Bak wondered how a man so reluctant to speak would fare with a small group of fishermen dwelling in an isolated camp on the shore of the Eastern Sea. Were they garrulous men who would resent his silence, or taciturn men who would welcome his failure to speak?

"Where did you practice your trade, Nebenkemet?"

The carpenter stared at Bak, saying nothing, as if trying to decide whether or not he should answer. "I toiled at a shipyard in Mennufer."

Rough work among rough men, so Bak had been told. He had never seen the shipyards, but he doubted the building of ships could account for all the scars on the carpenter's hands and lower arms, and those on the back of his legs looked like the marks of a whip. Perhaps he had failed to obey a hard taskmaster. Or maybe he was a man who became aggressive when besotted and involved himself in numerous brawls.

Nebenkemet released the donkey and let it trot to the well, where a drover was drawing water and pouring it into a deep, wide-mouthed bowl buried almost to the neck in the sand so thirsty animals would not tip it over. Another donkey was already drinking, so the new arrival had to wait. Bak caught the halter of the nearest laden donkey and drew it close. As the carpenter lifted a jar from its back, Bak removed the container from the opposite side. The two men's eyes met across the animal's back. Nebenkemet looked quickly away, as if he feared his eyes were windows through which Bak might read his thoughts.

If only such were the case, Bak thought. "Where will you get building materials for use at the fishing camp?" he asked, thinking a less personal question might open a path through the man's defenses. "I've been told that the coastline all along the Eastern Sea is as barren as these desert wadis."

"Amonmose will see that I get whatever I need for the boat. As for the huts, I'll build them of stone."

Bak glanced at the high walls of the wadi, at its floor littered with fallen boulders and rocks, and gave the carpenter a wry smile. "There'll be no shortage of stone, I'll warrant."

A suspicion of a smile touched Nebenkemet's face, but again he failed to pursue the opening Bak had provided.

"Do you expect the tasks to keep you long at the fishing camp?"

Nebenkemet shrugged as if indifferent.

Bak was becoming irritated. Normally a man would at least participate to some extent in a conversation. Talking to this man was like talking to a tree. "Did you ever meet Minnakht? Speak with him?"

Rather than the negative Bak expected, Nebenkemet said, "Amonmose did all the talking. I watched and listened."

"You were toiling for Amonmose even then?" Bak asked, surprised.

"His wife wanted a shrine in her garden. I built it."

That Amonmose would ask a man he knew and trusted rather than a stranger to accompany him on a hazardous journey such as this made sense. That the merchant would take a tough-looking man with him when searching through the rough houses of pleasure along the waterfront of Waset made more sense. "What was your impression of Minnakht?"

"He was a man whose dreams outstripped reality."

Bak was intrigued that a man of no learning should have seen something in the explorer that the worldly Amonmose had missed. "In what way?" he asked, openly curious.

"He talked of this desert as if the future of the land of

Kemet lay here. As if all good things could be found if a man would but seek them out. His enthusiasm knew no bounds." Nebenkemet eyed the land around him with a contemptuous scowl. "He may've been right in thinking that here can be found gold and precious stones. What he never once considered was how hard won they'll be."

The long speech was a measure of the craftsman's skepticism, Bak felt sure, but he also sensed a depth of feeling he could not account for. "User believes there's something out here to be found."

"He speaks with more caution than Minnakht did. He sees the world more as it truly is."

"What do you think happened to Minnakht?"

Glancing at the high, nearly vertical walls of the wadi, at the stones scattered along its floor, Nebenkemet returned the same wry smile Bak had given him earlier. "There's no shortage of rock in this desert, or of steep slopes down which a boulder could fall."

Bak did not know what to make of this man. He felt sure that one as powerful as he could slay another with ease, but would he take a life? Under what circumstances? Their unsatisfactory conversation had revealed nothing of his character.

Bak lay beneath an overhanging rock, trying to rest. His men, sleeping close by in the narrow strip of shade, had planted spears in the ground and had fastened sleeping mats between them to stave off the hot wind, but the stifling air and tumbling thoughts would not let him nap.

His discussions through the morning had given him much to think about. He had come no closer to identifying the dead man or the one who had slain him, but he had learned enough about his fellow travelers to realize how unlikely each man was to have set off on an untrodden path through an empty and unknown land. Except for User, the lifelong explorer.

The willingness of these men to venture so far afield, he suspected, was a measure of Minnakht's persuasiveness, his excitement when describing his adventures. Here he faced
another exception: Nebenkemet, the skeptic.

Few men had the ability to draw others in their wake. What
had Minnakht said to lure them into this rocky wasteland?
Had he altered his tale to fit each man's need? Or had he se-
duced them with a single tale and a pledge of secrecy?

Bak could think of no more disparate a group of people on
what promised to be a hard and dangerous journey. Which
man would prove strong enough to go on, no matter how difficult the circumstances? Who would falter and have to be
helped? With the donkeys able to carry a minimum of water
and supplies, with wells or springs as much as three days
apart, they could not offer unlimited aid to a seriously injured
man. What would they do if faced with such a decision?

Would they be able to find nomads willing to help? Where
were the nomads? Nebre and Kaha had found fresh tracks
around the well and signs that a small group of people had
camped in the shade. A shallow puddle had remained in the
bottom of the bowl, indicating that they had watered their animals not long before Bak and the others had arrived. Why
had they moved on in the heat of the day? Where had they
gone? Had the nomad Nebre and Kaha seen earlier in the
morning warned them of the approaching caravan? Even if
he had, their leaving made no sense. If the people of this
Eastern Desert were anything like the tribesmen on the
southern frontier, they were a garrulous lot, as eager to speak
with strangers as they were to pass news to friends.

His thoughts settled on questions more relevant to his
mission: What happened to Minnakht? Was he alive or
dead? If he was as highly respected by the nomads as everyone seemed to think, how could he have vanished with no
one the wiser? In what way was his disappearance related to

the dead man and to the man who had gone missing nearly a
year ago?

Bak awakened to the sound of falling water, droplets striking the earth around the edge of his shelter. He shook off
sleep, looked out into the bright sunlight, snapped his eyes
shut. Sunlight and rain? He sat up abruptly, nearly bumping
his head on the stone above, and glanced around. Another
smattering of sound. Small stones peppering the earth
around him. Someone or something was standing above his
shelter on the rim of the steeply inclined wadi wall.
Nebenkemet's words came back to him: "There's no shortage of rock in this desert, or of steep slopes down which a
boulder could fall."

He scooted out from the shade and, leaping to his feet,
yelled, "Move! Away from the hillside!"

Psuro and the Medjays, accustomed to acting without
question, obeyed instantly. Bak darted away from the overhang and at the same time looked up the long, steep slope of
eroded grayish rock. He thought he glimpsed something at
the top, but could not be sure. Whatever it was vanished as if
it had never been.

User, accustomed to life in the rough and attuned to danger, had been as quick to act as the Medjays. Nebenkemet
moved almost as fast. The other men left their resting places
half asleep and grumbling. The carpenter stared up the incline above Bak, then flung a quick glance at the officer, evidently remembering the words he had spoken so short a time
before.

"What happened?" User asked, hurrying to Bak's side as
the Medjays gathered around.

After a brief explanation, Bak sent Nebre and Kaha out to
find a way to the top of the incline. "I may be unduly worried," he admitted, "but we did find a man slain this morning."

Looking grim, User nodded. "I'm no lover of nomads, as

Minnakht was, but I have to say I've never known one who slew another man without reason. That reason may not always be valid in our eyes, but it is to them. A blood feud, maybe, or a war between tribes. Neither of which would apply to men new to this desert, such as yourself and the Medjays."

"Perhaps you've earned an enemy among them."

The explorer scowled. "I doubt a nomad would've mistaken the slain man for me, Lieutenant."

Bak, who had spoken in haste, hurried to make amends. A rift between him and User or among any of the others would multiply ten times ten any danger they might have to face. Clapping the explorer on the shoulder, he smiled. "That was a thought, no more. I'm a soldier, trained to be always on the defensive. An animal may've set those rocks to falling, not a man. Nebre and Kaha will soon learn the truth."

"A man was up there, all right." Nebre knelt beside the small fire Minmose had made, using a dead bush for fuel. He had built the fire on the wadi floor, well away from the hillside. Its fiery coals made a tiny patch of cheer beneath the cooler light of the stars and moon. "The man with the worn sandal, the one whose footprint Kaha found north of Kaine."

"We followed him for more than an hour," Kaha said, laying his bow and quiver with those of Nebre and squatting beside his friend. "He must've feared we'd catch him, for he put something on his feet to smudge his prints, a woolly sheepskin, I'd wager. Because the prints were so unclear and he traveled across rock as much as he could, we lost his trail."

Nebre scowled as Minmose broke up a crusty chunk of bread and dropped it in the onion and lentil stew warming on the coals. He was not irritated by the food being stretched to go around, but by the difficulties they had faced. "The lord Amon alone knows how much time we wasted walking in circles, trying to find him again. Not wishing to spend the night in an unfamiliar landscape, we thought to return before the lord Re entered the netherworld."

The smell of heated onions reminded Bak of how hungry he was. "Who can he be, I wonder? Why is he watching us?"

Nebre shrugged, as did Kaha. Psuro offered no comment, nor did Minmose or Rona.

"Could he have slain the man we found this morning without leaving behind any sign of his presence?"

Nebre shrugged. "Anything is possible, but I don't see how."

Bak looked down the wadi toward the small fire around which the men of User's party could be dimly seen. They, too, had thought it best to camp well out on the wadi floor. Night had fallen swiftly. The wind had died and the heat of the day had vanished with the sun. Most of the donkeys, sated with water and forage, were lying down, better able to rest in the cool of night.

He scanned the faces of the Medjays sitting around the fire, making sure he had their undivided attention. "From now on, one of you must stand watch every night, taking turns, and two of you must serve as scouts during each day's march. I know Nebre and Kaha are the best trackers among you, but you must all share the task. The days are too hot, the landscape too rough for the same two men to bear the burden day after day." He wrapped his arms around his bent legs and added in a deliberate voice, "If you see the man who's been watching us—or if you see anyone else, for that matter—you must bring him to me if you can. If he's too far away to talk to, you must give chase, but not for any great distance."

Kaha threw him a pained look. "But, sir!"

Bak raised a hand to silence the Medjay. "I doubt any of you would get lost, even in this wild and barren land. You've too much experience in the desert. But I don't want you walking into a trap. Nor do I want you injured by chance somewhere far from help."

"Sir!" Nebre said. "That's like leading a goat to water and not letting it drink."

"With luck and the help of the gods, before this journey is over, we'll find a way to draw the watching man into a trap of our own."

Chapter 6

They left the well before dawn to cross a low divide and enter another wadi, this many paces wide. Striking off in a more northerly direction, it carried them into a world totally different than that of the previous two days. The grayish limestone cliffs that had lined the lower wadi slid away behind them, replaced by yellow and brown sandstone. Golden dunes climbed the sides of the slopes, a few so tall they spilled over the top. Scattered boulders and stones of all sizes spread across the coarse sand on the wadi floor, casting long blackish shadows before the rising sun.

Nebenkemet's appraisal of Minnakht refused to fade from Bak's thoughts. Ani, Wensu, and Amonmose alike had described a man whose enthusiasm and way with words enthralled those with whom he spoke, filling the hearts of the most unlikely with dreams of adventure, wealth, and fame. Even User, admittedly envious of his competitor, thought the young explorer a man who loved the life he lived, the land he trod, and the nomads who dwelt in that land.

Bak had known men from all walks of life whose astute observations placed them above their fellows. Could Nebenkemet be one of them? Or did he, like User, harbor jealousy in his heart? Resentment of a man endowed with the wealth and opportunity he had never had.

* * *

"Look at this, Lieutenant." Ani scooped up a handful of sand and sorted through it with a finger, revealing granules of pink, white, and beige. "Feldspar and quartz washed down from those mountains." He pointed toward the northeast, where tall, rugged peaks reached up to the turquoise sky, catching wisps of cloud on their craggy tops. Towering above them all was a reddish mountain whose innumerable pinnacles caught the morning sun. Those peaks, several days' walk ahead, marked the place where the wadis drained eastward rather than toward the west as they did here. "Mere bits of rock, but beautiful, aren't they? Especially when one considers how small they are and how far they've traveled."

Bak hated to dampen the jeweler's enthusiasm, but he feared for his safety. "They're very much the colors of a viper, Ani. You must take care when you reach down like that. The snakes bury themselves close to the surface of the sand, and are quick to attack when they feel themselves threatened." He had long ago exchanged his baton of office for a spear to probe the sand ahead of his feet.

"So User has told me, but I forget."

Belaboring the subject would be a waste of breath, Bak felt sure. "Could the man we found slain at the first well have been mistaken for Minnakht? Did they resemble each other in any way?"

"I wouldn't think so." Ani let the granules fall to the ground and wiped his hand on his kilt. "The dead man was about the same age, but was of medium height and build. His face was unremarkable, with no distinguishing features that I recall." The jeweler screwed up his face, trying to remember. "I'm sorry, Lieutenant. I'd never before seen a man slain in his sleep. I guess I was more upset than I thought."

"Can you describe Minnakht?"

A smile lit up Ani's face. "That's easy enough. He was tall, taller than the dead man by more than a hand's breadth. He had thick, dark hair, slightly curly, lively dark eyes, and a most expressive face, bright with vitality and good humor."

Bak wondered how many hundreds of men would answer to that description. "Did he wear any jewelry of note or any special amulet?" This, he felt certain, Ani would be able to answer in detail.

"I saw him only the one time, and that in Waset," the jeweler reminded him. "He wore a broad collar much too fine to wear into the desert, and bracelets and armlets of an equal quality. He wore a bronze chain around his neck. I remember wondering why he chose bronze instead of gold. I couldn't see what hung from the chain. Whatever it was was hidden beneath the collar."

Bak would have given his best pair of sandals to know what hung from that chain. "You told me how you met him and how he swept you away with his tales of the desert and of the many beautiful minerals and stones found here. Did he talk of himself at all?"

"He wasn't an individual who enjoyed speaking of personal matters. He did say . . ." Ani stopped himself, reluctant to reveal what another man had told him, if not in confidence at least as one man to another. "I suppose, since he's been gone so long . . ."

"Anything you tell me might help. The most unlikely bit of information could be of infinite value."

"Well . . ." Ani bent to pick up another handful of sand—giving himself time to think, Bak suspected. Paying no heed to the possibility that he might disturb a viper. "You see, Lieutenant, he wanted my assurance that I could go off into the desert, leaving no one behind uncared for. I told him I dwelt alone, that my wife of twenty years had gone to the netherworld not six months earlier and my children were wed and had homes of their own. I told him my overseer, the chief jeweler in the royal house, would allow me to go with his good wishes and a prayer that I'd return with many unique and beautiful stones."

Ani ran a finger through the sand he held. Finding nothing special, he tipped his hand, spilling out the grit. The hot breeze was strong enough to carry away the dust but too weak to deflect the path of the falling granules. "He spoke of a young woman he had loved and lost. One who had vowed to be his forever. He left her behind to come into the desert, confident she would wait and wait again each time he set out to explore this barren land. Upon his return, he found her wed to another, a young nobleman who had given her a fine home and would never wander from her side." Brushing the dust from his hands, Ani added, "Six or seven years ago, it was, but he made no secret that the loss still hurt."

Bak wondered if the tale had been offered casually. Or had its telling been calculated to win the jeweler over? Ani had told Minnakht of a wife gone to the netherworld, and the explorer had offered up a mutual loss. A tie that had bound the older man to the younger, personally as well as professionally.

The wadi narrowed to half its former width. The yellowish sandstone walls rose higher, contrasting with the sky above, making the blue more intense. Bak walked a few paces to the left of the caravan, following the tracks of gazelle that had traveled this way sometime in the recent past. The day of their passing was unimportant, the event memorable for only as long as the tracks remained.

Ani's description of Minnakht had been sketchy at best, but Bak doubted the man at the well had been mistakenly slain in place of the explorer. Minnakht had vanished two months ago. If the people of the Eastern Desert were anything like those who dwelt on the southern frontier—and he assumed they were—news traveled faster than locusts laying waste to the land. All the world would have long ago known of the explorer's disappearance.

Which meant that the unknown man's death was a separate incident—but was somehow related, he felt sure. That the dead man had carried no means of identification was not unusual, but was frustrating nonetheless. His appearance had been ordinary, his few personal items and clothing of reasonably good quality but not the best. His traveling supplies had been much like those Bak and his men had brought into the desert. His thick wrists and muscular arms looked to be those of an archer. He might have been a soldier, but could as easily have been a man who ofttimes practiced with the bow. Nothing but the gold chain and pendant, both of fine quality and workmanship, had been noteworthy.

Shoving aside thoughts that led him nowhere, Bak crossed a stretch of sand whose grains sparkled in the sunlight and climbed a large reddish outcrop that angled upward until it was twice the height of a man. From the more elevated perspective, he looked up the wadi as far as he could see and scanned the clifftops to either side. He thought he glimpsed a figure on the southern rim, but the glare of sunlight made it impossible to be certain. Kaha and Minmose had slipped away from the caravan as they broke camp, and he assumed they were somewhere above. The figure might have been one of them.

User strode across the sand and climbed up beside him. "You've kept to yourself much of the morning, Lieutenant."

"I've been thinking about the dead man we sent back to Kemet. Wondering who he was."

"I pray someone in Kaine recognizes him. I, for one, wouldn't want to be buried nameless."

They stood in an uncomfortable silence, enshrouded by the thought. The loss of his name would doom the dead man to the destruction of his memory and would deprive him of existence in the netherworld.

"I've also been thinking of Minnakht," Bak said. "I've come to realize I have no idea what he looks like."

User smiled unexpectedly. "Never fear, Lieutenant. If you should come upon him while you're with this caravan, the rest of us will recognize him."

Bak had to laugh. "Are you so pleased with my company that you wish me to stay forever?"

"So far you've made no demands on me or my drovers or my animals." User had become dead serious. "In fact, you've given more than you've taken. I've not the men to scout ahead, and that's a task I'm beginning to think we sorely need."

"Because the nomads are leaving the wells before we appear? Or because someone has been watching us from afar?"

User eyed the passing caravan, the men and animals trudging in an irregular line up the dry, sunstruck riverbed. "I've never known the people to be so shy, and I can't explain it. They usually come to talk, to hear news of other nomads, and they come to trade for items hard to find out here in this remote land. Each time I enter this desert, I bring cloth, beads, honey, needles, and other small objects they need or desire. They've come to expect them, so why has no one approached thus far to see what I've brought?"

"Could they believe you responsible for Minnakht's disappearance?"

"I don't see why they would. I've not been out here since last he left Kaine." User looked up the wadi toward Senna, marching at the head of the caravan. "I'm more inclined to believe they don't trust your guide."

Bak's eyes followed User's. Did the nomads hold Senna directly responsible for Minnakht's disappearance, or did they simply consider him a man who had failed in his duty? "What did Minnakht look like?"

User barked out a cynical laugh, as if he had guessed Bak's lack of confidence in Senna. "He looked a bit like the dead man, but may not have been quite as tall. He had a lot of straight dark hair and dark eyes, and his skin was ruddy from too much sun."

Interesting, Bak thought. Ani, a short man, had described Minnakht as tall. User was tall; therefore, he thought the young explorer short. One man remembered his hair as curly, the other said it was straight. The truth must be somewhere in between. After taking a final look along the clifftops, reassuring himself that all was well, he walked down the sloping rock to the wadi floor. The older man kept pace with him stride for stride.

"He had a way of walking that struck me as an affectation, although I doubt it was," User said. "I know his father was a military man, and I guess he taught him to move like that, but he marched rather than walked. Chin high, long strides, spine as straight as that spear you're holding. It gave him the appearance of supreme self-confidence. A man invincible."

"Did he wear any special jewelry that he never took off, something he wore even when traveling through the desert?"

User shrugged. "I seem to remember a chain with some kind of pendant. Exactly what, I paid no heed."

"Sorry, Lieutenant, but I'm no good at guessing how tall people are." Amonmose walked up the gradually narrowing wadi between Bak and a donkey, his gait rolling like that of the sailor he had been in his youth, his stride easy. "I judge a man by his actions. If he's hard-working and honest, he's tall in my eyes. If he's indolent and a sneak, I think of him as small."

Bak could not help but smile at so simplistic a way of looking at others. "Did you see Minnakht as tall or short?"

"Hmmm." Amonmose probed his teeth with a sharpened twig, thinking. "Interesting. I thought him tall, but I recall standing before him, looking him straight in the eye."

"What else do you remember?"

"He was well-formed in body and face. What more can I say?"

Bak eyed the trader at his side. As he had before, he marveled that such a portly man could walk in the sun for hours on end without undue suffering from the heat. Too bad his powers of observation were not as powerful as his stamina. "From what you told me yesterday, the man who vanished ten months ago was a stranger to this part of the desert."

"So I assumed." Amonmose frowned, thinking back. "If the people who spoke of him had known him, their voices would've held more warmth or chill. More sympathy for the man, more passion at his failure to return."

"Did he know Minnakht, do you think?"

"No one said." The trader took the twig from his mouth and threw it away. "No more than a half-dozen men explore this desert year after year, Lieutenant. The area between the southern trail that runs east from Waset and the northern trail that connects Mennufer to the Eastern Sea is vast. They might never come face to face, but they'll surely have heard of each other."

Bak looked back along the caravan, thinking to ask User if he had known the missing man. The explorer was standing off to the side of the line of passing donkeys, watching a drover reload an animal whose burden had shifted on its back. He would have to wait for a better time.

An hour or so before midday, they stopped beside a strip of shade at the base of a cliff on the south side of the watercourse. The wadi had narrowed to a quarter of its original width. After checking the welfare of men and donkeys, Bak thought to speak with Wensu, another man who might better describe Minnakht than had Ani or Amonmose or User. On the other hand, having seen the explorer as a heroic figure, his description might be as influenced as theirs by his feelings about the missing man.

Wensu had rolled out his thin sleeping mat in the most comfortable place in which to rest, a wider than average swath of shade free of fallen rocks. While Nebenkemet and Amonmose had helped the drovers unload the donkeys, while Ani had wandered across the wadi floor in search of interesting stones, he had surrounded himself with his possessions, wasting precious shade better used by men and donkeys than by objects.

"I must speak with you, Wensu." Bak lifted the young man's waterbag, inadvertently trailing sand along the youth's leg, and moved it into the sun so he could sit in its place.

Clearly annoyed, Wensu brushed away the sand and moved the waterbag back into the shade, placing it on top of a basket of clothing and toiletries. "I'm not accustomed to rising so early in the morning, Lieutenant, nor am I used to walking so far. I'm tired and need to rest."

Unimpressed, lacking in sympathy, Bak said, "I never had the good fortune to meet Minnakht. If I'm to find him, I must know how he looks. Can you describe him for me?"

Wensu appeared torn, reluctant to give up his petulant attitude but eager to speak of the man he had admired above all others. The latter won out. "He's an admirable man, one who lives a life of adventure and excitement. A brave man, who daily risks his life so our sovereign and the noble ladies of our kingdom can bedeck themselves as befits their lofty stations in life."

Bak wondered if Wensu's father had risen through the scribal ranks by spouting similar trite phrases to his superiors. "I seek Minnakht's physical description, not your assessment of his character."

If Wensu noticed the cynicism, he gave no hint. "I see." The wrinkled brow, the slight frown, made Bak wonder exactly how well the youth remembered the man he professed to admire so much. "He's a fine figure of a man, much taller than average and broad shouldered, as well formed as a statue of our sovereign's deceased husband, the Osiris Akheperenre Thutmose. He has short dark hair, piercing eyes as black as night, and the sun-darkened skin of an outdoorsman."

"What was he wearing when last you saw him?"

"A thigh-length linen kilt. A very fine broad beaded collar and bracelets. A lovely gold chain from which hung amulets representing the ibex, gazelle, and falcon." Wensu gave Bak a supercilious look. "You'll not find him adorned like that out here, Lieutenant."

No, Bak agreed. What Wensu had described was finery one would expect a young man of substance to wear in Waset. He wondered if the gold chain was the same as the bronze chain Ani had noticed, the lesser metal turned to gold under the uncritical eye of the young admirer. "Did he reveal anything of himself to you?"

"He told me a few of his many exploits. He spoke of the time he climbed the red mountain, which he said was the tallest in the Eastern Desert. And the time he got caught up in a flash flood and . . ."

"Did he speak his innermost thoughts?" Bak cut in. "Did he tell you of his dreams, his fears, his failures?"

"Failures? Fears?" Wensu looked shocked at the very idea. "I doubt he fails at anything he attempts. I'm certain he fears nothing."

Bak prayed to the lord Amon for patience. The youth was so blinded by admiration that he refused to see Minnakht as an ordinary man with ordinary feelings and dreams. "Other than his love of adventure, did he give any reason for spending so much time in the desert and so little time at home in the capital?"

"His father is a commander in the army, assigned to the garrison at Waset." A look of contempt fell upon Wensu's face. "An overbearing man, he is, one who wants Minnakht to walk in his footsteps. Where he should support his son's explorations, he never ceases to argue in favor of the army."

Interesting, Bak thought. Inebny's every word and action had made him seem a doting father, inordinately proud of his son and the young man's journeys into the desert. Had Minnakht truly believed his father disapproved of him? Or had he created an image that would appeal to Wensu, one whose father pushed him to rise through the ranks of the scribal hierarchy. Or had Wensu heard what he wished to hear?

As the sun moved westward, the shade widened, sheltering both men and animals from the burning heat. A light breeze blew up the wadi, stirring the air but offering no relief. Everyone slept except Rona and Nebre, who each took a turn standing watch. When Bak relieved Rona at midafternoon, the Medjay reported that all was quiet, the wadi deserted. A couple of times, he had heard pebbles fall down the cliff face, but had seen nothing on the rim above.

Seated alone in the sparse shade of an acacia, Bak mulled over the inconsistent and ofttimes contradictory descriptions of Minnakht. He tried to blend them together to recreate the man in his thoughts. A dozen images came and went, none in which he had any confidence.

They were slow to leave the shade. A donkey had stepped on a stone early in the day, but had given no sign. After walking on it for several hours and embedding it deeper in his hoof, it had begun to bother him. When the drover began to load him, he favored the one leg. The drover tried to dig out the stone, but succeeded only in hurting the animal and making it fractious. User finally ordered the man away, approached the donkey with gentle words and hands, and performed the task, exercising an unexpected gentleness and patience.

By this time, Bak had begun to worry about Kaha and Minmose. He had heard nothing from them since they had walked up the wadi before daybreak. As if to justify his fears, he more than once saw Nebre and Rona looking up or down the wadi and at the clifftops to either side, their faces clouded by worry.

With the lord Re an hour above the western horizon, preparing to descend into the netherworld, and the caravan already on the move, the two Medjays appeared far up the wadi. Instead of walking down the dry watercourse to meet the caravan, as they normally would have done, the pair sat down in the first patch of shade they found and waited. Their decision to rest told Bak truer than words how tired they were.

He grabbed a goatskin waterbag and hurried on ahead of the caravan. The pair made motions of rising as he approached, but he signaled them to remain where they were. He handed the waterbag to Kaha, who drank from it greedily. As he had suspected, after so many hours walking the hot and barren land, their waterbag was empty.

"What kept you?" he asked.

Kaha wiped his mouth with the back of his hand and passed the bag to Minmose. "Where yesterday we found a few isolated footprints at widespread points overlooking the wadi, today we found a multitude of tracks. Not here, but farther upstream. We spent much of the day following them."

"They were fresh?"

"Each print was distinct, not blurred by time. I'd guess a day or two at most."

Bak imagined the rough terrain to either side of the wadi. No man would choose the much more difficult path over the sandy floor of the dry watercourse without good reason. He did not like the implication. "You say a multitude. Can you be more specific?"

"Fifteen to twenty men," Minmose said. "Possibly more."

Kaha's expression was grim. "Men alone, with no women or children."

Bak muttered an oath. "Warriors, do you think?"

"It would appear so."

"Nomads?"

Minmose nodded. "Most were barefooted. A few wore sandals that were old and worn."

"Was the watching man among them?"

"No, sir," Kaha said. "I looked specifically for the print of his sandal, but never found it."

"Our caravan is small," Bak said, thinking aloud. "Fifteen men total, with just six of us equipped and trained to fight. Why did they not wait for our approach? I wonder."

"They may have thought our force stronger than it is," Minmose said. "Maybe they went off to get more men."

Kaha broke the long silence that followed that dire prediction. "We thought to follow them, to find their camp, but after leaving this wadi, they scattered. None took the same path as any other, but in general they went in a northeasterly direction. Heeding your orders not to go too far afield, we followed none for longer than an hour. Each time we had to return to this wadi to pick up another trail. With so much going and coming, we were able to follow five men, no more."

"No wonder you came back exhausted."

"One thing we know for a fact: not a man among them remained behind."

Bak thought of the falling pebbles Rona had heard and was not so confident.

The wadi narrowed further. The pale glow of sunset faded from the sky, replaced by the light of the moon and a magnificent display of stars. Bak, walking with Senna at the head of the caravan, felt as if he were traveling up a river of silvery sand running between high walls of sandstone whose striations had lost their color with the setting sun, turning to shades of gray. Boulders and stones fallen from above were islets rising from the streambed, and wind-formed ripples in the sand had become minute swells whose form was fixed in time. The soft plop-plop of the donkeys' hooves were like bubbles bursting in water.

The section of wadi through which they were walking was beautiful, magical almost, but he looked forward to a safer stretch of landscape. The men who had left the footprints Kaha and Minmose had found had come to the wadi for a reason. That reason had to be the caravan. Since they had not shown themselves, he had to assume the worst.

"We must camp tonight well out in the open," he said, "where alert guards can spot in the moonlight any approaching men and where boulders can't fall from above. How long must we travel to find such a place?"

He had earlier told his Medjays, User, and both nomad guides of all Kaha and Minmose had seen. Senna had evidently given some thought to their situation:

"In a half hour or so, we'll reach a long bend in the wadi. It gradually widens out until we come upon a line of trees. They grow along the latest channel to be cut through the ancient streambed, near the center of the wadi. We'll sleep there, where . . ."

The guide's words were lost to the rumble of a falling boulder and a smattering of smaller stones. A huge rock struck the wadi floor not ten paces ahead of the two men, sending a burst of dust and shards into the air. Other rocks began to fall, thundering down the cliffside and crashing onto the wadi floor. Senna froze. Bak grabbed his arm and hustled him toward the opposing cliff. The foremost donkey, not far behind, cried out in fear and tried to jerk away from Minmose, who was leading the string of animals. The Medjay whacked it on the shoulder with his short whip, frightening it further.

Shoving Senna forward, Bak grabbed the rope halter and shouted at Minmose to use the whip on the animal's flank. As the lash snapped against its flesh, the donkey shot across the sand, nearly running Bak down and half-dragging the six animals roped together in a line behind. Rona grabbed the halter of the last donkey, urging it forward, and screamed a blood-curdling cry to keep the string moving. Within moments, they reached the center of the wadi and safety.

By this time, boulders and rocks were falling all along the southern rim of the cliff above the strung-out caravan. The larger missiles struck the earth with a solid thud, settling into the deep carpet of sand. Others fell with a clatter, striking the boulders among which they fell and the stones scattered along the wadi floor. Many burst upon impact, sending sharp bits of stone flying in all directions. The donkeys in User's string brayed and snorted and squealed, terrified by the noise, by the heavy boulders crashing down and the bursts of shards. Guide and drovers cursed and yelled at the animals, pulling and shoving and whipping them toward the opposite side of the wadi, away from the danger. Psuro, Nebre, and Kaha ran to help.

Bak looked upward toward the top of the cliff down which the stones were plummeting. He glimpsed men standing on the rim, pushing the rocks over the edge. The nomads Kaha and Minmose had tried all day to find, he felt sure. They must have come a day or so before to seek out the best place from which to attack. They had gone away, leaving conspicuous and confusing tracks for the Medjays to follow, and had returned by way of a circuitous route to await the caravan. Were they all above, shoving rocks over the rim? Or were a goodly number waiting around the bend to set upon the caravan?

Fearing another attack from the opposing cliff, Bak yelled at Rona and Minmose to hold the frightened donkeys in the middle of the wadi. Senna ran to help. Bak swung around, thinking to offer aid to User, but the other, larger string of animals had been brought under control and the nomad drovers and Medjays were hustling them well away from the cliff and the stones plummeting down.

With nothing left below to hurt or destroy, the number of

rocks falling from above gradually lessened, and the sounds of impact grew sporadic.

"Help! Help!"

Bak glanced quickly around, fearing someone had been caught in the barrage. The men and donkeys strung along the wadi floor were tense and uneasy, but none were missing and none seemed to be hurt.

"Help!"

Rona, Minmose, and Senna flung him a startled look. They, too, had heard the call. It had come from up the wadi in the direction they had been traveling.

Bak ran toward the sound and Senna followed close behind. A third cry for help drew them to a steep and narrow cut in the northern wall of the wadi. The moon beamed down from the far end, throwing its light on the rocky floor of the ravine and pockets of sand that had collected in the low spots. About midway, a man half-crouched on a strip of sand. He looked to be injured and appeared to be trying to get away.

"I'll see what I can do for him," Bak said. "Go tell Psuro where I've gone."

While Senna hurried to obey, Bak climbed upward. The floor of the cut was steep, and a tumble of craggy rocks slowed him down to a hard, fast scramble. He had a vague impression of rough walls to either side and the moon hanging dead center of the opening at the top. A vague thought struck that this man might be Minnakht, but as he neared the figure, he realized he was a nomad.

He knelt beside the man. "You called for help. What . . . ?"

A blow struck him on the side of the head and the world around him went black.

Chapter 7

Bak heard voices, men speaking softly in a tongue he did not understand. He opened his eyes but could see no one. His head throbbed, the pain radiating out from a spot above his left ear. He had no memory, could not imagine where he was or how he had gotten there. He lay on his stomach on a warm bed of sand, his right cheek pressed against the grit. The world around him was dark and he faced a stone wall. His hands were behind him tied at the wrists.

He tried to roll onto his side. A sharp voice—a reprimand or an order—cut through the murmurs. He heard the rustle of movement and a strong hand clutched his shoulder to hold him down. He tried to struggle free. A sharp blow brought him up short, sending agonies of pain through his head, extracting a moan from him.

He lay unmoving, letting the pain ebb. Bits and pieces of his life began to creep into his thoughts. The desert. The Eastern Desert. Walking at the head of a caravan up a gradually narrowing wadi. Rocks falling all along the wall of the watercourse. Men and donkeys scrambling for safety.

Afraid for them, he struggled to rise, to go to them. A spat-out warning and another clout, a fresh wave of pain so sharp it took his breath away. He lay as if paralyzed, waiting for the torment to subside, wondering how he had gotten himself into such a dreadful situation.

He thought he heard the hoof of a horse strike stone. Surely not. Not out here. Not in this desert where the lowly donkey served man's needs. Not . . . Memory came flooding back: a man calling for help, running up the wadi with Senna, the man in the ravine. He cursed himself for a fool. How could he have let himself be led into what had clearly been a trap?

What had happened to the caravan? To his Medjays? To the other men and the donkeys? Had they all been slain? Or had the falling stones been a distraction, giving these men the chance to snare him?

Was this what had happened to Minnakht? To the man who vanished almost a year ago?

A man hissed, silencing the murmurs. Bak felt the tension around him and strained to hear. Other than soft breathing and the thud of a hoof in the sand, the world was silent. He had a feeling they were hiding, allowing other men to pass them by. His Medjays searching for him. Praying fervently to the lord Amon that such was the case, that his men were alive and well, he tried to roll over, to call out. A callused hand came down hard on his mouth, muffling him. Another man dropped onto his thighs, pinning him to the ground.

How long they remained so still and quiet, he had no idea. A long time, long enough for his legs to grow numb. Gradually the tension eased and the voice of the man Bak took to be the leader issued a quiet but firm order. The man on Bak's legs stood up and he and the one who had silenced him moved away.

Bak rolled from his stomach to his side. No one seemed to notice. From his improved position, he could see that he was in a rough, natural enclosure of boulders, with an overhang forming a roof of sorts. Three men stood at the far side, looking out toward the starry sky and what Bak supposed was a wadi. Nomads, he took them to be.

A donkey stood deep inside the enclosure, held there by a

fourth man. No, the creature was too big to be a donkey. A horse? Out here in the Eastern Desert? A horse wouldn't survive a month in so hot and dry a place, with forage too rough for all but the hardiest of animals.

No sooner had he rejected the possibility than the creature turned its head and flicked its long ears. In other, better circumstances, he would have laughed. It was neither donkey nor horse, yet it carried the blood of both. It was a mule. A creature of which Bak had little knowledge. It would be sturdier and hardier than a horse, he assumed, but not much better adapted to this barren land. What were these nomads doing with a mule?

The man in charge barked out a command to the others, who abandoned their observation spot to gather together goatskin waterbags and weapons, preparing to move on. Eyeing Bak, the leader took from a ragged bundle a pottery container much like a beer jar and removed a hardened mud plug held tight by a square of fabric. He crossed the rough floor of the enclosure, knelt, held the jar to his prisoner's mouth, and signaled him to drink. Thirst vying with mistrust, Bak took a careful sip. He tasted an unfamiliar bitterness and jerked away. The man grabbed a handful of hair; yanked his head back, jolting his pounding head; and pressed the jar to his lips. Bak doubted the liquid was poison. If these men had wished to slay him, they would have silenced him with a dagger, not kept him quiet by brute force.

Unless they were beginning to feel the pressure of pursuit and no longer wanted to be burdened with him.

He let the liquid trickle down his chin. The man barked out an order. Another man came, held Bak's nose, and pried his mouth open. Bak choked on the liquid the leader poured inside—and swallowed much of it.

By the time the men were ready to move out, he was so groggy he needed help to sit up. The men untied his hands and dragged him to the mule. His eyelids drooped and he knew no more.

Bak came half-awake. He was straddling the back of the mule, his feet tied together beneath its belly, his arms secured around its neck. The creature's gait was rough, its breathing labored. Each step it took made Bak's head pound, but time—or maybe the sleeping potion—had eased the pain, which was neither as sharp nor as intense as before.

The leader trotted a few paces ahead, while one man led the mule and two others hurried along behind. They, like their charge, were breathing heavily. The sun, which held the warmth of early morning but not the heat of midday, beat down on Bak's back. As fuzzy as his thoughts were, he concluded that they had traveled through the night, keeping up the fastest pace they could to put as much distance as possible between themselves and the place where they had taken him from the caravan.

He remembered lying in the rocky enclosure, the nomads silent and tense, and clung to the hope that they had been hiding from his Medjays. That the stones falling into the wadi had been a diversion and his men, User, and everyone else in the caravan had come away unscathed. That no further attack had occurred and sooner or later they would find him.

The man leading the mule said something to the leader, who snapped out a sharp disagreement. The other man argued. The leader remained adamant. Dropping back a pace or two, the man ran a hand down the creature's neck and held it up so the leader could see how lathered up it was, how badly in need of a rest. The men behind spoke up, evidently agreeing. With angry reluctance, the leader allowed them to stop, giving the mule the respite it needed.

While the man in charge of the mule gave the creature a drink, another man wiped the animal down, working around

Bak's limbs as best he could, and the third massaged its trembling legs. The leader paced back and forth, looking at the sun at irregular intervals, silently nagging them to hurry. His impatience failed to move them. They dithered and fussed over the mule, giving themselves a rest as well as the animal.

Bak was too drowsy to consider escape, but was alert enough to know that he could not allow himself to become too lost. The thought was so ludicrous he almost laughed aloud. He had been senseless for hours. He had not the vaguest idea of how far they had come or in which direction they had traveled. Nonetheless, certain natural features stood out above all others and they would not have changed.

Letting his cheek rest on the mule's wiry mane, Bak forced himself to concentrate. Mule and men stood on a narrow trail that wound around a steep hillside on which were strewn chunks large and small of a dull yellowish sandstone. Spread out around them was a vast broken landscape of hills, ridges, and tablelands in various shades of yellow, brown, and beige. He glimpsed the pale gold of sand far below and a hint of green, the floor of a wadi containing a few trees or bushes. They had evidently left the system of wadis Senna had been leading them through and were following a track across the higher elevations.

Slightly off to the right, beyond a range of dark gray hills, Bak spotted the same high reddish peak he had seen the previous day. Thanking the gods for its very existence, he studied its jagged profile. It appeared closer than it had before and the perspective was somewhat different, but it gave him a general idea as to where he was. They had to be traveling in a similar direction to the caravan. If the caravan was still on the move.

One of the men noticed that Bak's eyes were open. He said something to the leader, who pulled out the jar containing the sleeping potion. He grabbed Bak by the hair and twisted his head around, indifferent to the sharp jolt of pain he brought

on, and forced the liquid down him. Bak was asleep before
the mule moved on.

When next Bak came to his senses, he was lying on the
sand in the shade of an upturned slab of dark gray granite that
had long ago fallen from above to form a room open at both
ends. His hands were bound behind his back with a leather
thong. Ten or so paces away, the mule stood in a similar deep,
shaded passage, nibbling the leaves and a few stubby
branches broken from a shrub Bak did not recognize. The animal's caretaker dozed nearby.

Bak felt weak and drowsy. The pain over his ear was modest, no longer a thing to fear and avoid. He squirmed around
until he could rise on shaky knees and made his way to the
end of his shelter. They were, he saw, in a narrow wadi whose
floor was covered with drifted sand and along whose walls
the fallen chunks and slabs of rock formed rooms of various
odd sizes and shapes. The leader and another man lay sleeping in the shade twenty or so paces to his left. The fourth man
was nowhere to be seen. Bak guessed he was sitting in some
sheltered aerie, keeping watch.

Or maybe he, too, was asleep.

Even as he thought of sneaking away, Bak felt himself
nodding off. How could he hope to escape when he could
not keep his eyes open? Shaking his head to wake up, jarring
the sore spot above his ear, he began to probe the sand,
searching for a sharp bit of rock, thinking to cut himself
free.

He glanced toward the leader of the nomads, who lay still
and silent, watching him. With a grimace, the man sat up,
fished through the ragged bundle beside him, and withdrew
the container holding the sleeping potion.

Bak next awoke lying in a band of shade at the base of a
cliff whose black face rose into a blue-white sky. A faint

breeze wafted past, drying the film of sweat on his body, soothing him. The quiet was absolute.

He struggled to a sitting position. Licking his dry lips, longing for a drink of cool, pure water, he watched a grasshopper fly downstream in search of a tastier meal. He began to realize how hungry he was.

His head felt heavy and his body felt thick and sluggish, but he was more aware of his surroundings than he had been for . . . For how long? How long ago had the nomads captured him? At least one night and one day. Possibly longer. Several days could have passed without his knowing.

Other than the insect, a pair of larks, and a lizard, he saw no sign of life. He was alone in the wadi, and if the creatures' lack of fear told true, he had been for some time. Had his abductors decided to abandon him, to leave him here to die? He thought of the two men who had vanished, the one who had been slain. Would he be the next to disappear?

Commonsense said no. They had gone to too much trouble to abduct him and to carry him across a landscape that had to have been molded by the lord Set himself. Set was the god of the barren desert, of violence and chaos, and such was the land Bak vaguely recalled: deep and rugged wadis; high, barren plains; narrow trails up steep escarpments so rugged the nomads had trouble placing one foot in front of another, where the mule had dropped down on his haunches and had had to be dragged forward.

Yes, they had gone to considerable trouble to bring him to this place. Why, then, had they left him alone if not to abandon him to death? He must free himself.

He had just located a thin black stone he thought would slice through the leather thongs binding his wrists when he heard voices approaching up the wadi. A nomad rose from among a shaded pile of rocks a dozen paces away. He had been there all along.

* * *

A half-dozen nomads, men Bak had never seen before, hustled him over a low rise. From the greater height, he saw a huge orange sun drop behind a haze-shrouded horizon. They descended into a broad, open wadi, with a smattering of acacias across its surface. As they strode out across the rocky streambed, swerving around the trees and clumps of silla, he saw in the lingering twilight fifteen or so seated nomads scattered loosely around a small fire. Not far away, the failing sunlight glinted on the mirror-like surface of water that filled a depression in the center of the dry watercourse. The mule and a half-dozen donkeys stood at the edge, nibbling shoots of greenery someone had gathered for them.

A man left the camp and walked out to meet them. Bak's heart sank as he recognized the leader of the quartet that had abducted him. The man withdrew a dagger from a sheath at his waist and, approaching the captive, snapped out an order. Someone pivoted Bak around so his back was to the weapon. His skin crawled and he could practically feel the dagger plunged deep into his flesh.

Another man grabbed his hands and jerked them back, away from his body. The blade struck the leather thong binding his wrists together and sliced it in two. Bak was so astonished his mouth dropped open. Laughing, the leader, beckoned and stalked toward the camp.

A tall, thin nomad stood up as they approached. His arms and legs were as bony as those of an adolescent boy, but stringy muscles hinted at stamina and power. "Ah, here you are." He eyed Bak curiously. "You seem to have fared well enough during your journey."

"You speak the tongue of Kemet," Bak said, surprised.

"While a young man, I spent three years with your army, serving as a scout and guide. I've a talent for languages, I discovered."

The heavy scent of roasting meat drew Bak's eyes to the fire, where the carcass of a young lamb had been tied to a stick raised above hot coals. He could not recall when last he had been so hungry. "What did you do to my men? What's happened to the caravan I traveled with?"

The man spoke a few words in his own tongue. A tiny, grizzled old man who was sitting close to the fire, tending the meat, handed Bak a beaten metal bowl filled with water. He took a careful sip. The taste was good, undefiled by the bitterness of the sleeping potion. He took another sip and another, taking care not to drink too much at any one time. Relaxing enough to look around, he counted twenty-two men and a youth. They were, he felt sure, the same men who had left the many footprints Kaha and Minmose had found.

"Did you take the other men as your prisoners after you abducted me?" He refused to believe the worst: that not a man or animal in the caravan had survived except for these few donkeys.

The tall, thin nomad, who looked to be about thirty years of age, sat on the sand near the fire and folded his legs in front of him. He signaled his captive to sit beside him. "Who are you?"

Bak could see that he would get no answer until he supplied a few of his own. "I'm Lieutenant Bak. And you are?"

"My name would mean nothing to you. The explorer Minnakht called me Nefertem."

Nefertem, a primeval god associated with the sun, a name most appropriate for a man who dwelt in this sun-baked land. "You knew Minnakht?"

The nomad's eyes narrowed. "You speak of him as if he's no longer among the living."

Bak could see he had stumbled into a sensitive area. "You spoke of him as if in the past. I followed your example."

Evidently not sure of his use of a tongue he seldom spoke, Nefertem thought over what had been said. A curt nod acknowledged his acceptance of the charge. "Do you know him?"

"I've heard much of him, but I've never met him."

The nomad's voice hardened. "You've heard of the gold he's been seeking, I'll wager."

Wary of the sudden flash of anger, of the bitter cynicism, Bak said, "I've been told he's looking for gold, yes. Precious stones and minerals have also been mentioned. No man has said for a fact that he's found them."

The old man dipped a shallow cup into a bowl of oil and poured it slowly over the meat. Drops fell onto the fire, making it crackle and smoke. Bak breathed in the aroma and his stomach cramped from hunger.

Nefertem leaned toward him, his eyes glittering, his expression hard. "Why have you come into this desert, Lieutenant?"

Bak did not know what to say. If this man had been a friend of Minnakht, the truth would serve better than a falsehood. If these men were ruffians who had attacked the caravan out of malice and greed, if they were responsible for the disappearance or death of Minnakht and the other two men—and the lord Amon alone knew how many others—a lie might serve him better.

"How well do you know Minnakht?" he countered, probing for a clue as to what best to say.

"You claim to be an officer. You and your men act and fight like soldiers. I repeat: Why have you come into this desert?"

Praying he was making the right decision, Bak admitted, "We are soldiers, yes. Commandant Thuty, my superior officer, has known Commander Inebny, Minnakht's father, for many years. The commander persuaded my commandant that Minnakht must be found. Commandant Thuty sent me into this desert to look for him."

"You lie!" Nefertem stood up and slapped Bak hard across

the face. "You walk at the head of a caravan filled with men seeking wealth, men whose honesty is less than it should be."

Infuriated by the insult, Bak shot to his feet and reached for his dagger. His hand fell on an empty sheath. A half-dozen nomads leaped up, caught his arms, and manhandled him to the ground.

"Release him!" Nefertem ordered scornfully. "He can hurt no one. He's as helpless as a newborn puppy."

Bak shook off the restraining hands, scrambled up, and, forming a contemptuous look, laughed. "Without a shield of men, Nefertem, you'd be as helpless as you've made me."

For an instant, he thought he had gone too far. Nefertem took a quick step toward him, his hands balled into fists, his expression murderous. Controlling himself with obvious effort, he clamped a hand on Bak's shoulder so tight the bones grated and pushed him to the ground. "Sit, Lieutenant Bak." The nomad loomed over him, his stance, his face, his voice calculated to intimidate. "I want the truth. Why have you come into this desert?"

"I came to find Minnakht."

"You've come for the gold you think he found," Nefertem insisted.

"If that's what you wish to believe, so be it. Listen to your own thoughts and pay no heed to anyone else. Dismiss the truth and shrug off any words of advice I or anyone else might offer."

Bak braced himself for another blow. To suggest to a proud and intelligent man that he preferred to live in ignorance was as much of a slap in the face as the one he had suffered.

The nomad glared, furious, and at the same time he shifted his feet, as if the accusation had struck home. "Rumors abound in Kaine, I've been told. Why would you search for a missing man when the lure of gold is stronger?"

"I'm guided by my commandant's wishes, not by tales of wealth that sound more like dreams than reality."

Nefertem crossed his arms in front of his chest. After a long, thoughtful silence, he said, "Let's say you speak the truth. Why, then, are you traveling with that wretched guide Senna? And with User, who's come into this desert for many years in an endless quest for gold."

"Senna didn't want to come any more than I did, but Commander Inebny gave him no choice. He believed I should travel the same route Minnakht followed on his last journey, and Senna knew the way. I had to accept, had to trust him to lead me along a safe and true path."

"You bargain with the lord Set." Shaking his head in exaggerated sympathy, Nefertem dropped to the ground beside his prisoner.

The darkness was complete, allowing Bak to glimpse in the scant light bits and pieces of Nefertem's men: a knee here, a face there, arms and legs and hands. A scene from the netherworld, he felt sure.

He thanked the lord Amon that he was no longer befuddled by the sleeping potion. "I've answered you as best I can. Will you not tell me what's happened to my men? To the caravan?"

"Why are those men so important to you, Lieutenant? If you've not come to find gold, why should you care about them?"

"I stand at the head of my Medjays. Not only are they my responsibility, but I care for them as brothers. As for the other men, I took it upon myself to travel with them. I'd be negligent in my duty not to care for their safety."

"Bah!"

That one tiny word infuriated Bak. "Have you taken all their lives, the innocent along with the guilty? Are you also the man responsible for Minnakht's disappearance? For all the other dead and missing men in this area?"

"No," the nomad growled through gritted teeth.

"Have I nothing to look forward to but death?"

Nefertem literally spat out his answer. "My father was Minnakht's guide for many years. We are as brothers."

"Your . . ." Bak clamped his mouth shut and gave the nomad a sharp look. Should he have guessed the connection? "Your father died about a year ago, I've been told, and Senna took his place."

"He did not die. He was slain at the hands of another."

Bak should have been surprised. He was not. Too many men had died or disappeared in this wretched desert to take the nomad lightly. "Tell me."

"A year ago, he came home to our camp in the mountains, suffering from a mysterious malady." Nefertem's voice pulsed with anger. "He was convinced he'd been poisoned, but knew not when or how or by whom. Within a few days, he breathed his last. Minnakht knew I wasn't free to serve as his guide, nor was my brother, so he asked Senna to travel with him."

"Did your father say why he thought someone wished him dead?"

"He could think of no good reason."

"Senna is not a man of this desert. Where did Minnakht find him?"

"A friend recommended him, he said."

Bak studied the nomad thoughtfully. "Why did you make me your prisoner, Nefertem? You guessed my men and I are soldiers. Did you not realize we were traveling with User's caravan but apart?"

"You walked in front, leading the way." Nefertem spoke with a stubborn certainty.

"I preferred not to breathe the dust of the other men and their donkeys throughout our journey," Bak said with a wry smile.

Nefertem was not amused. "Your men served as guards and scouts."

"We knew we were being watched. I was concerned for

our safety, as well as the well-being of the caravan." Bak glanced around, found the water bowl, and sipped from it. "As I was right to be. The watching man must've kept you well informed as to our whereabouts."

"My people, those who travel with their flocks to water and forage, told us where you were and what you were doing. I had no need to send a man to watch you."

"Oh?" Bak raised a skeptical eyebrow. "Who is he then?"

"I know not." Nefertem frowned. "My people have told me of his presence in this desert, but they don't know him. He's wary of them. He lets no one draw near enough to see his face."

The two men eyed one another, the nomad seemingly as puzzled as his prisoner. With no answer in sight, Bak asked, "Did you think, if you took me away from the caravan, the other men would return to Kaine?"

"User is a hard man to turn around. I doubted your disappearance would persuade him to do so." Nefertem glowered at Bak. "I knew or thought I understood why he and the others came into this desert. You were unknown to me. I wanted to know who you were and what you expected to gain from your journey."

"Has the caravan turned back?"

Nefertem hesitated as if he thought to make further use of his silence, but at length he answered. "No. User's guide Dedu is leading it instead of Senna, and your Medjays are wearing themselves out, scouring the land through which they travel, searching for you."

"Was anyone hurt after you took me?"

"To injure men and animals was not our intent."

Bak offered a silent prayer of thanks to the lord Amon. "I suppose the many footprints your men left the day before the attack were designed to confuse my Medjays when they tried to follow those who took me."

"The new tracks got lost among the old," the nomad said,

nodding. "They wrapped the mule's hooves, making them indistinct, and walked over the vague prints he left."

The scheme was so simple Bak vowed to use it himself should the occasion arise. "Now that you have me, what are you going to do with me?"

"You swear you've come in search of Minnakht?"

"I do."

Nefertem stared at Bak, letting the silence grow. "You'll never find him if you remain with the caravan, traveling through the wadis from one well or spring to another, following the path Minnakht took. We searched that route when first he vanished and came up empty-handed. We've since looked farther afield."

"This land is so vast and rugged that he could be anywhere. If I was more familiar with this desert, I might know better where to look. But if you haven't been able to find him . . ." Bak let the thought hang and took another sip of water. "Senna claims he last saw him on the far side of the Eastern Sea at the port that services the turquoise and copper mines. I'd like to know if anyone other than the guide saw the men with whom he sailed away."

"I've never believed Senna's tale, but could it be true?"

"I've asked myself that same question. I've found no answer." Bak watched the old man cut into the meat. He hated the thought of begging, but he was so hungry he vowed to kiss Nefertem's feet if need be. "I suspect Minnakht went missing somewhere near the Eastern Sea, whether on this side or the other, I don't know."

"If he's on the near side, he's no longer among the living, and that I'm not prepared to accept."

The old man drew close a basket filled with thin, round loaves of bread and called to the others. They pressed forward out of the darkness. Nefertem took a loaf from the basket, offered one to Bak, and handed the container to one of his men, who sent it on around the circle. The old man cut off a chunk of meat and placed it on the bread Nefertem held. The nomad signaled him to give Bak the second piece. The other men held out their loaves and, laughing and joking, appeared to be urging the old man to hurry. Bak wolfed down a few bites, then ate in a more seemly manner. He had never tasted food so good.

While they ate, Nefertem questioned him about his time in the army. When he learned he had been posted in Wawat, he showed a keen interest in life on the southern frontier and in the people who dwelt there. Not until they finished eating and cleansed their hands in the sand, did he return to their previous discussion. "You may go back to your Medjays and the caravan, Lieutenant. I wish you to continue your search for Minnakht across the sea. We're a different people than those who dwell in that barren land. We know few men there and have no friends among them."

Bak smothered a smile. The nomad was appealing for help without bending so far as to come straight out and ask.

"You must search with all due diligence," Nefertem added. "If you merely go through the motions and come up with nothing, you'll never leave this desert alive."

Relieved at being set free, yet resentful of the threat, Bak pointed out, "If Minnakht has been slain, his body buried in some secret place or dropped into the Eastern Sea, I doubt I'll ever find him. How can you in all good conscience say I haven't tried when in fact I've done my best?"

"What you learn, you must tell me. I'll be the judge of how well you've tried." Nefertem untied a soft leather pouch from his belt, pulled open the bound neck, and shook out a rough chunk of quartz hanging from a leather thong. Flecks of gold gleamed within the stone. "When you've learned Minnakht's fate, send this to me."

Chapter 8

Bak was beginning to think he was imagining things. Maybe the sleeping potion had lingering effects that were addling his thoughts.

For the third time in less than an hour, since breaking camp at daybreak, he had glimpsed—or imagined—a movement on the steep, rugged slope to the south. When he had studied the hillside in the gray light of early dawn, he had seen nothing. Later, as the sun rose, he could have sworn he saw a man darting through the long, deep shadows of early morning. When he had drawn attention to the spot, Imset, the lean young nomad whom Nefertem had sent with him to serve as his guide, had shaken his head. Either the boy had seen no sign of life or he simply did not understand what Bak was trying to tell him. Until they had set out the previous morning, he had had no knowledge of the tongue of Kemet.

"Rock." Imset touched with his toe a lump of granite half buried in sand. The stone's black facets gleamed like silver in the light of the rising sun.

"Yes," Bak nodded. "Rock."

The youth, whom he guessed was about twelve years of age, scooped up a handful of sand and held it out. "Sand."

The boy, whom Nefertem had suggested he call Imset after one of the lord Horus's children, was bright and eager to learn and was vastly pleased with himself each time he got a word right, but Bak wished the landscape varied more so he could expand his vocabulary. "Sand," he agreed.

"Donkey." Imset threw his arm around the neck of the dark gray beast plodding along between them. The creature was laden with water and food, the bare necessities required to get them to the next well and to take the boy to his mother's camp somewhere deep in the mountains. It also carried the spears and shields Nefertem had provided, fearing they might come upon a prowling hyena or leopard.

"Bird!" The boy swung his arm, tracing the path of the small winged creature as it flew past.

"Look!" Bak said, and pointed up the wadi. He had quickly tired the previous day of repeating the names of the objects around them and had gone on to words describing actions.

Grinning, Imset placed his hand above his eyes and stared in an exaggerated manner in the direction his teacher pointed.

Bak tried to think of a way to vary the pattern established the day before, but had second thoughts. Perhaps he could use the youth's enthusiasm to advantage. He pulled a waterbag off the donkey. "Walk," he said. While the youth strode along beside him, he unplugged the bag. "Trot."

Imset leaped forward to jog a half-dozen paces ahead. He pivoted and, smiling broadly, trotted in place until his companion caught up. Before Bak could issue the next order, Imset spun around, shouted, "Run!" and darted forward a dozen paces. He stopped as quickly as he had started and, turning for Bak's approval, laughed with delight. At the same time, Bak raised the waterbag to his lips, his eyes on the hillside to the south. If the boy's loud laughter and actions did not draw out the man who was watching—if someone was in fact keeping an eye on them—nothing would.

He spotted a movement in the shadow of a protruding boulder, the head and shoulders of a man. "Look!" he said and pointed.

Imset's eyes followed his. The laughter died in his throat and his expression grew puzzled. The man ducked behind the boulder, out of sight.

"You see?" Bak asked, pointing at his eyes and toward the spot where the man had vanished.

The boy nodded.

"Friend?"

The youth looked confused.

Bak knelt and drew with his finger two stick figures in the sand, men standing close together, their arms around each other's shoulders. "Friends," he said. A pace or so away, he drew two widely spaced figures, one face-forward, the other looking away. "Strangers." In another place, he drew two men facing each other, each carrying a spear in a threatening stance. "Enemies."

Not until Bak pantomimed the three actions, using the somewhat mistrustful youth as a second party, did his pupil begin to understand. Bak pointed toward the spot where they had glimpsed the figure. "Friend?"

Imset shook his head vehemently.

"Stranger? Enemy?"

The youth looked at the two sketches, his finger wavering uncertainly between them.

Bak went to the donkey to retrieve their weapons.

The following day, long before the sun peered into the gorge in which they had spent the night, Bak bade a reluctant goodbye to the young nomad. They had spotted the watching man several times during the intervening twenty-four hours, and he feared for the boy on his own. His efforts to convince him to remain with him had been futile, partly because of their mutual lack of words but mostly because Imset was determined to move on. Nefertem had told him to go to his mother, who needed him, and he refused to do otherwise.

The youth had packed a small bag of food, filled a waterbag, and wrapped his arms around the donkey's neck, bidding it a fond farewell. It could not travel the terrain he intended to pass through to evade the watching man. He had collected his weapons, and, with a stouthearted smile, had pointed in a northerly direction toward the red granite peak, which could not be seen from deep within the gorge where they stood. "Home," he had said.

They had clasped each other's shoulders, a silent goodbye, and the youth had walked up the gorge between overhanging cliffs to enter a wider area, where the brightening sky revealed several open pools of water. Beyond the uppermost pool, he had climbed the irregular steps of a dry waterfall. Whether the single word meant simply that he was going home, or whether it meant he knew this barren and desolate land better than any stranger, Bak had no idea. He prayed that the latter was the case. Or, better yet, that the watching man would choose to remain behind.

As he watched Imset vanish around a rock formation, loneliness descended upon him and he clutched the leather pouch hanging from his belt. Inside he felt the pendant, his sole way of contacting Nefertem. He had had to trust the nomad that the boy would guide him to a safe place where he would find food and water and where he could await his Medjays and the caravan. Now that he had reached that place, he had to believe they would come. If not, surely a nomad family would bring their flocks to drink.

Shoving aside the nagging thought that Nefertem had sent him here to be offered up as a sacrifice for some purpose of his own, he stowed the remaining food and waterbag in a niche in the rocks, hobbled the donkey, and collected his weapons.

The nomad had told him large numbers of sandgrouse came early each morning to drink, and he wanted to see for himself this source of food. Leaving his small camp, he walked out of the gorge to the pools. What Nefertem had called a well looked to him like natural springs. Green grass, reeds, and thorny shrubs grew in and around the lower pools, while the water in the uppermost was held in a bare pit of sand.

He climbed a cut in the hillside that looked out upon the water, found a rocky nook where no one could creep up behind him, and settled down to wait. Not long after sunrise, the birds began to arrive. Finches came first, a whirling multitude of stubby, dark gray birds twittering a high-pitched nasal song. They darted back and forth as if to make sure the pools were safe and finally settled around the upper pool. Other birds came in smaller numbers, and several lizards darted through the grass around the lower pools in search of insects.

Next came the grouse, brownish birds twice the size of the finches. They wheeled swiftly around in groups of twenty or more, circling the pools as their predecessors had, voicing something that sounded to Bak like a man fluttering his tongue while expelling a loud breath. Always keeping to their own flock, they landed on the hillside to preen themselves, their color so nearly like the earth and rocks that they were difficult to see. After a short time, they flew swiftly to the wadi floor to walk to the pool, where they lined up around the edge to drink. Satiated, each flock walked away from the pool, faced down the wadi, and leaped upward to fly off toward the open desert. Bak watched enthralled. Not until the final flock had taken to the air did he think of the birds as food. He certainly would not starve if forced to remain here.

He walked back to the gorge to get the donkey and turned it loose in the fresh grass. Keeping his weapons close by in case of need, he took off his clothing and, using the metal bowl Nefertem had given him, poured water over himself, washing away the desert's grime. He stayed well clear of the pools so as not to foul them. The water here, Nefertem had told him, attracted not only large numbers of birds and animals, but nomads from all across this part of the Eastern Desert. It was nothing less than a gift of the gods and must be treated as such.

While he bathed and washed his clothing, he studied the surrounding terrain. He did not spot the watching man, but he located near the mouth of the gorge a shaded crevice in which a man might hide through the morning hours. Finished with his bath and feeling considerably better for it, he donned his wet loincloth, kilt, and tunic, then led the donkey into the gorge and hobbled it so it would not wander back to the grass. Returning to the open area in which the pools were located, taking care not to be seen from above, he climbed up to the crevice, laid his waterbag beside him, and settled down to wait. With luck and the help of the gods, the watching man would grow curious—or fearful that his quarry had slipped away.

The sun climbed slowly into the sky. The day grew hot and the lizards indolent. A flock of cheeping sparrows flitted from shrubs to reeds to the grass and the bare ground, while a pair of larks walked among the rocks. Watching their determined but serene quest for sustenance, Bak grew drowsy.

Abruptly, amid sharp chirps of warning, the birds shot into the air. Bak started, came fully awake. Something had frightened them. The watching man? He had been hidden for over an hour if the sun's passage told true, plenty of time for curiosity to eat away at a man. He gripped his spear and shield and rose to his feet, as silent as the lizards that had darted in among the rocks.

A stone clattered down the slope some distance to his right. He eased into a fresh position, trying to glimpse the intruder. A jumble of rocks that had rolled down from above cut off his view. He could see no farther than the uppermost pool and considerably less of the slope. Quelling his impatience, he remained where he was, listening for another sound, hoping to determine the intruder's exact position. He heard nothing. The man, if indeed the noise had been made by a man, had to be a nomad to creep so silently down a hill as steep as this one and as covered with loose sand and rocks.

The time stretched to an eternity. Unable to stand the strain any longer, Bak stuck his head out of the crevice far enough to see around the rocks. A man wearing the ragged garb of a desert nomad was climbing downward, watching where he placed his feet. He was a half-dozen paces above the wadi floor at a point almost even with the uppermost pool. His hair was long and unkempt. He carried a bow, and a quiver filled with arrows hung from his left shoulder.

He stopped and looked to his left, down the wadi toward the mouth of the gorge. With nothing there to see, he shifted his gaze—and looked directly at Bak. Bak jerked back into his hideaway, but too late. Skittering rocks and the sound of feet half-sliding down the sandy slope verified the fact that he had been seen.

Shield in one hand, spear in the other, he burst out of his hiding place. He scurried down the slope, sending a miniature rock slide before him, and hit the wadi floor running. The nomad stood beside the upper pool, seating an arrow, pulling the string taut. Bak gave a blood-curdling yell, a fearsome sound made by attacking tribesmen on the southern frontier, and charged toward the man. The arrow sped past, too high and too far to the left.

Bak raced forward undeterred. He had not lain in wait for more than an hour to turn tail and run.

The nomad quickly tugged another arrow from his quiver, seated it, and let it fly. It sped past no closer than its predecessor. Bak sprinted on. The man spun around and ran to the dry waterfall. He raced upward, climbing the irregularly shaped and sized rocks as if they were the smoothest of steps. Unfamiliar with the terrain, Bak took longer to reach the top. The last thing he wanted was to break an ankle. He had no idea what had set the nomad to flight: the all-out charge, the howl of the southern desert tribesmen, or simply a sudden fear that he might get caught.

Above the fall, the wadi widened out and low dark gray mountains rose in all directions. Bak raced after the nomad up the most recent channel to be cut through the ancient watercourse, dodging fallen rocks and boulders and a few widely spaced silla bushes clinging to life in the dry sand. Instead of slowing to an easier pace, as he should have, and biding his time, he ran hard and fast. Sweat poured from him. His breath came out in loud gasps and he had a pain in his side. He knew that if he lost sight of the man in this playground of the lord Set, he would never find him. Worse yet, if the man was at all familiar with this landscape, he could circle around and lay in wait until his unsuspecting victim returned to the spring.

He kept up the pace for as long as he could, but finally slowed to a fast trot. The man ahead also decreased his speed. Bak saw him pause and raise his waterbag to take a drink. He, too, was thirsty—but he had left his water behind. When the realization struck, he cursed himself for a fool. He knew he should turn back then and there, but he plodded on.

The wadi gradually swerved to the left and the single channel split into innumerable shallow dry ditches. Ahead, he could see the gaping mouths of several intersecting wadis. No matter which way he looked, the landscape was the same: streams of coarse golden sand dotted with rocks flowing between low gray mountains whose surfaces were rough and broken. Later, he thanked the lord Amon for giving him the good sense to pay heed to his surroundings, for that awareness probably saved his life.

A thousand or so paces farther on, the nomad veered into a gap that angled off to the right between two peaks. Bak lost sight of him, but his footprints were clear in the sand. When he followed the tracks into the gap, he saw that the man had stopped and turned around to see if he was still being pursued. Spotting Bak, he ran on.

Bak slowed to a walk, lifted the tail of his tunic to wipe the sweat from his face, and looked around. This gap was about the same width as the wadi he had just left and the peaks to either side looked exactly the same. The similarity troubled him.

Breaking into an easy trot, he resumed the chase. The stitch in his side eased, but his mouth was as dry as the sand beneath his feet. Another thousand or so paces took him through the gap, where he saw some distance ahead a forked intersection, with wadis opening to right and left. The nomad turned into the latter, glancing back as he did so. Bak followed him as far as the fork and stopped to study the terrain ahead. The mountains looked no different than those all around, the wadi looked the same as the series of wadis behind him.

Common sense dictated that he not follow any farther. He was tired and an ache at the back of his head told him how badly in need of water he was. To allow himself to be led deeper into this maze of identical mountains and wadis would be sheer folly.

Reluctantly, he turned around, giving up the chase.

"I can't tell you how happy I was to see you." Bak smiled at Nebre and Kaha, who had come upon him trudging back to the pools. "Never again will I go off without a waterbag."

"You think he wished you to lose your way and die?" Psuro asked.

Bak leaned back against the wall of the gorge, well out of the strip of sunlight that fell between the overhanging walls. He had had enough sun for one day. "I've no doubt he did, but whether that was his original intent, I've no idea. He

may've known no other way to get me off his trail. On the
other hand, he came down to the pools to look for me. He
may've seen Imset leave and thought to take advantage of my
being alone."

"You're certain the boy didn't know him?" Nebre asked.

"I don't believe he did. He'd not have left his donkey behind if he'd felt he could safely travel the usual, easy paths."

Kaha scowled. "You said he looked to Nefertem as at a
god. If he told him to sacrifice the donkey, would he not have
done so?"

"All I know is that after I drew his attention to the man
who was watching us, he was as wary as I was."

"Who is this Nefertem?" Psuro asked.

Bak sipped water from the metal bowl, replacing the moisture he had lost during his futile chase. He felt considerably
better than before, but was disgusted with himself for having
gone off so ill prepared. "He said his father, who was slain a
year or so ago, was Minnakht's guide before Senna. Minnakht is as a brother to him."

"You believed him."

"He was very angry about his father's death and worried
for Minnakht."

"At least he had the good sense to send you here," Kaha
said. "Compared to the wells we've seen, this sheltered place
and pools are like the Field of Reeds." He referred to the domain of the lord Osiris, a place of abundance men hoped to
reach in the netherworld.

Bak, Psuro, and Nebre followed his glance, looking up the
gorge to the pools. User was supervising the taking of baths,
making sure no one wasted a drop of water or soiled the
pools in any way. Minmose and Rona, seated at the top of the
dry waterfall in the shade of an overhanging rock, were keeping watch.

Bak and his companions sat on the sand, surrounded by
the water jars, supplies, and weapons they had brought from

Kaine. Their donkeys and the animal Imset had left behind stood or lay in the shade inside the mouth of the gorge, dozing. User's camp and animals were farther back in the gorge.

From what the Medjays had told Bak, the caravan had arrived at the well not long after he had chased the nomad up the wadi. They had found the hobbled donkey, the meager supply of food, the abandoned waterbag, and the spent arrows. Their first thought was that the donkey's master, whoever he was, had vanished as Minnakht had.

Nebre, while watering one of the donkeys, had spotted the print of a sandal near the pool and, thanks to a small V-shaped cut at the heel, had recognized it as Bak's. The Medjays were stunned. The man they had been seeking for the past four days had been here, possibly awaiting them, but had vanished once more—maybe not of his own volition. While Rona and Minmose had remained behind with Psuro to tend to the animals and make camp, Nebre and Kaha had gone out to look for him. The sand carpeting the wadi floor was too soft to leave clear prints, but they had gradually come to believe they were following two men. They could not tell if Bak was pursuing the other man or if he was that man's prisoner.

Later, after returning to the pools, Bak had pointed out the slope on which he had first seen the nomad. Kaha had climbed the incline. Higher up, he had found a print of the sandal worn by the watching man.

"The boy went off alone, you say." Psuro adjusted his seat on the hard ground. "If he was truly what he said and was no friend of the watching man, do you think he got away unharmed?"

"Coming back from my foolhardy chase, I looked specifically for his footprints," Bak said. "I found the place where he left the wadi to climb a hillside too rough and rocky to leave traces of himself. From that point on, I walked in reverse the path he took when he left here, covering all sign of his passing. I saw nothing to indicate that he'd been followed, and I doubt he can be now."

Kaha and Nebre exchanged a look. The latter spoke for them both. "User wishes to spend the night here. We should have plenty of time during the cooler hours of evening to track the man you chased."

"I'd wager the last drop of water in this bowl . . ." Bak held up the container from which he had been drinking. ". . . that he's even now somewhere above the pools, watching us."

The Medjays looked distinctly uncomfortable with the thought.

Kaha broke their long, unhappy silence. "Nefertem must've sent him. How else would he have known to look for you here?"

Bak could not bring himself to trust Nefertem without reservation, but the nomad had been true to his word as far as the pools were concerned and the caravan had come as predicted. "I first saw him watching us a day's walk down the main wadi that descends to the west. Is that not the way you came?"

Nebre shifted a blade of dry grass from one corner of his mouth to the other. "We did."

"Either that's the only way to reach the pass we crossed to get here, or someone in the caravan told him the route you meant to take and he hurried on ahead to intercept you. My coming along may've been a surprise."

Bak spoke reluctantly of a traitor in their midst. He had been greeted like a long-lost brother, with every man in the caravan clapping him on the back, expressing his joy at his return, and letting him know in a multitude of ways how worried they all had been for his safety. He had described his abduction as briefly as possible and had evaded further questions, saying the nomads had known few words of the tongue of Kemet.

"We've a snake among us, you think?" Kaha spat out a curse.

"Why take such interest in this caravan?" Psuro asked. "We've done nothing of note, nor are we likely to."

Bak gave him a wry smile. "Nefertem seemed to think we're seeking the gold Minnakht is rumored to have found."

"Bah! User's been looking for gold for years. He's never found a thing."

"Will he be all right?" Bak asked.

Dedu let the donkey's hoof drop to the ground. The creature sidled away, favoring the one leg. "A night's rest will help. After that, we'll see."

User's nomad guide was at least ten years older than Senna, closer in age to the explorer than to any of the other men in the caravan. White hairs were visible among the black and deep wrinkles etched his face.

Bak knelt beside him to help him gather together tweezers, a small knife, a razor, and several other bronze tools suitable for use when men or animals needed medical care. "Do you always travel with User when he comes into this desert?"

"When I was a young man . . ." Dedu flashed a smile, corrected himself. "When he and I were young, I served always as his guide. But I took a wife and she bore me many children. Responsibility weighed heavy on my shoulders, and my days of wandering came to an end."

Bak smothered a smile. The nomad may have ceased to wander far from his wife, but in the ensuing years, he and his family had without doubt roamed far and wide over the Eastern Desert. "Your children have grown, I suppose, allowing you more time away?"

Dedu dropped the tools into a soft leather bag along with a dozen small packets of herbs. "While at the market in Kaine, I heard men talking about User and this journey he planned. I've long wanted to increase my flock and I know he gives fair exchange for labor." A twinkle came to his eyes. "And if the truth be told, I missed the old days."

Smiling, Bak stood up. "So you offered your services."

"This, I think, will be my last journey. I thought never to say so, but I long for my wife."

Laughing, Bak eased the guide toward the hillside overlooking the pools, where the rock-strewn slope lay in shadow. A gentle breeze ruffled the grass and reeds, the leaves on the bushes. Most of the men had entered the gorge for their evening meal, and the limping donkey was nibbling his way toward his equine companions hobbled within the overhanging walls.

"Did you know Minnakht?" Bak asked, sitting on a flattish rock near the base of the slope.

Dedu chose a rock not far away. "Each time he came through my family's territory, he stopped for a day or a night. He was a good man. Should he not return—and after so long a time, I think it unlikely—we'll miss him."

"Did he bring Senna with him?"

"Since a year ago. I envied Senna his task. The gods surely smiled upon him when they sent him to Minnakht."

"Had you ever met him before? He told me he's a man from the north, but said he first came here many years ago."

Dedu placed the leather bag on a rock close to his feet. He adjusted the way it lay and adjusted it a second time. Evidently sensing Bak's eyes upon him, he said, "Once before, I saw him. Five years ago or longer."

Bak gave him a speculative look, wondering why the delay in answering. "Was he serving as a guide at that time?"

Another hesitation. "He was."

Giving no sign that he noticed Dedu's reticence, Bak said, "He mentioned toiling as a boy for a man who wanted above all things to find gold. Was he traveling with him at that time? A man your age or older, I'd guess."

"No."

The nomad had been very forthcoming earlier. What had stolen his words? "Minnakht's father sent me into this desert to find his son, Dedu. So far, I've learned nothing. I don't even know if I can trust Senna."

"I know nothing to Senna's discredit."

"Something happened five years ago. What was it?"

Dedu shook his head. "Nothing."

"You claim you liked Minnakht. Why will you not help me in my quest?"

"What happened to me and mine has nothing to do with his disappearance."

"I can't be sure until you tell me."

Dedu lowered his head, covering his face with his hands. When at last he spoke, his voice was thick with distress. "Senna came to our camp in the mountains. The man he traveled with was not old. Twenty years, no more." He raised his face to Bak, letting him see his shame. "My daughter, a child of beauty and innocence, was twelve years of age. She was betrothed to the son of one of our clan leaders, a youth she claimed to love above all others. That man with Senna smiled upon her and she in turn smiled at him. They went off together for a night and a day and another night. If her betrothed had been any other man, her loss of purity would've been of no significance, easily forgiven and quickly forgotten. But the son of a chief must keep the line pure. That man with Senna ruined her in the eyes of her betrothed."

Bak laid a sympathetic hand on the nomad's arm. "What part did Senna play?"

"He went out to find them and brought my daughter back." Bitterness entered Dedu's voice. "Later, we learned she was with child. She lives with me yet, she and the girl, and she refuses to wed any other man, convinced the swine will one day come back for her."

"What was the man's name?"

"I don't know."

Bak felt certain he did know, but to press for an answer might silence him altogether. "When I came back this morning and found the caravan here, I talked of my abduction. One thing I failed to mention was the name of the man who led the nomads who took me away. You've dwelt here a lifetime, so you must know him. I was never told his birth name, but he said Minnakht called him Nefertem."

The guide's relief at the change of subject turned to surprise. "He's our tribal chief, the one man standing at the head of all our clans. Why would a man of his stature abduct you?"

Bak also was surprised, but for a different reason. He had not guessed Nefertem was of such import, though when he thought back on how quick the nomads had been to obey his every command, he should have. "He spoke of his father as Minnakht's guide, not as a tribal chieftain."

"His father was a good man highly regarded by all, but not a leader. His uncle, who died two months ago, leaving behind no sons of his own, named Nefertem to succeed him."

"He believes his father was slain at the hands of another. If he was so well thought of, why would anyone wish him dead?"

The question hung in the air between them with no answer to be found.

Chapter 9

Bak awakened, rolled onto his back, and groaned. What now? he wondered. The donkeys were moving around, blowing, making small noises. Something had disturbed them.

This was not the first time the creatures had grown restless. He and Psuro had gotten up earlier in the night to walk among them, calm them, and search for a reason. At the same time, User's drovers had dealt with the larger string of animals for which they were responsible. He had no idea how long ago that was. The gorge, whose overhanging cliffs had cut off much of the moon- and starlight, had been very dark. Even with eyes accustomed to the deep gloom, they had had trouble seeing. Unable to find anything wrong, they had gone back to sleep.

The narrow strip of light between the cliffs told him the lord Re had begun to rise from the netherworld. He rolled over and looked toward the mouth of the gorge. The pools glowed like mirrors in the clear light of dawn. Ordinarily the caravan would have been ready to leave, or already on the way, but User had decided they needed fresh meat. The large numbers of sandgrouse that came to drink offered too tempting an opportunity to resist. They would remain until evening.

Bak sat up and glared at the donkeys. They were not going to settle down without a gentle touch and soft words of encouragement.

"What's gotten into them?" Nebre grumbled as he, too, sat up.

The two men scrambled to their feet and walked into the small herd. As they calmed the animals, they examined the ground and the walls of the cliff and probed the supplies and forage scattered around, trying to discover what had made the creatures so restless. A single thought lay unspoken between them: a snake. In the better light, they could see fairly well, but were no luckier than before. Whatever the donkeys had sensed had either gone away or hidden itself.

They walked deeper into the gorge to help the drovers with User's donkeys. Again, they found no apparent reason for the animals' distress.

When they returned to their camp, Psuro, Kaha, and Rona were seated around their makeshift hearth, where the long-dead fire had turned to ash, eating a skimpy morning meal of bread and dried fish. The sandgrouse would make a welcome change to so dreary a diet.

Psuro glanced out through the mouth of the gorge toward the dry waterfall and the rocky steps on which the men assigned to guard duty often sat. "Someone must relieve Minmose." His gaze traveled from one man to the next and settled on the slender Medjay seated beside him. "You slept through the night, Kaha, unlike those of us troubled by the donkeys."

Kaha sighed dramatically. "I thought for a while that I was blessed by the gods. Now I see they favored me through the night to deprive me of the opportunity of slaying a few birds."

The sergeant rolled his eyes in mock despair. "Leave your spear behind and take a bow and quiver. The lord Inheret might by chance send the grouse flying your way." Inheret was the god of war and hunting.

With a quick smile, Kaha rose to his feet, scooped up a chunk of bread and a couple of dried fish, and strode to the weapons leaning against the cliff wall.

While the Medjay selected a bow, Bak looked across the
pools toward the dry waterfall. The morning was cool, the
sun pleasant rather than fiery hot. Why was Minmose not
seated on the rocky step at the top the men on guard duty preferred? His thoughts returned to the donkeys' behavior, and
concern entered his heart. He picked up a spear and shield
and walked with Kaha out of the gorge.

The Medjay scowled at the place where his fellow policeman should be. "If Minmose saw or heard anything, sir, he'd
have raised an alarm."

"If he could have, he would've."

Grim-faced, the two men picked up their pace, passing the
pools with long, fast strides. They stopped at the bottom of
the dry waterfall to study the slopes to either side. Minmose
was nowhere to be seen. Exchanging a worried look, they
raced up the natural stairway. At the top, a desert lark burst
out from among the rocks, calling an alarm, and fluttered up
the rocky hillside to their right. Other than the bird, they saw
no living creature in the wadi beyond.

Their eyes were drawn to a good-sized patch of disturbed
sand that would have been immediately behind a man seated
on the top step facing the pools. A shallow hollow in the sand
had smudged the vague footprints Bak, his pursuer, and the
Medjays had left the previous day. Traveling in an upstream
direction from the hollow was a depression about a cubit
wide, cut by two narrow indentations. The wider was the
path of a man's body, the narrow were the marks of his heels
dragged along behind.

Praying to the gods that Minmose was unhurt, Bak trotted
up the wadi, following the depression, with Kaha at his side.
As they neared the rock formation behind which Imset had
vanished the previous day, Bak heard—or thought he
heard—a low moan. Kaha sucked in his breath. He had also
heard the sound. They broke into a run. Behind the formation, they found Minmose trying to sit up, holding the back

of his head. Muttering a quick prayer of thanks to the lord Amon, Bak knelt beside him, while Kaha helped him to rise.

The usually cheerful young Medjay pulled his hand away from his hair and stared perplexed at the rusty red stain on his fingers. "What happened?"

Bak parted the hair, which was matted together with dried blood, and looked at the wound. When he touched the bump, Minmose flinched. The small break in the skin had bled a considerable amount, but was entirely scabbed over. Bak's knowledge of head wounds was limited to the few times when his father, a physician, had taken him along when he dealt with such injuries. He had been a mere boy, easily distracted, and had not learned as much as his parent would have liked, but he doubted Minmose was badly hurt.

"What can you remember?" he asked.

"I was sitting at the top of the dry waterfall. The moon was high and I was watching a herd of gazelles, seven or eight of them, drinking from the pools." Minmose wrinkled his brow as if trying to squeeze out what had happened. "I'm sorry, sir, but that's all I remember."

While Bak reassured him, Kaha studied the sand upstream. "Whoever did this walked the same path we did yesterday. The sand is too churned up to leave distinctive prints. I'd wager this weapon . . ." He touched the bow lying beside him on the sand. ". . . that he climbed down a hillside close by to leave as small a sign of himself as possible before creeping up behind Minmose."

Bak's thoughts leaped backward to the night and to his broken hours of sleep. "And I'd wager that he struck Minmose so he could enter the gorge unseen." He took up his weapon and walked around the rock formation so he could look downstream. "Stay where you are, Minmose. I'll send someone to you." To Kaha, he said, "We must examine the floor of the gorge before the donkeys and men trample any sign he might've left."

* * *

"Here you are!" User hurried to the mouth of the gorge to meet Bak and Kaha. "We must get into position before the finches fly in. If we frighten them off, I doubt the grouse will come."

Signaling the explorer to come with him, Bak called out to Psuro. The sergeant stood with Senna, Nebre, and Rona, selecting weapons for the hunt. User had set up a few snares, but the Medjays, proficient archers that they were, preferred the bow.

"Minmose was struck on the head in the night." Bak quickly explained that the young Medjay was not seriously hurt, told Rona to bring him back to camp, and, paying no heed to the Medjay's disappointment that he would miss the hunt, explained where the injured man could be found. To User, he said, "I fear the one who attacked him slipped in among us while we slept."

"The grouse . . ." The explorer clearly wanted to go on with the hunt, but was not sure they should.

"Gather together your hunters and go," Bak said. "Kaha and I will search this camp while you're away."

Psuro and Nebre offered to remain behind, but Bak shook his head. "If we're to have enough grouse for every man in this caravan to get more than a bite, you'll have to join the hunt. I doubt if anyone else can use the bow to as good effect."

"I'll help you, sir," Senna offered.

Bak shook his head. "The two of us will suffice. The fewer men in the gorge, the more likely we are to find some sign of the intruder."

User summoned the men traveling with him, who had been standing around his campsite, and strode toward the mouth of the gorge. A drover armed with a bow and quiver and carrying a basket in which to gather up the slain grouse accompanied them. Ani and Nebenkemet took no weapons with them and made no pretense of hunting. They wanted to

see the vast numbers of birds Bak had described. Wensu carried a bow, but Bak suspected the other hunters were in more
danger from his arrows than were the grouse. He did not
know what to think of Amonmose's skill as an archer. Since
the journey had begun, the man had continually surprised
him with his abilities and talents, his endurance.

As the hunting party hurried toward the pools, Bak said to
Rona, "If you think Minmose well enough to remain alone
for a time, you must join the hunt."

Rona flashed a smile of thanks and followed the men trailing behind User. The explorer and his party scrambled up the
slopes to either side of the pool where the birds drank. Rona
hurried on to climb the dry waterfall.

Bak watched the men settling down among the rocks.
Dedu, he noticed, was not among them.

Bak and Kaha thoroughly searched their campsite. Finding nothing of note, they walked the short distance down the
gorge to User's camp. The remaining drover, who had chosen not to participate in the hunt, had separated five donkeys
from the rest and was spreading a greenish unguent over
galls caused by poorly balanced loads. He understood few
words of the tongue of Kemet, but Kaha, in his slow and halting manner, made him understand that Minmose had been
struck down and an intruder had entered the camp.

"Like us, he and the other drover looked for a snake during
the night," Kaha told Bak.

"Ask him where Dedu is."

Bak could tell from the troubled look on the nomad's face
that he had no answer, and so Kaha reported. The man turned
back to the donkey he had been tending. Speaking through
Kaha, Bak continued to interrogate him. The Medjay stumbled through the questions, pausing often to think of a word
or a phrase, trying to make himself understood. The answers
came no easier to him. Could Dedu have been prowling

around in the night? Would his familiar figure have upset the donkeys? Not likely, nor—and here the drover grew defensive—would he have had reason to strike Minmose senseless. A stranger had entered the gorge, a man unknown to the donkeys. Why had he come? Kaha asked. The nomad shrugged, unable to answer.

"Does he believe Dedu has merely gone off somewhere, soon to return?" Bak asked. "Or does he fear he was lured away by someone he knew or by the stranger? What does he think happened in the night?"

The more questions Kaha asked, the more agitated the nomad became. Bak recalled User saying the drovers were Dedu's kin. Telling himself he was worrying needlessly and had upset the man for no good reason, he allowed him to finish with the donkeys while he and Kaha searched Dedu's meager possessions, abandoned where he had left them. As far as they could tell, the guide had left all his personal effects behind. They offered no clue as to where he might have gone, but hinted at a hasty or unexpected departure.

The drover, when shown the missing man's razor, medical kit, and cooking pot, shook his head over and over again, denying what his eyes told him might well be true. Dedu had walked away from the camp in the night. Maybe not of his own volition.

"Sir!" Kaha called.

Bak hurried to the Medjay's side. "You've found something."

"This footprint, sir." Kaha, kneeling close to the base of the cliff, pointed to an impression in the fine sand. "It's like the one I saw on the hillside north of Kaine."

Bak stared at the print. "The watching man."

"I'll look for more, but if I'm to find any, all the gods in the ennead will have to smile upon us." Kaha stood up and glanced around. "He walked this way, believing the donkeys would erase his tracks—for good reason."

"He took a chance, coming this deep into the gorge."

Putting himself in the intruder's sandals, Bak doubted the man had returned the way he had come. He looked down the wadi toward the north, in the opposite direction from the pools. He could not see beyond the nearest bend, but he remembered the way the walls gradually spread apart, with broad expanses of sand carpeting the floor and rocky slopes rising to either side. He would have gone that way rather than double his risk of being spotted.

He left the Medjay to continue his search and moved on to the place where User and his party ate and slept. He searched through every bundle and basket, but came upon nothing unexpected or suspicious. Kaha found no second print.

"Let's walk down the wadi," Bak said. "You'd best tell the drover. User will want to know where we've gone."

"I'll try to set him more at ease. We don't know yet that Dedu has met with some misfortune."

Trying to sound soothing, Kaha stumbled through an explanation of where they were going and why. The drover's expression grew stubborn, his voice doggedly insistent. In the end, Kaha explained, "This man insists on coming with us." He shot an annoyed look at the drover. "He wants to bring along a couple of donkeys. He fears one might be needed should we find Dedu injured. As for the other, User told him to collect green plants for the animals and dry brush for the fires on which to cook the grouse. He wishes to obey."

Bak had thought to search the wadi unencumbered, but the drover was right. Dedu could as easily be injured as dead. Also, if the many donkeys were allowed to graze around the pools, which they would have to do if other food was not gleaned, they would leave insufficient fresh grass for the nomad flocks that would come later.

"Let him come," he said, nodding so the man would know he agreed. "As long as he keeps busy, doing what he's been told to do and helping us search at the same time, he'll not feel so helpless."

They set out right away, planning to retrace the caravan's path all the way to the large wadi up which men and animals—and Bak a few hours ahead of them—had traveled from the west. He had scant hope of tracking Dedu or the stranger, but they had to try. The caravan had followed the same path the nomads used when bringing their flocks to water. The donkeys and the goats before them had churned up the sand, making it too soft to hold definite shapes. An ideal path for a man hoping to travel undetected.

"I'm very concerned about Dedu," Bak said. He, Kaha, and the drover had returned to the campsite hot, tired, and discouraged. They had found no sign of the guide, nor had they seen any prints of the man who had passed among them in the night.

"It's not like him to go away without a word." Frowning, User tore a leg from a bird browned to perfection. "At the very least, he'd tell the drovers where he meant to go."

"He isn't a large man, but neither is he small. No man could've carried him for any great distance. He had to have walked on his own two feet."

"I'd guess he spotted the watching man and followed him. He'll probably show up in a day or two."

Bak did not like the lack of conviction he heard in the explorer's voice. "I don't know where else we could look without remaining here and searching the nearby wadis and mountains."

"As much as I'd like to stay, we can't. These pools are fragile, and we've too many donkeys to feed and water." User took a bite from the bird's leg, barely chewed the succulent flesh, and swallowed. "The nomads count on them to water their flocks, yet none have come since you arrived two days ago. Their animals will be needing a drink."

For a man reputed to have no love for the nomads, User was very aware of their needs. Not only did he bring as trade items necessities unavailable in the desert, but he valued their water supply and the plants their animals needed to survive. Bak had to respect his decision. "I know you don't trust Senna—and I'm not sure I do—but with Dedu gone, we've no other man to guide us to the Eastern Sea."

User scowled, unhappy with the thought. "On this side of the mountains, all the wadis drain into the sea. I've explored a few and heard men talk of others. If he tries to lead us down an untrodden path, I'll know."

"When I asked where we should travel from here, he spoke of two wells, one to the north and the other to the east, each about a day's march away." Bak took a sip of water from the metal bowl Nefertem had given him. The grouse looked and tasted like the food of the gods, but he had already eaten so much that not even the rich odor of well-cooked meat could tempt him. "He recommended we go east, water our animals, and travel from the well to the sea. Do you think his plan good?"

Amonmose, standing a few paces away, helping Nebenkemet pack up the birds that had been cooked and set aside for the following day, abandoned his task to join them. Lowering his bulk to the ground, he said, "The men who fish in my fleet know the coast well. They say there's no fresh water anywhere along this section of shoreline."

"So I've been told." User tore away a wing and nibbled the flesh from the bones. "We'd be better off traveling north. Tomorrow we'll reach a gorge with pools, similar to this one, and I've heard of a well three days beyond. It's near the sea, so they say." He threw the tiny bones onto the embers dying within the makeshift hearth. "Dedu thought to travel that way and will expect us to. He'll probably intercept us somewhere along the route."

Bak prayed to the lord Amon that such would be the case.

"If I'm not mistaken, the well you mentioned is where my fishing camp is located," Amonmose said. "We could go there, yes, but must we travel so far between sources of water?"

User stared at nothing, thinking. "I suppose we could go straight down the wadi from the pools. The nomads take that path and camp on the shore while they fish and dry their catch." He focused on the trader and shook his head. "No. That's a single night's march, and we'd still have three nights' march up a waterless coast."

"My men have told me of those nomads." Amonmose picked up a dried twig and prodded the embers, which flickered to life each time the breeze touched them. "A couple of islands lie offshore, and around them the fish have a tendency to school. A few boats in my fleet usually toil in the area. If such is the case, we should be able to signal them. I don't know about you, but I'm ready to leave this vile desert, and that might be the way to do it."

User glanced at Bak. "Well, Lieutenant? Do you agree?"

"We can't abandon the donkeys on a coast barren of water, and I doubt the nomads can care for so many animals for long. If we find any nomads there."

A short silence ensued, broken by Amonmose. "Our sovereign's ships sail those waters throughout the months when the mines are being worked on the far side of the Eastern Sea. I could send a boat to intercept one of them. Ofttimes the decks of the cargo ships have empty space, and I've found their captains to be an obliging lot."

"If we must wait more than a couple of days for transport, a few of us will have to return the donkeys to the pools for water." User flung the last of the bones onto the fire. "To travel both ways will take two nights."

"If ships arrive while you're gone, they'll wait," Amon-mose assured him.

Bak prayed to all the gods in the ennead that User's knowledge of the desert and the merchant's confidence in his fellow men would prove to be accurate. He preferred not to die a slow and lingering death from thirst and hunger on the barren coast of the Eastern Sea.

The caravan left the pools and retraced its path to the main wadi, where it turned in a northeasterly direction. Ahead, the red mountain rose into the sky, catching small puffy clouds tinted orange by the sun dropping toward the horizon. Nebre and Rona met them not far beyond the intersection.

"We walked the heights paralleling the wadi all the way from the pools," Nebre said. "If Dedu came this way, he took care to hide his footprints. We found no sign of him."

"I'm certain something's happened to him." Bak glanced down the broad dry watercourse toward the west, where long fiery fingers of light reached into the sky. "User's trying to convince himself that he's not worried, but he's as concerned as I am."

The trio fell in beside the string of donkeys twenty or so paces behind Senna. With Dedu gone, Minnakht's guide walked once again at the head of the caravan. He should have been happy that he had regained his position, but he was sulking instead. He resented the fact that Bak had allowed User and Amonmose to choose the route they would take to the next well, and took every opportunity to remind him that he was the sole man among them who had earned his daily bread by guiding other men through this barren desert.

Bak had had to bite his tongue to keep from reminding him that he had been Minnakht's guide when the young explorer had vanished.

"Did you happen to spot the watching man?" Bak asked.

"No," Nebre said. "Nor did we see another print like the one Kaha found in the gorge."

"Do you think . . ." Rona looked at Bak and Nebre. He had no need to finish the question. The glum look on their faces made it clear that they feared the watching man had lured Dedu out of the gorge and had slain him somewhere in this vast wasteland.

Dusk was falling when three large birds, their calls loud and jarring, drew Bak's attention. The ravens dropped out of the sky to perch on the tallest of the many craggy boulders that formed a shoulder of rock nudging the south side of the wadi. They cocked their heads, watching the men below and the world around them. Their brownish black neck feathers shone iridescent in the setting sun. Another harsh call sounded at a distance. As if summoned by the lord Set himself, they bounded into the air and streaked up the wadi to swerve into an intersecting watercourse a couple of hundred paces ahead.

When the caravan drew closer to the intersection, Bak heard more birds, their bold, demanding calls carrying across the empty landscape.

"Something has died," Kaha said.

Bak glanced at the Medjay, whose expression was as grim as his own. "Let's go see."

The two men picked up their pace, told Senna where they were going, and trotted up the wadi. To their left, looking in the clear air almost close enough to touch, rose the precipitous southern side of the massive red mountain that dominated the Eastern Desert. The birds had flown up a narrow, steep ravine that cut into the base of the mountain. Its slopes rose steeply to either side, intimidating masses of broken and craggy red granite.

Beyond a strip of sand fifty or so paces long, the floor of the defile rose up the side of the mountain in rough and irregular steps. Some distance up and scattered on the rocks to either side were twenty or more ravens. Not far below them, a huge brown-black bird flapped its long, broad wings, trying to frighten the smaller birds away. Each time it turned its back to probe among the tumble of rocks on which it stood, the ravens hopped closer, only to be chased away as before.

"The vulture doesn't want to share," Kaha said.

"If that's what I fear it is, we'd better hurry."

They ran forward, yelling and waving their arms to scare off the birds. The vulture fluttered awkwardly up the slope to watch them from a flattish boulder. The ravens darted a few steps away to settle on rocks projecting all around and to scold and watch and wait. As Bak and Kaha climbed up to where the vulture had been, they saw among the rocks the right shoulder and upper arm of a man, the flesh torn away by the sharp beak of the bird. Someone had buried him, but not well enough.

Bak handed his spear and shield to Kaha and knelt beside the dead man. He shifted a few rocks off the head.

"Who is he, sir?"

"Dedu. As we feared." Bak remembered the guide's denial that he knew the name of the man who had defiled his daughter. He regretted his failure to press for the truth. If he had done so, would Dedu still be among the living? Or had the lie been a senseless act, having nothing to do with his death? "How was he slain, I wonder?" he asked, more to himself than to the Medjay.

He flung more rocks aside, baring Dedu's torso. Flies swarmed over and around a bloodied wound below the guide's breastbone. The birds had not been able to get to this part of the body. As he waved away the insects, he felt as if he were reliving the moment when first he had seen the wound of the man who had been slain at the well north of Kaine.

"He seemed a good man," Kaha said, his voice softened by compassion.

Bak began to replace the rocks he had moved. "We weren't very careful where we walked, but you'd better look for tracks. I'll go to the caravan and bring back help. We must bury him here, but not on this slope where a multitude of scavengers can reach him."

Chapter 10

After burying Dedu deep in the sand and covering him with stones, the caravan continued down the main wadi and around the red mountain. User was very quiet, speaking only when spoken to. The drovers went on with their tasks, as silent as the explorer. The loss of their incessant chatter and easy smiles, the empty space where the guide once had trod, affected everyone, and much of the time no sound could be heard but the braying of a donkey, a hoof striking a stone, or a smattering of curses when the sand was especially soft, making walking difficult.

Like everyone else, Bak walked in silence, weighted down by Dedu's death. He could not understand why the guide had had to die. True, his death fit a pattern of sorts. Minnakht was an explorer, as was the man who had vanished almost a year earlier. The man slain north of Kaine looked to be a soldier, an archer, perhaps a man who patrolled the desert. Bak smiled grimly at himself, acknowledging a guess stretched to fit the known facts.

Dedu had served as a guide, as Nefertem's father had, and both had traveled with explorers. Unlike the tribal chief's parent, Dedu had not led any men or caravans through the desert for many years. What could have happened in the nine short days he had been with User that had made him a target for death?

As the sun dropped behind the red mountain, leaving the eastern slopes in shadow and the surrounding heights bathed in the hot glow of late afternoon, clouds enveloped the tops of its craggy pinnacles. Senna and the nomad drovers grew wary, constantly looking toward the hidden peaks. User mumbled something about rain.

Dusk deepened the shadows. The breeze lost its heat. The faraway roll of thunder could be heard and long spindly fingers of lightning flickered through the clouds, reaching out to the peaks hidden among them. User suggested they look for higher ground on which they could spend the night should the wadi be inundated by floodwaters.

Bak, who had long ago witnessed a desert storm while hunting in the broken landscape west of Waset, knew the power of the torrents that infrequently filled the dry watercourses, washing away everything in their path. He had also seen the wadis on the southern frontier filled with racing water from storms so far away that not a cloud could be seen. He sent Nebre and Kaha on ahead to scout the hillsides and the tiny feeder wadis, telling them to seek a safe haven.

The clouds dropped lower over the mountain, enveloping the slopes below the pinnacles. The flashes of lightning drew closer, so bright they blinded the men trudging along the wadi. The thunder was loud enough to awaken those who dwelt in the netherworld. The donkeys grew uneasy and threatened to bolt. Minmose and Rona strove to calm Bak's string of animals, while Amonmose, Nebenkemet, and even Ani and Wensu stepped in to help the drovers control User's string.

While the gods were rampaging over the mountain, the sky above and to the south and east was twilight bright and empty of clouds. None but the moon and the most brilliant stars could outshine the firmament. The wadi was filled with an eerie yellowish glow, which drained the landscape of its reddish color. The air smelled different, clean and damp.

User, walking with Bak near the head of the caravan, pointed to three gazelles ascending a hillside farther to the north. "They fear a flood. They're climbing to safety."

"If my men don't find a safe place soon, we'd better follow their example and drive the donkeys up into the rocks."

"These storms don't usually last for long, but they can drop a significant amount of water. With no soil or sand to absorb it, huge quantities can race down the mountainside, carrying away boulders as large as a house."

Not to mention men and animals, Bak thought, shuddering.

The storm ended as quickly as it had begun. The lightning and thunder faded away. The clouds fragmented and scattered, leaving a silhouette of the mountain displayed against a flaming sunset sky. The features of its pinnacles were lost in the deep shadow of dusk. The donkeys grew calmer, but their ears remained cocked and alert. Whether they sensed a threat or could feel the men's unease, no one knew.

The lord Re entered the netherworld and darkness fell. The moon glowed its brightest and stars lit up the sky, allowing the men to see a surprising distance ahead. Bak and User were watching two gazelles, a mother and her young, climb a steep, rocky slope when Nebre and Kaha appeared around a bend in the wadi. The Medjays hurried up the watercourse to meet the caravan.

"We found a place to camp, sir," Nebre said. "A wide, flat shelf too high for floodwaters to reach. It offers plenty of space for all of us, men and animals."

"How far away?" User asked.

"At the pace you're traveling, it's almost an hour's walk down this wadi. And there's no clear path up to the shelf. We may have to unload the donkeys to get them up the slope."

"Nothing closer?"

"No, sir."

"The gazelle have been climbing to higher ground for almost an hour," Bak pointed out.

"We saw a few, and a couple of ibex." Kaha, looking none too happy, eyed the mountain, a dark mass looming above the wadi to the northwest. "We can climb up into the rocks at any point along the way, but getting the donkeys to safety wouldn't be easy. If water comes racing down this wadi, we wouldn't have time to unload them."

"We must push them harder," Bak said, "and tell the men in the back to close ranks. We don't want the caravan spread out should we have to save ourselves."

Looking grim, User swung around and walked back along the row of animals.

Thanking the lord Amon that the explorer was proving far less difficult than he had originally seemed, Bak walked with the Medjays back to his sergeant. "You must take our donkeys on ahead, Psuro. Kaha will show you the place where we'll camp. The two of you must find the best paths up to the shelf and clear them of obstacles if need be. The rest of us must stay behind to keep User's caravan moving."

"What of Senna?"

Bak eyed the nomad guide leading the caravan. "You won't need him. We will."

"We're about two-thirds of the way to the shelf where we'll camp," Nebre said, eyeing a large monolithic rock projecting from the wadi floor.

Bak accepted the statement as fact. While on the southern frontier, his Medjays had learned from the desert tribesmen to use such formations and other less obvious natural forms to find their way across the desert.

Nebre paused, raised a hand for silence, and listened.

Bak heard it, too, a faroff roaring sound. "A landslide?"

"You might call it that." User scowled at the mountain towering off to their left. "That's water rushing down a slope, carrying rocks and boulders with it."

Feeling the worm of fear creep up his spine, Bak tried to sound hopeful. "It sounds too far north to flood this wadi."

"The mountain must be draining in that direction. The first rains fell there, I'd wager."

"Would the rain have traveled with the lightning as it came this way?"

User gave him a grim smile. "You never know what the gods intend, Lieutenant, but I'd not be surprised to see water before sunrise."

"Pull him up!" Amonmose yelled and slapped the donkey hard on the flank.

Nebenkemet, standing at the animal's head, holding a rope that had been tied around its neck and forequarters in a fashion Bak thought exceedingly clever, literally hoisted it up the steep, narrow gap between two boulders.

While the craftsman urged the donkey on up the hill to the shelf where Minmose and Psuro waited to unload the supplies it carried, Bak went to the next animal in line. There he found Ani standing a couple paces up an incline covered with loose rock chips, tugging ineffectually on a donkey's halter. The animal's two front hooves were on the slope, but it refused to climb farther on the treacherous surface. Bak whacked it on the flank and shoved. With a furious bray, the creature lunged up the slope, sending rocks clattering down behind it. Ani scurried out of its way and hurried along beside it, guiding it to the shelf.

Bak helped Rona coax a donkey up a steeper but more stable path and waited to help Wensu follow with another animal. He and User had decided not to unload the donkeys except as a last resort. They had to assume their time was limited, and they did not have enough men to carry the heavy water jars and other supplies and, at the same time, urge the tired and stubborn creatures up the difficult slope.

"How many more?" User called from above.

Bak glanced back at the animals yet to be urged to safer ground. "Four."

Nebenkemet plunged down the slope. Sweat poured from him as he stopped beside the first donkey in line and began to tie the rope around it so he could haul it up the gap while the other men urged the remaining animals up the easier paths.

Catching the halter of the second donkey, Nebre urged it up a sloping rock along which, six or eight cubits above the wadi floor, a diagonal channel filled with sand made an easy path to the shelf. Just below the channel, the animal's hooves slid on the granite and it fell to its knees. Amonmose climbed up to help pull it erect.

Wensu started down the hillside to get another donkey. Bak heard what at first sounded like a child rolling rocks around the inside of a pottery bowl. To the southwest, somewhere up the dry watercourse. The sound became a faraway rumble, which steadily grew louder.

"Go back, Wensu!" he yelled. He grabbed the rope halter of the third donkey and flung it at Kaha. "The water's coming!"

Terrified by the sound, which had grown ominous enough to frighten the lord Set himself, the donkey bolted, practically dragging the Medjay up the slope. A wide-eyed Wensu met him part way, let him pass, and stood in the one spot as if turned to stone. Amonmose and Nebre got their donkey on its feet and urged the frightened animal onto and up the diagonal path.

Flinging a quick look up the wadi, Nebenkemet tied the final knot and hurried to the head of the donkey he meant to haul upward. Bak slapped it hard on the flank, getting it started, and swung around to grab the halter of the last animal. The creature, terrified by the rumble of rocks, which had swelled to a dreadful roar, swung away from his hand. Bak caught the strap holding the water jars in place, halting its flight. The donkey flung its head and kicked out, trying to break free. Staying well clear of those mean little hooves, Bak dragged it to the slope up which Kaha had gone. Amonmose met him, managed to catch the halter, and began to pull the animal upward.

Bak glanced up the wadi and saw, coming around a bend, a wall of water taller than he was, gulping up rocks and boulders, dead brush and trees. Its roar was horrendous. The donkey, white-eyed with fear and braying wildly, fighting to free itself of Amonmose's grip, blocked his path. He slapped it hard, hoping to get it moving. It kicked out, forcing him to duck onto the slope covered with rock chips.

Senna came down the incline above him, half-running, half-sliding on the loose surface. To slow his headlong plunge, he grabbed hold of a projecting crag, his feet slid out from under him, and he kicked Bak into the wadi.

Bak fell against the wall of water so hard it knocked the breath from him, and he thought his back was broken. The flood sucked him up, tumbled him like the rocks and debris around him, and swept him downstream. The rumble of the rushing water and rolling, twisting rocks was deafening, the sand swirling around him blinding. Trying not to breathe, forced to close his eyes, he was caught up in dead brush and pelted by rocks, chunks of wood, and the lord Amon only knew what else. He was too shocked, too paralyzed by fear, to think. Unable to tell up from down, one side from another, he curled into a ball, trying to spare his face and chest from the battering, and let the current carry him downstream.

Along with a craving for air, the will to live rushed through him. He recalled falling against the wall of water, the trememdous impact. Could he save himself?

Praying to the lord Amon that his back was not broken, he

uncurled his body and stretched full length. He was sore but uninjured. Vastly relieved, he looked as best he could through the swirling sand. What he had thought was the wadi floor below was brighter than the water above. Pushing away the dead, spiny limb of an acacia, he rolled over and fought his way toward the light. He broke the surface, gulped air, and took in some gritty water with it. Coughing, he tried to see over the roiling surface, searching for the nearest land.

The leading edge of the flood had passed on down the wadi, which was filled with swift-moving, turbulent water from wall to wall as far as he could see. Each small wave glistened in the moonlight, a gleaming silver shard that shattered as fast as it formed. Stones rumbled over the floor of the wadi beneath him, driven by the water, while brush and trees, dead lizards and birds and insects, were swept downstream on or near the surface.

He was about twenty paces from a hill that looked much like the one on which the caravan had found shelter. He was not surprised to find this slope empty of life. At the speed he was moving, he had to have been swept a considerable distance downstream.

Twenty paces to dry ground. An easy swim at the best of times. An intimidating expanse with the surface so rough and the current so strong, with so much debris floating around him and so many rocks and boulders tumbling below him, their clatter muted by the water to an ominous growl. With no other choice, he set out, swimming diagonally across the current. He could and he would save himself.

A large water jar bobbed past him, caught in the limbs of a dead bush. It had to be one of the vessels the caravan had brought into the desert. It reminded him of that wretched donkey. And of Amonmose. They had surely been swept away as he had been.

Praying they, too, had survived, thanking the gods for so bright a moon and starlight, he looked around, searching for donkey and man. Fifteen or so paces back and about halfway between him and the shore, he spotted the donkey, its muzzle held above the dirty, choppy swells. The jars and supplies were gone from its back and it was swimming with the current. Would its burden have come loose without the help of a man? Promising himself to wring the creature's neck if it had brought about the merchant's demise, he scanned the choppy water around the beast. He thought he saw a human head on the far side, but could not be sure.

Praying he had found Amonmose—or Senna; he had forgotten how close the nomad guide had been to the wadi floor—he swam across the raging waters to intercept the donkey. He fought the pull of the current, the tumbling debris and brush. He could see that the initial force of the flood had lessened, but not enough to ease his journey. Slowly he approached the animal. The filthy and sometimes foaming swells marred his view, preventing him from verifying whether or not he had seen a man.

As he drew close, the donkey flung its head and thrashed around, afraid of what must have seemed to it another of many threats to its safety. Bak let the current carry them on a parallel course, giving his tired muscles a rest, and spoke to the creature, trying to reassure it.

"Lieutenant?" Amonmose, peering over the donkey's back, had to yell to make himself heard. "I thank the gods. I thought never to see you again."

Bak swam closer to the donkey and clutched its brushlike mane. "When I thought of you and this wretched beast . . ." He gave the trader a rueful smile. "I must admit I feared the worst."

"If I hadn't been holding onto him when the water struck, I'd not be here now. I'm not much of a swimmer."

"I'm surprised you both didn't drown."

"He fought me and for a while I feared he'd fling me away. But I held on tight. I knew I'd never reach safety in these untamed waters without help." The need to speak loudly failed to check Amonmose's garrulous tongue. "Fortunately, as afraid as I was, I had the good sense to unload him. He was having trouble staying afloat with those big jars on his back. He must've realized I'd helped him. He grew more sedate and let me stay with him, clinging to his neck."

Bak nudged the donkey toward the nearest hillside, a steep slope of rough and broken rocks. "We may not be able to get ashore right away, but at least we'll be close if we find a likely place." Or if we get desperate, he thought.

"Where are we, do you know?" Amonmose asked.

The hill looked no different than any of the others. The moonlight had stolen away the reddish color of the landscape, turning the rocks gray and the intervening spaces black. He had no idea how fast they were moving or how long they had been in the water.

"Not so far, I pray, that the caravan won't come upon us early tomorrow." Thinking to lighten the situation, he said with an exaggerated sadness. "I fear our fellow travelers will eat the remaining grouse, Amonmose, leaving none for us."

The trader flung a very wet but wry smile across the back of the donkey. "One thing we know for a fact: we won't suffer from thirst."

"The donkey's tiring," Amonmose called. "If the truth be told, so am I."

"We can't give up yet." Bak, as exhausted as his companions, eyed the hill they were sweeping past. He had begun to swim ahead, looking for a place where they could climb out of the wadi.

Thus far, every hillside had been so rough and craggy that it had been virtually impossible to seek safety on its slope. His greatest fear was not the land they could see, but the rocks that lay below the water's surface. After the donkey's

valiant struggle to swim along with them, supporting Amonmose to an ever increasing extent, he dreaded the thought
that it might break a leg and have to be slain.

Several times, he had swum toward the shore, feeling with
his feet the surface below. Each time he had found hidden obstacles too rugged and sharp-edged to allow the donkey to
reach higher ground. And each time he had had to bolster his
will to carry on. The speed and force of the water was abat-
ing, but so was his strength. According to the passage of the
moon, they had been caught up in the flood less than half an
hour, but it seemed to him forever.

Dreading the thought that they would have to risk the donkey's legs, he beseeched the gods to look upon them with favor. No sooner had he uttered the plea than he spotted a
steep-sided cut that split apart a ridge to the east. Praying
sand had blown up the defile, covering any rocks on its floor,
he fought the swift waters sweeping past its mouth and swam
into a narrow, calm bay. Within moments he felt sand beneath his feet. Blessed sand. As he waded farther into the cut,
the water level dropped from his shoulders to his waist to his
knees. A few paces ahead, he saw dry sand.

He could not have found a better refuge.

He heard the sharp bleat of a goat. Looking toward the end
of the cut, he saw in the moonlight four adults with their
young. They must have sought safety in the defile when the
wadi flooded.

He waded back into deeper water and swam quickly toward the wadi. He had to catch Amonmose and the donkey
before the floodwaters swept them past the cut. He, the
trader, and the donkey were all too tired to fight the current
for long. As he feared, they had drifted on by, but not far. He
thought he had the strength to get them back—if they had the
strength to help.

"I found a good, safe place to stop," Bak called, swimming

to the donkey's head. He caught its halter and turned it against the current. It fought him, not wanting to swim counter to the flow, but was too tired to resist for long.

Amonmose saw Bak urging the creature upstream and shook his head. "I can't fight the water any longer."

Bak had never seen him look so tired and worn, or sound so dispirited. "Grab the donkey's mane close to his withers, stroke with one arm, and paddle your feet." As Amonmose clutched the donkey, Bak felt the animal falter. "Don't make him carry your weight," he said sharply. "Swim! It's not far."

Amonmose summoned a last burst of energy and obeyed. With Bak urging on man and donkey—and himself, if the truth be told—they fought the current back to the cut and swam into the still water inside.

When Bak stood up to test the water's depth, it reached to his shoulders. Amonmose stared like a man not sure he could believe in their salvation and also stood erect. Bak waded forward, pulling the exhausted donkey until it stumbled to its feet. There it dug its hooves into the sand and refused to move another step.

"We can't leave the wretched beast here," he grumbled. "It needs to dry off, to get warm."

As if in a daze, Amonmose plodded around behind the animal and shoved it forward while Bak pulled. When all four hooves were on dry sand, he let go of the halter, dropped to his knees, muttered a few words of thanks to the lord Amon, and rolled onto the warm sand to rest. Beyond the donkey's trembling legs, he saw Amonmose collapse. His eyes closed and he slept.

Bak heard a sharp, strident word and someone poked his shoulder. He opened his eyes to sunlight, glimpsed a small face above him. Shading his eyes with a hand, he looked at the boy peering at him, then sat up slowly, testing his weary

muscles. The child quickly backed away as if afraid. A smile
failed to reassure him.

Amonmose lay where he had fallen, but the donkey was
gone. And so was the water. Bak stared down the cut. Its sandy
floor was exposed all the way to the wadi. That, too, had been
drained of much of its water. For long stretches, the sand was
a mottled damp and dry. In other places, large shallow pools
mirrored the sky above. He glanced at the boy and smiled.
What the gods gave, they took away, sometimes very fast.

His thoughts turned to his Medjays and the caravan. He remembered the last few men and animals he had seen struggling up the hillside. He thought they had been high enough
to escape the flood. Of them all, Senna was the most likely to
have been caught up by the raging waters. Bak prayed such
was not the case. The guide's one act of carelessness might
well have cost Bak and therefore Amonmose their lives, but
no man should have to face death because he brought about
an accident. If losing his footing had indeed been an accident.

User was a rational man who knew the caravan must continue to the next well. In the extremely unlikely event that he
chose not to press on, Psuro and the other Medjays would
surely continue down the wadi to look for the missing men.
The likelihood of another flood was minuscule. The sun had
barely risen above the peaks to the east. They must be well on
their way.

Both Bak and Amonmose tried to talk to the boy. He
could speak no tongue but his own. He sat at a distance, too
shy or afraid to come near, and watched them with wide, curious eyes.

"When the caravan comes, we must give him some food,"
Amonmose said.

"Also a gift. He didn't save us, but he cared for the donkey
while we slept."

After a long silence, Amonmose said, "I don't recall ever being so hungry." He patted his substantial stomach. "I fear I'll waste away to nothing."

"We've plenty of fresh water," Bak said, smiling.

"I can't bear the thought of it." Amonmose eyed a long scratch on his arm, which he had gotten when becoming entangled in the branch of an acacia. "That Senna. I'd willingly slay him at the slightest provocation."

"He didn't mean to push me into the water."

"With your help, I might've been able to get the donkey higher up the hill. The chance was slim, I know, but it was a possibility. Without you, we were both lost to the flood."

Bak remembered how hard he had hit the water and he doubted a dozen men could have saved any of the three of them. "Senna may've been carried off, as we were."

"He didn't have to kick you."

"He was sliding on the rocks, out of control."

The trader looked unconvinced. "User told me the day he joined our caravan that he was not to be trusted."

"I agree that he shouldn't have let Minnakht go off with two strangers, but if Minnakht insisted, what could he do?"

"How can you be sure Senna didn't slay him? Or that man at the well north of Kaine? How do you know he didn't slay Dedu?"

"He was on the trail with my men and me when the man at the well was slain. As for the night Dedu was slain, at least one of us would've heard him if he'd left our camp."

"User told me you didn't entirely trust him. Now you're defending him."

"As you well know, I'm a police officer. I must not make hasty judgments."

"Grant me this: it's possible that Senna deliberately pushed you into the flood."

Bak laid a hand on the trader's shoulder. "Don't fret, Amonmose. I'll never again turn my back to him."

Chapter 11

"Are you sure you're all right, sir?" Psuro, seated on the damp sand at the edge of the wadi with Bak and Amonmose, seemed not to know whether he should laugh with delight at finding them alive and well or worry about their many bruises, scratches, and cuts.

Bak finished eating the grouse and threw away the last of the bones. Cold though it was, it was as delicious as the warm birds he had eaten the previous day. "You've no need to worry, Psuro. Considering how fast the water flowed and the many objects it carried with it, we fared very well."

"I thank the gods you came when you did." Amonmose glanced toward the goats, waiting patiently for their small shepherd. "I was beginning to look upon those lambs as a tasty meal."

Bak eyed the child, who stood a few paces away with User and Senna. He was small, dark-skinned, and dressed in rags, a miniature version of Imset. "The boy would never have forgiven you. Those animals are his responsibility, and he must return them to the family flock."

The child's reserve had melted away when User had given him a grouse. He had gobbled the food and eagerly accepted a second bird. After he finished eating, however, when the explorer had summoned Senna and tried to talk to him, his shyness had returned tenfold. He seldom raised his eyes from the wadi floor, did not know what to do with his hands and feet, and seemed to have lost the ability to speak.

User, with the guide translating, was trying to learn where the boy's family might be found. The child had nodded when asked if he had been caught in the defile while searching for strays, but had shaken his head when asked where his mother was camped with their flock.

"They can't be far away," a frustrated User said. "Why won't he tell us where they are? His mother might wish to trade for medicines or cloth or needles, or any of the other necessities I've brought that she'll never be able to find in this wretched desert."

"He knows where they are," Senna said, openly irritated. "Why he won't tell, I can't say."

"Something has to be troubling him," Bak murmured to his companions.

"You should try, sir." Psuro stood up and took the halter of the donkey, prepared to return it to User's string of animals, gathered at the edge of a puddle spread across the wadi floor. "He's seen with his own eyes that you're a brave man, the way you survived the flood. And he knows you're an officer, the one we Medjays look to for guidance. For those two reasons alone, he might speak."

Bak studied the two men and the boy. The latter had displayed no shyness toward User until he began asking questions. Could Senna's presence have inhibited his speech? "Summon Kaha, Psuro. I wish to use another translator."

"Yes, sir," the sergeant said, not bothering to hide his approval. He had not witnessed Bak's fall into the floodwaters, but he had heard the tale from men who had. Like Amonmose, he had aired his mistrust of the nomad guide.

After cleaning his hands on the sand, Bak rose to his feet and joined User, Senna, and the boy. "The caravan must move on, Senna. If you wish to walk at its head, go with Psuro."

"But, sir . . ."

"We've a long journey to the next well." Bak's voice was curt, allowing for no disagreement.

Senna flushed. "Yes, sir."

The guide, who had managed to cling to the crag, thereby saving himself from being torn away by the flood as Bak and Amonmose had been, had begged forgiveness. He had since been subdued, self-effacing. Bak had not meant to belittle him, but he wanted no argument from the man who might well have brought about his death.

Amonmose hoisted himself to his feet, threw away the last few bones, and walked to the boy. With a broad smile, he ruffled his hair and bade him goodbye. The child's smile was shy, wistful almost, as if he thought himself losing a friend.

"Could I have a word with you, User?" Amonmose asked.

The explorer gave him and Bak a speculative look, evidently realizing he was being steered away. He offered a farewell smile to the child and strode toward the waiting caravan with the trader.

When Kaha hurried up, Bak told him of User's failure and asked him to question the boy further. "Rather than asking where his family is camped, try this time to discover why he won't reveal where they are."

Kaha stumbled through the question. The boy shrugged as if he did not understand. The Medjay tried again, receiving in return another shrug. After several further attempts, Kaha flung a desperate look at Bak and tried a fresh approach. He knelt before the boy and delivered a long, painfully difficult speech, looking often at Bak. After a while, the child began to offer a word when the Medjay failed to find one. His eyes grew wide and he often glanced Bak's way.

"If you make him fear me, Kaha, he'll never tell you what we wish to know."

The Medjay chuckled. "I'm telling him how brave and

strong you are and how clever you are when you face an enemy, using guile as well as arms to win the battle."

Smiling at the boy, Bak said, "You'd best tell him that I
have no intention of harming his family. Or any other nomad
in this barren desert unless we're forced to protect ourselves."

Kaha passed on the reassurance. The boy gave Bak a grave
look and nodded. He said something to Kaha, a few brief
words. The Medjay asked a question. A stubborn look appeared on the child's face and he uttered the same words he
had spoken before. Kaha stared long and hard as if willing
him to say more. When he failed to respond, the Medjay
picked up the basket containing the four remaining grouse,
spoke a few words, and handed the container to him. The boy
flung a quick smile at Bak and ran up the defile to his goats.

"What did he tell you?" Bak asked.

"All he'd say was that we travel with a bad man."

A bad man. As if Bak needed to be told that. He suspected
the boy spoke of Senna, but he could just as well have meant
any of the other men in User's party—or the watching man.
One thing he knew for a fact: the child had had no reserva-
tions about Amonmose.

So they could reach good shade in which to rest through
the heat of the day, the caravan moved on. The sun beat down
on the wadi floor, drying its surface. Birds appeared from out
of nowhere to drink from puddles and gazelle could be seen
in the distance, drinking their fill. Minmose claimed he could
see new leaves already popping out on the silla bushes.
Amonmose refused to allow the donkey he swore had saved
his life—as it probably had—to be loaded, saying it needed
more rest. User adopted a severe demeanor, insisting he'd
spoil the beast, and flung Bak a good-natured wink. The
abundance of water had lifted the spirits of everyone.

Even the drovers seemed less disheartened, but they remained as watchful as they had been since Dedu's body had

been found. Bak had a feeling they no longer trusted anyone, not even User, the man for whom they toiled. They continued to accept Nebenkemet's help with the donkeys and the loading, but were much more taciturn than before. When Bak sent Kaha to sound them out, they shook their heads, pretending not to understand.

No one had seen any sign of the watching man since leaving the gorge where last they had seen Dedu alive. Was he still watching them from afar? Or had the guide's death been his ultimate goal, releasing the caravan from his constant scrutiny?

Convinced they were not yet free of him, Bak sent Kaha and Rona to scout the land through which they were traveling, telling them specifically to look for the watching man. After they left, he walked to the head of the caravan to inquire about the day's trek. He found Senna to be unusually informative and anxious to please.

"Minnakht was more interested in this area, sir, than in any other place." Senna motioned toward the rugged reddish hillsides all around them. "We spent almost two weeks exploring the mountain slopes and the wadis, never straying more than a day's march from water: the pools where we were when Dedu died, the well to the east that you and User spurned, and the gorge where we'll spend this night."

"Did you always remain within the triangle formed by those three water sources?" Bak asked.

"Now and then, he'd spot a faroff landform that he thought interesting or would find a stone that had been washed down a wadi from afar. If he believed them promising, we ventured farther afield."

Bak wondered if Minnakht had restricted his explorations solely because of the proximity to water or if something had convinced him that he would find what he sought in the triangular area Senna had described. User had never ceased to study the landscape through which they walked. He had displayed no special interest in anything he saw and derided the idea that gold would be found this far north. Eyeing the broken and eroded granite around them, Bak was inclined to agree.

"If you wish, sir, we could part from this caravan and I could take you to the places we explored. Minnakht might've seen something I missed and kept it to himself." Senna spoke with a growing enthusiasm. "Who knows what we might find if we travel the path he took!"

Bak smothered a smile. He regretted that Amonmose was not close by to hear the offer—and the lure of wealth that made it sweeter. The trader's mistrust of the guide far surpassed his own and his reaction would have been interesting to behold.

"I thought myself close to Minnakht," Senna went on, "but I'd not be surprised if he kept to himself whatever he found. You've no idea how secretive these explorers can be when they think they're close to finding something of value."

The guide surely knew Bak did not entirely trust him. Was he so naive that he believed the thought of discovering gold would break down his defenses? "I think it best that we remain with User. We can explore these wadis and mountains more thoroughly on our return journey to Waset."

Senna flung him a surprised look. "You plan to come back this way, sir?"

Bak could not be sure, but he thought he heard a touch of dismay in the nomad's voice. "Unless I find Minnakht elsewhere, we must. His father and Commandant Thuty would expect no less."

"It's clear to me," Nebre said. "Senna wishes to separate Lieutenant Bak from the caravan and slay him."

"Where the lieutenant goes, we go," Psuro said. "He knows that."

Bak leaned back against the wall of rock behind him and

watched the pair fill a goatskin waterbag, pouring water from a large pottery jar. "I must admit I was tempted to go with him, if for no other reason than to learn if he's as innocent as he claims."

"You wouldn't, sir!" Psuro said, horrified.

"Not without taking precautions, no, but it might be worth the risk. If we knew for a fact that he wishes me dead, we could in all good conscience force the truth from him about Minnakht. As for the men who've been slain since we set out from Kaine, he couldn't have taken either life, but I'd not be surprised to learn that he knows who did."

"Do you think, as you did before, that one of the men with User slew them?"

"I'm not sure what to think. The absence of all other footprints at the first well pointed to one of them; the footprint in the gorge indicated that an intruder slew Dedu."

"The watching man."

"So it would seem."

The two Medjays stood with Bak in a broad wedge of shade cast by the almost vertical wadi wall. Three half-asleep donkeys shared the space with them, while their remaining animals and those in User's string stood or lay in the shade at the base of the wall farther south. The explorer and his party lay slightly apart from their animals, sleeping. Minmose, assigned to keep watch, sat with Senna beneath an overhanging rock across the wadi, playing throwsticks. The vantage point was not good, but offered the only shade large enough for two men.

A hot breeze blew sporadically up the wadi, rippling the surface of puddles that had not yet dried, offering no relief from the midday heat. Water trickled through the rocks in the bed of the deeper channel, flowing down the center of the watercourse. Brown sparrow-like birds flew among the branches of four acacia trees that grew on the edge of the channel, catching flying insects, while grayish finches hopped across the sand among roots laid bare by the raging floodwaters, seeking grubs or seeds washed to the surface. Their bright voices carried through the still air.

Psuro plugged the waterbag and set it aside. "Minnakht was experienced in the ways of this vile desert and he was beloved by the nomads who dwell here." He picked up another bag and held it out so Nebre could fill it. "Of equal import, he had a good life in the land of Kemet, a life of ease and luxury. Would a man whose days were filled with advantage choose to disappear?"

"Unlikely," Nebre said.

"If he didn't trust Senna any more than we do, he might've gone off on his own," Bak pointed out for argument's sake.

"Would he not have gone to his nomad friends?" Psuro asked.

"Nefertem claimed he wants to know as much as I what happened to Minnakht." A large brown lizard darted down the cliff face, drawing Bak's glance. Something above must have startled it, a bird hunting its midday meal most likely. "He may've been leading my thoughts astray, but I don't think so. I think his people have searched everywhere they know where to look. That's why he wants us to seek Minnakht beyond the sea."

"I suppose we must take Senna with us," Psuro said with a notable lack of enthusiasm.

"If I can't convince all the men in User's party to go, I fear I'll lose all my suspects except him."

A grating of stone against stone sounded above and a pattering of rocks on the face of the cliff, pebbles skittering downward. Dirt and small stones pelted Bak's head and shoulders, and the donkey beside him awoke with a start. The birds cheeped a warning and darted into the air.

"Someone's above us," Bak yelled. "Move!"

He shoved himself away from the wall and slapped the donkey on the flank, sending it and its startled brothers out into the sunlight. Psuro tore the goatskin bag away from the stream of water and ran. Nebre raised the neck of the jar, saving the rest of the precious liquid, and raced out of the shade with Bak and the donkeys.

A huge granite boulder came crashing down from above, bringing smaller stones with it. It struck the ground with a solid thud, smashing a water jar leaning against the wall within a hand's breadth of where Bak had stood. Smaller stones clattered down the cliff face, and quiet descended.

Bak looked at Psuro and Nebre to be sure they were unhurt and at the three donkeys, who had stopped their headlong flight near the trees. Farther to the south, men and donkeys stood in the sunlight, confused by their abrupt awakening, their burst of speed to get away from the cliff. He offered a silent prayer of thanks to the lord Amon that no one had been injured. He had only to look at the water jar to see what could have happened. Reddish shards lay at the base of the fallen boulder in a puddle of water.

"Sir!" Minmose came racing across the wadi floor. "I saw a man looking down from above. He must've pushed the boulder over the cliff."

"Which way did he go?"

"North, I think."

"Let's go, Nebre."

"I'll come, too," Psuro said.

Bak tore the half-full waterbag from Psuro's hand, shoved it at Nebre, and scooped up the bag the men had filled earlier. "No, Sergeant. Someone must look after the caravan while I'm gone." He paused over the pile of weapons, decided a bow and quiver would be less ungainly to handle than a spear and shield and armed himself.

Nebre, far more talented with the bow than Bak, chose a similar weapon. "I noticed a cleft between this hill and the next, around the bend a couple hundred paces to the north. We can climb to the top there."

* * *

They ran down the wadi, ignoring the anxious calls of the
men in User's party, the shouted questions as to what had
happened. Lizards darted out of their path and the birds
wheeled around to settle on and among the acacias behind
them. Rounding the bend, they glimpsed the defile and seven
or eight gazelles standing close to the top of the hillside beyond, watching a female urging a tiny baby up a lower slope
of rough and broken rock.

"I'll wager he set those gazelles to flight," the Medjay said.

"He must've come down this way, thinking to cross the
wadi and enter the rougher land to the west." Bak looked toward the foothills of the red mountain and the multiple peaks
beyond. "In land so rough, he'd have an easier time of evading us."

"Could he have reached this point ahead of us, I wonder?"

They hurried into the defile. The first thirty or so paces
were almost flat and were floored with drying sand. A half-
dozen shallow runnels left by the receding water retained
some moisture. Loose rocks dotted the surface. Bak and Nebre slowed their pace so the Medjay could search for prints.

"Sir." Nebre knelt to look at a reddish stone and a wet indentation where it had recently lain. "Someone came this
way not long ago."

A dozen paces farther, the Medjay spotted the print of the
outer edge of a sandal. Bak sucked in his breath, let it out
slow and long. The sole was old and worn, curled to fit the
foot of the man wearing it, and it had a slight cut near the
small toe.

"The watching man." Bak arose and glanced up the cut.
"He looks to be heading down to the wadi."

Seeking confirmation, Nebre walked deeper into the defile. A couple dozen paces farther, up the slope where the
sand was dryer, they found a long indentation that ran along
the edge of a runnel and cut down into it, the sign of a man

who had skidded on the loose, rocky soil. Where his other foot had come down hard when he saved himself from falling, he had left a print that matched the one they had seen before.

The man they sought had been in a hurry, racing down the defile, no doubt hoping to cross the wadi before they could round the bend and spot him.

Nebre gave Bak a humorless smile. Bak stared out across the wadi toward the red mountain. He was no more eager than the Medjay to follow a man into a landscape constructed by the lord Set himself, but the task must be done. The sooner they laid hands on the watching man, the sooner their many questions would be answered.

"How many times have we spotted him?" Bak asked.

"Four." Nebre scowled at the high reddish walls of the wadi up which they were walking. "Each time we lose his trail or can find no footprints, he reappears. Too far away to catch, too close to miss seeing him."

"So I was thinking." Bak eyed the way ahead, the narrowing gorge whose stone floor had been washed clear of sand. Water filled holes etched deep into the stone. The early part of the storm, which had struck the red mountain from the north, had drained this way. "Those opportune appearances worry me, Nebre. Is he trying to get us lost? Or is he leading us into a trap?"

Nebre responded with a noncommittal grunt.

Kneeling beside a pool, Bak splashed his face and upper body. The water was clear and warmed by the sun. "Let's walk to the end of this gorge and no farther. We've been away from the caravan too long. Psuro will be wondering where we are."

"We're to let the man ahead slip away again?" Nebre asked, chagrined.

"He knows this land. We don't." Bak walked on up the

gorge. "Would it not be foolhardy to let him lead us to our deaths?"

"If we always turn back, sir, we'll never lay hands on him."

The Medjay was like a dog, Bak thought. Once he had scented his prey, he'd risk his life rather than give up the chase. "We must find some other way of snaring him."

"How?"

Bak flung the Medjay an annoyed look. "If I knew that, Nebre, we'd not be here now, debating whether or not we should allow our quarry to tempt us deeper into his lair."

Nebre had the good sense to say no more.

They walked on, following a stream that meandered from pool to pool. Bak feared the gorge would narrow further, forming a trap they could not evade, but around the next bend, the walls spread wider. Wisps of cloud passed across the brilliant blue sky and an eagle soared overhead.

They rounded another tight bend and stopped dead still. The gorge ended thirty or so paces ahead, blocked by a high wall. The stream poured out of a groove eroded over the top and plummeted downward, a silvery, gurgling waterfall splashing down narrow steps of waterworn red granite, each step taller than a man.

The climb to the top was possible, Bak thought, and tempting, but commonsense prevailed. "We'd best turn back."

Nebre looked half around, turning a wary eye to the gorge through which they had come. "Could this be the trap we've been expecting?"

"I can think of no better place."

Eyeing the high walls to either side, the steep waterfall in front, not sure if they expected one man to set upon them or an army, Bak and the Medjay eased backward toward the nearest bend in the gorge. Suddenly a solitary man came out from among the rocks at the top of the fall and stood beside the lip over which the water spilled. He stared boldly at the two men on the floor of the gorge, then knelt to cup his hands and drink. The action was deliberate, a gibe at Bak's decision not to follow, a sneer at their worried retreat.

Bak muttered an oath, echoed by Nebre.

The man rose to his feet, stretched, and yawned, making further mockery of the men below. He was tall and thin and had the same dark skin as Nefertem and his tribesmen. His clothing—a dark brown kilt, probably leather, and a ragged, long-sleeved tunic discolored by age or dirt or both—was that of a nomad. He carried a long staff or maybe a spear, difficult to tell which at so great a distance

"I'd like to know his purpose, Nebre. Do you think you can disable him?"

Baring his teeth in a eager smile, Nebre drew an arrow from his quiver and seated it. "I'd rather slay him, sir, but since I'm forbidden to do so, will an arrow in the thigh satisfy you?"

As the Medjay raised the bow, the man on the clifftop flung himself sideways, out of sight. The arrow sped through the air where he had been, traveled high into the sky, and arced downward.

Nebre spat out a curse and strode toward the waterfall. "I'll get him for you, sir!"

"No!" Bak barked out the word, an order meant to be heeded.

"But, sir . . ." Nebre stared in angry frustration up the waterfall.

"If he allowed us to climb the cliff unmolested—and I doubt he'd miss so tempting an opportunity—he'd be far away by the time we reached the top." Bak glared at the Medjay, waiting for him to see reality.

As Nebre turned around with obvious reluctance, Bak added, "We must return to the wadi the caravan is traveling. I, for one, would not like to spend the night in this wretched land, with a man who wishes us dead lurking about."

* * *

"Would you recognize him if you saw him again?" Bak asked.

"He was too far away." Nebre scowled. He had come to see the sense in their retreat, but his irritation had not entirely fallen away. "Would you, sir?"

"I doubt it," Bak admitted. "He made sure we got a good look at him, but not good enough."

He studied the craggy slopes to either side. The sun had dropped behind the mountain, leaving the landscape around them in shadow. Hills and precipices, ledges and steep defiles, merged together in the near distance, the loss of light turning them an identical shade of deep red and stealing away depth of vision. Even the patches of sand that had blown into the nooks and crannies had a reddish tinge, as if reflecting the flaming sky.

He guessed he and Nebre were about a half-hour's walk to the main wadi, which they should reach as darkness fell. The caravan would have moved on an hour or two earlier, but they could easily catch up with it in the cooler hours of night. Signs of the recent passage of men and animals would be clear on the freshly washed and smoothed sand, eliminating any risk of getting lost.

He eyed the glittering wound on the side of a boulder where, during their outbound trek, Nebre had chipped away a piece of rock to mark their path. "I thank the lord Amon that we had the good sense to leave a clear trail when we entered these mountains."

Nebre looked back over his shoulder. "I haven't spotted anyone behind us, sir, which surprises me. If the man we followed is trying to slay us, he'd surely come after us."

"He has to have guessed the caravan's destination—and ours. He may know a shorter way than the route we're taking."

"If only I'd been quicker with the bow! The threat of leaving him untended where he lay would've set him talking soon enough. We'd have no further doubt as to why he's been watching us."

"He probably believes we'll lead him to the gold Minnakht is rumored to have discovered."

"We've found no gold, and User swears we never will."

Bak scowled at the landscape around them. "Who knows what we'd find if we'd stay in one place and explore the land all around."

"The watching man must know we've done no searching."

"The merest thought of great wealth can besot a man far more than the strongest date wine—and a besotted individual is often a man of irrational determination."

"What of Dedu and the other slain man? Did he fear he'd have to share with them?" Nebre asked.

"What of the man who went missing almost a year ago? The one Amonmose heard of in Kaine. And don't forget that Nefertem swore his father was slain."

"The foul deed of Senna, you think? To guide Minnakht would've been a desirable task, I'd wager."

"If he slew Nefertem's father so he might toil for Minnakht, why would he then slay Minnakht?"

While they puzzled over the problem, they turned into a wadi paved with loose stones ranging in size from a man's fist to his head. They were forced to walk single file along a narrow path the nomads had painstakingly cleared by shifting the rocks off the sandy bed of the watercourse. Low cairns rose at irregular intervals, marking the course of the track. Out in the open as they were, with no way to go other than the path they were following, they felt exposed, easy game for a man thinking to ambush them.

They hurried along, studying the landscape to either side, tense with anticipation. They must have been a quarter of an hour's walk from the main wadi when they rounded a bend and saw a man on a hillside ahead, two hundred or so paces away. He was looking toward them across the mouth of an

intersecting wadi as if he had anticipated their arrival. He
was tall and slender. His kilt and tunic looked white in the
uncertain light, making him appear more a man of Kemet
than a nomad. Instead of spear and shield, he carried a bow
and quiver. His features were indistinct from so far away, and
it was impossible to discern the color of his skin in the late
evening glow.

Nebre tore an arrow from his quiver, but was too confused
to seat it. "Is he the man we saw before, or isn't he? Can there
be two of them, do you think?"

"I don't know," Bak admitted, equally at a loss.

The man stood where he was, watching them, as if waiting
for them to draw near. What is the range of his weapon? Bak
wondered. Is he carrying an ordinary bow? Or a composite
bow such as those carried by Nebre and me? Far superior
weapons to the older type, and with a range markedly longer.
Weapons not easy to lay hands on in a barren wilderness.

To leave the path and risk a broken ankle would have been
foolhardy, and neither Bak nor Nebre was in any mood to
turn around and run. Assuming the man's bow to be ordinary,
praying it was, they quickened their pace and forged ahead.

Scraps of white caught Bak's eye. Several men striding
into the wadi from an intersecting watercourse fifty or so
paces beyond the hill on which the man stood. Kaha, Minmose, and Amonmose. Spotting Bak and Nebre, the portly
trader placed his hands in front of his mouth to form a horn
and shouted. Bak could not make out the words, but assumed
a greeting. He raised a hand and waved.

"They must've thought us lost," Nebre said, breaking into
a smile.

Bak pointed toward the man on the hillside. "Shall we
snare him?"

"Yes, sir!"

As they ran forward, the man hurried across the slope,
moving to a spot from which he could see the Medjays and

the trader. He stopped beside an upended slab of rock and peered around it. He must have realized he would be caught between Bak and Nebre and the other men, for he swung around, wove an upward path through the broken rocks cluttering the slope, and vanished over the hill's crest.

"I couldn't be certain," Bak said. "He was too far away. But he might well have been a man of Kemet."

"Nomads sometimes move to Kemet, seeking a better way of life, and adopt the clothing and ways of our people." Amonmose, fully recovered from his experience in the floodwaters, strode beside Bak with the vigor of a youth. "Perhaps the man you saw has come home to visit his kin."

The evening had cooled, and a steady breeze blew along the eastern slope of the desert heights. In the clear air, the moon and stars glowed bright and clean, illuminating the hoofprints and droppings left by the donkeys in the caravan. Their small party had followed the tracks down the main wadi and were crossing a low divide of gravel banks covered with sand, making their way to the next watercourse and the well.

"After following one man and losing him, you can imagine how surprised we were to see another. If he was a different man."

"Are you sure the one who led you into the mountains is the same man who sent the boulder crashing down?"

"I'd wager my best kilt that he is. I know for a fact that he entered the gorge the night Dedu was slain."

Thinking back over the chase through the foothills, Bak felt exceedingly frustrated. He had told Commandant Thuty that he knew nothing of the Eastern Desert and had thus far proven it over and over again. Their quarry had led him and Nebre through the rugged landscape as if he held them on a leash, then had evaded them with the ease of a lizard in a thicket of thorny brush.

"I must admit I prayed you'd snare him," Amonmose said.

"I'd not like to lead him to my fishing camp. If he's treading the sands of this desert, slaying men for the fun of it, he might think my men fair game."

Bak thought of the men who had been slain or had gone missing and might well be dead. Five men, at least four of them involved with exploring this vile land in search of riches. He doubted the fishermen were in danger, but still . . .

"Would it not be wise to send them across the Eastern Sea to the port that serves the turquoise and copper mines? They could sail out daily and would have a ready market for their catch. I think it safe to assume they'd be in no danger there."

"Hmmm." Amonmose's brow wrinkled in thought. "The fishing is better around the islands on this side of the sea, but the men's lives are worth more than a small profit." He stubbed a toe on a rock, muttered an oath. "I suppose I'd have to cross the sea, too. They'll need passes and other documents. Would you object if Nebenkemet and I travel on with you?"

Pleased that he would not have to cajole the merchant into accompanying him, Bak smiled. "You must vow that we'll have no more swims in a flooded wadi."

The trader laughed. "Not so much as a bath, Lieutenant."

His good humor fading, Bak asked, "Now that User no longer has a guide, do you think he'll alter his plan to remain in the Eastern Desert?"

"Ani's been talking of turquoise since leaving Kaine. If he has his way, he'll convince User to go on. If he can't, I'm certain he'll wish to tag along with us. Would User not be foolhardy to remain here, with no one to travel with but Wensu?"

Bak made a silent promise to himself to have a word with the explorer. Whether or not someone in his party had slain the man found dead north of Kaine, he wanted them all to stay together and to accompany him across the sea, if for no other reason than to keep them alive and well.

Chapter 12

Bak awoke to the stirring of donkeys. Long ribbons of red colored the sky to the east, heralding the rising sun. A stiff northerly breeze blew across the eastern reaches of the granite peaks, swirling fine dust across the wadi floor. Shivering, he rose from his sleeping mat and stretched muscles that ached more after his night of rest than they had the day before, immediately after his strenuous swim in the flood.

He and his companions had found the caravan camped in a wadi lying between high gravel banks. Several acacia trees stood at the edge of the latest channel cut into the ancient riverbed. The men were sleeping and he did not disturb them. Psuro had told him User had decided to remain until evening, opting to travel on to the sea in the cool of a single night.

Bak looked toward the trees where, before falling asleep, he had seen Rona relieving Minmose. The Medjay was no longer there, nor could he be seen anywhere else. Thinking he had either grown thirsty or was more conscientious than most men assigned to guard duty, Bak walked up the wadi. There the pools were located, so Psuro had said.

He followed the channel to a massive tumble of fallen boulders that rose to the top of a sheer wall of granite. Beyond the cliff, the reddish slopes of the mountain glittered in the early morning light. The dry watercourse took him around an angle formed by gigantic rounded boulders to the

spring-fed pools. The songs of birds greeted the dawn and a
large greenish lizard clung to the side of a boulder, awaiting
a careless insect. Their indifference told him Rona was not
here.

Several pools were located near the foot of a dry waterfall,
reminding him of the place where the men had slain the
grouse. The similarity ended there. Where the earlier gorge
had preceded the pools, here the water was found inside the
gorge, and its rocky floor discouraged the growth of the lush
vegetation found at the other site. According to Psuro, the
men had grown excited when they saw the pools, hoping for
another feast. They had been sorely disappointed when User
told them no grouse drank here; the birds preferred more
open water.

Bak strode toward the pools. Three squawking ravens
launched themselves into the air from behind a mound of
rocks. Curious, he walked closer. A dark, bare foot caught his
eye. Muttering a curse and a hasty prayer to the lord Amon
that he would not find what he feared, he hurried forward.
Rona lay on his side behind the rocks, his form inert, lifeless.
Blood had drained from a slit in his back, and flies had gathered in vast numbers on the dry, caked blood around the
wound. Bak felt as if he had been struck hard in the stomach.

He forced himself to take several deep breaths, to collect
his wits. Jerking a branch off a half-dead bush, he brushed
away the flies and knelt beside the dusty body. Gently, as if
the Medjay could still feel pain, he turned him onto his stomach, revealing a pool of dried blood where he had lain. A long
thin streak on his cheek betrayed the fact that he had also
bled from the mouth. His body had barely begun to stiffen.

Tears flooded Bak's eyes. In the years since he had stood at
the head of his company of Medjays, he had lost only one
man. He had vowed at the time never to lose another. Now he
had. Out here in this godforsaken desert where he could not

be buried as a man should be. Where he could not be sent off to the netherworld with the proper spells and incantations.

Gathering himself together, he stood up and looked around. The gorge was deep, flanked on either side by the huge rounded boulders piled to the tops of the cliffs. He could imagine many thousands of nomads coming for water through the ages, a daily parade of humanity and their live-stock. A place dark and forbidding at night. A place of myth and superstition, he felt certain. Why had Rona come here?

"Sir!" Psuro called, hurrying to Bak's side. He spotted the Medjay, let out a deep, heart-wrending cry, and dropped to his knees. "How did this happen, sir?"

"He must've seen something . . ." The words caught in Bak's throat. "Something that made his life forfeit."

The sergeant rose slowly, like an old stiff man, aged by the death of a longtime friend. "I must tell the other men."

"Send Nebre and Kaha to me." Bak's voice grew hard, res-olute. "We must not let his slayer slip through our hands."

With Bak looking on, Nebre and Kaha, both grim-faced and determined, painstakingly examined the stony ground around the body. The few patches of sand had been thor-oughly churned up by donkeys and goats and men. Nonethe-less, they persisted. They finally found, partly hidden by a scrubby bush, one small pocket smoother than the rest where some telltale sign had been rubbed out. This hint of stealth spurred them on and they gradually expanded their search. They had been toiling at their grim task for about a half hour when Psuro ran into the gorge.

"Sir! Senna is gone!" The sergeant stopped well back on a slab of rock where he would disturb no sign of the slayer. "We've looked everywhere. I'd wager a jar of the best brew in the land of Kemet that he slew Rona and fled."

Bak snapped out an oath. "He must've sneaked away from

our camp to meet the man who slew Dedu. Rona probably followed."

"Into this gorge?" The sergeant eyed the towering walls and the boulders heaped to their summits and shuddered. "At night this place must be as black as a sealed tomb."

Bak followed his glance. The ravens had circled around to drop onto the rocks about a quarter of the way up the mound. Their loud, raucous cawing merged with that of two others, perched on boulders slightly apart. "Why he allowed himself to be drawn into a place with no way out, I can't imagine."

"We'll track Senna down like the snake he is," Psuro growled. "I know you believe the cudgel a faulted means of questioning a prisoner, sir, but surely in this case it's fitting. We can strike him and strike him again until he reveals the name of his partner in crime."

In his heart, Bak applauded the sergeant's enthusiasm for the hunt—and hunt down their prey they would—but he wanted Senna alive, not beaten to death. The nomad must face the law of the land of Kemet, his guilt weighed on the scales of justice, not meted out in this wretched desert. The punishment would be no less severe.

"Should we go on with our search, sir?" Nebre asked.

"We're seeking two men, not Senna alone," Bak reminded him. To the sergeant, he said, "Go find men to carry Rona to our camp. We must see that he's buried at once."

"But, sir, the sooner we go after Senna, the better."

The harsh scolding of the ravens jarred Bak's senses, waking him to another possibility. He studied the birds perched on the piled boulders, cocking their heads one way and another, peering expectantly at . . . At Rona's body and the human intruders into their domain or at something else? He glanced higher. In the brightening morning sky above, three vultures circled the gorge.

"Look at the birds, Psuro. What do they tell you?"

The sergeant barked out a curse. An instant later, he and

Bak had thrown off their sandals and were climbing the steep, irregular boulder pile. Four or five paces above the floor of the gorge, they came upon a brownish smear, blood drained from a man being dragged upward. They followed other smears until, about ten paces higher, they found a second body stuffed in among the boulders. A man jammed headfirst into a narrow cleft. They had to pull him out to know for a fact that he was the one they sought.

Like Rona, Senna had been stabbed. Unlike the Medjay, the dagger had been plunged into his breast. He must have known and trusted his slayer.

Using spears with sleeping mats fastened between, the Medjays made two makeshift litters on which to carry Rona and Senna down the wadi to their camp. Bak hated to leave Rona in this wretched desert, but he had no choice. The caravan was too far from Kaine to send him back and the land of turquoise lay far to the north and beyond the Eastern Sea.

He and Psuro located a suitable burial spot on the south bank that was high enough to escape flooding. After the bodies were moved to their final resting place, he sent Nebre and Kaha back into the gorge to continue their search for signs of the slayer. While Psuro and Minmose set about digging the graves, he examined both bodies more thoroughly.

Finding nothing of note on either man, he hurried back to his campsite. While he searched through Senna's possessions, seeking he knew not what, he heard raised voices coming from User's camp. By the time he finished his task, having found nothing but the personal items one would expect, the volume of the voices and the intensity of the argument had escalated dramatically. He hastened to the explorer's camp to look into the problem.

User stood with Amonmose, Nebenkemet, Ani, and Wensu, facing the drovers. His face was ruddy from anger and the effort of getting across a message in a tongue of which he had limited knowledge. He spotted Bak, snarled, "Where's that wretched Medjay of yours? Kaha? Maybe he can talk some sense into these men."

"What's wrong?" Bak asked.

"As soon as they learned of Rona's death they started whispering to each other. Then Psuro told us Senna had been slain. That did it." User glared at the two men. "They've packed up their belongings, preparing to leave."

Bak noted the way the nomads' eyes strayed toward the south and the men digging the graves. "They're afraid."

"Aren't we all?" User snapped.

"Dedu was kin to them," Bak reminded him. "I'm surprised they've remained as long as they have."

"I know. I know." User looked contrite, but only for an instant. "They stayed when he was slain. Why must they leave now?"

Bak could see that the explorer had worked himself into a state that would allow him no retreat. He flung a resigned look at the portly merchant. "Go to Kaha, Amonmose. Explain what's happening and tell him we need him." He doubted the Medjay's far-from-expert knowledge of the tongue of the nomads would help, but he must try. Watching Amonmose hurry away, he asked User, "If the drovers go, will they take the donkeys with them, leaving you with no means of carrying supplies and water?"

"They're my donkeys. I bought them in Kaine and hired these swine to care for them."

Bak thanked the gods that such was the case. Without the animals, User's party would be in dire trouble. "Can we not go on without these men?"

"They're the nearest thing to a guide that we have."

"You said yourself that you should be able to lead us to the Eastern Sea. Senna told me that once we reached this gorge, all we had to do was follow the wadi to its outflow."

"We need these men to set me straight should I err."

Bak wanted to shake him. "I doubt they know this part of the desert any better than you do."

User's expression grew more stubborn. "They agreed to care for our donkeys throughout our journey. I insist they do so."

"Here's Kaha." Bak stepped aside and urged User to come away with him. "We must let them talk."

The Medjay spoke with the drovers for some time. He stumbled and fumbled and searched often for words but persisted in a sensible, calm voice no matter how angry and insistent the nomads became. At last he turned away and shook his head. "They refuse to stay with us, sir. They fear they'll be slain in the night as Dedu was, and as Rona and Senna were."

"Tell them I doubt their lives are at risk," Bak said, "but since I can't guarantee their safety, I'll do nothing to prevent their leaving. They can collect half what User owes them in Kaine, but not until this caravan returns to Kemet."

Kaha explained. With obvious relief, the drovers picked up their scant possessions and hurried away. They climbed the gravel bank to the south, veered around the dead men and the unfinished graves, and hurried on across the ridge as if they intended to retrace the caravan's path. Bak hoped they had kin in the area who would see they reached Kaine safely.

"What are we to do without them, Lieutenant?" User shifted his angry gaze from the drovers to Bak. "Travel south along the sea until we reach the southern route in the faint hope that we'll find men there to replace them?"

"We can't turn back now!" Ani stared at the explorer, appalled. "We're too close to the mountain of turquoise."

"I plan to cross the Eastern Sea with Lieutenant Bak," Amonmose told the jeweler. "He's convinced me that my men will be safer fishing out of the port that serves the mines than remaining here with a slayer on the loose. I must see that they get official permission. Nebenkemet will travel with us. Why don't you come, too?"

"Should you wish to travel with us," Nebenkemet said to User, "I can take charge of the animals." He glanced at Ani and Wensu. "I'll need help gathering food for them and with the loading and unloading, but that shouldn't be too great a burden."

"I'll be glad to help," Ani said, flinging a defiant look User's way.

"I've come too far to turn back," Wensu agreed, "but you must show me what I'm to do."

User scowled at the men around him, but made no comment. Whether he would continue on across the Eastern Sea, remain in the Eastern Desert, or return to Kemet, Bak could not tell.

Bidding a grim farewell to the stone-covered graves in which Rona and Senna lay buried, the caravan set out an hour before dusk for the Eastern Sea. Bak led them down the wadi, stopping each time the way grew confusing to consult with User, whose sense of this desert was much better developed than his. Pacified by the show of trust, the explorer's anger abated.

Though the water jars were filled to their brims and the donkeys were fully loaded, they behaved well for their inexperienced drovers. The trek through ever lower elevations in the cool of night was swift and easy. They left behind the high reddish mountains and surrounding peaks and passed through an equally barren but less rugged land of gray granite. Ahead lay the coastal plain, a broad expanse of sand and rocks that dropped toward the Eastern Sea. Far down the wadi, where the stars vanished on the horizon, Bak imagined he could see the sea. User swore he could hear the sound of water splashing the rocky shore and smell its salty-fishy odor.

The sky was brightening and the stars fading into its pale yellow expanse when they reached the fringe of the highlands. The wadi broadened out. On either side rose chains of hills that looked small and insignificant, mere mounds of rock when compared to the heights they had left. Acacias and silla grew in the shallow watercourses that spread out across the plain. By User's estimate, they were less than two hours' walk from the sea.

Bak had dropped back to speak with Psuro when he spotted Kaha coming around the southernmost of a cluster of hills off to the left. The Medjay raced toward them, bow in his hand, quiver slung from his shoulder. A man in a hurry with news to impart. Nebre, who had gone with him to scout ahead, was nowhere in sight. They should have remained together. Spitting out an oath, fearing another man had been hurt or worse, Bak and Psuro dashed out to meet him.

"Sir!" Kaha stopped to stand before them, his breath coming in quick gasps. "We found a man. Nebre said to tell you . . ." He bent over, hands on knees, trying to breathe more evenly. "He's the man you saw two days ago in the mountains. Not the one you followed, but the second man. He wishes to speak with you."

"Nebre's all right?" Bak demanded.

Kaha nodded. "He's holding the man at arrow point, unwilling to trust him."

"Where are they?" Psuro asked.

"Around that hill," Kaha pointed. "The man wishes to speak with you and you alone, sir, with none other than us to see him."

Bak knew Nebre would take no unnecessary chances, but one man alone might not be able to face the unexpected. Fearing for the Medjay, he ordered Psuro to stay with the caravan and strode rapidly down the wadi, with Kaha by his side. "This isn't a trap, is it?"

"We saw no one else throughout the night, but Nebre told him that if any stranger came near, he would shoot him in the stomach so he would die a painful and lingering death."

"The man asked specifically for me?"

"Yes, sir. He said your name. Lieutenant Bak."

Bak's steps faltered. "He knows who I am?" Eyes narrowed, and not from the brightness of the sky, he stared thoughtfully toward the hill around which Kaha had come. "Did he offer a name of his own by chance?"

"No, sir." Kaha slung his bow over his shoulder. "There's something else, sir. He's a man of Kemet, not a nomad."

"Lieutenant Bak." The man stood at the base of the grayish rocky hill, looking out across the sand toward the approaching men. Nebre had placed himself ten paces to the right of his prisoner, too far away to be leaped upon in a surprise attack.

Bak stopped the same distance away. "How do you know my name?"

The man was taller than he but not as broad across the shoulders, and was about the same age. He was slender of build, with muscles that looked solid and well honed. His dark hair was cropped short, his skin darkened by the sun to a golden brown. Like everyone who walked the paths of this wretched desert, he was none too clean, but his tunic and kilt retained some semblance of white and his sandals appeared to be fairly new. His back was to the bright splash of orange reaching into the eastern sky, making his features difficult to see.

"Senna told me. You're a soldier, he said, sent by your commandant into this desert to search for Minnakht."

Bak's suspicions sharpened. He thanked the lord Amon that he had never entirely trusted the guide and had not revealed that he was a policeman. Could he trust this man? Had he rather than the nomad they had followed pushed the boulder over the cliff above their resting place? "You knew Senna?"

"Your Medjay told me he's been slain. He was a good man, dependable to a fault and exceedingly loyal. I shall miss him."

"How long have you known him?"

"Long enough to trust him. Unlike you, so he told me."

Bak took a couple steps forward and off to the side, hoping to turn the man more toward the rising sun, making his face easier to read. "You've talked to him since we left Kaine."

The man bowed his head in amused acknowledgment. "Three times we met in the night. He said your Medjays are like cats, awake at the slightest sound. He had trouble slipping away unseen, so we met less often than we wished."

Neither Medjay gave any indication that he had heard what Bak suspected was meant as a compliment. "Did you expect to see him last night?"

"He knew where I normally camp outside the gorge. I thought he'd come if he could."

Sidling closer, Bak maneuvered him around more toward the lighted sky. "Someone has been watching our caravan. You or another man?"

"I've watched you now and then. The nomads are also keeping an eye on you."

"How have you avoided the men I sent out as scouts?"

The man's eyes slid toward Kaha and he laughed. "Over the years I've explored every wadi and hill and mountain, every pinnacle and ledge. Each time I saw them, I simply dropped down behind a boulder or slipped into a niche between rocks or lay in a patch of deep shade."

"What of the nomads? Do they know of you?"

"They're more difficult to evade, but I've managed to stay far enough away to make any men who saw me believe I'm just another nomad, unworthy of a closer look."

The man was so self-confident he might be called arrogant. Bak supposed he had every right to be if he could elude men who had dwelt in this desert through a lifetime. "Who are you and why did you wish to see me?"

"You've not yet guessed, Lieutenant?" Smiling, he bowed

low as if to make an offering of himself. "I'm Minnakht. The man you've been seeking."

"If you're who you claim to be, why have you not shown yourself?" Bak, whose surprise had immediately given way to skepticism, sat on a large rock that had tumbled down the hillside to half-bury itself in the sand.

Minnakht, taking care not to approach too close lest Nebre or Kaha send an arrow his way, chose a rock at the base of the hill. "I fear for my life."

"Who wishes you dead?"

"If I knew his name, I'd not be hiding from the world."

Bak noted the dubious looks the Medjays were giving their prisoner and he almost smiled. Having lost one of their own to a knife in the back, the man who called himself Minnakht was in far more danger from them than from some mysterious man he claimed he could not name.

"Explain yourself," he said.

"As Senna surely told you, I went off to the mountain of turquoise, thinking to see the mines. Because I traveled with a military caravan, I left him behind. Upon my return to the port, I found him ill. We agreed to meet later at my usual camp near the pools where you spent last night, and I sailed away with two men who claimed to be fishermen. They brought me across the Eastern Sea and left me on the shore. There two men awaited me, nomads they were, men I didn't know. They beat me senseless, trying all the while to make me tell them where I'd found gold. I could tell them nothing. I'd located no gold. In the end, they left me for dead."

While he spoke, Bak studied him, trying to find a resemblance between him and Commander Inebny. Other than their height and a vague similarity in facial features, the two were as unlike as a pomegranate and a pea. "I've been told this coastline is barren, with no water anywhere."

"Few men would've survived, I know, but you must remember that this land is no mystery to me."

Bak thought of the men he had questioned about Minnakht and the contradictory answers he had received. He could not recall any man mentioning this utter lack of modesty, unless the tales the explorer had told in the houses of pleasure had been so filled with excitement that those whom he had questioned had been too enthralled to notice.

"I've no memory of that time." Minnakht, if he was indeed Inebny's son, went on with his tale. "I somehow made my way to a place where water seeps through the sand. The nomads seldom go there; the water is too slow to come to sustain animals. The men who beat me had scattered my possessions, but the will to live is strong, and I had the good sense to wrap myself in my sheet to save myself from the burning sun. At the seepage, I spread the sheet over some bushes, forming a tent, and there I lay for . . ." He spread his hands wide and shrugged. "How long, I know not. All I remember is digging for water and drinking."

An improbable tale, Bak thought, but not impossible.

"As soon as I could, I bathed my wounds and moved on, traveling through the night to the closest well. I didn't want my assailants to come back and find me alive."

"If they left you for dead at a place other than the seepage, how would they have known where to find you?"

"I doubt I was thinking clearly." Minnakht smiled at the two Medjays as if he felt a need to convince them. Their unsmiling faces could not have been encouraging. "I made my way to the place where Senna was to meet me and there I waited, licking my wounds, so to speak. He came and he took me to a well high in the mountains, where we camped. As I knew not who had set upon me, whether friend or foe, I had him pretend to search for me, thinking my enemies would reveal themselves. They never did. I've been running and hiding ever since."

"Your father is eager to know your fate. Why did you not send a message with Senna when he went to Kemet to report you missing?"

"My father loves me too well. If he knew I lived, he'd proclaim the news as a farmer sows grain during the season of planting. All the world would know and he'd unwittingly commit me to death." Minnakht rubbed a thin scar on his right arm. "I've another reason for caution: not quite a year ago, a man closer to me than a brother, Ahmose by name, vanished in this desert. I suspect he was slain, as were Senna and the others who've died since your caravan set out."

Ahmose, Bak guessed, was the missing man Amonmose had heard of in Kaine. "You didn't recognize the men who beat you, yet you knew not if they were friend or foe. That makes no sense."

"They referred often to someone they called 'he' or 'him.' 'He' would be angry if I didn't reveal where the gold was. They feared to tell 'him' of my stubborn refusal to talk. 'He' had no love for me and wouldn't mind seeing me dead."

The argument failed to convince Bak that Minnakht had good reason to turn his back on all men, especially his father. Perhaps he had been too much alone and had begun to see danger where no peril existed. "Do you have any idea who that man might be?"

"I've thought long and hard through many lonely days. I believe him to be User."

Bak eyed him thoughtfully. He had begun to like User—his quiet competence, his acceptance of his own strengths and limitations—and he preferred not to think of him as a slayer of men. "Explain your reasoning."

"Through the years, he's made no secret that he hopes to find gold or precious stones. Now his wife is ill and he has a need in addition to an obsession. He's one of the few men who knows this desert almost as well as I, and I'd wager he'd need no guide should he plan a deed he'd want no other man to witness."

"I think you err."

"Senna suspected that you believe someone in the caravan murdered the man found dead north of Kaine. Who else but User? Who but he could've kept in constant contact with the nomad you call the watching man, the man Senna believed took the lives of all who've died since you left that first well."

Minnakht seemed exceedingly sure of himself, but Bak had heard no proofs, nothing but a few generalities. Also, User's skepticism about the possibility of finding gold seemed very real.

He glanced at the two Medjays. Both men had relaxed to an extent, but neither had laid his weapons aside. Both appeared to be absorbed by Minnakht's tale, and both exhibited a healthy mistrust.

"Why did you choose to make yourself known to me?"

"You've been wasting your time searching for me." Minnakht flashed a smile. "I thought to set you on a right and true path."

Bak eyed this man, essentially a stranger. He thought him arrogant, but he might merely be overcompensating for his fear of an unknown enemy. His tale was well rehearsed, but would it not be after so long alone in the desert? For a man who had been described as close to the nomads, why had he not gone to them for help?

"Did you follow me when I was abducted by the nomads?"

"Senna told me later that you'd been taken. I'd gone on ahead of the caravan, so I knew nothing of your absence until I saw you with the child." Minnakht eyed Bak narrowly. "What did they say of me?"

"I was threatened with death if I didn't help find you. Does that not tell you in what great esteem they hold you?"

Minnakht's brow wrinkled in thought. "They might wish

your help so they can slay me. Or are they, like User, looking for gold?"

Bak decided to assume the question rhetorical. "I'd planned to cross the sea and go to the mountain of turquoise, but with your father so eager to see you, we must return to Kemet without delay. I suggest we travel south along the coast and go back by way of the southern route. At this time of year, with caravans coming and going, transporting supplies for the mines and carrying ore to the land of Kemet, we should be able to travel in complete safety."

"Will User remain with you?"

"I believe he will."

"If I were to travel with you, I'd be placing my life in his hands."

"Maybe," Bak said doubtfully.

"I can see that you're unsure of me, and I don't blame you. We've barely met." Minnakht gave him an understanding smile. "You need more time to reconcile yourself to the fact that I still live. I suggest you go on to the mountain of turquoise, and I'll meet you upon your return."

"You wish me to drag out your father's agony? No. We'll travel to Kemet immediately."

Minnakht stared at him, unhappy with what amounted to a ultimatum. "I've two donkeys hobbled north of here, far from food or water. I must go get them. I'll follow you to the sea, and meet you there before day's end."

"Kaha and Nebre will accompany you."

"You trust me so little?" Minnakht's laugh carried a hint of bitterness. "Trust goes two ways, Lieutenant. If you send them with me, I'll slip away and you may never see me again."

"What would you do?" Bak jeered. "Slink off into the wilderness and hide forever, living like a frightened animal?"

"I do miss the land of Kemet," Minnakht said with a rueful smile. "I'll meet you, that I promise. If not today, then tomorrow." He must have noticed the lack of conviction on Bak's face. His smile faded. "If for some unaccountable reason, I fail to do so, I'll follow you wherever you go. Senna told me you were a man of your word, one who never fails to do his duty. If I'm ever again to see my home and my father, you're the man who'll keep me safe.

"All I ask is that you watch User and wait for him to reveal himself as a slayer. I grant the possibility that the guilt lies elsewhere, but I think the likelihood small." Minnakht leaned forward, as if to physically impress Bak with his plea. "Whatever you do, you must tell no one I live. Ahmose vanished nearly a year ago and other men have since been slain. I'd not like to follow them to the netherworld."

Bak studied the man seated before him, letting the silence build. He found him to be likable in spite of what he suspected was an irrational fear. He could not and would not entirely trust him—Minnakht or not, he was a stranger—but he saw no reason to spread the word that the young explorer lived. "I'll say nothing, that I vow." He glanced at Nebre and Kaha and added, "My men will also remain silent."

Chapter 13

"The nomads have gone," User said, stating the obvious.

Bak scowled at the empty fishing camp, built on the shore of the Eastern Sea. "They've avoided us throughout our journey. Why should this place be any different?"

He was thoroughly irritated with Nefertem. He did not know for a fact that the tribal chief had told his people to stay away from the caravan, but he strongly suspected such was the case. Why could the man not help rather than hinder?

He and the explorer led the caravan into the camp, where men and donkeys gathered on the beach between two rough huts and the water's edge. The shelters could not have been more basic. Spindly acacia branches supported roofs covered with brush held in place by rocks. They would not provide much shelter during a storm, but would suffice for men wishing to sleep through the heat of the day. A larger, rectangular hut farther along the beach showed signs of occupation by animals—donkeys and goats, Bak guessed.

He strode to an unpainted wooden boat lying on its side well above the waterline. It and three similar vessels had been overturned and left in a row to dry in the hot sun. He squatted to feel the sand beneath the small craft.

"They've not been gone for long," he said, standing up and brushing damp sand from his hands.

Bak's Medjays and the other men, long deprived of baths, eyed the sea with eager anticipation. Wensu abandoned his fellows and ran into the water, which splashed around his legs.

"Not so fast!" User growled, wading in to grab his arm and usher him back to the shore. "The donkeys must come before your pleasure."

Wensu had the grace to blush.

Bak stood at the water's edge, where the tiny swells washed over his feet. The beach was a long, empty stretch of pale sand curled around a bay whose waters were a deep blue green. The sand was soft, stirred up all around the huts and boats by the nomads, and in one place he noticed a gridlike pattern where a net had been stretched out to dry. For as far as the eye could see to north and south, not a tree or bush interrupted the shoreline. Seabirds were everywhere: soaring overhead, diving for fish, standing on the beach to dry their wings.

"I don't see any of my boats," Amonmose said, striding up beside him and staring out to sea.

"How best can we raise a signal?" Bak refused to think that help might be slow to come.

"Let me show you."

The merchant walked slowly along the line of boats, studying the wooden masts resting on the ground. He stopped at the tallest and called to Nebenkemet, who was poking around in a basket tied to the back of a donkey. The carpenter pulled a roll of whitish fabric from the container. He shook it out, revealing a long-sleeved tunic that was none too clean, and hastened to Amonmose's side.

Bak helped the merchant tip the boat, raising the mast off the sand so Nebenkemet could tie the tunic to the upper end of the long, straight pole. Curiosity drew the other members of the caravan, who stood close by, watching. The merchant demanded rocks. While the men scattered, he, Bak, and

Nebenkemet scooped out a shallow hole and set the vessel upright, its flat bottom resting in the cavity. The men returned with enough stone to anchor the hull in its sandy berth. The northerly breeze caught the fabric, making it blossom out and flap in the sun.

Smiling his satisfaction, Bak asked the men standing around, "Who wants fresh fish for our evening meal?"

They all raised their voices in eager anticipation.

Bak held out what looked like a bundle of loose, knotted cords he had found tucked into the prow of the upright boat. "Have you ever fished with nets, Psuro?"

"I can learn, sir."

"I have," Wensu said, surprising them all. "My father has an estate a short way inland from the Great Green Sea. As a youth, I sneaked away with the men who fished its waters."

A half-hour later, two boats were sailing out to sea. From the foremost, with Wensu in command, Kaha was paying out the net between his craft and that of Psuro and Nebre.

"I hope they don't get lost out there," User said, scowling at the vessels.

Bak flung off his filthy tunic, kilt, and loincloth and waded into the water. Nebenkemet was settling the donkeys in the shade of the elongated hut, while Minmose was excavating a shallow pit for a fire. Ani and Amonmose had finished their tasks and were enjoying their first real bath in days. "Wensu vowed they'd never lose sight of the shore."

"He's better than he was at the beginning. At least now he tries." User stripped bare, as Bak had, and waded into the water beside him. "But he's just about the most useless man I've ever met."

Bak smiled. "Psuro will see that they return safely."

The explorer followed him into deep water. "You usually know what you're doing, Lieutenant. I hope you do this time."

* * *

About three hours before nightfall, after a long swim and a rest, Nebenkemet and Minmose led a half-dozen donkeys up onto the coastal plain in search of fuel and forage for the animals. The sun was hovering over the western horizon when Bak spotted the men and the laden animals returning to the sea. He walked out to meet them. As the trio trudged into camp, they saw three fishing boats sailing toward the bay, the northerly breeze driving them along at a fast pace. The two smaller vessels had to be those Psuro and Wensu had taken out. The third was considerably larger, a seaworthy fishing boat.

"That's one of mine, Lieutenant!" Amonmose was practically dancing with excitement. "Wensu and Psuro must've hailed it."

Joy—and relief—flooded Bak's heart. He could not believe how glad he was to see that boat, how much he looked forward to leaving this wretched desert.

"I suppose I could take one or two of you with me." The master of the fishing boat, a short, muscular man of thirty or so years, eyed the men standing around him, burned by the sun, their clothing stained, their hair unkempt.

Amonmose ignored what was patently an insincere offer. "If you sail at daybreak tomorrow, how long will it take you to find one of our sovereign's cargo ships?"

"Ten or fifteen days if we sail north and have to go all the way to the port across the sea. Four or five if we sail to the southern trail, where they may even now be loading supplies brought across the desert from Kemet. A lesser time if we're fortunate enough to intercept a vessel along the way."

"I suggest you sail south—and I pray you meet a north-bound ship. We can't remain here for long." Amonmose pointed toward the animals standing in their shelter. "We need a vessel with enough deck space for all those donkeys. I'll not condone abandoning a single animal, you understand?"

"Yes, sir."

* * *

"Minnakht's not coming, is he, sir?" Psuro kept his voice low so no one else would hear.

"He said today or tomorrow. We'll see."

They stood near one of the huts, while the other men sat on the sand, encircling the shallow pit in which a fire glowed. The fishermen sat among them, enjoying the company of men who had, little more than two weeks earlier, trod the streets and lanes of Waset, a city they had not visited for months. The odor of cooked fish came and went as a chill breeze fanned the air around the cooking pot. The nomads' vessels lay beached nearby, while the larger fishing boat was anchored offshore.

"If he doesn't show up?" Psuro murmured.

"We should have time to go back to the place where we met him. With luck and the favor of the gods, we can trace his path from there."

"You're not thinking we should stay in this wretched desert!"

Bak laughed at the horrified look on the sergeant's face. "If he meets us here as he vowed he would, or if we can find him, we'll take him back to Kemet without delay. Otherwise, we'll leave him to his own resources and go on to the mines across the sea."

"The mountain of turquoise?" The sergeant gave Bak a puzzled look. "Why? Surely not to satisfy Nefertem. We've seen Minnakht. We know he lives and can tell him so."

"Our brief meeting yesterday left many questions unanswered, and many new questions have come to me since we spoke. If Minnakht fails to join us, fresh questions will arise. Questions related to him as a man and to his integrity. A journey to the mines might well answer those questions and at the same time help us snare the man who slew Rona."

* * *

The fishermen bade them goodbye at sunrise, weighed anchor, and sailed away, driven south by a stiff wind. The ten men stood at the water's edge, watching the vessel vanish over the horizon. From the looks on their faces, each and every man felt cast adrift, as Bak did. He prayed fervently that a ship would soon come with plenty of space on its deck, that they would not have to return to the pools where Rona and Senna had been slain.

Throughout the day they busied themselves with the small tasks of camping in the desert. User sent men out in search of additional fuel and forage. Wensu had caught considerably more fish than they needed and had left the net in the sea, thinking to keep them close and alive. They pulled the net in, let the smaller fish swim away, and killed the larger. They cleaned those they kept, gave a few to Minmose for the cooking pot, and laid the rest out to dry. They repaired torn clothing and rope halters, cared for the donkeys' hooves and medicated their sores, swam and rested. Bak looked often toward the wadi down which they had come, but Minnakht failed to appear.

At day's end, he leaned against a pole supporting one of the huts, watching what appeared to be an idyllic scene. They had an abundance of food and would never starve with fish so plentiful. They were getting the rest they needed. Water was the problem. In two more days, they would have to send men and donkeys back to the gorge to refill the jars.

Psuro suggested they walk along the beach. When they reached a point where no one would hear, he said, "I'm disappointed in Minnakht, sir. I was hoping we could go home."

"You'd think a man like him, as accustomed to the desert as he is, would take advantage of our offer to help him." Bak did not bother to hide his irritation. "If he won't trust the nomads, we're his next best alternative."

"Did he not tell you he fears User?"

"An unrealistic fear, I'm convinced. User's been striking out at the least provocation since Dedu was slain. He's as angry about the guide's death as we are that Rona's life was taken."

"Maybe Minnakht's been too long alone, sir."

Bak looked westward, where the sun, a huge fiery ball, was dropping behind the high mountains, leaving the eastern slopes in shadow while coloring the sky a brilliant red. "Tomorrow we must make an effort to find him, but I suspect he's already too far away to make the journey worthwhile."

"Do you think he'll be safe?"

"I think he's more capable of taking care of himself than you and I and all our Medjays together."

Psuro threw a surprised look his way. Seldom did Bak allow such sarcasm to cross his tongue. "We shouldn't have let him slip through our fingers, sir."

Bak was not entirely convinced that he had made a mistake in allowing Minnakht to go his own way. The very fact that the explorer chose to remain in the desert rather than return to his father in Kemet revealed something about him, something that gave pause for thought.

Minmose had obtained a small bag of grain from the master of Amonmose's fishing boat. He had found a suitable stone on which to grind it and a deep pot in which to bake bread. As they had run out several days before, the yeasty smell emanating from the pot drew the men close as nothing else could. Bak was no exception. He sat down with User, who occupied a patch of sand downwind of the hearth.

The odor made Bak's mouth water. "While in Kaine, Amonmose heard of a man who walked into this desert about a year ago and was never seen again. You must also have heard the tale."

User gave him a wry smile. "For many years, Lieutenant,

I've bought donkeys and supplies in Kaine. I know everyone
in the village, from the smallest baby to the oldest grandfather. I doubt anyone with the ability to talk failed to tell me of
the missing man."

"How long ago did you hear?"

"Six or eight months, I suppose. When he failed to return,
men began to talk."

"He was an explorer, Amonmose was led to believe."

"Ahmose by name, yes."

As the merchant had said, few men explored this wasteland and those who did were bound to know of one another.
"You knew him?"

"I've heard of him, that's all. He trod the desert far to the
north, in the vicinity of the trail that connects Mennufer to
the Eastern Sea."

"What was he doing this far south, I wonder?"

The explorer pulled his legs up and wrapped his arms
around his knees. "I heard a few years ago that he knew Minnakht. Perhaps he heard the rumors of gold and thought to
get a share." He frowned, shook his head. "No, that couldn't
be true. The first I heard of gold was when Minnakht failed to
return to Kaine, long after Ahmose vanished."

Minmose and Kaha lifted the pot off the fire, holding the
hot vessel between two flexible sticks. Minmose pried the lid
off to let the loaf cool. The smell of the fresh bread made the
onlookers moan with anticipation.

"Have you decided to travel on to the mountain of
turquoise?" Bak asked.

"Amonmose told the fishermen to sail south, you may've
noticed." User's laugh held equal parts of cynicism and humor. "Any ship they meet, whether at the end of the southern
trail or on the water, will most likely be sailing north. The
odds are great that we'll travel to the port that serves the
mines whether we want to or not."

* * *

"No, Lieutenant, we can't remain. As soon as the donkeys
are loaded, we must sail." Captain Kheruef stood on the bow
of the largest of the three cargo ships that had sailed into the
bay an hour after daybreak, while Bak and Nebre were arm-
ing themselves, preparing to walk up the wadi in search of
Minnakht.

Resting his hands on the railing, the captain looked out
across the water, watching a donkey struggling to get away
from Kaha, who was swimming it out to the ship on which
the animals would travel. "We carry plenty of food and water
for ourselves, but ten extra men will strain our resources. As
for the donkeys, you're fortunate we're transporting hay and
grain for the caravan animals kept at the port."

The three vessels, the largest in Maatkare Hatshepsut's
fleet, had been built several years earlier to sail to the distant
land of Punt to trade for incense trees, exotic animals, ebony,
and other luxury items. Rather than break the ships down and
carry the pieces across the desert to be reassembled in Waset,
as had been done with the rest of the fleet, these three had
been left intact to haul men and equipment, and the turquoise
and copper they mined, across the Eastern Sea. As User had
guessed, they had been traveling north to the port when inter-
cepted by the fishing boat.

The ship on which the animals would travel had anchored
as close to the shore as its broad, nearly flat bottom would allow. Often used to transport donkeys, it had been an easy
matter to clear the deck of cargo so pens could be raised. A
half-dozen sailors stood on the deck near the open railing
where the gangplank would normally be. Their task was to
lift the donkeys on board, using a sturdy wooden winch. Beneath them, Nebenkemet and two additional sailors caught
the fractious donkey and slipped a sling beneath its belly. A
man yelled and the donkey rose upward, kicking out and

screaming in fear. Within a short time, it stood on deck as docile as it had been on the beach.

"You've done this before," Bak said, appreciative of the ease with which the task was performed.

"There are few quays along the shores of this sea, Lieutenant."

"We'll be gone for four hours, no more," Bak said, continuing a plea that had thus far fallen on deaf ears. "I wish to know if Minnakht stayed near."

"From what you've told me of him, I'm more inclined to believe he's deep in the mountains, hiding from shadows."

Bak had had no qualms about relating his tale to the captain. He had thought it best to share with a man of authority the fact that Minnakht still lived. "We could—and probably should—refill the water jars at Amonmose's fishing camp."

"So I mean to do. We must also instruct the fishermen there to move across the sea to the port." Kheruef watched another donkey, this one more sedate, being hoisted onto the ship. "I know you think them safe, and I'm inclined to agree, but we must warn them anyway. A short delay, but necessary, making a hasty departure from this bay even more urgent."

Chapter 14

"Not quite what you expected, Lieutenant?" Lieutenant Puemre, his eyes twinkling, stood with Bak on the bow of Captain Kheruef's cargo ship.

The vessel and its two attendant ships were anchored in front of the port that served the mines. A smaller, fleeter traveling ship—used to carry messages, Puemre had explained—was moored with them. Bak likened it to a small, graceful dove sitting with three ostriches.

"No, sir," Bak admitted. "Not even the southern frontier, with its barren and empty landscape, prepared me for this stark coast and no doubt lonely outpost."

The two men stood at the railing, looking at the port for which Puemre was responsible across a narrow stretch of water so clear Bak could see fish swimming around the hull. Within a wall built of stones, the various colors muted by dust, were a dozen or so single-story interconnected buildings inhabited by soldiers, a somewhat larger structure that served as military headquarters, and a storehouse easily identified by its vaulted roof. A rough stone quay jutted into the sea in front of the enclosure. A more casual village lay outside the wall. A few dwellings were similar to those of the army, but most consisted of a framework of spindly poles supporting mud-coated brush walls. Donkey paddocks lay south of the dwellings. A large plain spread out beyond the port, with haze-shrouded hills rising behind and jagged peaks in the faroff distance.

"You think it lonely now," Puemre said, "you should visit us during the heat of the year when the mines are closed down."

"I'm amazed that anyone remains."

"This is a military base, and we must keep it manned throughout the year. Nomads come and go, and a surprising number of people dwell in the few oases scattered along the flanks of the mountains or in the wadis that cut through the highlands. And the fishermen come. Amonmose's men and others who fish the Eastern Sea or the waters around the southern tip of this peninsula."

"They all come to trade?" Bak asked, thinking of User and the objects he had brought across the Eastern Desert in the vain hope of trading with the nomads.

"Every ship brings items not easy to get in this empty land. A goodwill gesture by our sovereign, well worth the effort."

Bak pointed out User, seated on the deck between the massive oarlike rudders of the next ship in line, playing knucklebones with Ani and Wensu. Several sailors toiled at the bow, singing a bawdy song while they scrubbed away the manure dropped by the caravan's donkeys. He asked if the explorer's trade goods would be welcome at the port. They would, so Puemre said.

Amonmose had long since disembarked and was walking north along the shore to the place where his fishermen had begun to set up their camp. Psuro had gone with Nebenkemet to see to the donkeys' well-being, while the other Medjays had boarded the third vessel to watch a final wrestling match in what had been an ongoing competition among the sailors.

The ship rose and fell on gentle swells, its hull and fittings creaking. At irregular intervals, schools of small fish surfaced, drawing seagulls in large numbers. The squawking birds plummeted out of the sky to gather on the water and feed. Amid the frenzy, a half-dozen terns swooped down to snatch fish on the fly. Several small boats lay on the shore above the waterline, and three feral dogs fought over the torn remains of a gull. Farther down the beach, a group of naked children were splashing in the shallows, their laughter ringing through the clear air.

"Who dwells in those huts?"

"Men who've chosen to remain for one reason or another, usually because they've wed a nomad woman and are raising families. We've the usual number of camp followers, of course. Men who wager, hoping to lay hands on a few chunks of turquoise, women no better than they should be, men who jump ship and find themselves with no way to earn their daily bread. And so on." Puemre glanced at Bak and smiled. "As you can imagine, when we're not organizing the unloading and loading of ships, our primary task is to maintain law and order."

Bak had seen many impoverished villages on the southern frontier. This was no better than the worst. "I have endless respect for you and the soldiers who man this desolate outpost."

"All things eventually come to an end, Lieutenant, whether good or bad." Puemre, a short, squat man with a slight paunch and thinning grayish hair, turned his back on the port and, with Bak by his side, walked along the deck. "I'm to be relieved at the end of this mining season. With luck and if the Lady of Turquoise chooses to smile upon me, I'll be posted to a garrison in Kemet." The goddess of whom he spoke was a local version of the lady Hathor.

The two men ducked beneath the woven reed roof of the deckhouse, whose colorful mat walls had been rolled up to allow air to pass through. On a small boat tied to the side of the ship, the two soldiers who had rowed Puemre across the water argued in a good-natured way.

"According to Captain Kheruef, you're not what you appear to be," Puemre said, sitting on a mat and crossing his legs before him.

Bak, who had raided Kheruef's beer supply, broke the plugs from two jars, handed one to his companion, and sat down on the mat. He revealed his identity as a policeman, explained his mission, and told of the caravan's journey across the Eastern Desert and the men who had been slain along the way. He spoke of the watching man, who might well be the slayer, and of how he had managed to slip away untouched. He failed to mention that Minnakht was alive and well. He had concluded that he would glean more information if the men he spoke with remained in ignorance, if he lumped the explorer's probable death in among the others.

A snarl drew Bak's glance toward the shore. A gull had dropped onto the sand and, wings flapping, was trying to chase the dogs away from a new prize, this a dead fish. He skipped over the long voyage north and across the Eastern Sea to conclude his tale. "Now here we are, twelve days later, safe at our destination."

Puemre took several sips of beer, evidently reviewing the account, and licked the foam from his lips. "I'm surprised Amonmose came with you. Even more surprised that he's ordered his men to abandon their camp. He must indeed be worried."

"Many men have died within the past year."

Puemre studied him with interest. "You're determined to snare the slayer, I see."

"He took the life of one of my Medjays." Bak's voice was hard, grim. "I mean to see justice done."

The port officer shifted on the mat, uncomfortable with the promise of vengeance. "Why come across the sea? From what you've told me, he's in the Eastern Desert, not here."

"I can't be certain, but logic tells me the many deaths are related to Minnakht's disappearance." Bak sipped from his beer jar, letting the slightly bitter brew wash over his tongue. "Minnakht hasn't been seen since he left this port. I hope to learn more of his last few days. I don't even know why he ventured so far from the land he knew so well."

Puemre toyed with his beer jar, thinking. "Too many men traveling with you have died, that I grant you, but why? Why concentrate on your caravan?"

"I know nothing of the man who was slain at the well north of Kaine, but, with the exception of my Medjay, all the others who've died were at one time or another involved in a quest for gold." Bak drew close a basket containing dried dates and offered them to Puemre. "Minnakht made no secret of the fact that he hoped to find gold, and User has been seeking the riches of the desert for many years. Because we've been following Minnakht's last route across the desert, the slayer may believe we can lead him to gold. Or he might fear we'll stumble upon a vein he's already found."

"Do you suppose he's followed you across the sea? Neither my men nor I have any experience with murder."

Bak could find no answer. Silence hung between them, an invisible curtain of puzzlement and frustration.

"I suppose Minnakht has gone to the netherworld." With an unhappy sigh, Puemre bit into a date. "I'm sorry. I liked him, as did most men who met him."

"According to User, Minnakht had never before left the Eastern Desert. Why did he abandon a lifelong pattern? Why did he stray so far from his usual haunts?"

"He wanted to see the mountain of turquoise. He was, after all, an explorer, one who year after year studied the land in search of the wealth it offered."

Bak was not surprised by the answer, but he wondered if it was not too simplistic. "Tell me of his visit."

"The hot months of the year were upon us, so we were closing the mines. Lieutenant Nebamon, our caravan officer, was readying men and donkeys for their final journey into the mountains to bring back the few remaining miners and soldiers and the fruits of their labors. I insisted Minnakht travel with them." Puemre nibbled the pulp from the date and flung the seed overboard. "He remained here a couple of days, waiting. From what I heard, he spent much of the time in what passes in the outer village for a house of pleasure. He drank beer and talked about his adventures in the desert, filling the ears of all who would listen. Then he joined the caravan and set out for the mountain of turquoise."

"According to his guide Senna, he left this port soon after returning from the mines."

"He meant to leave the following day, but he altered his plans." Puemre took a healthy drink of beer and nodded his appreciation. It was probably the best brew he had drunk in a long time. "He'd talked with the overseer of the copper mines west of the mountain of turquoise, and he wished also to see the mines a considerable distance to the south. He asked for a guide to take him, but I refused to supply one. Those mines, quite a long journey from here, were also being shut down. I insisted he wait until the overseer came in with another caravan. Which proved to be a delay of only three days."

"If he was seeking gold, why would he want to visit copper and turquoise mines?"

"The more a man knows, the more able he is, I suppose." Puemre shrugged, uncertain of the answer. "He asked endless questions about anything and everything. That's why he was so well liked. People enjoy talking about themselves and what they do day after day."

A gull dropped onto the forecastle rail, drawing Bak's glance. "Did you know Senna?"

"I knew Minnakht brought a nomad guide." Puemre flung a date pit at the gull. The bird merely tilted its head, showing its disdain. "I heard, while he was away at the mines, that Senna tried to befriend a few local nomads, but he was an outsider and was treated as such. By the time I learned he was ill, Minnakht had returned. I thought all was well, so paid no further heed. I was surprised to hear a few days later that Minnakht had left without him. By the time I sent a man to see if he still ailed, he'd gone."

Bak sipped from his beer jar, taking care not to stir up the sediment, thinking over what he had learned. Nothing much new, certainly nothing of significance. "I've vowed to follow in Minnakht's footsteps. Will you clear away any difficulties I might face while I'm on this side of the Eastern Sea?"

"A caravan will leave before nightfall tomorrow to deliver men and supplies to the mountain of turquoise. The officer in charge is Lieutenant Nebamon, with whom Minnakht traveled a few months ago. He'll welcome your company."

Bak flashed a smile of thanks. "How many of the men who are presently working the mines are the same as those with whom Minnakht spoke?"

"The officers and overseers, most of the miners, and about half the soldiers are the same. The prisoners who toil on the goddess's mansion, adding the new chambers our sovereign wishes built, differ from year to year."

Bak set aside his empty beer jar and stood up to stretch his back. "All the men in User's party will wish to come, and I want my Medjays with me. Is that too much to ask?"

"If you've a reason for taking so many men, it can be arranged."

"I have no idea who the guilty man is," Bak admitted, "and I've thought at times that we have a snake among us." He gave Puemre a humorless smile. "If I keep them all together and within arm's reach, I hope to prevent another death."

The following afternoon, the caravan left the port. The walking was easy for men and donkeys as they crossed the vast flat plain between the sea and the hills. Its sandy floor was strewn with chunks of gray and red granite, pink

feldspar, and black basalt that had many centuries ago been
swept down from the mountains. Ani ran from one rock to
another, delighted with the display. He picked up innumerable colorful shards but, mindful of the difficulty of transport, left most where he found them.

Along with the soldiers serving as guards and tending the
donkeys and Bak's small party, the caravan included thirty
prisoners, men who would toil on the mansion of the Lady of
Turquoise. Bak did not envy them their punishment. The lord
Re had dropped behind the western horizon, offering a magnificent showing of color, but the day was slow to cool. A prel-
ude to the many more long, hot days the men must endure.

Leaving the plain behind, they entered higher ground, following a series of dry watercourses carpeted with golden sand
and hugged on either side by hills and escarpments, some yellowish, some a glittering gray, and others shades of brown, all
losing their color as night fell to blend together in shades of
gray. A surprising number of acacias dotted the wadi floors, as
did silla bushes and a kind of shrub the donkeys refused to eat.
Subsidiary wadis went off in all directions, a confusing maze
of dry valleys cutting through the barren rock.

"You've no idea what you're looking for?" Lieutenant
Nebamon drew Bak aside, allowing his sergeant to lead the
caravan around a shoulder of rock by way of a narrow trail
covered with a thick layer of soft sand. A steep bank fell
away to the right, dropping fifty or so paces to the wadi floor.
Sand displaced by the animals spilled over the rim and slid
down the slope with a gentle whisper.

They eased past several donkeys to stand beside a large
boulder poised on the edge of the trail. A small grayish bird
flitted out from above, startled from its sleep. The heavily
laden donkeys passed one by one, their hooves mired in the
deep sand. Several brayed their irritation at such strenuous
effort.

"Did Minnakht ever explain why he wished to see the mines?"

"Not specifically." Nebamon pushed back his lank black hair. He was of medium height and stick-thin. He looked to be about Bak's age but his face was lined and leatherlike, victim of the harsh sunlight. "He questioned me about the way the men locate the copper ore and the turquoise and how they extract and process what they find." He smiled at the memory. "I'm afraid I disappointed him. I've no interest in watching men burrow in the ground or toil over blazing furnaces, so I seldom go beyond the miners' camps."

Puemre had said this was Nebamon's third year as caravan officer. Bak could not imagine spending so long a time in what had to be an exceedingly boring outpost without seeking distraction. As far as he could see, no diversion existed except the mines. "Aren't you the least bit curious?"

"I once climbed the mountain of turquoise. I saw a few holes in the ground and men hacking away at the rock. I thought the lumps of stone they found small reward for the effort of transporting men, food, and supplies over inordinately long distances and of grubbing the rock from the earth."

"Men and supplies most often come from Mennufer along a trail some distance to the north, I understand. That has to be shorter than the southern route from Waset."

"The journey is shorter, both by land and sea, the voyage made faster by northerly breezes. Still, the effort is substantial for so modest a gain."

"Our sovereign takes immense delight in the jewelry made from those chunks of stone," Bak pointed out.

Nebamon leaped out to steady a donkey that had stepped on an unstable rock at the edge of the trail. "I assume Puemre told you she's adding chambers onto the mansion of our Lady of Turquoise." He shook his head in disapproval. "She's never been here, of course, nor will she ever set foot in this wretched land, but I suppose she believes that enlarging the structure will increase her stature." With a cynical laugh, he added, "While I was up there, I entered the mansion to bend a knee to the goddess. I almost broke my neck, stumbling over the stones lying about, awaiting placement."

Bak enjoyed the lieutenant's irreverent attitude, but foresaw grief in the future. Should the officer be posted to a garrison in Kemet, he would have to bite his tongue to keep himself out of trouble. "Did Minnakht ever find a man who could answer his questions?"

"I heard that he spent a considerable amount of time with one of the miners. A man who toiled in the mines for several years, traveling all the way from the land of Retenu."

Puemre had told Bak that many of the miners came from afar. They spoke a tongue other than that of Kemet and worshipped different gods. For some reason Puemre could not fathom, the mansion of the Lady of Turquoise satisfied their devotional needs.

"Has that man come again this year?"

"I haven't seen him. He was older than the other miners. Too old for rough labor, I thought, and he seemed to know it. He talked of leaving this life of deprivation and toil so he might spend his final years in his homeland, close to his wife and children, and their children."

Bak muttered an oath. Thus far the gods were doling out the information he sought in such small bits that he feared he would die of old age before he learned the truth.

The prisoners trudged past, watched closely by their guards. Where they might flee in this waterless landscape, he could not imagine. Their hands were tied behind their backs and they were roped together in a loose chain. Their faces were impossible to see in the darkness, but he sensed their lack of hope. He could not help but feel pity, but they had offended the lady Maat and justice must be served.

Justice. He prayed that soon he would be able to offer to

the gods the name of the man who had taken Rona's life and the lives of so many others. At times he felt a glimmer of hope that he would do so; at other times he felt no closer to the truth than he had the day he and his men had set out from Kaine.

The caravan reached the camp at the base of the mountain of turquoise the following morning. Bak pitied the soldiers posted to this hot and sun-bleached valley, and he was certain the miners and prisoners who toiled atop the mountain suffered a harsher existence.

The camp was basic—primitive almost. Several groups of rough stone huts had been erected near the scree-covered base of a reddish sandstone mountain. A small flock of goats and four donkeys, tended by a nomad family, were permanent residents, satisfying the scant needs of the army. Because the caravan animals had to bring their own food from the port and water had to be carried from a distant well, they never remained more than two or three days. Like the houses, the paddocks were walled with stone. Acacias fanned out across the valley floor, providing some relief from the sun.

A half-dozen soldiers stood guard, while others performed the small, tedious duties necessary in a desert outpost. Their primary duty, Bak suspected, was to care for the caravan animals during their brief but regular sojourns. A few men branded as prisoners suffered the harshest duty, repairing tools, cleaning manure from the paddocks, and so on. Nomads came and went, men who had left families and livestock in distant wadis while they came to trade.

Like the soldiers who had brought in the caravan, Bak and his party slept through the day. Not until after the evening meal did he have the opportunity to speak with Lieutenant Huy, a slim, ruddy-faced man who, according to Nebamon, treasured his senet board and playing pieces and pressed all who came near into playing the game with him.

"I'm eternally grateful, Lieutenant." Huy sat on a low stool beneath an acacia and set up the board, which had folding legs and contained a drawer in which to store the pieces. "I seldom get to challenge anyone new."

Bak, seated on a similar stool, watched him place the pieces in their appropriate squares. "Nebamon said you'd want to play."

What the caravan officer had actually said was, "If you want him to answer your questions, you must play at least one game with him. But let me warn you: he fancies himself an expert, and he doesn't like to lose. His goodwill is important to the smooth running of this mine, and I can't tell you how difficult it is to think of new ways to let him win."

"He must've told you, then, that each time he comes, we compete." Huy, who had given Bak the white cones and had taken the blue spools as his own, made the opening move without throwing the knucklebones, as he should have, to decide who would begin. "I enjoy our games, but I can predict his every move. He plays with no imagination whatsoever."

Bak took a sip of beer, smothering a laugh, and began to play. After allowing Huy to take his third playing piece, he said, "I understand Minnakht asked many questions about mining the turquoise while he was here."

"He did." Huy pounced on another piece. "I helped him as best I could, but finally sent him to Teti, the overseer." He noticed Bak's curious look and smiled. "I'm responsible for the mines, yes, but my primary task is the smooth running of this camp and seeing that the men are supplied with all their needs, modest as they are. Teti knows the mines and mining better than any living man, so I entrust him to oversee the activities atop the mountain of turquoise."

Bak saw an opening on the game board so obvious a blind man could have spotted it. He could not resist taking one of Huy's pieces. "I understand he also asked about copper mining."

The officer eyed the board and his mouth tightened, but as the number of spools exceeded the cones, he had no grounds for complaint. "He inquired about the workings west of here and those much farther away to the south. I told him all I knew, which isn't much. I've been to the former, of course, but I've never seen the more southerly mines."

"He visited the closer location, I understand." Bak noted a careless move on Huy's part and was sorely tempted to take advantage. He resisted the urge.

"He did, and he asked for a guide to take him south. I refused. We were closing these mines for the season and none of the men who remained had sufficient experience to lead him through the mountains. I also warned him that those mines might already be shut down."

"After I climb the mountain of turquoise, I wish to see the copper mines he visited. Would that be possible?"

"When Nebamon returns to the port, his caravan must make a detour to those mines. They've a load of copper ready to transport to the sea, the first of this season."

Nebamon and his men had set up camp near the donkey paddocks, as had User and his party. Bak and his Medjays had elected to sleep twenty or so paces away and an equal distance from the nearest cluster of huts. At dusk, while Minmose prepared an evening meal of fish cooked with onions, Bak strode across the sand to the caravan officer's camp.

Nebamon saw him coming and motioned him to sit on the sand beside him. Handing his guest a jar of beer, he grinned, "How did your game progress, Lieutenant?"

"Unfortunately I failed to win," Bak said, forming an unhappy look that would have convinced no one—except perhaps Lieutenant Huy.

"I trust you made up for the loss in another way."

Bak took a sip of beer and grimaced. It was one of the bitterest brews he had tasted since leaving the southern frontier.

"Tomorrow I'll climb the mountain of turquoise and speak with the overseer."

Nebamon smiled at Bak's reaction to the beer. "Teti."

"You know him?"

"I've seen him here at the camp a couple of times." Nebamon sipped from his beer jar, then set it on the sand between his bare feet. "The miners say he's a hard man, but one who can smell turquoise where none believe the stones exist. They say he enters a shaft and strolls around with his hands locked behind his back. He tilts his head one way and another, peering at the walls, and finally points a finger. Eight times out of ten, the miners find turquoise in that very spot."

"If he's so competent, why would Minnakht have spent so much time with the miner from Retenu?"

"Teti probably didn't want to be bothered with him."

If the overseer had no time for one man, Bak wondered how he would feel about ten, strangers one and all, demanding a personal tour of his domain. "Huy said I could climb the mountain and descend in one day."

The caravan officer raised his beer jar and twisted it in his fingers, making a show of studying it. Bak was reminded of the old woman Nofery, his spy in Buhen, and the way she doled out information, hoping to make a better bargain. Nebamon, however, responded freely enough. "My sergeant, Suemnut, and his men must escort the prisoners up the mountain tomorrow and must deliver the supplies we brought. They'll leave at first light. You can walk up with them. The trail isn't difficult, but can be confusing to one who's never climbed it."

"How long will they remain atop the mountain? I'll need time to speak with Teti and I'd like to see the mines."

"They won't tarry." Nebamon glanced toward the paddocks and said in a too-offhand voice, "If the donkeys are rested by the time they return—and they should be—I thought to leave in the early afternoon."

Bak gave the officer a speculative look. He was convinced he wanted something, but what it might be, he could not imagine. "I've come too far to make such a hasty journey."

Nebamon drank from his beer jar. Screwing up his face in distaste, he nodded. "I agree."

Bak hated to ask the question. The answer might be costly. "Could I convince you to stay an extra day?"

Nebamon's lips twitched. "On one condition."

"That is?"

"When at last you reach the land of Kemet, I'd be obliged if you'd send back to me twenty jars of the finest brew you can find, and a single jar of a good northern wine."

Bak burst out laughing. "Done."

"I'd like to go with you, sir." Psuro untied his rolled sleeping mat, clutched the edge, and flung it out on the sand. "We're surrounded by soldiers, true, but if the man who's been trying to slay you is close by, you're no safer here than you were in the Eastern Desert."

"I insist you accompany me, Sergeant, and Nebre and Kaha as well." Bak glanced toward User's campsite. "I feel certain User and Ani will wish to go and probably all the other men who came across the Eastern Sea with us. Any one of them may be as much at risk as I am."

"I doubt that, sir."

Refusing to argue with him, Bak picked up his sleeping mat, untied it, and shook it open. A long, thick brownish snake writhed free and dropped to the ground. A viper. Snapping out a curse, Bak leaped backward. The deadly reptile sped across the sand toward Psuro, who stood paralyzed with shock. Too far away from their weapons cache to grab a spear, Bak tore his dagger from its sheath. Uttering a hasty prayer to the lord Amon, he flung the weapon. The slender blade impaled the snake just below its head. While it whipped its tail, trying to shake itself free, Bak leaped toward

the spears, grabbed one, and slashed the head from the creature. Moments later, the snake writhed its last.

Psuro stared, appalled, at the reptile. "How could a viper
get into your sleeping mat?"

"Not by itself, I'd wager."

The sergeant tore his eyes from the creature. "As I said before, sir, you're no safer here among all these soldiers than
you were in the solitude of the desert."

Chapter 15

"Someone tried to slay me last night." Bak looked at each of the men scattered around User's camp, registering their reactions. "When I unrolled my sleeping mat, a viper fell out. An angry viper bent on avenging its captivity."

User, honing the edges of his spear point, showed no surprise at this new attack on a member of the caravan, but his usual grim expression turned grimmer still. Nebenkemet looked up from the cooking bowl he was cleaning with sand and muttered a curse. Ani, who was tucking a dirty square of linen into his belt with the expectation of collecting a few samples of turquoise, looked appalled. Wensu, seated on the ground, the last to finish his morning meal, glanced quickly at the sand around him and scrambled to his feet.

Amonmose slipped his arms into the sleeves of his filthy tunic and pulled it over his head. "I thought we'd left that vile criminal behind when we crossed the sea."

"Could not the snake have crawled inside to escape the heat?" Wensu asked.

As far as Bak could tell, each of the men had reacted in a predictable manner. "The mat was rolled too tight. Only because the lord Amon chose to smile upon Psuro did he avoid being struck by its deadly fangs."

"And because you were quick with the dagger, sir." The

sergeant stood with the other Medjays at the edge of the camp, watching the men in User's party as closely as Bak studied them.

About thirty paces away, Lieutenant Nebamon stood with Sergeant Suemnut, a hard-muscled man of medium height, in front of the hut in which the supplies had been kept safe until they could be transported to the mines atop the mountain of turquoise. They watched the soldiers who had come from the port with the caravan scurrying around, placing yokes on the prisoner's shoulders and checking for balance the baskets and bundles of supplies and the water jars suspended from either side. When they finished that task, more than half the soldiers, grumbling among themselves, assumed identical burdens. The remaining men stood off to the side, fully armed and awaiting Suemnut's signal to depart.

"I know several attempts have been made to slay you, but were they true attempts on your life?" User asked. "All who've vanished or have died were men familiar with the Eastern Desert. As I am. You'd think I'd be the next target, not you." He raised his hands to stave off comment and bared his teeth in a sham grin. "Don't get me wrong, Lieutenant. I'm grateful. But I'm also puzzled."

Bak gave him a sharp look. "You knew the man we found dead at the well north of Kaine?"

"If I knew him, I'd have said so." User scowled, irritated. "You're not the sole man in this caravan who's capable of reaching the vast sum of two after adding one and one together. No sane man would travel the desert alone if he didn't know it well."

Bak ignored the sarcasm. "You're right. To keep to his pattern, he'd wish you dead instead of me. Unless he's more afraid of me than you."

"If it's wealth he's after, he has no reason to fear me. I'm no closer to finding gold today than I was twenty years ago."

User's laugh was humorless, directed at himself. "As for you, Lieutenant: If I planned some vile deed abhorrent to the gods, I'd want you out of the way. You may not know this land, but you're tenacious. And you're a soldier free of the burdens of official duty, the nearest thing in this godforsaken land to a policeman."

"I am a policeman."

Bak glanced at Amonmose, the sole man among them who had known who he was. The trader smiled, relieved at the disclosure. Ani looked startled, while Wensu appeared annoyed. Nebenkemet's expression shut down, a man refusing to reveal himself.

User burst out laughing. "I should've guessed. The questions you've asked, the way you examined the men we found dead, and most of all, the Medjays. Not many ordinary officers command a troop of Medjays."

"How could you not tell us?" Wensu demanded. "We had a right to know. Men have been slain beneath our very noses, yet you sat back and did nothing. Said nothing. We needed protection, reassur . . ."

"Silence!" User snarled. "If the lieutenant and his men hadn't joined our caravan, we might all be dead by now. His Medjays have walked ten times the number of steps the rest of us have taken, scouting ahead, searching for him when he was abducted, following suspicious footprints. I've not seen you put forth one-tenth the effort."

Thoroughly chastised, Wensu swallowed whatever else he thought to say.

"I came not as a policeman," Bak said, "but as a soldier given a task by his commandant. If we'd not found the man dead at the well, I'd have revealed myself sooner. But men answer questions more readily when asked by a friend or acquaintance, so I decided to keep secret the fact that we're policemen."

"You thought one of us slew the stranger," Ani said, clearly surprised.

"My men found no sign of an intruder."

User eyed him thoughtfully. "You've been watching us ever since, saying nothing, hoping to pounce on the rat among us."

"The night Dedu walked away to be slain, we found the footprint of an unknown party in your camp, a man whose print Kaha first spotted between Kaine and our initial campsite, the man who's been watching us ever since. That print cleared no one of suspicion, but it suggested that someone other than any of you might've slain the first man."

"What of Senna and Rona?" Amonmose asked.

"The floor of the gorge was too rocky, the patches of sand too disturbed to reveal footprints."

"Do you continue to believe one of us is the guilty man?" Ani asked. "Is that why you've come to us this morning?"

"I don't know the name of the slayer," Bak admitted, "nor am I convinced he's among you. Whether or not he is, wherever he is, I intend to snare him. If one of you has been helping him, you'll suffer a like fate. Make no mistake about that." He scanned the faces of the men before him. "I keep no secrets. I share with my men all I know and suspect. I've reported to the captain of the ship on which we crossed the Eastern Sea and to Lieutenant Puemre at the port. Any attempt to silence me or to stop my investigation will be in vain."

"I can't believe any of them is a slayer." Psuro, walking behind Bak up the narrow trail that led to the mines atop the mountain of turquoise, hoisted his quiver higher onto his shoulder. "Wensu's all talk, too weak to face a man with a dagger. Ani wouldn't know what to do with a weapon. As for the others . . ."

"You don't think User could slay a man?"

"I do—for a good reason or in the heat of battle. I doubt he'd slay several men, one after the other, or creep up behind a man and stab him in the back." Psuro glanced down the long, steep slope to their right, which was covered with broken chunks of reddish sandstone. "I believe the same to be true of Amonmose."

Bak nodded, in full agreement. "What of Nebenkemet?"

"I've no doubt that he could slay a man, but would he?"

They walked on, following Sergeant Suemnut and four armed soldiers who led the supply train. Not a sound could be heard in the still air except the crunch of sandals on rock, a muttered curse now and then, and the faint call of a falcon soaring overhead. At the end of a long traverse around the curve of the mountain, they scrambled up a vertical section of reddish sandstone, split by erosion into thick, flat plates lying one on top of another.

Bak turned to watch the row of men ascending the path behind them. Nebre and Kaha were first in line. A dozen paces back, User led the men in his party, checking often to be sure Ani and Wensu were keeping pace. Next plodded the soldiers and prisoners laden with water jars and supplies. Armed soldiers were spread along the line, maintaining the pace, preventing gaps, and watching for raiders. Attempts to steal supplies were rare, Lieutenant Huy had said, but not unknown.

The trail, which had been heavily trodden through the years, was not difficult for a man accustomed to strenuous activity, but the heat was pervasive, with not a breath of air to offer relief. Bak feared for Ani, the most likely among them to suffer from the climb.

He examined the barren landscape around them. The deep defiles, the steep slopes, a total absence of vegetation. A land endowed by the gods with turquoise and then abandoned to the lord Set. The sandstone was a different shade of red than that of the granite peaks in the Eastern Desert. Where those had had a pinkish cast, the stone here was tinted with gold, as if burned by a fire from within as well as by the sun without.

Psuro, following Bak on up the trail, continued their conversation as if it had not been interrupted. "Do you think one of them the guilty man, sir? You haven't said."

"I believe the man who's been watching us the most likely slayer. Whether someone among us is his ally, I can't say."

"You speak of the man you and Nebre followed into the mountains."

"The one who led us into the mountains, you mean." Bak grimaced, unhappy with the memory.

"The man I should've slain," growled Nebre, walking close enough to hear.

"Would he have followed us across the sea?" Psuro asked.

"A good question, Sergeant. One for which the answer eludes me."

"I pray to the lord Amon never to have to toil in a place such as this."

Bak smiled at the intensity in Psuro's voice, though he agreed wholeheartedly. The mountain of turquoise was not a place where he wished to spend many hours. "You'd best check on Ani, Sergeant. He looks ill. I think the climb was too difficult for him."

"He must drink more water, sir. He's not taken in enough to make up for what he's lost."

"I've seen all manner of men enter the mansion of the Lady of Turquoise," User said, joining them. He handed the Medjay a waterbag. "Get him inside, into the shade. If anyone complains, send him to me."

Psuro strode down a slope of coarse, hard-packed sand as red as the rocks around them. He said a few words to Kaha, standing with the weapons and goatskin waterbags they had brought from the valley camp. Together they approached the plump jeweler, who sat hunched over, his forehead on his knees, and offered him a drink. After Ani took a few careful sips, Psuro took his arm, helped him to his feet, and led him across the grit. Kaha, taking the waterbags and weapons with him, followed them around a chamber being built against the southern wall of an open court. They vanished through a side door into the mansion of the Lady of Turquoise.

Like Bak, User watched to be sure an overly officious priest did not turn the men out. "Amonmose told me of how highly regarded you were in Wawat, Lieutenant. I'm suitably impressed."

He did not sound the least bit impressed, Bak thought. "I'm not sure why. Since we left Kaine, three men, including one of my own, have died beneath my very nose."

"What was your intent this morning? To make us all suspicious of one another?"

"Any man with good sense would've been looking over his shoulder long ago. I believe you to be a man of good sense."

User's laugh held not a shred of humor. "Why do you think I agreed to bring Ani and Wensu with me into the desert? To let Amonmose and Nebenkemet come along?"

"You told me you needed additional wealth to pay for physicians," Bak reminded him.

"I do, yes, but I much prefer traveling alone with a nomad guide. So I intended this time." User flung Bak one of his humorless smiles. "I must admit to a certain relief when Ani and Wensu approached me, wishing to come with me. I'd heard, as I told you before, that Ahmose had vanished. Then Minnakht failed to reappear. Both of them explorers. It set me to thinking."

He obviously thought himself guilty of a weakness, but Bak called his concern commonsense. "Amonmose and Nebenkemet must've been easier to accept."

"The merchant at least knew something of the desert."

Bak saw Kaha leaving the goddess's mansion empty-handed. He must have found a safe place to leave the weapons and waterbags out of the sun. "You seemed none too happy when we came along."

"I didn't know if you were friend or foe. You outnumbered us and you were better armed. If Amonmose had told me who you were . . ." User shrugged. "He didn't. He kept the knowledge to himself."

"I asked that he do so."

The two men stood on a rise of rock-strewn red sand south of the goddess's mansion, looking across the low walls that would one day form a large chamber being added to the building by Maatkare Hatshepsut. Ten men toiled at the wall, increasing the height of a ramp up which the next course of stones would be hauled and placed. Prisoners they were, but they chattered constantly as all men do who toil together day after day. An overseer watched, barking out orders, while a guard sat dozing in a slice of shade beside the wall. A sledge containing two large sandstone blocks stood idle on the chamber floor and seven or eight additional blocks lay ready to load. Bak guessed they had been cut the previous season and left for the new crew to place.

"Where's that overseer, the one called Teti?" User grumbled. "I've no desire to spend the night up here."

The hill on which they stood sloped from south to north, allowing them to look beyond the new chamber and the open court to what had been, many generations ago, another structure, now partially destroyed. Kaha had joined Wensu and the pair were walking among a dozen or so monolithic memorial tablets that rose into the sky or lay in the sand at either end of the fallen building, reminders of past kings and long-ago expeditions to the mines. Now and again they stopped so Wensu could read an inscription to the Medjay.

Beyond the building, the irregular surface of the plateau

sloped toward the north until suddenly it dropped away. The high, steep cliff overlooked a deep wadi cut through the sandstone by raging waters many generations ago.

The mansion of the Lady of Turquoise, built of the reddish stone taken from the mountain, looked a part of the land around it. It was not large, four or five rooms, Bak guessed, and angled off to the south at the rear of the open court. Lieutenant Huy had told him the goddess's shrine and that of the lord Sopdu, patron god of the eastern frontier, were cut into the rock beneath the high ground behind the structure. An impressive stand of bushes somehow managed to survive in front of the building, adding life to the hot, dry, and otherwise lifeless land.

Other than the prisoners toiling on the building and the soldiers and prisoners resting from their ordeal of carrying water and supplies up the trail, few men were visible on the tableland atop the mountain. Bak guessed that its uneven reddish surface concealed the mines and those who dug the turquoise from within. A young man wearing the long kilt of a scribe was talking with Sergeant Suemnut, and four men were approaching up a slope farther to the west.

"I thought this place would be busier," User said, as if reading his thoughts, "an ant hill."

"According to Huy, too large a number of men would be impossible to supply. Necessity limits the population to about a hundred and twenty."

"Thirty prisoners came with us from the port to help build the mansion of the goddess, and I count ten men raising the ramp in the new chamber. Do you suppose our sovereign knows her generous offering to the Lady of Turquoise is being carried on at the expense of her mining operation?"

"Someone will have told her. From what I've heard, she keeps a close eye on the amount of precious minerals and stones received at the treasury. She'd question a shortage."

User grinned. "You speak as if you don't know her personally, Lieutenant."

"The earthly daughter of the lord Amon? You jest."

Bak wondered if Amonmose had heard of his exile to Buhen and had told the explorer. He probably had. Such tales were the stuff of legend, far more interesting than talk of skirmishes in the desert or the arrival at a garrison of a beautiful young woman.

Sergeant Suemnut called out and one man of the four turned aside to join him. The sergeant pointed toward Bak and User. Words were exchanged, not all of them agreeable if the intensity of their gestures told true. The sergeant snapped out a final order and the man strode across the sand.

"I'm Teti," he said. "Which of you is Lieutenant Bak?"

The overseer of the mines was a few years older than Bak, of medium height, and well muscled. He wore a dirty knee-length kilt and carried a short baton. His snapping black eyes and the angry set of his mouth promised an interesting tour if not a pleasant one.

"This is one of our bigger mines, and at present our most productive." Teti stopped beside a large square hole in the ground. At the bottom, a horizontal tunnel led off to the right. "Do any of you want to go down?"

Bak knelt to look. The sound of voices could be heard issuing from the tunnel, along with the tapping of mallets on chisels. "I'm going." He had made his expectations clear to the sergeant, and felt sure the message had been passed on. Evidently Teti had not wished to hear.

"As are we," Psuro said, signaling Nebre and Kaha to come forward.

"And I," User said.

"After coming so far?" Ani rubbed his hands together in anticipation. "I wouldn't miss it."

"Nor would I," Nebenkemet said, kneeling beside Bak and looking down the shaft.

Amonmose knelt beside the carpenter. "How do we get down?"

"Are you well enough?" User asked Ani.

The jeweler, whose face remained flushed from his arduous climb, formed a resolute smile, took a waterbag from the Medjay sergeant, and raised it to his lips. "Psuro was right. The more water I drink, the better I feel."

Openly irritated by the growing number of men who wished to accompany him, Teti frowned at Wensu. "You're not coming, too, are you?"

The young man stared into the hole, which looked to be less than the height of two men. "Are all the mines so deep?"

"If we could find turquoise on the surface, do you think we'd be burrowing in the ground like sand rats?"

Wensu swallowed hard but refused to back off. "I wish to go down this mine, not wait until we reach the next one."

Teti swung around, eyes blazing, but before he could argue Bak raised a hand to silence him. "Yes, Teti. The next and the next and the next. As many as we must. The sooner we learn what we came for, the sooner you'll be free of us."

"I thought you wanted to know about Minnakht, not spend your time watching other men labor."

"I want to use this day to its greatest advantage. Shall we go?"

Teti took them down what proved to be one of three shafts sunk through the reddish stone from the top of the hill to the mine below. They followed him along the short horizontal tunnel to a gallery about twenty-five paces wide and half as deep. Its floor was irregular, made uneven and treacherous by earlier excavations never filled in. The mine was better lit than most and had plenty of air. In addition to the shafts to the surface, the gallery had been cut all the way through the ridge, leaving a large opening at one end that overlooked a valley.

Nine miners were chiseling away the rock face, five within subsidiary chambers separated by walls or pillars of stone left intact to support the roof. Each chamber was taller than a man and wider, allowing plenty of space in which to search for stones embedded in the matrix. Fine dust hung in the hot air, and the miners smelled strongly of sweat. To a man, they turned around, curious to see who had come. Spotting Teti, they quickly returned to their task.

Staying well out of the way, Bak and his companions watched the men chiseling out small, careful bites of stone and letting them drop around their feet. Any turquoise they found, they cut free of the matrix and threw into pottery bowls placed nearby. At irregular intervals, ordinary work-men—nomads who dwelt in the surrounding mountains, Lieutenant Huy had said—loaded the waste into baskets and carried it away.

The miners' task was hot, filthy, and laborious, and could be dangerous. Sweat poured from them. Their knuckles were barked, their legs and feet scabbed. These men were not pris-oners. A few had come from the surrounding villages, the rest from lands much farther afield. They would receive payment in kind at the end of the mining season and would return to their homes and families wealthier men. Bak would not have exchanged places with them for any number of riches.

Amonmose caught Bak's eye and grimaced. Psuro looked on with distaste, and Nebre muttered a few words in his own tongue, a prayer no doubt. Of them all, User, Nebenkemet, and Ani appeared the least troubled. The explorer had seen other mines and quarries, and if this offered any surprises, he gave no sign. The burly carpenter wandered around the gallery, peering closely at the walls, examining tools dulled by use and thrown aside to be resharpened, and watching the way the miners performed their task.

Ani looked around with avid interest. "How much turquoise do you get each day?"

Scowling, the overseer walked along the row of miners, picking up the bowls behind them. He brought them back and displayed their contents. Each held three or four blue-green stones from the size of a pea to as big as a man's thumbnail. "We've been working the mines since daybreak, three hours at most. When the workmen sort through the waste, they may find a few more nodules, but this looks to be a typical day."

Ani looked disappointed. "Are the stones always so small?"

"Most, yes, but now and again . . ." Teti glared at him beneath lowered brows. "I suppose next you'll want to see all we've recovered since our last delivery to the port."

Ani's already flushed face turned even redder. "I mean no disrespect, sir, but I earn my daily bread by making jewelry, toiling in the workshop at the royal house. I've seen a few large stones, yes, but I longed to see them here, in the place where they . . ." His voice tailed off, his expression wistful.

"You make jewelry for our sovereign?" Teti eyed the chunky little man with interest—and a new respect. "I never thought to meet such a man. Certainly not out here in this desolate land." A smile blossomed and he ushered Ani to a shallow chamber near the deepest end of the gallery, "You must see this, sir. It's the most promising vein we're following."

User winked at Bak and they hurried after the pair. Teti tapped the miner on the shoulder and issued an order in an unfamiliar tongue. The man stepped out of the way and the overseer motioned Ani into the chamber. Bak and the others gathered around.

Teti pointed to several blue-green lumps about the size of chickpeas, all more than a hand's length apart, embedded in a diagonal line down the wall. "It doesn't look like much, I know, but I've a feeling about this vein. I think we'll get some good pieces out of here."

"Could I have one of these?" Ani asked, running his fingers along the row of stones.

Teti looked taken aback. "I'm sorry, sir. If I gave away bits of turquoise to everyone who asked . . ." He paused, laughed. "Why not? They're neither large nor especially precious." He turned to the miner, hesitated, asked Ani, "Would you not prefer a bigger and more perfect stone? We can pick one out from among those we mined earlier this week."

"I want this piece, one I've seen in its natural state. In fact . . ." Ani's plea faltered, then took on a new strength. "Could I have the sandstone around it, with the turquoise enclosed within?"

They visited a dozen other mines. One was more than twenty paces across, lined with small galleries in which men were chippping away the stone. Another was thirty paces wide and half as deep, cut on two levels, with the men following layers of reddish sandstone sandwiched between bands of yellow stone. They descended a sloping shaft barely large enough to admit a man bent over, where they found a solitary miner. A couple of mines were shallow, gaping mouths whose rough stone faces occupied men fortunate enough to toil in the open air. Much of the roof had recently fallen in an older mine, making access impossible, and a cloud of squeaking bats forced retreat from a small but deep shaft.

All the while, Nebenkemet hovered close to their guide. His first few questions verified Bak's initial impression that he was more interested in the mining process than in the turquoise. Teti, who must have reached the same conclusion, began to divide his attention between the craftsman and Ani. Bak watched with interest this man who seldom spoke but sometimes revealed hidden depths.

As they walked from one mine to another, they passed several tall memorial tablets left by long-dead kings whose desire for the blue-green stone was as great if not greater than that of Maatkare Hatshepsut. Teti pointed out the small quarries from which sandstone was taken for the mansion of the Lady of Turquoise and a multitude of open-air shrines where the men bent a knee to their gods.

They peeked into long-abandoned mines, some shallow, others deeper and more heavily shadowed, which had been converted to rough dwellings by the miners and prisoners. Stones outside, etched with unfamiliar symbols, identified the team of men who had laid claim to each shelter and dwelt within. Similar stones identified old mines converted to storage magazines and the shaft the scribe had taken as his own. The whole formed a small village of poor dwellings and storehouses better identified and therefore easier to find than those in the capital city of Waset.

They shared a brief, inadequate midday meal of bread and beer in the shaded opening of a storage magazine. By that time, the supplies and water had been safely stowed away, so Suemnut ate with them. Lieutenant Nebamon had told him to remain atop the mountain until Bak was satisfied he had seen enough, but the sergeant urged them to hurry. They would descend by way of a different trail, one too dangerous to risk in poor light.

"As you can see, this place of worship is small," Teti said, leading them through the open court in front of the mansion of the Lady of Turquoise. "Our sovereign has plans to enlarge it further, but I see no need. You saw the many shrines scattered over the mountaintop."

He led them around a square column lying on the ground. A workman was smoothing the stone face of the Lady of Turquoise carved at the top. The goddess had the ears of a cow, as she did in her true form of the lady Hathor. "Our scribe serves as priest, making offerings to the Lady of Turquoise. One of the miners, a wretched foreigner, makes offerings for his people. Rather than the lady Hathor, they think of our goddess as their own lady Ashtoreth."

Passing through a doorway in a high wall, they walked into a court partly roofed to form a portico. An open doorway led into the sanctuary. Bak was surprised when Teti said they could look inside. In the land of Kemet, none but priests dared tread so close to the dwelling place of the deity.

The rockcut chamber was small and illuminated solely by the light falling through the doorway. Its walls had originally been smoothed as had the surface of the single pillar that supported the ceiling. Prayers for officials who had long ago led expeditions to the mountain of turquoise covered the walls. Many had faded or were flaking away. Recesses held sacred symbols of the goddess: a sistrum, a thick, beaded menat necklace, and a fist-sized chunk of turquoise. A squarish altar supporting the enclosed shrine in which the statue of the Lady of Turquoise dwelt stood in one corner. Thick smoke, reeking of incense, drifted from the tops of several cone-shaped altars placed around the room.

Bak felt exceedingly uncomfortable. The paintings of ordinary men, noble though they may have been, on the walls. The heavy scent of incense. The oddly shaped altars. The very fact that he stood so near the deity's dwelling place. All seemed too much of a compromise with a world he did not know.

He swung away from the sanctuary and, motioning Teti to follow, hurried through the building, not stopping until he reached the open court with its bright sunshine and air free of the cloying scent.

Sitting on the edge of a stone libation tank, he asked, "Where do you store the turquoise you mine?"

"In the goddess's mansion, where the stones will be safe." Teti sat on a large block of sandstone, shaped for placement in a wall of Maatkare Hatshepsut's new chamber. "We send them down the mountain each time the supply caravan returns to the port."

Bak nodded his understanding. The fewer the number of stones kept on the mountain, the less tempting they would be.

"Have you seen what you came to see?" Teti asked.

"I've seen everything and more. You've outdone yourself in showing us this place. I thank you."

Teti failed to hide how pleased he was. "I resented your intrusion, I freely admit, but Ani and Nebenkemet made the day a pleasure." He laughed. "I couldn't resist the jeweler's enthusiasm, and as for the other . . . I assume you saw him point out the direction he believed a vein to go."

"Do you think his guess right?"

Teti gave him a sharp look. "He knows mines and mining, Lieutenant. He never said?"

"He came across the Eastern Desert with Amonmose, who has a fishing camp on the sea. He claimed to be a carpenter, planning to build a fishing boat and huts in which the men will dwell."

"What a waste. I'd wager a chunk of turquoise the size of a goose egg that he knows as much as I about taking minerals and stones from the depths of the earth."

This man's approval, Bak thought, was praise indeed. He vowed to speak with Nebenkemet, to press for the truth. "Tell me of Minnakht's visit. What was his mission when he came?"

A harsh yell drew Teti's eyes to the wall and the prisoners building Maatkare Hatshepsut's new chamber. The ramp was finished and they were pulling, with difficulty, the heavily laden sledge up the slope. "He wished to learn about the way we mine turquoise. I answered his questions and he had more. I finally sent him to a man from Retenu, one with many more years' experience than I."

"Did that miner by chance return this year? I'd like to speak with him."

"He bade me goodbye when he left, saying he'd never come back—and he didn't." Teti spotted a waterbag someone had left on the wall and went to get it. "This new season has barely begun and I miss him already. He could accomplish twice in a day what these younger men barely manage to do in two days' time."

"Do you have any idea what he told Minnakht?"

"We were closing down the mines, so I hadn't much time to speak with him before he departed." Teti took a deep drink and handed the waterbag to Bak. "According to what he told me, I made a wise choice in sending Minnakht to him. Through the years, he'd dug in the earth for minerals as well as stones at many different sites. From what he said, Minnakht questioned him about the mining at each of them."

Bak sipped from the bag, thinking of the man rumored to have found gold, the man who denied that he had. "Tell me of Minnakht's appearance."

"You've never met him?"

"His father asked me to find him long after he vanished."

"Let me think." Teti took the waterbag, plugged it, and laid it on the stone beside him. "He was tall and slender, his face and body as well formed as the statue of a god. He walked stiff and straight and he had a way of raising his chin as if he thought himself better than any other man. I believe that the pride he took in himself, not a display of superiority."

The description was similar to others Bak had heard but unadulterated by admiration. "He had no marks on his body? No special way of talking?"

Teti shook his head. "Other than his good humor and a readiness to speak of his adventures, I can think of nothing more."

Later, as they trod an easy trail across the top of the plateau to the place where they would descend the mountain, Bak had the leisure to think of all he had learned. He was a long way from discovering the truth, he knew, but at last he felt as if a ray of light had penetrated the darkness within his heart.

Chapter 16

"I see why you wished to descend before dark." Bak stood at the top of what looked to be a high and steeply stepped waterfall—except he doubted any water had flowed down for many generations.

Sergeant Suemnut eyed the ragged line of men standing on the narrow trail behind them. "I pray to the lord Sopdu that none who came with you has a fear of high places."

Bak followed his glance. His Medjays, who carried their weapons and waterbags, led the procession. Next came four soldiers, two armed with spears and shields and each of the other two carrying a leather bag of turquoise. After them came User and his party. Standing between a steep red slope on one side and the rough face of a low cliff on the other, they could see nothing from their vantage point except the gap where the path dropped away. Farther back, the soldiers who had delivered the supplies to the mines straggled across the plateau, walking easily, carrying yokes from which nothing was suspended. The remaining soldiers, having no prisoners to guard, mingled with their fellows, no longer fearful of raiders. Suemnut had explained that past experience had proven the supplies to be of more value to plundering nomads than the turquoise.

Bak looked again into the deep wadi down whose side they must climb. The dry waterfall seemed to fall away for-

ever. An elongated black peak rose on the far side. Because
of the complicated folds of land, he could not see the bottom,
but he suspected for the sake of the fearful among them that
ignorance was preferable to knowing what lay ahead. The
climb down would be long and difficult.

"Should one of them be afraid, could he not return to the
lower camp by way of the path we ascended this morning?"

"This late in the day, the shadows hide details on that side
of the mountain. It's easy to get lost or take a wrong step.
He'd have to stay overnight with the miners and come down
tomorrow."

"I'll talk to them." Bak walked back and gathered the men
around him. He described the path and the alternative of remaining on the mountaintop. "I suggest you stand with
Sergeant Suemnut and look down. If you think you can't descend, tell us. A soldier will take you back across the plateau
to the mines."

Standing close by, he watched the men as one after another peered over the edge. None of the Medjays were troubled by what they saw, nor were User, Amonmose, or
Nebenkemet.

Ani looked down, sucked in his breath, and took a quick
step back. He offered Bak and the sergeant a timid smile and
hesitantly stepped closer to the edge to look down a second
time. "I'm terrified, but I can do it." He glanced back at
Psuro, added, "If you'll help me, Sergeant."

The Medjay studied the small plump man, weighing fear
versus determination. At last he nodded. "I'll stay with you."

Wensu moved closer and looked down. His face paled, but
he remained at the drop-off, staring at the steep incline. "I,
too, am afraid and may need help."

Such an admission from such a headstrong young man was
astonishing. With a hint of a smile, Nebre volunteered his aid.

"Once you start down, you must go all the way," Bak reminded them. "There'll be no turning back."

The two men, so different from each other, spoke as one: "I'll climb down this way."

At a point Suemnut said was about halfway down the trail, they stopped to rest on a flattish and relatively wide ledge overlooking a short, steep ravine-like drop in the dry waterfall. On the opposite side of the ravine, miners had, many generations earlier, etched reliefs on the dark surfaces of huge smooth-faced boulders. Immediately above the ravine, Psuro had had to help Ani down a particularly difficult section of trail where the stone had crumbled, leaving the natural rock steps loose and treacherous. Sweat poured from the jeweler and his face was fiery. The descent had thus far been difficult, but his fear had to have made it many times harder.

He dropped onto the ground, wiped his face, and gave Bak a haggard smile. "My knees are shaking. But so far I've managed to hang on to this." He patted the bulging square of linen hanging from his belt. It held the turquoise Teti had given him.

Psuro handed him a waterbag. "You've done well, sir. When I saw that narrow stretch of trail where the rock alongside projected outward, I feared for you. Looking toward the rock as you did instead of facing the slope was wise."

"I was so afraid, I feared I'd lose my midday meal."

The sergeant clapped him on the back and laughed. "Bread and beer. No great loss, I'd say."

Bak smiled at the two of them. Psuro was not one to easily call a man "sir." He had come to respect the jeweler. Bak felt the same. Ani had never been high on his list of suspects, but the more he saw of him, the more convinced he was that he would not, could not, slay a man. This journey up the mountain of turquoise had proven he had immense inner strength and tenacity, but was lacking in physical strength and had no ease of movement in the natural world. With sufficient will, he might be able to bury a dagger in a man's breast or back, but he could never slip away unseen from a campsite where men were sleeping all around.

Wensu flopped down beside Ani and, with a grateful smile, accepted the waterbag with shaking hands. Where the jeweler was flushed, the younger man's face was pale and drawn. "My father will never believe me when I tell him of this trail."

Nebre laughed. "Send him to me. I'll tell him how often you've shaken off my hand, spurning aid."

User and Amonmose, sweating profusely but undaunted, continued a good-natured argument they had begun halfway down the dry waterfall. The explorer claimed a bird soaring overhead was an eagle. The trader swore it was a vulture. As it was hardly more than a black speck, Bak suspected they were arguing simply for argument's sake. Nebenkemet, no more troubled by the descent than they, sat with the soldiers carrying the turquoise. They were flipping a small flat stone they had dug out of the bag and were betting on which side would turn up when it fell.

Suemnut studied the sun and the shadows, which were growing longer and deeper. Bak could see he wanted to move on but, evidently believing Wensu and Ani needed more time, he let them rest. He ordered one of his men to take charge of the soldiers straggling down the trail and signaled all but four to pass them by and go on ahead.

Suemnut paced back and forth along the ledge, waiting for the two weaker men to regain their strength. Gradually, some of the flush faded from Ani's face and Wensu's color returned. Very much aware of how anxious their guide was to get off the mountain before darkness fell, Bak stood up and suggested they leave. The sergeant flashed him a grateful smile.

The men responsible for the turquoise reluctantly quit their game and hefted the bags of precious stones. Their

guards and the Medjays scrambled to their feet and took up
their weapons. The men in User's party hauled themselves
off the ground. Suemnut, in his haste to be on his way, strode
down the steep slope at the lower end of the ledge.

Bak, several paces behind, started down the slope. A sharp
crack stopped him short. He glanced around, not sure what
had made the sound. Seeing nothing, he walked on. Perhaps
a rock had rolled off a ledge and shattered. Or could stone
burst apart when exposed to too much heat and suddenly
chilled by shade?

Another sharp report, this so close that small shards of
broken stone erupted from the rock beside him. He ducked
and looked around. A movement on the hillside high and to
his right caught his eye. A man on the opposite side of the
ravine. One who looked to be tall and slender. Too far away
to see well and standing with his back to the sun, Bak could
not discern his features. From his stance, from the way he
pulled his arm back and flung it forward, Bak guessed his
weapon.

"Get down!" he yelled, throwing himself sideways. "I see
a man using a sling!"

A stone struck him hard on the right thigh, dropping him
onto the rocks beside the path. Cursing mightily, he scrambled into the inadequate shelter of a broken boulder. Suemnut crouched low and slid down the slope to a bulge in the
hillside. Psuro, Nebre, and Kaha hustled everyone else to the
base of the trail down which they had come. Huddled against
the hillside in a corner of sorts, the man with the sling could
not see them.

Bak glanced at his thigh. Except for a slight redness, he
saw no sign of the impact, but a hint of soreness promised an
impressive bruise. He had no illusions about the power of a
sling in the hands of an expert, and he thanked the lord Amon
for his good fortune. Men were trained in the army to kill

with the weapon and could strike a man's head with practiced ease and deadly force. He had heard that the desert nomads used slings to slay gazelle and ibex and to take the lives
of one another in tribal disputes.

The man with the sling heaved another rock. It skidded
across the top of the boulder behind which Bak lay, sending
bits of stone flying around him. Suemnut yelled at the soldiers he had sent on ahead, ordering them back. His voice
echoed through the wadis, the words lost in repetition. In the
unlikely event that his troops heard, Bak doubted they would
understand the summons.

The man flung another rock, silencing the sergeant. Psuro
leaped out into the open and fired off an arrow. The angle was
not good, and the missile fell short. The man stood his
ground and may even have laughed, reminding Bak of the
man he and Nebre had followed deep into the foothills of the
red mountain.

Snarling an oath, Psuro ducked away. He spoke a few
words to Nebre and Kaha. The former seated an arrow and
raised his bow, ready to leap out into the open.

Favoring his thigh, which was beginning to throb, Bak
made motions as if to leave his shelter. If he could draw the
man's attention . . .

"Stay there, sir!" Psuro yelled.

The man sent another rock flying. With an angry crack, it
slammed into the boulder near Bak's head. At the same time,
Nebre stepped out, the look on his face venomous. He raised
his bow in a careful and deliberate fashion and fired off an arrow. It struck the man in the left side, but flew on past. A
glancing blow at best. The Medjay snapped out an oath and
seated another missile.

The man touched his side, raised his hand to look at his
fingers and what had to be blood, and slung a rock at Nebre.
The stone grazed the Medjay's arm, causing him to fumble

the arrow. Kaha stepped out to aid his fellow policeman. The man swung around and began to run. Kaha's arrow flew high, missing its target. Nebre's missile struck the boulder behind which the man vanished.

The Medjays grabbed their quivers and a waterbag, ran toward the stepped waterfall above the ravine, and scrambled across a slope of loose rocks on the opposite side, following the man who had ambushed them. The two guards raced after them. Bak leaped up from his shelter, grabbed a spear, and followed.

"No!" Suemnut yelled. "You can't go after him. It's too near nightfall and you don't know the mountain."

Bak slowed his pace, torn between common sense and a desire to snare the attacker.

"Come back!" Suemnut yelled.

Snapping out a curse, much against his wishes, Bak ordered the men back. Though he had not had a good look at the man with the sling, his basic physical appearance was too familiar to ignore. He had to be the watching man. The man who had, less than two weeks earlier, tried to entice him and Nebre into an ever more confusing landscape, where they might well have become lost, where they could easily have died from lack of food and water.

Bak plodded down the trail behind Suemnut, seething with fury. The man he sought had an uncanny ability to choose a place and time that would give him the advantage. Bak had vowed to snare him, and he knew he would, but when and how?

The path was no longer as difficult as it had been, but each step he took jolted the bruise on his thigh, making it ache with the intensity of an open wound. A dark lump had formed and was beginning to extend downward, blood spreading below the skin from the injury. To make matters worse, the day had been long and he was tired and hungry. The deepening shadows of the peaks to the east were spreading across the landscape, harbingers of night. At least the heat of the day was waning.

"There you are, sir." Suemnut stopped and pointed almost straight down.

Bak looked upon the wadi below with mixed emotions. He thanked the gods that their goal had shown itself at last, but it looked impossibly far away. Huge slopes of broken red sandstone fanned out below them. A thin pale line traversing the lower incline marked the path to the wadi floor. Acacia trees sent long, late-evening shadows across the broad strip of burnished sand, which meandered away between high reddish hills, maybe spurs of the mountain of turquoise.

"We're not far from the nearest slope of fallen rock," the sergeant said. "After we reach that, it's simply a matter of placing one foot in front of the other."

The troops who had passed them by, physically fit and accustomed to the descent, were nowhere in sight. Bak assumed they had gone around a shoulder of the mountain or had descended into a ravine and would reappear on the path below. Or they might have already reached the wadi and walked on to Huy's camp. A depressing thought considering the distance he and his companions still had to travel.

With a quick glance backward to be sure the men for whom he was responsible were keeping up, Suemnut walked on. Bak also looked back. Psuro was close behind, walking with Nebre, trying to convince him that even if they had gone after the man with the sling, they could not have caught him. The Medjay, furious at having to let him slip away yet another time, wore a scowl that would have sent fear into the heart of the lord Set himself. Bak, who felt no less angry, sympathized.

*   *   *

Bak sat on a thick pillow stuffed with straw, his leg stretched out before him in the faint hope that he could ease the pain in his thigh. No amount of pampering would heal the injury, he knew. Only time would erase the ghastly black bruise and the constant nagging ache.

Lieutenant Huy, eager for another game of senet, had urged him to accept the pillow. Now the officer sat on a stool on the opposite side of the game board, setting up the playing pieces. As before, he had taken the blue spools for himself and had given Bak the white cones. Lieutenant Nebamon sat on a rock, his back to the wall of the rough stone structure Huy and his scribe used as a dwelling and office. His face was hidden in shadow, while the light of the torch mounted on the wall behind him illuminated the game board and the two men preparing to play. A yellow dog lay at Nebamon's feet, twitching and moaning in its sleep.

Bak allowed Huy to take three of his pieces before he asked, "How many men who toil here are nomads?"

"Twenty or twenty-five. They labor atop the mountain, carrying away waste taken from the mines, helping in the quarries, and performing any number of other tasks that are easy to learn and require physical strength rather than wit or talent."

Huy studied the pieces on the game board. Blind to an opening Bak had given him, he made an ineffectual move. A partially smothered chortle escaped from Nebamon's lips.

If Huy noticed, he gave no hint. "Three women and their children remain in this camp to care for the livestock we keep, while their men toil on the mountain." He studied the board, then nodded his satisfaction. "You'll have noticed that any number of nomads come and go, seeking to trade or to cadge some small item they need."

Bak was forced to take the spool Huy had moved. "Do any men come from the Eastern Desert?"

"Not many," Huy said, blinking surprise that he had lost a

piece, "and they seldom remain for long." With his mouth tight and determined, he moved another spool. "The local men look to us as a source of wealth. They resent sharing with outsiders."

"Are any here now?"

"Possibly. My scribe would know."

"All who wish to toil at the mines report to the scribe when they arrive," Nebamon explained. "Each day a man remains, his foreman makes a mark on a shard. When he's ready to leave, the shard goes to the scribe and he gives the nomad a token to deliver to the port for payment in kind."

Bak muttered an oath. A man could pass through the camp and climb the mountain of turquoise without ever reporting his presence. An individual from the Eastern Desert, shunned by one and all, might come and go virtually unnoticed or, more likely, would be looked upon as invisible. He was willing to wager a month's rations that the man with the sling had walked in and out without so much as attracting a glance.

Bak lost the game by a narrow margin and insisted Nebamon play the next. He found losing to be much more difficult than winning. Offering the caravan officer the pillow, he moved to the rock. The dog woke up, curled into a tight ball, and went back to sleep with a grunt of contentment.

While the officers played, Bak's thoughts turned to the attack earlier in the day and to the man who had used the sling. The watching man, he felt sure. Had someone in User's party told him they meant to come to the mountain of turquoise? Or had he simply followed them, with no one noticing? His knowledge of the wadis and mountains on this side of the sea was especially puzzling. While Bak and his Medjays were tied by their ignorance of the land and its people to the caravan and the army, as were User and his party, their foe traveled with no such constraints. How did he manage?

The question turned Bak's thoughts to Minnakht. He had vowed to stay close, but had he? Bak thought about the man he had met in the Eastern Desert, the man he had heard so much about through the last few weeks. A man of courage who traveled the barren land undeterred by adversity. One who . . . suddenly, without conscious intent, a new idea leapt into his heart, a thought that would not be dislodged. "Do you know of a place nearby where a man might find water, where he could stay alone and undisturbed by other men?"

"Where you find water, you'll find nomads." Huy's voice was curt, agitated. "Women and children bringing their flocks to drink. Sometimes a man or two."

Realizing something was wrong, Bak glanced at the senet board. Nebamon had taken more than half his fellow officer's pieces.

"The closest spring is at the copper mines west of here," the caravan officer said, capturing another spool.

Bak did not know if Nebamon's thoughts were elsewhere or if he believed Huy had had enough pampering for one night. "I'm seeking a more solitary place, one where a man might slip out of sight should nomads bring their flocks."

Huy gave his opponent a cool look. "Your return journey to the port often takes an inordinate length of time, Nebamon. Puemre tells me that you stop at an oasis north of here, allowing your troops to play when they should be hastening to the sea with their valuable burden."

Noticing the venom in Huy's voice, Nebamon looked more closely at the board. He was clearly surprised by what he saw. "Often? No. Now and again, yes." He placed a white cone in jeopardy, glanced at Bak, grinned sheepishly. "There's an open, running stream in the next large wadi to the north. The journey to the port is longer, but I sometimes return that way, giving my men an opportunity to bathe themselves and the donkeys. The water has an odd smell and

we can't drink it, but washing away the dust refreshes man
and beast alike."

He studied the game board as if trying to decide what he
should do next. "A few nomads go there, but a man who
wished to remain unseen could easily walk a short way up
the wadi, where the stone has been carved by wind and water
as if by the hand of a man."

Bak watched him sacrifice another white cone. From the
look on Huy's face, he would soon be placated. "With no
drinkable water, he couldn't stay there for long."

"There's a larger oasis closer to the sea and to the south.
We get water there for use at the port. It's frequented by the
nomads, so a man couldn't remain unseen for long, but he
might slip in and out at infrequent intervals, taking only
enough time to water his animals and fill his jars." Nebamon moved another cone into the path of the spool Huy
was driving toward the final square. "Do you think the man
who attacked today might be camping at one of those
oases?"

"Perhaps." Bak shifted his position, waking the dog and
the pain in his thigh. "You must remember that I'm also looking for Minnakht."

"He's not been seen since he left the port," Huy said, his
disposition soothed. "Most men believe he sailed back to the
Eastern Desert."

Bak stayed as close to the truth as he could. "I vowed I'd
follow his path from the beginning of his journey to the end.
I know he visited the mountain of turquoise and the copper
mines west of here. There's a chance that he sailed away
from the port, but returned to this barren land. A place with
water would be a necessary destination." Noting the doubt on
their faces, he gave them a humorless smile. "Unlikely or
not, I must leave no possibility unexamined. If I find no sign
of him, I must return to the Eastern Desert and remain in that
wretched land until I learn his fate. I prefer the company of

men of Kemet to seeing nothing but footprints of nomads who vanish each time we draw near."

Giving him a quick, sympathetic smile, Nebamon offered up his last white cone.

Huy made a final move. "You wish to visit those oases," he said, his voice ringing with triumph.

"You'll have to go by yourself," Nebamon said, hiding a smirk from the victor. "I can't take the caravan the long way around this trip. We've another load of supplies awaiting us on the vessels on which you crossed the sea."

Bak thanked the gods. If the man he sought had indeed gone to one of the oases and if he saw an approaching caravan, he would slip away faster than a desert fox. "Can you give me a man to serve as a guide?"

"I can send a nomad with you," Huy said. "One I often trust to carry messages to the port."

"Such a man would serve me well." Not merely because he would know the wadis better than any soldier, but because the man he hoped to find would have no reason to hide from one who wandered this land. "I'd like first to see the copper mines. When do you plan to move on, Nebamon?"

The caravan officer dropped his playing pieces into the drawer and smiled. "You've had enough of the mountain of turquoise, Lieutenant?"

"More than enough," Bak said, glancing at his throbbing thigh.

"I thought to leave tomorrow before nightfall."

"I'll tell User and the others." Bak stood up, yawned. "I wish them to travel to the port with you, not come with me. I trust you've no objection?"

Nebamon gave him a long, speculative look. The kind of look one man gives another when he suspects him of a hidden purpose. "User's good company, and so is Amonmose. I'll keep them and the rest out of your way."

* * *

"You understand what you must do." Bak spoke softly so his instructions would not carry to User's camp or to any soldiers.

He sat on his sleeping mat, his leg stretched out, trying again to ease the ache in his thigh. His Medjays sat around him, leaning close, faces intent. The yellow dog, which had followed him from Huy's dwelling, lay at his feet. The sky was black, the multitude of stars resplendent, the moon large and luminous.

"I'd rather stay with you, sir." As if seeking support, Kaha glanced at Psuro, sitting beside him on the sand. "Cannot Minmose or Nebre deliver your message?"

Minmose squirmed, uncomfortable with the thought, and Nebre grunted. The sergeant remained mute.

"They can't speak the tongue of the men of the Eastern Desert," Bak said. "You can."

"They understand no more than half of what I say."

"As long as you can convince them that you must speak with Nefertem, the rest matters not. Once you reach him, you'll have no trouble. He speaks our tongue as well as you or I."

"What if I never get to him?"

Bak's patience was coming to an end. He understood Kaha's reluctance to go off by himself into the wilderness, but an order was an order. "I told you before: seek out a family of nomads, show them the pendant, and say you must go to Nefertem right away. Someone will take you to him."

The Medjay, who could not have missed the impatience in Bak's voice, stared unhappily at the chunk of quartz in his hand. "If I manage to speak with him, what am I to tell him?"

"Tell him I'll soon cross the sea, returning to the Eastern Desert. I hope to be traveling with Minnakht. I wish Imset to meet us when we disembark at the quay where our sovereign's cargo ships anchor at the eastern end of the southern route to the sea. The boy must take us to Nefertem, whom I hope to meet at the place where he found this." Bak lifted the pendant from Kaha's hand and held it up, letting the quartz dangle from the leather thong.

Several dogs began to bark, momentarily distracting them, and a sheep voiced alarm. The dog at Bak's feet raised his head and cocked his ears to listen. Bak guessed a predator of some kind was lurking close by in the dark. A ewe had given birth to a lamb during the day. The fragile creature would be a tasty morsel for a large feline or a hyena.

Bak returned the pendant to Kaha and handed him a tight roll of papyrus. "Take this to Lieutenant Puemre. In it I ask that he rush you across the sea to the Eastern Desert. The traveling ship we saw at the port, which he uses to carry messages, is manned by soldiers and is fast. You should have plenty of time to contact Nefertem."

"Am I to await you at the shore with the boy?" Kaha asked.

"You will stay with Nefertem."

Kaha gave him a dismal look. "I'm to be his hostage."

"I plan to give him what he wants. He'll not harm you."

"Aren't you getting ahead of yourself, sir?" Psuro walked with Bak around the walled pen in which the sheep and goats were kept. They looked to be the sole men awake in the warm, still night. "How can you be so certain we'll find Minnakht at one of those oases?"

The yellow dog, lured by the other dogs who dwelt in the camp, had run off into the darkness, his voice merging with theirs. Their furious barking gradually faded away as they chased the predator away from the camp. The flock, which Bak and the sergeant had found milling restlessly within the rough stone walls, had begun to settle down. The lamb was safe among them.

"If we don't find him, if he didn't follow us as he vowed he would, I must still meet with Nefertem. We alone can never hope to find one man in an area as vast as the Eastern Desert.

We need the help of a tribal chieftain, one whose people can sweep across the landscape, letting no one and nothing slip out of their grasp."

"They didn't find him before, sir."

"They didn't know what they were looking for."

"You vowed to tell no one that he still lives. Now you plan to tell Nefertem. Is that wise, sir? What if he's right and the nomads wish him dead?"

Chapter 17

"You're staying behind?" User, shaking the dust from his tunic, eyed Bak with suspicion. "Did you not vow to snare the man who's been prowling the Eastern Desert, slaying first one man and then another?"

"I will snare him," Bak stated.

He stood at the edge of User's camp, studying the men scattered around. He had caught them filling the time with small tasks while they waited for Nebamon's order to load the donkeys for the short trek to the copper workings and the longer journey to the port. His Medjays were similarly occupied in their own camp. The sun hung low over the western peaks and the day was beginning to cool, so their departure was imminent.

"Clearly, he followed us across the Eastern Sea," Amonmose said, looking up from several unusual barbed harpoon points he had received in trade with a nomad. "His ambush on the mountainside left no doubt that he wishes you dead. Would you not be safer if you remained with us?"

"Four men have died within a few paces of your campsite," Bak reminded him.

"And yours," Wensu muttered.

"If the slayer follows us rather than you, more may die," User said in a grim voice. "We've neither the means nor the ability to protect ourselves, as you well know."

"Your trek to the port with Lieutenant Nebamon should be safe enough," Bak said. The cargo ships moored there will sail as soon as they unload the remaining supplies and load the copper and turquoise he'll deliver to them. I suggest you cross the sea on one of those vessels. If you remain on board all the way to the southern trail, you can cross the Eastern Desert with the soldiers who'll transport the stones and copper to Waset. Any caravan carrying so precious a load is bound to be well guarded."

"I say we do as the lieutenant suggests," Wensu said. "I, for one, have had enough of sand and rocks and death."

"Yes, that would be best." Ani looked resignedly at the three small bags of stones he had collected since leaving Kaine. "I feel I've seen very little of what I came to see, especially in the Eastern Desert, and—for the very practical reasons Lieutenant Bak long ago pointed out—I'll not return to the royal house with many stones, but I've no wish to see other men slain to satisfy my desires."

User studied the two men he had led into the desert. His face wore no expression, but Bak could guess his thoughts. In spite of his preference to travel alone, to seek gold and precious stones unencumbered, he had agreed to bring them along in exchange for payment in kind—and because he did not wish to vanish as had Ahmose and Minnakht. Better to return to the land of Kemet with nothing to show for the journey than to risk their lives and his.

"In many ways, this trek has been easy, but the toll on men's lives . . ." The explorer's voice tailed off in resignation. "I concur. Best we sail on one of our sovereign's ships and cross the desert with the army."

Bak thanked the lord Amon for the man's strong sense of duty. "Will you go with them, Amonmose? Or will you remain with your fishing fleet on this side of the sea?"

The merchant spread his hands wide in a gesture of indecision. "Only when my men can safely return to their camp can

Nebenkemet build huts and another boat. We could wait, but should we?" He flung a rueful smile at Bak. "If I thought you were close to laying hands on the slayer, Lieutenant . . ."

"I suggest the two of you cross the Eastern Sea with User," Bak said, side-stepping the question.

The merchant eyed him with open curiosity. "That sounds ominous, as if you think never to snare the vile criminal."

Bak failed to rise to the bait. Instead he said to User, "Once our sovereign's ships are loaded, they'll not tarry. If they sail a day or two after your arrival, as I believe they will, I'll not reach the port in time to board. I'll need another way of crossing the sea." His eyes darted toward Amonmose and he flashed a smile. "A fishing boat perhaps."

The merchant grinned, acknowledging his failure to learn more. "How large a boat will you need?"

"One big enough to carry four or five passengers, the fastest in your fleet."

"The moment we reach the port, I'll speak with Nufer. You'll find his boat and crew awaiting you."

User looked with a marked lack of enthusiasm toward Bak's camp, where Minmose and Kaha were packing their belongings, while Psuro and Nebre examined the three donkeys on which they would carry weapons, water, and supplies to the oasis where they hoped to find Minnakht. "You're taking all your men with you?"

"Minmose will remain with you and will see that our donkeys are transported back across the sea. Kaha has an errand that will take him to another destination. Psuro and Nebre will travel with me."

User grunted, in no way comforted.

"I doubt we'll be more than three or four days behind you," Bak said. "I've been told there are wells at the near end of the southern trail and a village of sorts called Tjau. A contingent of soldiers, their task to check all who come and go along that route, dwell there, along with a few nomads and camp followers. I suggest you wait for us there."

"If we wait, we'll lose the safety of the caravan."

Bak realized that he had to give them an incentive to delay, had to rouse their curiosity. "With luck and the help of the lord Amon, I expect by then to have found the answers to all your questions and mine."

The caravan set out at dusk. The trek to the copper mines was short and the donkeys, carrying nothing but the food and water needed for the return journey to the port, made good time in the cooler hours of night. What could have been a single load of turquoise was, for safety's sake, divided up and concealed among the more mundane objects on the backs of a half-dozen animals.

A small forest of widely spaced acacias dotted the floor of the wadi that served as the center of copper production in the area. They camped a short distance from the trees and away from the well—to keep the donkeys out of the overseer's garden, Nebamon explained. Bak walked with him through the night to a grove of palm trees rising above a dark drystone hut. Along the way, they passed a cluster of interconnected stone huts in which the workmen dwelt and several slag heaps that marred the simple beauty of the moonlit watercourse. The cool night air smelled of dust and goats and of a tangy plant he could not identify.

Nenwaf, overseer of the copper works, roused himself from his sleeping mat and welcomed them with a broad smile and a gush of words. His nomad wife barely made an appearance and that not a happy one, but his five small children leaped from their sleeping mats and rushed to Nebamon's side for the treats they had come to expect each time he passed through. With faces and hands sticky from the honey cakes they quickly devoured, they hovered around, staring wide-eyed at the two officers talking with their father.

The next morning, the garrulous overseer escorted Bak and the men in User's party over the surrounding hillsides, delighted to show off his domain. The mines, scattered throughout the area and especially abundant in the next wadi to the east, were much like those on the mountain of turquoise but were more widespread, more abundant, and larger. Here, too, the miners were men from afar, come to toil for Maatkare Hatshepsut and the generous earnings they would take back to their faroff homes. From shafts penetrating deep into the hillsides, narrow galleries followed the ore, often widening into underground halls. The tunnels formed complicated networks through which the heavy loads of ore had to be dragged and, in the end, lifted up to the surface.

Ani and Nebenkemet asked a multitude of questions, and Nenwaf immediately warmed to them both. Unlike Teti, he allowed Ani to sort through the piles of malachite brought to the surface and take as many chunks of the bright green stone as he wished. It was less valuable than turquoise and not as appealing to the eye. Nonetheless, the pudgy jeweler avidly picked up one chunk of rock and another, filling the filthy square of cloth he carried. When he had a good-sized collection, he spread them out on the ground and sorted through them, ultimately saving just two or three choice pieces.

As the morning wore on, Nebenkemet's knowledge of mining became ever more apparent and Nenwaf began to speak to him on equal terms. Bak was intrigued. He doubted Amonmose would have brought this man into the desert if he thought him unable to build huts and a boat, but he was no simple carpenter.

After a midday meal of bread and beer supplemented with green onions and cucumbers harvested from Nenwaf's garden, the overseer led them across the wadi floor past slag heaps containing greenish black lumps of malachite from which much of the copper had been drained. On the hillside beyond, he escorted them to a dozen furnaces where men toiled in the heat. He stopped at one of the few not being worked. It had recently been used, he explained, and had been left to cool. A pile of greenish rock, crushed for easier smelting, lay beside the furnace.

"As you can see," Nenwaf said, "we're using the latest methods of extracting the ore from the stone."

Nebenkemet hovered close, hands clasped behind his back, studying the clay-lined pit dug into the hillside. Rather than the more common goatskin bellows on which men stood to pump air into the furnace, the newer pot bellows were used. Here, a leather top on the flared opening of a pottery nozzle could be pumped up and down by hand or by foot, blowing air into the furnace to make it burn hotter, allowing for a more efficient production of copper from stone.

"By locating the pit on the hillside," Nenwaf said, "we can take full advantage of the wind that usually blows up the wadi, causing the fire to burn more fiercely."

"What do you place in the furnace to aid in the separation process?" Nebenkemet asked.

"Several materials found locally."

Nenwaf went on to discuss the process in detail. As far as Bak could tell, the method was cruder than that employed at the fortress of Buhen to smelt gold, but similar. He glanced at his companions. Other than User, who looked a bit bored, all but Nebenkemet appeared overwhelmed by the description. The carpenter followed the overseer's explanation with no trouble and at times asked questions as difficult to comprehend as were the answers.

Bak was about ready to shout "Enough!" when the overseer pointed out the shallow pit flanked by stones in front of a hole in the base of the furnace. At the bottom, a lump of molten copper had begun to congeal as it cooled.

Ushering them on, Nenwaf showed them every phase of

the process: men crushing the stone, loading the furnaces, operating the bellows. If User had not noticed that a long line of donkeys was being led to the place where the ingots were stored for transport, the overseer would probably have gone on for the rest of the day.

As they walked back toward the caravan, Bak drew Nebenkemet aside. "Who are you, Nebenkemet? What are you?"

The man looked him straight in the eye. "I don't know what you mean."

"You may well be a carpenter, but you've a knowledge of mining that few men can claim. You grasped every word Teti said, and while Nenwaf's explanation was beyond my understanding, you spoke with him on equal terms."

During the ensuing silence, a breeze rustled the leaves of an acacia and a desert lark sang its solitary song. The blowing and complaining of donkeys marked the progress of the loading, along with the shouts of soldiers and an occasional laugh.

"I've a natural curiosity, that's all."

"No."

Nebenkemet swung around to face him, his mistrust apparent, his dislike for what Bak represented if not for the man himself. "I've known other men like you, Lieutenant. Quick to charge a man with some foul deed and quicker yet to take away his life, sending him far away from home and family, ofttimes to his death."

Smothering resentment at so offensive an assumption, Bak kept his voice level, unemotional. "You were a prisoner," he guessed.

"You may as well speak the truth," Amonmose said, hurrying up to lay a hand on Nebenkemet's shoulder. "You know nothing of pretense. A blind man could've seen that you know as much if not more about mining and smelting than Nenwaf himself."

Nebenkemet shook off the hand and glared at Bak. "Do you think to accuse me of slaying the men who've died since we set out from Kaine?"

"I seek the truth, nothing more."

Amonmose hovered close as if he feared they would clash. "I believe the lieutenant to be a fair man, Nebenkemet. If you say nothing, he'll be bound to believe the worst."

"He'll think the worst no matter what I say."

"Are you in truth a carpenter?" Bak demanded. "Or are you a miner?"

"Tell him," Amonmose urged.

"The knowledge may not help me find the slayer," Bak said, "but if it serves to eliminate a single individual—you— I'll be one step closer to snaring that vile criminal. Closer to saving the life of yet another man who might stand in the way of his dagger."

Nebenkemet looked at Bak and at his friend, his defiance slowly crumpling, turning to indecision.

"What you've done in the past is of no concern to me." Bak veered around the branch of an acacia. "I came into this desert with a task to perform, and that I mean to do. I've no interest in anything other than that."

Nebenkemet glanced at Amonmose for support, received a quick nod of encouragement. Staring straight ahead, into the past, he said, "I labored in a shipyard in Mennufer, apprenticed to a boat builder. Young and foolish, thinking to make myself look more of a man, I stole a small bauble for a woman I coveted. I was caught within the hour." He glanced again at Amonmose, who urged him on with a concerned smile. "I was sentenced to spend four years toiling in a mine in the desert east of Abu. Unlike my fellow prisoners, I liked mining, and I had a nose for following the veins of ore. The overseer raised me to the level of assistant and asked me to stay when my punishment ended. I refused." He expelled a bitter laugh. "I thought to return to my old life in the shipyard in Mennufer, but my master turned me away. I was a criminal, a man who couldn't be trusted."

Amonmose, seeing his friend's distress, took up the tale. "I knew Nebenkemet as a youth. When I came upon him in a house of pleasure, angry and besotted, talking of revenge, I took him away and washed the beer from him. When I heard his tale, I asked him to come with me."

"So here I am, a prisoner of another sort." Nebenkemet laughed softly. "A man more besotted with the desert, the quiet and the solitude, than with any woman I'll ever meet."

Bak smiled. He believed the tale, that Nebenkemet had been punished as a thief. Would he slay a man—and another and another? He had lived a hard life, to be sure, but from what Bak had seen through the long journey across the desert, he was as steady as a man could be, easygoing, unencumbered by pride, a man who took pleasure in the simple things. Greed and the quest for gold were not a part of him.

"You remained behind for a purpose, Lieutenant?"

Nenwaf, seated on a mudbrick bench in the shade of the palm grove, glanced at the five children straggling up the wadi. The two largest, both girls, carried a basket between them, sharing its weight. They had followed the caravan to collect the dung dropped by the donkeys. The manure they had picked up, along with the waste the animals had left at the camp, would be formed into flat, round cakes and laid out to dry for use as fuel.

"Do you recall the explorer Minnakht?" Bak sat on a fallen palm trunk facing the overseer, while Psuro rested a shoulder against a tree.

"How could I forget?" Nenwaf offered Bak a handful of dates. "He seemed a fine man and was a joy to speak with."

"Did he say why he came?"

"To see the mining and smelting." The overseer smiled at the memory. "He wished to know all there was to know about following the veins of ore while at the same time keeping the tunnels safe, and he was most interested in the furnaces and in the way we take the metal from the stone. Other than Nebenkemet, I've known few men to ask so many apt questions." He laid the dates in a pile on the bench beside him. "He wanted also to visit the larger mining area to the south. I assured him that the furnaces they use are outdated, as is their way of smelting the ore."

"All the mines aren't operated in a similar manner?" Bak asked, surprised.

"The southern wadis have been mined for many generations, far longer than here. The quantity of copper-rich stone is dwindling. Soon it'll no longer be practical to send men and supplies to dig it from the earth. As a result, no attempt is made to modernize the process." Nibbling the flesh from the seed of a date, Nenwaf eyed Bak curiously. "He seemed determined to go there, so I suppose he went anyway."

Bak was well satisfied with the information he was gleaning and Nenwaf lived a singularly uninteresting life. To satisfy the man's curiosity was small reward. "Because it was so late in the season, Lieutenant Puemre wouldn't supply a guide. He urged him to wait at the port until the final caravan came in from the south. Minnakht did wait, and Puemre believes he spoke with the overseer."

"I trust he learned enough to make the wait worthwhile."

Bak gave him a sharp look. "You don't believe he did?"

A small naked boy climbed onto Nenwaf's lap, while another child laid her head on his thigh. A boy of four or so years ran to Psuro and chattered in a mixture of tongues picked up from the miners and those who smelted the ore. The two older girls had carried the basket to the hut, where their mother sat on the ground, grinding grain for bread.

"He wished also to learn about the mining and processing of gold." Nenwaf adjusted his legs beneath the child's bony bottom. "I could tell him nothing except that I suspect the effort is much the same as here. I doubt anyone else in this god-forsaken land knows any more than I do. We seek turquoise and copper, not the more precious metal."

Bak exchanged a quick glance with Psuro, who had never allowed the demands of the child to distract him from the adult conversation. "Minnakht was an explorer, an adventurer who wandered the Eastern Desert in search of precious stones and minerals. Did it not surprise you that he showed so great an interest in such mundane tasks as digging out the ore and smelting it?"

"I've met men like him before. Men who have a natural curiosity about the world around them. I took his questions for granted."

"I've never met him, but from what I've been told, he was liked and admired by all who knew him. He evidently drew men to him, made each see what he wanted to see. Every man I've questioned has given me a different description." He eyed the overseer curiously. "How did you see him, Nenwaf?"

"Nenwaf's description of Minnakht was very much like that of Teti. As far as I could tell, neither was colored by Minnakht's charm or adventurous spirit," Bak said, glancing up at the stars to be sure they were traveling north as they should be. He did not mistrust the nomad guide Huy had loaned them, but should anything happen to that guide, he thought it best that they know exactly where they were.

Psuro, trudging along at his side, said, "They're both practical men, too knowledgeable to be swayed by what might be taken as flattery."

"Unlike the men in User's party." Nebre, walking a few paces ahead with the guide, led their three donkeys.

Bak studied the wadi along which they were walking. The

bright, clear moonlight made the sand glow and deepened the shadows on the stony hillsides. What had looked in the sunlight to be bright, multicolored mounds and plateaus were flat and dull in the lesser light. An army could be hidden along the slopes and remain undetected.

"I know we're traveling to the oasis because you believe Minnakht is there," Nebre said, shifting the strap of the quiver hanging from his shoulder, "but why would he follow us across the sea?"

Psuro grunted agreement. "Why would he approach us, for that matter, then hide himself as if he doesn't trust us?"

As before, Bak eyed the slopes to either side, assuring himself that they were too far away for a man to hear what he had to say. "When he failed to appear on the shore of the Eastern Sea as he vowed he would, a thought struck me, one I couldn't shake. Since then, I've asked a multitude of questions and have gleaned innumerable answers, many of which have strengthened that thought. It's time I told you of my conclusion and of what I plan. Go tell our guide to walk on ahead. What I have to say is for your ears alone."

"Listen to the night birds, the squeak of bats," Nebre said, studying the oasis they were approaching. "I'll wager he's not here."

Bak stared at the long, irregular row of palm trees and tamarisks. What appeared to be a tangle of undergrowth lay partially concealed within the deep shadows beneath the trees. He had hoped to arrive before the moon dropped so low, but his revelations to Psuro and Nebre had taken time, and the hour they had spent refining his plan had been well worthwhile. Now, with the darkness so deep, he mistrusted the oasis and the shelter it offered. Anyone camped there would have heard their approach. Common sense urged him to proceed with caution.

He pointed to a broad sandy spot midway between the

hills rising to either side and at least two hundred paces from the shadowy oasis. "Let's camp there, where no man can come upon us out of the shadows."

"I'll stand watch," Psuro said.

"Don't watch from afar, but stay among us. To stand apart might be risking death—and we've already lost Rona."

Nebre pointed toward a thick layer of ash lining a hollow dug in the ground, a jumble of footprints and the imprint of a woven reed sleeping mat, and traces of two hobbled donkeys. "A man camped here for some time, sir."

"His donkeys are ailing," Psuro said, standing over a mound of fresh, loose manure buzzing with flies. "He's not been gone for long. A few hours at most."

Bak knelt beside the shallow stream that gave life to the palms and tamarisks, the tall rushes that grew along its banks, and the brush that grew among the trees. According to the guide, the water appeared from out of nowhere and vanished in an equally mysterious fashion. It had an odd smell and tasted brackish, but was not so salty that it discouraged the presence of wildlife. Birds, lizards, and insects abounded, and the prints of gazelle and other larger animals revealed occasional visits, probably to eat rather than to drink the disagreeable water.

Hoping to learn where Minnakht had gone, Psuro and the nomad guide walked upstream while Bak and Nebre followed the slowly moving water in the opposite direction. As the guide had predicted, the stream trickled away, leaving behind a few patches of damp sand and a row of tamarisks clinging to the bank of a dry channel cut through a wider bed of gravel over which long ago had flowed a substantial river. Beyond the scrubby trees, Nebre found signs partially obliterated by wind of the explorer's arrival from the west, but no prints indicating that he had left.

"Did he bring so much water with him that he had no need to replenish his supply?" Bak asked.

"Could he have brought enough for himself and two donkeys?" Nebre gave a disapproving grunt. "I'd wager not."

Psuro and the guide met them at the abandoned campsite. They had had better luck.

"He's run away," the sergeant said. "He took his donkeys and walked upstream. The lord Amon alone knows how far he's gone."

Bak's smile was grim. "I suggest we go hunting."

Leaving their donkeys in the care of the guide, Bak and his Medjays walked up a wadi barren of water and life. The high walls to either side entrapped the sun's heat and the carpet of gravel absorbed it, turning the wadi into an oven. Sweat poured from the men, and the water they drank failed to quench their thirst.

Armed with bows and arrows, they ranged the width of the wadi floor, looking for signs of a man's passage. The gravel made footprints difficult to find, but swarming flies drew them to two disturbances of pebbles which, when dug into, covered piles of manure similar to the one they had found in the oasis. Bak wondered if Minnakht had allowed the donkeys to drink the brackish water. Whatever had caused their distress, he doubted they could go on for long without proper care.

Frequently, he called out, "Minnakht! We've parted from the caravan and are traveling alone. You can show yourself now."

Sometimes he shouted, "Minnakht! Your donkeys are ailing. If they should die, you'll not survive a week alone."

More than an hour after they set out, they rounded a bend and spotted ahead a man walking toward them. Two laden donkeys plodded along behind him, stumbling at times on the loose gravel. As he and the weary animals drew near, Bak and Nebre identified the man who had approached them in the Eastern Desert. Minnakht. His tunic and kilt were clean and bright, but he needed a shave, his hair was too long, and his face looked haggard. He carried a bow and arrows. A spear and shield and a harpoon were suspended from the load on one of the donkeys.

He walked slowly toward them, cautious, mistrustful. A dozen paces away, he offered a tentative smile.

Bak smiled in return. "You've been alone too long, Minnakht. You must learn anew that some men can be trusted. My Medjays and I among them."

With a sharp laugh, Minnakht dropped the rope leads of the donkeys and rushed forward. He greeted Bak like a long-lost friend, clasping his shoulders and giving him a broad smile. "I can't tell you how glad I am to see you, Lieutenant. I feel as one with the Eastern Desert and don't mind its solitude, but here I'm like a bird with a broken wing, unable to fly or care for itself."

"No more," Bak said, laughing. "You'll remain with us until we see you home."

Minnakht jerked back, startled. "I told you before. I can't go home. If anyone were to learn that I still live, word would spread like fire in a stiff wind. Those who tried to slay me would search me out, beat me to learn a secret I don't hold in my heart, and take my life without a qualm."

"Your father longs to see you again. You must go to him."

Minnakht glanced at Nebre, who had taken up the ropes, ready to lead the donkeys back to the oasis, and at Psuro, standing off to the side, bow in hand, waiting. "I'd never complete the journey across the Eastern Desert."

Bak held out his hand, signaling that they must return to the oasis. "Why imprison yourself in the desert wastes? Do you not wish to bathe in a true river, to walk through lush fields, to lead the life of a man of ease, one free to go where he wishes in a land of plenty such as Kemet?"

Reluctantly, Minnakht fell in beside him and they strode together down the wadi, followed by the Medjays and donkeys. "I'd like nothing better, but . . ."

"Do you not hold your father close within your heart? Would you not like to see him?"

"You know I would! But I fear you'd deliver nothing to him but the few small items I carry with me and news of my death."

"I guarantee your safety."

Minnakht's mouth curled in a cynical smile. "Senna told me how many men were slain while you crossed the Eastern Desert. As he also died in the end. And all the while, you and your men slept nearby."

Bak bit back a sharp retort. The accusation had merit, but stung nonetheless. A hiss behind him told him what Psuro thought, or maybe Nebre. "My men and I will never let you out of our sight, that I vow. We'll guard you day and night."

"You tempt me with freedom," Minnakht said with a bitter smile. "but you'd make me your prisoner."

"I don't deny that we'll hold you close, but only for the time it takes to cross the sea and the Eastern Desert. When you reach Kemet, you can tell all the world that you found no gold and your life will no longer be at risk."

Minnakht flashed a smile that failed to hide his irritation. "All right, Lieutenant. I'll come with you. But should I be injured or slain, I pray your conscience doesn't trouble you so much that never again will you rest easy."

Chapter 18

Bak knelt beside Sergeant Psuro, who was skinning a hare he had trapped, and spoke softly so his voice would not carry. "Will Minnakht's donkeys survive the journey to the sea?"

"If the sickness was caused by the tainted water in the stream, as Nebre and I believe, and if we share our good water with them, their illness should clear up and their strength return. We must also lighten their loads and not push them too hard. We've already tended the galls on their shoulders." Psuro spat on the ground, a sign of contempt he had copied from Troop Captain Nebwa. "That Minnakht. What kind of man is he to treat his animals so?"

"Fear can make a man push beyond endurance the creatures he needs most. Not wise in a desert such as this, where one's life is so dependent upon their well-being."

Psuro eyed with tight-lipped disapproval the man of whom they spoke, who was kneeling at the edge of the stream, washing his face and arms. "And he professes to be a man of the desert."

Because Minnakht's donkeys were weak and Bak's animals had to carry a considerable amount of extra weight, the journey down the wadi to the sea took two days more than it should have. Neither Psuro nor Nebre nor the nomad guide

bothered to hide their contempt for a man who would sacrifice his animals for himself. Bak, who wanted to set Minnakht at ease, took care not to register his own disapproval.

The wadi opened out onto the shore. After spending so
many days in the barren desert, the clear blue waters lapping
the sand drew them like ants to honey. Laughing like children, in too much of a rush to remove their clothing, they
raced into the water and indulged themselves in a long, refreshing swim. Later in the day, their guide led them south to
the next oasis, which was located at the base of rounded
grayish hills rising behind a narrow coastal plain. An open
pool containing drinkable water supported a lush palm
grove, grass, reeds, and tamarisk, and a tiny garden whose
ancient caretaker dwelt in a palm-frond shack. From their
camp, they could see the glittering expanse of water that
merged with the sky on the horizon.

Early the following morning, Psuro and the guide led the
donkeys south to the port. His mission was to take them to
the paddocks where Lieutenant Nebamon kept his pack animals, to find the fisherman Nufer and tell him where Bak
waited, and to purchase necessary supplies for the voyage
across the sea and south to the trail that would take them
home to Kemet.

Bak expected the Medjay to be away for no less than three
days. Rather than remain at the oasis, where Minnakht grew
irritable and furtive each time a nomad family came to water
its flocks, they walked each day to the shore. They swam
fully dressed to protect themselves from the hot sun. As had
been the case throughout the journey down the wadi, they
never let the explorer out of their sight. While Bak swam
with him, Nebre remained on shore with their weapons.
While Nebre swam, Bak stood watch.

Minnakht made no comment until the second day after
Psuro's departure. He flopped down on the sand and grinned.

"I know you vowed to keep me alive and well, Bak, but your scrupulous devotion to duty has begun to wear on my patience. Can I not at least walk alone along the water's edge? With no donkeys or supplies, I can go no great distance."

"A man might well be hidden among the rocks on that hillside, waiting for you to go off alone." Bak pointed toward a high rocky mound rising from the plain.

"No man, no matter how talented with the bow, could strike his prey from so far away."

"If he carries an ordinary bow, I agree, but have you not seen how far an arrow can fly when delivered by a composite bow?"

"How many men in this wasted land would have such a weapon?" Even as Minnakht scoffed at the idea, his eyes darted toward the bows laying on the sand beside Bak, both of the composite variety.

"Where you go, we go," Bak stated in a voice he hoped would conclude the argument. "You've told us time and again that you fear for your life. If you truly do, you'll talk no more of how weary you've grown of our company."

Minnakht drew a spiral in the warm sand in front of his crossed legs, then erased it with a brusque swipe of his hand. "I should not have let Psuro take away my donkeys and water jars. You've admitted you don't know the fishermen who're to take us across the sea. How do you know you can trust them?"

"I trust the man who told me of them."

Minnakht opened his mouth as if to pursue the argument, but Bak's closed expression forbade further debate. So he drew another spiral and eradicated it as abruptly as he had the first. He no longer bothered to hide his irritation. "Four of us cooped up on a small boat with the lord Set only knows how many fishermen. I've had nightmares no worse than that."

Bak stood up and brushed the sand from his buttocks and legs. "Do you or do you not wish to be safe?"

"You know I do." The explorer rose to his feet and formed a bitter smile. "I've no choice but to trust your judgment, but I don't have to like it, do I?"

Bak grinned. "You'll one day look upon this journey as a memory to treasure."

Minnakht's incredulous look melted into a rueful laugh. "Will we cross the sea to the Eastern Desert and sail south along its shore? Or will we follow the coastline of this wretched land before crossing over?"

That, Bak suspected, was the question the explorer had been edging toward all along. "I'll let the fishermen make that decision."

Psuro returned with the fishing boat, which its crew anchored a dozen or so paces off the beach. The sergeant dropped into the water, waded ashore, and, while he and Bak walked south along the water's edge, reported the success of his mission. As Amonmose had promised, the vessel was larger than most fishing boats that plied the waters of the Eastern Sea. In addition to its master Nufer, it had a crew of three. It offered plenty of space for four passengers and, in addition to the supplies needed for an extended fishing expedition, enough for Bak and his party during a journey that could take as long as three weeks. Satisfied with all Psuro had accomplished, Bak waded out and hauled himself on board, where he spoke at length with Nufer.

They sailed early the following morning.

"What a life this is." Minnakht placed his fishing pole between his knees to hold it steady, spread his arms wide, and stretched luxuriously. "If I didn't prefer to roam a larger world, I'd remain with these men forever."

Bak chuckled. "Not a day has passed that you haven't reminded me that you're a man of the desert, not the sea. Why this sudden affection for this vessel and the fishing?"

"Can I not enjoy the moment while at the same time I long to be free, to go where I please?" Laughing, the explorer took up his pole and dabbed the line up and down, making the wooden float bob on the water's surface. "I like you, Bak, and I know you mean well, but your constant companionship is burdensome. Yours and that of everyone else in this small space we inhabit."

"Thus far, we've made good time. These islands mark the halfway point in our voyage."

Bak swept his hand in an arc encompassing a multitude of brownish or grayish rocky outcrops rising from the water over which they were sailing. Some were islets barely large enough to support the nest of an osprey. Others were considerably more spacious, with sandy beaches that offered a safe haven to thousands of sea birds and their young. In the water below, a multitude of bright fish swam among plants that rose from the depths, waving long colorful arms in the sea's currents.

"Once we pass through them, we'll follow the shore of the Eastern Desert."

"At long last! You've no idea how much I long to sleep on the land I hold so close within my heart."

Nufer was a cautious man, one unwilling to sail through the brightest of nights. During the several days' voyage down the eastern shore of the sea, they had anchored at the water's edge and camped on the sand. The coastal plain had been bare and uninviting, the mountains to the east high and forbidding. Bak knew their task would be more difficult when they reached the Eastern Desert, but he was glad to leave behind that wasted landscape.

A smile spread across his face; his eyes twinkled with good humor. "You think we've held you close thus far, but what you've faced in the past is nothing like the way we'll guard you when you set foot on the land where your life is most at risk."

Minnakht rolled his eyes skyward. "Can I not breathe without taking in air you've expelled?"

For the next three nights, Nufer anchored his vessel in the shallow waters off small barren islands, lumps of rock and sand that rose in the sea off the coast of the mainland. Minnakht jested about the choice of camping places, asking Bak if he feared he would slip away. Bak had a feeling he was merely going through the motions of complaining.

On the fourth night, rather than camp on an unusually large island lying offshore, they anchored off the mouth of a wadi that cut deep into the Eastern Desert. For the first time since crossing the sea, they slept on the mainland. Minnakht displayed nothing more than a casual interest in what Bak had assumed would be a tantalizing route into the interior. Had he decided at last to place his trust in them? Or was he biding his time?

Late the following evening, they camped on a narrow spit of jagged black rocks edged with sand that arced around a pool of mirror-calm blue-green water. A ridge rose gradually from the tip of the tiny peninsula to merge into a low cliff that had roughly paralleled the shoreline throughout the day. Armed with harpoons, Psuro and two fishermen walked north in search of a quiet backwater where they might spear fish for the evening meal. Bak, Nebre, and Minnakht swam among a school of fingerlings that had sought shelter in the cove. Gulls wheeled overhead, squawking at the interlopers, while three white pelicans sat on crags, grooming their feathers. Nufer, who feared the water as no sailor should, sat on shore with the third member of his crew, trading ribald jokes.

Darkness descended and the night grew chilly. The moon and stars shone above, a slice of white among chips of light as bright as highly polished rock crystal. The gulls flew off to their nesting places and their raucous calls were replaced by the lonely song of a night bird. Nufer nursed a fire in the expectation that Psuro and the sailors would shortly return with fish. Minnakht waded out of the pool, silencing the bird. Shivering in his wet tunic, he wrapped his arms around himself and hastened to the camp. He trotted past the fire, heading toward his meager belongings, and merged into the night.

Bak and Nebre exchanged a glance none but they could see.

The time dragged. The waiting seemed endless.

A long, shrill whistle shattered the silence.

Bak and Nebre scrambled out of the water. Nufer dipped an oil-soaked torch into the fire. While a flame burst into life, the two policemen slipped on their sandals and scooped up spears and shields. A quick glance verified that Minnakht had bolted.

Bak had expected no less.

The sailor plucked the torch from the fire and sped with Bak and Nebre into the night, showering sparks behind them. They ran along the base of the stony ridge, dodging rocks that rose out of the sand, splashing through pools of water, crunching across stretches of broken shell as sharp as the best bronze knife. Bak thanked the gods that he had had the foresight to inspect the landscape earlier.

Another whistle told them they were on the right course and bearing down on their quarry. A dozen paces farther, he spotted four men ahead. Psuro and the two fishermen stood around Minnakht, holding him in place with harpoons casually held but aimed at his breast.

"I should've known my flight was too easy." Minnakht's smile was thin, his good humor as shallow as the trickle of water beneath his feet. "You'd see me dead rather than let me make my own way back to Waset."

Bak, refusing to answer smile with smile, motioned him to walk back toward camp. "Have I not kept you alive and well thus far?"

"You've kept me apart from all who might wish me ill, yes, but can you continue to do so?" Minnakht shook his head. "Not on a route as well traveled as the southern trail. We'll meet one man and another and another, and word that I live will spread like oil on swiftly moving water. An army couldn't save me from my enemies."

"We'll guard you well, never fear."

"I'll wager that the men who wish me ill are the same as those who slew Senna and the others."

"One man took their lives, not a multitude. If it's you he seeks rather than me, we'll snare him when he comes close."

Minnakht stopped walking and gave a cynical laugh. "So I'm the goat you're staking out to attract a hyena."

Bak took his arm and pressed him forward. "You'll remain with us. We'll see that you arrive in Kemet alive and well. After that . . ." He let the thought hang, leaving the future open.

"Is Minnakht still sulking?" Bak asked. A night and a day had passed since the explorer's attempt to slip away into the desert.

Psuro shook his head. "He can't maintain the pose. He's too genial by far."

So they could talk without Minnakht hearing, they had walked south along the water's edge, setting out as the sun dropped toward the western horizon. They were wading through the swells rushing onto the shore, splashing the sand and receding with a whisper. Garish red tentacles reached across the sky to be mirrored on the sea below.

They had camped on a barren shore, where the coastal plain was broad and the escarpment too far away to offer cover to a man attempting to run away. If a wadi drained the higher land, its mouth had widened out and had become lost in the flat expanse of sand and gravel.

"Never let him seduce you with his charm, Sergeant. He'll flee if he can."

Psuro frowned, perplexed. "Why he won't resign himself to our protection, I don't understand."

"Perhaps he doesn't entirely trust us," Bak said with a wry smile.

The sergeant chuckled, but quickly sobered. "Nufer believes we'll reach the southern trail late tomorrow or early the following morning. What are we to do with him then?"

Bak knelt to pick up the shell of a sea creature new to him. Smelling the stench of the occupant decaying inside, he flung it into the sea. "I think it best that you hold him on the boat while I go ashore. I must report to the soldiers, and I must see if User and his party await us, as I suggested. I must also look for the nomad child Imset—or Nefertem, but I think his coming unlikely."

"Could Kaha have found him so quickly?"

"If Nefertem wanted to be found, I'm certain Kaha reached him. If he believed in my message, he'll have sent the boy on his way within the hour."

"The desert is vast, sir."

"Yes, but one man alone can travel much faster than a caravan."

They stood together, looking out upon the sea and a flock of squawking gulls swooping down for a late evening meal, flapping their wings and splashing the water while they squabbled for fish.

"What if Imset hasn't come?" Psuro asked.

"We'll wait."

Bak prayed fervently that the child had arrived and even now stood on the shore awaiting them. The amount of food and water they had was limited. They could refill their water jars at the village well, but he doubted they could replenish their food supply unless they met a caravan carrying supplies destined for the mines across the sea.

"Lieutenant Bak!" The voice was childish but bordering on manhood.

Bak stepped away from the stone hut used as an office and storeroom by the soldiers who manned the outpost called Tjau at the eastern end of the southern trail. A well encircled by a waist-high wall was nearby, and a stone-walled paddock enclosed a small herd of donkeys.

He looked in the direction from which the call had come, toward a dozen rough mud-and-reed huts occupied by nomads. Imset, who had been gathering dead branches from a clump of tamarisks a hundred or so paces away, dropped the bundle of fuel at the door of a hut and loped toward him across the hot sand.

Smiling, Bak strode out to meet the boy, scattering a flock of goats along the way, and clasped his shoulders in greeting.

The woman to whom the animals belonged stood in the doorway of the hut, keeping a close eye on man and boy. A small dark-haired girl clung to her ankle-length tunic and a baby crawled around her feet. A shaggy white dog lay with its head on its paws, watching the goats. Bak wondered if the woman was Imset's mother or if he had joined her household to make himself less conspicuous while he waited.

Imset tugged from a leather pouch hanging from his belt the quartz pendant and a cloth-wrapped package. With a shy smile, he handed them to Bak. Bak unwrapped a limestone shard covered with writing. The message, written in the carefully formed script of a man who had long ago learned to write but seldom had occasion to do so, was brief and to the point: "I long to meet with my brother Minnakht. And with you, Lieutenant. You must travel west along the caravan trail. Your Medjay Kaha and I will await you at the well midway between the sea and Waset. From there, we'll travel on together."

Bak smiled. The response could not have been more to his liking. Sobering, he stared off to the west, taking a few moments to decide what best to do.

"Do you know User?" he asked, pointing toward a campsite shaded by a large acacia some distance away. The sergeant in charge of the outpost had told him the explorer and his party had arrived four days earlier. He had urged them to continue west with the caravan, but they had refused, saying they wished to return to Kemet with Bak.

Imset led him to the crude hut. The woman and children shrank away, fearful of the stranger. Inside, lying on a bed of goatskins, he saw a length of bright fabric, several bronze spear and harpoon points, and a jar that contained honey or some other desirable substance difficult to get in the desert.

"You traded with him?"

"Trade. Yes."

"Is User your friend?"

The boy nodded.

"Enemy?"

Imset shook his head vehemently. User had apparently won him over.

Signaling the boy to wait, he hurried to the building the soldiers occupied and asked for papyrus and writing implements. None of the men could read or write, so they were slow to take the request seriously. He snapped out an order, convincing them his need was real. The sergeant hastened to cut a small piece of papyrus from an inventory of supplies delivered some months earlier and a soldier located a scribal pallet so long unused that a thick layer of dust had to be scraped off before the ink could be moistened. Bak wrote a quick message to Nefertem, rolled it tight, and tied it with a bit of string. Getting into the spirit of the task, the sergeant secured it with a daub of mud and impressed it with a seal he had never before had occasion to use.

Bak tucked the cylinder beneath his belt and went in search of Imset, who had returned to the tamarisks to gather more wood. After helping the boy carry his gleanings to the hut, he looked toward the campsite he had yet to visit. "User," he pointed, "and you . . ." He touched Imset's chest. "Walk west." He pointed toward the place where the trail began.

The boy gave him an uncertain look. Either he did not recall the meaning of the word walk or he did not wish to remember.

"Walk." Bak moved two fingers like a man walking.

Imset gave a reluctant nod.

"You walk with User to the well. To water." Bak pointed again to the boy and toward the camp, placed the first two fingers of both hands side by side and made the walking motion, and pointed west. He cupped a hand and pretended to drink, reminding Imset of the meaning of the word water.

Imset shook his head. "I walk with you to water."

"You walk with User. I follow." Bak made the walking motion with his right hand followed closely by two fingers of his left hand.

A stubborn look settled on Imset's face and he turned to walk away.

Bak caught his arm to halt his flight, withdrew the papyrus from beneath his belt, and held it out. "For Nefertem."

Imset took the scroll and inspected the seal. He looked at User's camp, thought over what Bak wished him to do, and nodded that he understood: the message must reach Nefertem ahead of Bak. "I walk with User."

"You want us to travel on to the well without you." User gave Bak a suspicious look. "What're you up to, Lieutenant?"

Bak laughed. "I'll be no more than a day behind you."

"What are we to do when we get there?"

"Make camp and wait for me. The water is good, so the soldiers here say, and the man who dwells there is friendly. I'm certain he'll enjoy talking to someone new for a change, and his wife will appreciate the goods you have to trade."

Bak had left Imset to gather his few belongings and had walked to User's camp. Minmose had greeted him with a huge smile and Amonmose with the hug of a bear. The other men, though more restrained in their actions, were openly delighted to see him, but were concerned that his Medjays had not come with him. Upon learning that his men were alive and well, their smiles returned and they urged him to sit with them, share their beer, and tell them of his travels. He obliged, giving them a brief account of his journey. True to his word, he made no mention of Minnakht.

User, whom he had drawn away from the camp as soon as he decently could, looked across a stretch of sand toward the men packing up to leave in the cool of evening. "The trail is easy to follow and I know it well from my youth. Why is the boy coming with us? Not as a guide, I'd wager."

"He wishes to go west with me. I prefer that he travel with you."

User eyed him thoughtfully. "You've a reason, I suppose."

"One that should become clear when you reach the well."

The explorer scowled, not happy with the evasion. "Why did you not tell us to go on with the caravan? Now we'll be alone and at the mercy of the man who slew Dedu and Senna, Rona and the stranger. The one who's tried more than once to slay you."

"His attention will be focused on me. You'll be safer without me."

Looking unconvinced and not at all happy, User growled, "I pray to all the gods in the ennead that you're right." He realized the import of Bak's words, added, "And that you'll stay safe as well as us."

"The trek will be well worth your while, I assure you."

From the soldiers, Bak obtained three donkeys to carry water and supplies westward. Twenty-four hours after User's party moved on, he, Nebre, Psuro, and two armed sailors Nufer had loaned them escorted Minnakht along the trail. The explorer made no real attempt to slip away, but he constantly tested the men who were guarding him. Bak guessed he did not know this part of the desert well, and was waiting to make his move when he came to a place he knew better.

Before sunrise on the fourth morning after striking out from the sea, they strode into a large valley whose flat expanse was blanketed in golden sand. It was enclosed by brownish hills that appeared low at a distance but proved, as they walked forward, to be high and rugged, singularly uninviting. The sun, a sliver of gold, peeked above the horizon to the west, bathing the sky in red and orange, revealing near the center of the sandy plain a stand of trees. What appeared in the dim light of dawn to be squarish mounds of stone gradually revealed themselves as three drystone buildings and a walled structure that Bak assumed was the well.

Minnakht walked slower, reluctant to approach the tiny, isolated oasis. When the growing light and a fresh perspective revealed twenty or more donkeys in a walled paddock, he stopped. "You vowed to keep me safe."

"I've heard that the man who dwells here exchanges healthy donkeys for caravan animals that show a weakness or an illness." Psuro, walking beside the explorer, had never ceased to remind him in some oblique way of the manner in which he had neglected his animals. "He cures them and sees that they get good food and water until another exchange is needed."

Bak doubted such was the case, but the barbed comment seemed to ease Minnakht's doubts—at least for a while.

They strode on across the valley floor, walking on the hard sand alongside multiple paths softened by the hooves of many donkeys. The sun burst above the horizon to glare into their faces. The oasis slowly came to life. A donkey brayed and a goose cackled. Dogs barked, setting to flight a flock of birds, black silhouettes against the brilliant sky. Bak expected the dogs to come running and soon they did, a dozen scruffy mutts barking bravely from afar but too shy to come near.

The closer the men came to the cluster of buildings, the more tightly strung Minnakht became. He was not the only man to feel the strain. Bak adjusted his hand on his spear, balancing it better for use. He had to force himself to keep his pace regular and unhurried. Psuro, Nebre, and the sailors continually scanned the land to either side. Nebre retrieved his bow and quiver from the back of a donkey.

Two boys left the largest building and took a donkey from the paddock. The dogs streaked back to the oasis and followed them north up a broad subsidiary wadi. They had to have noticed the party of approaching men, but gave no sign of greeting. A short time later, a woman left the building to draw water. A small child followed and pestered her until she finished her task. As she turned away from the well, she looked their way, waved, and in a leisurely fashion, carried the heavy jar inside. A donkey brayed as if forgotten. Two others took up the plea.

Minnakht stopped twenty paces from the closest building. "You go ahead, Lieutenant. Make sure this place is safe."

Bak barked out a humorless laugh. "You'd sacrifice your mother if you thought it to your advantage. Would you not, Ahmose?"

The man who called himself Minnakht stiffened. "What?"

"Ahmose. Is that not your name?"

"You've lost your wits."

Bak stepped away from the explorer, as did Psuro. Out of arm's reach. The grim expression on their faces told truer than words how serious they were—and how unlikely they were to believe any denial.

Minnakht—or Ahmose—swung toward the sailors, the least wary and poorest trained of his guards. He flailed out at one man, shouldered the other aside, and began to run.

Bak, who had expected no less, raced after him, with Psuro, Nebre, and the sailors fanning out behind. Suddenly twenty or more men burst from behind the nearest building. Ahmose veered sharply away. Bak closed in on him, leaped at him, and with a flying tackle, pulled him to the ground. His prisoner tried to kick himself free and scramble away, but Psuro grabbed an arm, jerked him to his knees, and placed his spear point to his breast.

The men who had appeared from behind the building swept forward, led by Nefertem and User. The group included Imset, the members of User's party, and more than a dozen nomads. They encircled Bak, his men, and his prisoner.

"You vowed to bring Minnakht," Nefertem said, glowering. "This is not my friend."

"He's not the man I knew," User seconded the opinion. "Who is he?"

"I couldn't bring Minnakht, Nefertem. I fear he's dead. I brought instead the man who took his life." Bak grabbed a handful of hair and forced the captive to raise his chin so all could see his face. "His name is Ahmose. Like Minnakht, he explored the Eastern Desert—but farther north in the area where Senna grew to manhood. Senna was his guide and a longtime friend, but he slew him anyway, fearing I'd force the truth from him. I believe he also claimed to be Minnakht's friend. When the pretense failed, he took his life while trying to force him to reveal the location of the gold he believed he'd found."

The nomad chieftain, his mouth tight with anger, glared at the prisoner, then drew his hand back and slapped him so hard the crack of the blow echoed across the valley.

Chapter 19

"You're a dead man, Ahmose. You know that, don't you?" Bak, seated on a large rock in front of the well, had long ago lost patience with his prisoner, who refused to say a word. Nefertem's slap had not only raised four elongated red welts on Ahmose's cheek, but had sealed his lips. "Whether you remain here with the nomads or whether we take you back to the land of Kemet, your fate rests in the hands of the lady Maat. She's not a forgiving goddess."

"Nor am I a merciful man." Nefertem, who had been sitting on a low stool, looking on in silence, rose to his feet to tower over the man seated on the sand, his hands tied behind his back. "You risked death for what, you swine? For a faint hope of wealth? For gold you couldn't find but thought to steal?" The nomad hissed between his teeth, the sound of a snake preparing to strike.

Ahmose shrank back but remained mute.

User, perched on three mudbricks stacked to form a seat, pulled a stick from the smoldering hearth over which a gazelle cooked, and prodded the fire to make it burn hotter.

The Medjays, the men of User's party, and the nomads sat on the ground, forming a half circle around them. The dogs, which had returned in ones and twos, lay in a loose group behind the men, looking on like additional witnesses. The family who dwelt in the oasis sat in front of their house, watching. The men of Kemet were offering various ways of breaking the prisoner's silence, each more disagreeable than the one before. A young nomad who could speak the tongue of Kemet continually translated for his brethren, who built on the suggestions with ideas of their own.

User rotated the stick, examining its fiery tip. "Dedu was my friend. A good friend. You didn't just take his life. You left him for carrion." A calculated look settled on the explorer's face and he shifted his gaze to the prisoner. "I say we blind this snake and turn him loose in this barren land with no water or food."

A murmur of agreement swept through the onlookers. A donkey brayed, as if offering its consent.

"No!" Ahmose scrambled back, his horrified eyes locked on the stick. "You must take me to Kemet, Lieutenant. My offenses must be weighed on the scales of justice, not left in the hands of these desert swine."

"Ah," Nefertem said, dropping onto his stool. "He can talk."

Flinging User a hasty look of thanks, Bak shoved himself back against the wall that enclosed the well, startling a lizard that darted across the hot sand to the shelter of a broad-leafed vine. "Are we correct in believing Minnakht died rather than tell you of the gold you sought?"

Ahmose tore his eyes from the stick User continued to toy with. "I've searched the Eastern Desert for a lifetime, thinking to become a wealthy man. I know this land holds vast riches, and I knew that someday . . ."

User cleared his throat, urging him to omit the prologue.

The prisoner's quick response was gratifying. "I bumped into Minnakht in Waset—a year ago, that must've been—and he let slip hints of his good fortune. I thought to learn his secret. Later he would say nothing, and in my anger I slew him."

"Have you not failed to fill in the details of your black deed?" Bak asked in a hard voice. "When first we met, you told me you were brought across the sea, dropped on the shore, and were accosted by men who beat you and left you to die. Was that tale Minnakht's rather than yours?"

Ahmose hesitated, but finally nodded. "Yes."

User's mouth twisted in contempt. "You met him as a friend, then set upon him, bound him so he was helpless, and beat him to death. What kind of man are you?"

Ahmose's mouth clamped tight, which in itself was an admission of guilt.

Nefertem made a sound deep within his throat, part angry growl, part heartfelt pain. The nomads seated around them, who had thought of Minnakht as one of themselves, glared at the prisoner and murmured angry words. Wensu and Ani, Amonmose and Nebenkemet looked shocked and saddened.

The old man who cooked for Nefertem scurried forward. For a moment Bak thought he meant to slay the prisoner. Instead he spat on his face, turned his back to him in a gesture of contempt, and rotated the gazelle over the hearth.

As the old man retreated, Bak pressed on, not bothering to hide his disgust for so cowardly a murder. "Why did you send Senna to Minnakht's father? Why did he not simply disappear in the desert?"

"I thought to convince Inebny that his son was truly dead," Ahmose said, wiping the spittle onto his shoulder, "and Senna wished to collect the livestock and supplies he was due. It never occurred to us that the commander would find a man to take up the search—you, a seasoned police officer— and that he'd insist Senna serve as your guide. Or that you'd join User's caravan."

"I doubt we would have if a dead man hadn't been found when first we came upon them." Bak's voice grew hard, grim. "You slew that man, did you not?"

Ahmose hesitated. User shook the stick at him like the long finger of a teacher reprimanding a pupil. The tip had turned black as the heat dissipated, a fact the prisoner had to have noticed. Still, he answered with a nod.

"Who was he?"

"He was a soldier, Paser by name, a friend of Minnakht. He'd seen us together in Waset, heard us talk of the Eastern Desert and gold. I thought never to see him another time, but when he appeared at that well, I knew he must die."

User jabbed the stick in among the burning embers. "How did you slay him without leaving footprints?"

Ahmose curled a lip, betraying a superiority he was in no position to feel. "I'm far more a man of the desert than Minnakht ever was. He regularly returned to the land of Kemet, shrugging off his life as a desert wanderer, while I often dwelt throughout the year with Senna's clan." His eyes slid toward Bak. "I know more of tracking than you or your Medjays will ever know, Lieutenant, and I know how to hide any sign of my presence."

Bak glanced at his men, who looked as if they themselves were ready to commit murder. "From then on, you thought to watch us night and day."

Ahmose smirked. "The watching man, you called me."

Noting the pride he took in the appellation, Bak said, "You carried off well the look of a nomad."

"I dared not risk being seen by the people who came to the wells to water their flocks—they'd have known I wasn't one of them—and most of the transitory pools had dried up. I'd not bathed for some time. When Senna told me you believed me a nomad, I thought your error would serve me well."

He was so smug Bak had to resist the urge to strike him. "Why slay Dedu?"

"By then I was wearying of your pursuit. No matter what I did to discourage you, you refused to give up. So I thought to pass myself off to you as Minnakht. I couldn't risk Dedu seeing me. I knew him from long ago, and he wouldn't have forgotten."

"You were the man who destroyed his daughter's future," Bak guessed. "You're the father of her child."

Ahmose let out a barklike laugh. "When Dedu realized I meant to slay him, he tried to play on my sympathies by telling me I had a child, a girl. I didn't believe him, and I don't believe you."

"You slew your daughter's grandfather, Ahmose."

A look of self-doubt—or possibly pain—flitted across Ahmose's face. He erased it with a thin smile. "Dedu would never have told you, a stranger, a secret so painful to him."

"Believe what you wish," Bak said with a shrug. "You'll never have the chance to see the child."

The two boys who had traveled north earlier in the day walked into the oasis. Bak could see nothing but the donkey's head, feet, and tail, so heavily laden was it with dry twigs gleaned from the bushes that grew in the nearby wadis. Looking curiously at the gathering of men, the youths left the laden animal in the shade of a tree and hurried to the house to learn what they had missed.

"Why slay Senna?" Bak asked, "a man you claim was your longtime friend?"

"You know why. He pushed you into the face of the flood, trying to slay you. Sooner or later you'd have gotten the truth from him." Ahmose's mouth twisted into a cynical smile. "I once saved his life—you saw the scar on his shoulder—so I suppose I could say it was mine to take."

"What of Rona?" Bak demanded.

The prisoner glanced toward Psuro, sitting with Nebre, Kaha, and Minmose, their expressions dark, threatening. He lowered his voice, as if he hoped to prevent their hearing. "I held no ill will toward him. He saw me slay Senna."

Bak wanted to smash Ahmose in the face. Nebre, burning with rage, leaped forward, trying to reach the bound man. Psuro, no less furious, grabbed the Medjay's arm, halting

him, and snapped an order to Kaha and Minmose, forbidding
them to move.

"You met me and we talked," Bak said, suppressing his
anger with an effort. "If I hadn't insisted you join our caravan, which was made up of far too many men who'd know
you weren't Minnakht, would you have followed us across
the Eastern Sea?"

"I knew, when I failed to join you as I promised, that you'd
guess the truth." Ahmose wiped his face on his shoulder a
second time, as if he could still feel the spittle. "Senna had
told me you'd talked with Nefertem. I suspected you'd joined
forces, and I dared not slay you in this wretched desert. I
thought to follow you into that alien land, where I could slay
you and slip away, with no fierce tribe of nomads prepared to
avenge your death."

Leaning forward, elbows on knees, Nefertem spoke in a
voice as soft and rumbling as the purr of a lion. "Tell me of
my father, Ahmose. You took his life, did you not?"

Not a man present could mistake the threat, and Ahmose
was no exception. "I know nothing of his death."

User jerked the stick from the hearth and held its flame-red
end within a hand's breadth of the prisoner's eyes. "We want
no lies, Ahmose."

The bound man cringed. Whether he feared most the tribal
chieftain or the explorer, Bak could not begin to guess. "In
the beginning I believed that if I was to learn where Minnakht had found gold, Senna had to get close to him. He had
to serve as his guide. But as long as your father lived, he
would accept no one else." Ahmose saw the fury on Nefertem's face and quickly looked away. "I placed poison in his
waterbag. I meant him to die right away, but he drank too
small an amount. He lingered long enough to go home, and
there I heard he died."

Nefertem bounded forward, gripped him by the neck, and

began to squeeze. Ahmose pounded the earth with his feet, his face turned fiery. Bak shouted an order to Psuro, who leaped forward. Together with User, the three of them pulled the nomad from the man he meant to slay.

The tribal chief was still struggling, still trying to reach the man who had slain his father, when Bak shouted, "Nefertem! Stop! He must see the truth."

Bak's words seeped into the nomad's heart and he grew more calm. Staring at Ahmose, he shrugged off User's grip and Psuro's and wiped the sweat from his face. A harsh laugh escaped from his lips and he nodded. "Yes, let him see what a fool he's been."

Early in the evening, User's party, the nomads, and Bak and his Medjays left the oasis with their prisoner to travel north up the subsidiary wadi. Bak had thought Nefertem would object when he said he wished the explorer and his party to come along, but his fears proved unfounded. The tribal chief agreed they had every right to participate to the end.

They rested through the darkest of the night and set out long before daybreak to follow a series of smaller wadis deeper into the desert. An hour after sunrise, they arrived at a camp, simple in construction and inhabited by nomads. Several tents that looked suspiciously like those issued to the soldiers of Kemet had been erected near the base of a tall brownish hill. A rough wall of stone supported a lean-to of spindly poles and brush. A dozen or so donkeys stood in its shade, munching hay that might well have been stolen from a caravan crossing the desert between Kemet and the Eastern Sea.

A tall, thin nomad stood beside a tent, removing baskets of grain from the back of a mule. Bak smiled. This had to be the animal on which he had been transported during his abduction.

The man returned his smile. "Lieutenant Bak. I'm happy to see you again."

Bak stared, aware that somewhere in the past he had seen this man, but where? "Waset!" he said. "You were with your wife, preparing to leave the city."

"You came to our aid." The man glanced at Nefertem. "I told my brother of the service you did us."

"Your brother?" Bak looked at the tribal chieftain, surprised.

Nefertem gave him what might have passed for a sheepish smile in a man less regal. "When I took you captive, you were unknown to me. Some days later, Hor came to our camp. When I told him of you, he told me of the way you'd saved his life. His and that of his wife and unborn child. Not until then was I certain I could trust you."

Eyeing Hor in a new light, Bak guessed, "You'd gone into Waset to trade?"

"My wife was carrying our first child." Hor smiled at the thought, but quickly sobered. "I wished her to talk to a woman of Kemet who helps others give birth. I paid the woman dearly to reveal her secrets, thinking to improve their chance of survival during the ordeal."

"While in the city," Nefertem added, "they picked up a few items impossible to get in this empty land. We've a friend who helps us trade for what we need. What we can't carry on a single donkey, he brings later on a string of animals."

Bak thought of the besotted fools who had attacked Hor out of simple malice. If they had only known that he had arrived in the capital carrying the wealth of the desert. "Your wife is well, I hope?"

"I have a son," Hor beamed. "We call him Minnakht."

"I've never seen anything like it." User stared in awe at the gigantic slash in the earth.

"Nor have I," Bak said, as amazed as the explorer.

Nebenkemet shook his head, whether in wonder or negation was impossible to tell. "Not the best way of taking gold from the earth. Too much effort by far."

"I'd prefer toiling in the open air to burrowing in the darkness of a tunnel," Ani said, "but those high walls don't look safe."

Ahmose stood with them, hands bound behind his back, staring at the long ditch cut deep into the side of the high brown hill. A half-dozen nomads were breaking up the stone at the far end and a like number carried heavy baskets back along the cut, taking the broken stone to be processed. The prisoner's face looked gray. He had come so close to finding what he sought. Now here he was, looking upon his failure.

"You know mining?" Nefertem eyed Nebenkemet with interest. "Minnakht said there had to be a better way, but this is all we knew to do."

"I not long ago toiled in the gold mines east of Abu." Nebenkemet wiped the sweat from his brow, added, "I could make a few suggestions if you wish."

Bak turned away from the excavation to walk a half-dozen paces along a well-trodden track to where the bearers were emptying their baskets beside a second group of nomads. These men were seated on the ground, pounding the excavated rock, painstakingly reducing the stone to the consistency of coarse sand. Another man sprinkled the granules into a sloping metal basin partially filled with water. He sloshed them around, allowing the gold to fall to the bottom while the lighter stone remained on top.

"I guessed Minnakht had found gold when I was told of the questions he asked at the turquoise and copper mines," Bak said. "Or did you find the vein, Nefertem, and ask for his help?"

"We've been taking gold from this place for many years, but we believed the vein had run out. I knew we could trust Minnakht, so I brought him here. He urged us to dig farther. He was right. The vein went on and our ditch went ever deeper, its walls higher and less stable. One man was felled

by falling rocks, losing his life, and several have been hurt
when walls collapsed. Minnakht thought to cross the sea to
learn a safer way of mining."

A pottery bowl sat on the ground beside the man washing
out the gold. A mound of the precious metal sparkled within.
Bak glimpsed Ahmose's face, his look of unadulterated
greed.

"I suppose he found other veins in this wadi."

"He did." Nefertem beckoned a nomad who stood nearby.
The man poured the glittering grains of gold from the bowl
into a leather bag already bulging with earlier deposits and
handed it to the tribal chief. "My people have no need for
great wealth. We dig only what we require to keep us alive
and well in times of hardship. When we come to the end of
this vein, we'll go on to another."

"I've a need to relieve myself," Ahmose said.

"Can you not wait?" Psuro snapped.

"You must free my hands so I can lower my loincloth."

Psuro looked to Bak for a decision, but Ahmose groaned
and bent over, making his need clear. Not a man among them
failed to think of how awkward and unpleasant it would be to
clean a man in this place where every drop of water was in-
valuable. The sergeant nodded to Nebre, who jerked his dagger out of its sheath and slashed through the leather cord
binding the prisoner's hands.

Ahmose straightened, flung away the cord, and shouldered Nebre aside. He tore the bag of gold from Nefertem's
hand and raced down the trail toward the camp. He had run
no more than twenty paces when Hor and four other nomads
came around the shoulder of the mountain, blocking his path.
He swung around, saw Bak, Psuro, and Nebre speeding after
him, and veered aside to race up the slope toward the mine.

The rocks on the hillside were jagged and sharp-edged,
forcing Ahmose either to enter the huge ditch, which was a

dead end, or climb up the hill to right or left. All along both sides of the excavation, the surface had been smoothed by the miners to form a path from which they could suspend a few men to cut away more of the wall. Ahmose chose the path on the downhill side of the ditch.

Bak and his Medjays raced after him. Close behind came Nefertem and two nomads armed with bows. The other men were spreading themselves across the hillside, cutting Ahmose off should he try to return to the wadi. Bak sped up the slope, angry at the ease with which the prisoner had tricked them and determined to recapture him. Psuro, who was furious at having been made to look the fool, and Nebre, adding a new grudge to the old, ran so close behind that Bak feared they would step on his heels.

The hill rose toward the sky; the man-made chasm grew deeper. Bak slowly closed the gap between himself and Ahmose. Fifteen paces. Twelve. Ten. The fresher dirt near the top was softer, looser, slowing the pace. He began to fret. Soon they would reach the deepest end of the mine. Beyond, the hill rose untouched, a hazardous slope of hard-edged rocks and boulders. Ahmose knew better how to pick his way through these natural obstacles than they did, knew how to use this harsh landscape for cover.

Dredging up an added burst of speed, Bak narrowed the space between himself and his quarry by half. Ahmose must have heard the thud of his feet. He looked back—and stepped on a fist-sized stone. The rock rolled beneath his foot, tipping him toward the chasm. He raised his arms to regain his balance and Bak leaped toward him, reaching out to catch him.

An arrow sped past, missing Bak's shoulder by a hand's breadth, and plunged into Ahmose's back. He toppled into the gold mine.

"He had to die at my hands." Nefertem sat on his stool by the hearth, watching the old man add twigs to the fire over which a lamb stew simmered. "He slew my father and he took the life of Minnakht, a man as close to me as a brother. What I did was right and proper."

Bak had trouble resigning himself to the loss of his prisoner. In a way, the tribal chieftain had helped Ahmose escape the justice he had deserved, the wrath of the lady Maat. "I'd hoped to learn where he buried Minnakht. His father would wish him returned to Kemet to be placed in a tomb in western Waset."

"Minnakht loved this desert more than any other place, and here he should stay."

Secretly Bak agreed. Commander Inebny would not be happy that his son was truly lost to him, but so be it. "Did he have a woman here, a family?"

Nefertem stared at nothing, seeking an answer Bak was convinced he knew. After a long silence, he said, "You saved my brother and his wife and child. You found the slayer of my father and Minnakht and of Dedu, a man of high repute among my people." An unexpected smile spread across his face and he glanced toward Nebenkemet. "You've even provided me with a man who can tell us how best to mine the gold."

Bak returned the smile. The tribal chief and Amonmose had agreed that Nebenkemet could divide his time between the fishing camp and the mine, satisfying all concerned.

"I owe you far more than I can ever pay, but . . ." The smile faded away. "Did Minnakht take a wife from among my people? That I cannot tell you."

Bak understood. If Inebny learned he had grandchildren, he would not rest until they dwelt with him in Waset. Such would be intolerable to a tribal chieftain.

"Sir, look!" Imset caught Bak's arm and pointed upward.

A flock of several thousand white storks glided through the air over the ridge of mountains that separated the eastern slope of the desert drainage from that of the west. They were some distance to the north, but Bak imagined he could hear the wind streaming through their wings. They came to a rising current of air and circled around, gaining height. As their angle to the sun changed, their color turned from white to black and turned again from black to white as they completed the circle. Safely over the ridge, they spread their wings wide and let the air carry them onward toward Kaine and the river that made fertile the land of Kemet.

While growing to manhood, Bak had watched these flocks of birds travel to and from their summer nestingplaces, and a sudden yearning for home struck him. He thanked the lord Amon that his mission was finished and soon he would be returning to a land of plenty.